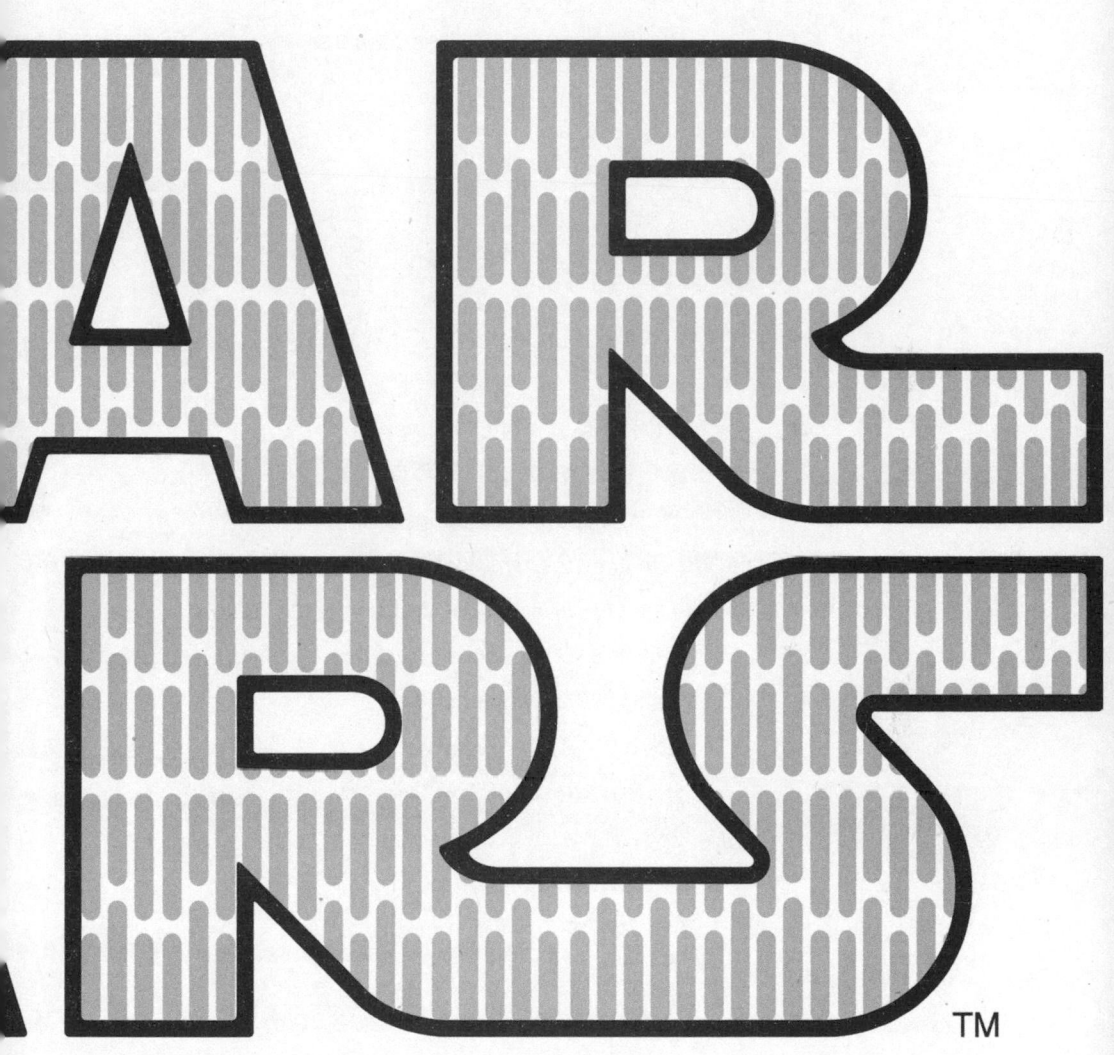

OTHER STAR WARS BOOKS BY TIMOTHY ZAHN

STAR WARS: Heir to the Empire

STAR WARS: Dark Force Rising

STAR WARS: The Last Command

STAR WARS: The Hand of Thrawn, Book 1: Specter of the Past

STAR WARS: The Hand of Thrawn, Book 2: Vision of the Future

STAR WARS: Survivor's Quest

STAR WARS: Outbound Flight

STAR WARS: Allegiance

STAR WARS: Choices of One

STAR WARS: Scoundrels

STAR WARS: Thrawn

STAR WARS: Thrawn: Alliances

THRAWN

TREASON

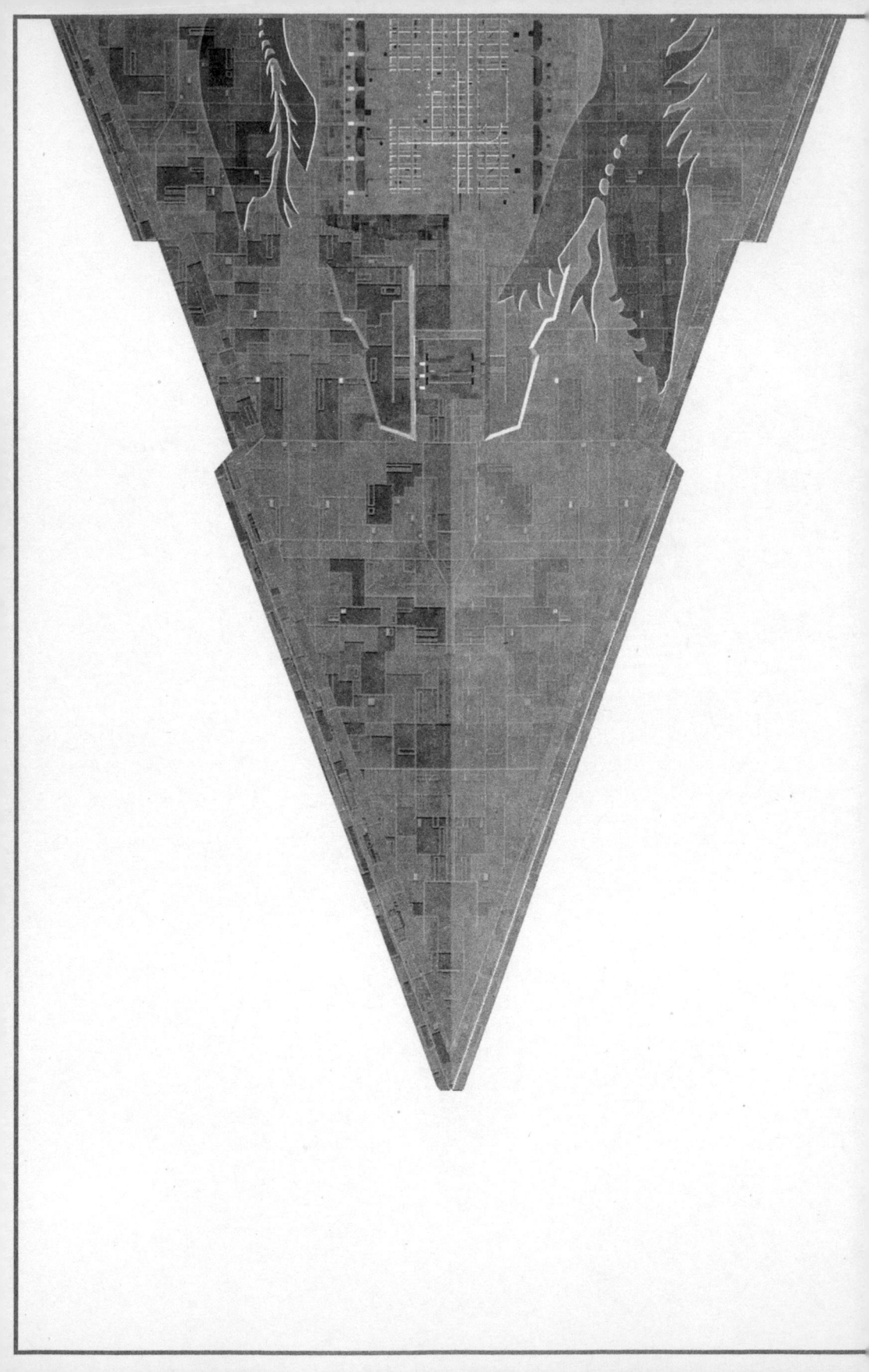

THRAWN
TREASON

TIMOTHY ZAHN

DEL REY | NEW YORK

Published in the United States by Del Rey, an imprint of Random House, a division of Penguin Random House LLC, New York.

DEL REY and the HOUSE colophon are registered trademarks of Penguin Random House LLC.

ISBN 978-1-9848-2098-3
International edition ISBN 978-0-593-12965-4
ebook ISBN 978-1-9848-2099-0

Printed in the United States of America on acid-free paper

randomhousebooks.com

2 4 6 8 9 7 5 3 1

First Edition

Book design by Elizabeth A. D. Eno

For all who have ever had to consider
the cost of doing the right thing

THE DEL REY
STAR WARS
TIMELINE

THE DEL REY

TIMELINE

A long time ago in a galaxy far, far away. . . .

THRAWN

TREASON

PROLOGUE

The Imperial Star Destroyer floated lazily over the blue-green planet below it, a hint of those colors reflected faintly against its hull in the shadows created by the distant sun. The warship reached the end of its patrol sweep and, apparently satisfied that there was nothing amiss in the vicinity, angled away toward deep space. It continued its leisurely course until it reached the edge of the planet's gravity well, then in a flurry of flashlines made the jump to lightspeed.

Seated in her command chair on the bridge of the Chiss Defense Fleet warship *Steadfast*, wrapped in darkness alleviated only by the stars outside and the handful of indicator lights still active, Admiral Ar'alani scowled. The accidental interloper was finally gone. The crucial question now was whether the *Steadfast*'s forced descent into full dark mode had given their quarry the time and distance it needed to escape. "Mid Commander Tanik?" she prompted quietly.

"A moment, Admiral," Tanik said softly. There was no real need for quiet—their quarry could hardly hear them across a thousand kilometers of vacuum—but Ar'alani had long noted that dark mode tended to have a silencing effect on a ship's crew. "Searching along the last known vector."

"Assuming they didn't take the opportunity to alter it," Senior Captain Khresh growled from his position beside Ar'alani's chair. "Imperial fools. The exact worst time, the exact worst place—"

"Patience, Senior Captain," Ar'alani admonished, gazing out at the starfield wrapped around the bridge viewports. She was just as frustrated as Khresh by the Star Destroyer's unexpected and oblivious interference with their mission, but that wasn't a reason to abandon his dignity and self-control.

She looked back at the sensor board. Especially not with Tanik sitting right there within earshot.

Sure enough, the sensor officer had a small smile on his face as he worked to relocate the Steadfast's target. No doubt the tale of Khresh's small outburst, mild though it might be, would wend its way back to the Ascendancy and there be thrown on the growing fire between their two families.

Unfortunately, Khresh also spotted Tanik's smile. "Is something amusing you, Mid Commander?" he demanded.

"No, Senior Captain, nothing at all," Tanik assured him calmly.

"Have you found the target? If not, I suggest you put thoughts of entertainment out of your mind and concentrate on the task at hand."

"Yes, sir." Tanik straightened in his chair. "Oh, wait, sir," he said with exaggerated brightness. "I stand corrected. Admiral, we have them."

"On the board," Ar'alani ordered.

"There," Khresh said, pointing at the glowing circle on the tactical board that marked the drive emissions. "Looks like they're maintaining their original heading."

"Ship's uncloaking, Admiral," Tanik said. "Still too far away for any configuration analysis." He shook his head. "I have to give them full marks for confidence."

"Confidence bordering on arrogance," Ar'alani agreed. The target ship had naturally activated its cloaking field the moment the Star Destroyer popped into the system, hiding itself from the potential enemy. But from its current position, it was clear that, instead of shutting down its drive and playing dead the way the Steadfast had, it had continued to track along its course, fully expecting that the Imperial ship wouldn't notice the telltales.

Which, of course, it hadn't.

"Looks like it's getting ready to jump," Khresh said. ". . . There it goes."

"Secure from dark mode," Ar'alani called. "Do we have their vector?"

"We do, Admiral," Tanik said as, all around them, the bridge and the *Steadfast* began once again to come to life. "Sending it to the helm."

Ar'alani turned her attention to the helm, and the young girl seated quietly in the navigator's seat. "Whenever you're ready, Navigator Mi'yaric."

"Yes, Admiral," Mi'yaric said. She braced herself as she took the helm controls, then bowed her head. She held the pose a moment, then drew a breath and huffed it out.

A moment later the *Steadfast* was in hyperspace.

"Let's just hope they're all as incompetent as the ones in that Star Destroyer," Khresh murmured at Ar'alani's side.

"They won't be," Ar'alani said, trying to hide her own misgivings. Tracking an enemy ship to learn its destination and purpose was one thing. Tracking it across borders toward the very center of alien territory was something else entirely. "Signal all senior officers. I want them in the bridge conference room in ten minutes to discuss the current situation."

"Yes, ma'am," Khresh said. "And . . . ?" He left the question hanging.

Not that Ar'alani didn't know perfectly well what he was suggesting. The problem was that the newcomer—the alien—was still not fully accepted by some of the officers and crew. In a crisis situation, or even a politically charged one, lack of trust could lead to hesitation, which could lead to disaster.

But she was likely to need information and analysis before this was over, and he was far and away the best resource the *Steadfast* had.

And a good commander never wasted or ignored resources.

"Yes," she told Khresh. "Go ahead and signal him, as well.

"Order Lieutenant Eli'van'to to join us."

CHAPTER 1

Communications to and from a Star Destroyer like the ISD *Chimaera* came from many directions, and at many different status and security levels. Each message carried a numerical code specifying the degree of importance, and those codes defined how and by whom each was to be handled.

Commodore Karyn Faro knew all of those codes. But somehow, in a still-youthful corner of her mind that years of Imperial military regulation and order hadn't quite eradicated, those codes also somehow ended up as colors.

Identification signals from nearby ships or status reports from mid-distant bases, routine matters handled by junior officers, came in shades of green or blue. The small percentage of more significant orders and reports from Coruscant—which was better known by the bureaucracy these days as Imperial Center—were pictured in shades of yellow or orange. Those were screened by the *Chimaera*'s more senior officers. The rare handful of vital or top-secret messages coming from the senior admirals of High Command, all of which were handled by Faro personally, moved into the range of darker shades of red or purple.

And the few—the very few—that came from outside the official navy chain of command, the ones that went directly to Grand Admiral Thrawn himself, were an unremittent black.

And they were never good news.

"Your TIE Defender program is at risk," Grand Moff Tarkin intoned.

Standing just inside Thrawn's office, with the image from the desk holoprojector facing away from her, Faro couldn't see Tarkin's expression. But she could see Thrawn's, and the subtle hardening of those facial muscles sent a small shiver up her back.

"Orson Krennic has been quite persuasive," Tarkin continued, "about diverting the funding to his own project: Stardust."

"The Emperor has assured me that he supports my project," Thrawn replied. His face was back under control now, Faro noted, and his voice its usual calm.

But there was an edge there that Faro had heard before. The Emperor and Thrawn had a special relationship that dated all the way back to Thrawn's first arrival on Coruscant. Rumor had it that especially in those early years the two men had sometimes disappeared for hours into the palace's strategic planning center, closeted with a few top admirals and trusted moffs, for conversations on still-unknown topics. If Krennic was playing fast and loose with one of the Emperor's favorites, he was treading on dangerous ground.

On top of the ridiculous political maneuvering, Krennic was risking the Empire's very survival. The TIE Defender assembly line Thrawn had established on the Outer Rim world of Lothal was poised to turn out the best starfighters the galaxy had ever seen: fast, maneuverable, heavily armed, and—in a radical departure from the rest of the TIE series—equipped with shields and hyperdrives. They could take on anything even the best-equipped pirate gang or uncooperative system could field, and could grind the slowly growing rebel movement into dust.

Without the Defender, Coruscant was in for a long fight on all three of those fronts. With the Defender, the Empire would be unbeatable.

"In my view, Director Krennic's project has been nothing but expenses and excuses for years on end," Tarkin said. "If construction of the Defender is to continue, you must make your case directly to the Emperor himself. I have already arranged the meeting."

"I'll leave immediately, Governor Tarkin," Thrawn said.

The holoprojector flicked off, and Thrawn tapped the comm switch. "Commander, inform Governor Pryce I'm departing for Coruscant," he ordered. "As soon as you have your course, make the jump into hyperspace."

The bridge acknowledged. For a moment Thrawn gazed at the desk as if considering his options; then he looked up at Faro. "Commodore," he said gravely. "Is that the communications report I requested?"

"Yes, sir," Faro said, coming forward and holding out her datapad. "I'm afraid we were unsuccessful in finding a pattern."

Thrawn took the datapad, and for a moment he studied the numbers in silence. Faro watched him, wondering if, like her, he was thinking that Commander Eli Vanto might have been able to dig something out of the seemingly random times, dates, and comm frequencies she'd collected. Vanto had been gifted at such things.

But Vanto was gone, disappeared without a trace one day from the *Chimaera*. And while rumors placed him everywhere from Wild Space to a secret planning group in the Emperor's palace to floating dead in deep space, the fact was that no one really knew what had happened to him.

Faro had asked Thrawn about it at the time. The grand admiral's response had been polite enough, but Faro had left the conversation with the clear understanding that she was never to ask that question again.

Privately, given the fondness Thrawn had had for the young man and the master–pupil relationship they'd shared as Thrawn nurtured Vanto's career, Faro was pretty sure Vanto was dead. She could think of no other reason for him to have left the *Chimaera*.

"Perhaps the rebels are being unusually cautious," Thrawn said, handing back the datapad. "It could also be that the group planning to rescue Hera Syndulla is small enough that it has no need of overt communications."

Faro felt her lip twitch. Yes, the group that was undoubtedly plotting Syndulla's rescue from Governor Pryce's detention block was certainly small. But it should by no means be discounted, if only because it included the former Jedi Kanan Jarrus and the young would-be Jedi Ezra Bridger.

In some ways, Faro would have preferred that Syndulla had died with the rest of her X-wing squadron in their abortive attempt to wrest the space over Lothal away from the *Chimaera* and the rest of Thrawn's force. Prisoners could be useful in a number of ways, but they also created headaches and focal points for new enemy operations.

With Thrawn completely in charge, Faro had no doubt he would turn those liabilities into assets. But Pryce had the prisoner, and she didn't have Thrawn's intelligence, subtlety, or sheer strategic skill.

Even worse was the fact that Pryce had allowed herself to become emotionally involved in the situation. The governor was taking the rebels' attacks on her planet personally, and that meant thinking with her heart instead of her head. Taking Thrawn's advice and influence away from Lothal, even for a few days, could mean disaster.

At the very least, Syndulla could die without rendering any useful service to the Empire. That would be a waste of a valuable resource, which Pryce also didn't seem to care about.

"I take it you disapprove of the *Chimaera* traveling to Coruscant?"

"Yes, sir, I do," Faro said. Thrawn had long since learned how to read her face and body language. Faro had long since accepted that ability without getting freaked out by it. "I don't think Governor Pryce has any idea what kind of nasty she has by the tail with Syndulla. If Jarrus and his team move to rescue her, I don't think Pryce can stop them."

"Agreed," Thrawn said. "On the other hand, losing Syndulla would be a relatively small defeat. Losing the TIE Defender program would be catastrophic. If Director Krennic's project is the one I think it is, it represents a strategically shortsighted approach to both offensive and defensive warfare. If he has indeed persuaded the Emperor to divert the Defenders' funding, the Empire's entire future would be strongly impacted."

"Yes, sir," Faro said. Lord Vader, she knew, had also expressed interest in the Defender, especially after his experiences flying one against the Grysk forces out in the Unknown Regions. That support should certainly weigh in on Thrawn's side.

But Vader spoke for the Emperor. If the Emperor turned his back on the Defender, so would Vader.

There was a chime from the comm. "Admiral; bridge," Commander Hammerly's voice came from the speaker. "We've just received a new set of destination coordinates from Governor Tarkin. We're now apparently to meet him aboard the *Firedrake,* currently in the Sev Tok system."

A hint of a frown crossed Thrawn's face. "Interesting. Did he indicate whether or not the Emperor would be present?"

"No, sir, there was no mention of him," Hammerly said. "But the message *did* state that Director Krennic and a few others would be present. I did an origination check, and the message and coordinates definitely came from Tarkin."

"Very good, Commander," Thrawn said. "Reset course to accommodate; jump to hyperspace when ready."

"Yes, sir."

Thrawn again keyed off. "Thoughts, Commodore?"

"Seems awfully cloak-and-blade," Faro said, punching up the *Firedrake* on her datapad. Imperial Star Destroyer, flagship of Grand Admiral Balanhai Savit and the Third Fleet. "If Tarkin wants to meet aboard a Star Destroyer, why not here aboard the *Chimaera*?"

"I'm sure Tarkin has his reasons," Thrawn said. "He generally does."

There was a warning tone from the office's repeater displays: The *Chimaera* was on the move. "Yes, sir," Faro said. "With your permission, Admiral, I'd like to return to the bridge and run an extra check on all of this."

"Certainly, Commodore," Thrawn said. "I trust you're relieved that one of your concerns, at least, has fallen away."

Faro frowned. "Sir?"

Thrawn's eyes seemed to harden. "It appears that we will not, in fact, be traveling to Coruscant."

"Admiral?" Captain Boulag called from the Star Destroyer *Firedrake*'s command walkway. "Director Krennic's shuttle has just docked in the hangar bay."

"Acknowledged," Grand Admiral Savit called back from the aft bridge, scowling to himself. Last-minute schedule changes, high-ranking persons intruding on his ship, politics upon politics upon politics—it was like the Republic had been reborn within the Empire, with every bit of the old headaches and frustration reborn with it.

"You seem unhappy, Admiral," the thin, gray-haired man standing at the comm station suggested.

Savit focused on him. And of all the political players in the Empire, he'd long since decided, Grand Moff Tarkin was one of the worst. "I doubt my state of mind was high on the Emperor's priority list when he decided to change the meeting site from Coruscant to the *Firedrake*," he said.

Tarkin raised his eyebrows slightly. "*Should* it have been?"

Savit's lip twitched. Politics at its worst, but at least Tarkin had a sense of humor. "Of course not," he conceded. "The *Firedrake* and I are here to serve the Emperor and the Empire that he commands."

"As are we all," Tarkin said. "I'm certain you can see the Emperor's desire not to waste any additional time by asking the participants to travel all the way to Coruscant. The *Firedrake*'s current location was a key factor in the decision."

Savit pricked up his ears. *A* key factor? "Of course," he said. "And the other factors?"

Tarkin favored him with a thin smile, then let his gaze drift past Savit to the main bridge. "Tell me, Admiral: What are your thoughts concerning Project Stardust?"

"An interesting question," Savit said, his mind dropping reflexively into combat mode. The Emperor's pet project—Krennic's pride and joy—Tarkin's own quiet interest . . . "It's a bold and unique approach to the question of Imperial security," he continued, choosing his words carefully. "I'm looking forward to its completion."

"As are we all," Tarkin said. "At the same time, there are . . . issues . . . particularly with regard to allocation of funds. Are you familiar with Grand Admiral Thrawn's TIE Defender project?"

"Somewhat," Savit said. "I've looked over the schematics, but haven't had a chance to see any of the fighters in action."

"Thrawn feels quite strongly about the navy's need for the Defender," Tarkin said. "It's also no secret that the Emperor holds him in high regard. But the Emperor also feels strongly about the need for Stardust."

"Indeed," Savit said. "We're both busy men, Governor. What exactly do you want from me?"

Tarkin's forehead furrowed slightly as he studied Savit's face. "Can you keep a secret, Admiral?"

Savit had to smile at that one. "Of course."

"I have reason to believe the meeting that will take place shortly will end in a challenge," Tarkin said. "Director Krennic will be on one side. Admiral Thrawn will be on the other."

"The makings of a fine contest," Savit said. "Which of them do you want me to help win?"

"Thrawn is a proud officer," Tarkin said, his voice going thoughtful. "Efficient, highly capable, but definitely proud." Another thin smile. "Much like you yourself, Admiral. He would never ask for help, nor would he willingly accept it."

"But if I were to happen to find a way to assist him without his knowledge . . . ?" Savit suggested.

"I feel such assistance would be of great benefit to the Empire," Tarkin said gravely.

Or at least, Savit thought cynically, of great benefit to Tarkin himself.

But that was how the game was played. And really, anything that took Krennic and Stardust down a few pegs was all for the best. "Understood," he said. "If you'll excuse me, Director Krennic will expect me in the hangar deck to personally welcome him aboard. You've signaled Thrawn about the change in venue?"

"Yes, and the *Chimaera* has acknowledged my message," Tarkin said. "Please add my greetings to Director Krennic, and I'll see both of you in a few hours."

"I'll do so, Governor." Savit smiled. "And I'll look forward to the meeting."

Three men are seated around the table in the Star Destroyer Firedrake's *command conference room. The room itself is a duplicate of the* Chimaera's *conference room, though the* Firedrake's *table and chairs are newer and somewhat more elaborate.*

"Ah—Grand Admiral Thrawn," Tarkin said in greeting. *His expression holds anticipation, perhaps an underlying calculation. His voice holds calmness, perhaps with the mental preparation of one going into combat.* "Allow me to introduce Grand Admiral Savit, commander of the *Firedrake* and the Third Fleet. I don't believe you two have met before."

"No, Governor, we haven't," Savit said. *His voice holds guarded welcome. His expression holds wariness and evaluation. His body stance holds a mixture of confidence and pride.* "Welcome aboard, Admiral."

"You may have heard of Admiral Savit through his family's music programs on Coruscant," Tarkin said. *The calculation in his voice increases. The tone holds warning, perhaps a heightened political awareness of the strong cultural position of Savit's family.*

"So I have. I would very much like to attend one of your performances someday."

"You'd certainly be welcome," Savit said. *His voice holds pride and a hint of smugness, reflecting his own awareness of his family's status.*

"And this—" *The stiffness in Tarkin's voice increases, perhaps accompanied by heightened combat awareness. His expression holds reserve, perhaps antagonism.* "—is Director Orson Krennic."

"Admiral." *Krennic's voice holds perhaps caution. His expression holds perhaps unfriendliness. His body stance holds perhaps anger, per-haps defiance.* "I understand you wish to take funding away from my Stardust project."

"Not at all. I wish only to preserve the funding I was already prom-ised."

"By the Emperor himself, I might add," Tarkin said. *He looks at Krennic for half a second, his eyes unblinking, then touches a switch on the console before him. There is a stiffness to his touch, perhaps holding combat readiness.* "Now that we're all assembled, I shall alert him that we're ready to proceed."

There is a pause of eleven seconds. No one speaks. Tarkin's eyes re-main fixed on Krennic. Krennic's eyes shift between Thrawn and Tar-kin. Savit's eyes remain on the table's holopad, his expression holding watchful calm.

The holopad lights up, and an image of the Emperor appears above it. "Good day, Governor Tarkin," he said. *His voice holds anticipation and interest. The shaky image renders his expression, currently in pro-file, unreadable.* "Director Krennic; Grand Admiral Savit; Grand Ad-miral Thrawn."

"Good day, Your Majesty," Tarkin said. *He inclines his head in greet-ing and perhaps respect. The others do the same. Krennic's expression includes a small smile, perhaps holding confidence.* "As you know, Project Stardust has run into a small problem, which I thought should be presented to you."

"Indeed." *The Emperor's face turns to Krennic. The corners of his mouth turn downward.* "I was under the impression that Stardust was proceeding at a satisfactory pace."

"The project itself is, Your Majesty," Krennic said. *His voice contin-ues to hold confidence.* "The problem is merely in the supply chain, and I assure you it's under control."

"Is it?" the Emperor countered. "Governor Tarkin seems to believe differently."

"Indeed, Your Majesty," Tarkin said. *His expression does not change, but there is a loosening of facial muscles that perhaps indicates a hid-den desire to smile.* "And as Director Krennic seems unwilling or unable to face the problem, I have invited Grand Admiral Thrawn here for consultation."

"So I see," the Emperor said. *The image turns, a small smile touching his lips.* "And what, pray tell, does Grand Admiral Mitth-'raw'nuruodo think of this situation?"

"Actually, Your Majesty, I've not had an opportunity to bring the admiral up to speed," Tarkin said. "With the extreme security surrounding Stardust, I deemed it prudent to keep any such details off the HoloNet."

"Very wise, Governor Tarkin," the Emperor said. "Perhaps, Director Krennic, you would be kind enough to explain your reading of the situation." *The corners of his mouth again turn down.* "For *both* our benefits."

The muscles in Krennic's throat tighten briefly. "As I said, Your Majesty, the situation is under control. We're merely having a few problems with mynocks at the equipment transfer point."

"Grallocs," Tarkin murmured.

"Grallocs are simply a cousin species to mynocks," Krennic countered. *His expression hardens, the skin flushing slightly. Possibly annoyance; possibly anger; possibly embarrassment.* "They live in vacuum, they attack power cables and couplers—"

"They're also considerably larger and tougher than typical mynocks," Savit put in. *His expression holds hidden amusement.* "Governor Haveland and her people have had a great deal of trouble with them in the Esaga sector."

"The point is that they're a nuisance and nothing more," Krennic said. *The skin reddening fades. His voice holds renewed control. His eyes are steady on Tarkin, perhaps holding challenge.*

"A *nuisance*?" Tarkin asked. *His expression holds triumph.* "Your own reports show the equipment and point-defense turbolaser transshipments are already three weeks behind schedule. I don't see how this qualifies as merely a *nuisance*."

"So you are saying Stardust is being held hostage by a group of *vermin*?" *The Emperor's voice holds controlled anger. His eyes focus on Krennic.*

"I assure Your Majesty that the problem is under control." *Krennic's voice holds fresh caution. But the confidence remains intact.*

"Admiral Mitth'raw'nuruodo?" the Emperor invited. "Do you share Director Krennic's assessment?"

"A delay of three weeks seems more than simply a nuisance. But I have duties to attend to on Lothal."

"We all have duties, Admiral," Tarkin said. "But Governor Pryce has the bulk of your force available to maintain order. Surely you can spare some time to deal with this problem."

"It appears that Admiral Savit has more information and experience with these creatures than I do. He would be better able to find a solution."

"Admiral Savit also has other duties," Tarkin said. "Furthermore, he lacks your tactical and problem-solving capabilities. Capabilities of which, I dare say, Director Krennic should already have been cognizant."

"I tire of this bickering," the Emperor said. "You, Governor, were the one who arranged this meeting. What precisely was your intent?"

Tarkin's eyes are steady, his face again holding triumph. "Director Krennic has suggested to Your Majesty that the funds earmarked for the TIE Defender program be transferred to Stardust. I propose that this delay in Stardust equipment shipments not only threatens the project's timetable, but also squanders funds that could and should be utilized elsewhere."

"So you propose a trade?" the Emperor asked. *His voice holds anticipation.*

"I do, Your Majesty," Tarkin said. "I propose that if Admiral Thrawn is able to solve this problem and destroy the grallocs, the necessary funds be restored to his Defender program."

"Director Krennic?" the Emperor invited.

Krennic is silent a full second. "I would be willing," he said at last. *His face is under careful control. His eyes are wary, as if watching a stalking animal.* "If Admiral Thrawn can destroy them within the next week."

"That's hardly fair," Savit objected. *His expression and voice hold contempt.* "As I said, Governor Haveland has been dealing with these things for years."

"If Admiral Thrawn can't solve it in that time, he's of no use to us," Krennic countered. "It would also, I daresay, bring his so-called problem-solving capabilities into serious question."

"Admiral Mitth'raw'nuruodo?" the Emperor asked. "I give you the decision."

"I accept Governor Tarkin's proposal. I further accept Director Krennic's conditions."

"Very well," the Emperor said. *The corners of his mouth turn up in a satisfied smile.* "One week. Director Krennic, you will provide the necessary coordinates. Admiral Savit, you will provide all the information Governor Haveland has gleaned about these creatures. Admiral Mitth'raw'nuruodo, you have one week." The image vanished, and the holopad went dark.

"One more thing," Krennic said. *His eyes turn to Thrawn. His expression holds tension, perhaps suspicion, perhaps simple animosity.* "I'll be sending a representative aboard to observe your procedure and the progress of your work."

"I hardly think that necessary," Tarkin said. "Admiral Thrawn's success record speaks for itself."

"Admiral Thrawn's record also speaks of some notable irregularities," Krennic said. *His voice is harsh, no longer pretending a veneer of civility.* "I know what you're up to, Tarkin. If I'm to sacrifice any Stardust funds, I want to ensure that proper Imperial procedures have been followed. To the letter."

"They will be. I will expect the transfer point's coordinates to be transmitted to the *Chimaera* within the quarter hour. Your representative will board within that same time period or be left behind."

"Not a problem, Admiral Thrawn," Krennic said. *His expression becomes a smile, perhaps mocking, perhaps triumphant.* "They'll arrive simultaneously, since Assistant Director Ronan will personally bring the data." *He looks at Tarkin, his smile fading, his expression turning hard but once again feigning civility.* "As Governor Tarkin said, this data is too sensitive to trust to transmissions."

Savit rises from his chair. His expression holds both amusement and disdain. "Come, Admiral. I'll escort you back to your shuttle." *He smiles, the amusement fading and the disdain increasing.* "Along the way we can talk about grallocs. And other predators."

The door to the suite slid open, and Brierly Ronan looked up to see Director Krennic stride through the opening, his long white cape swirling behind him. "Director," Ronan greeted him, rising quickly from his chair. "I trust the meeting went well?"

"No, it did not," Director Krennic said, biting out each word. "Are you familiar with Grand Admiral Thrawn?"

"Ah . . . I've heard the name, sir," Ronan said cautiously. "But that's all."

"Then you need to get an education," the director growled. "The terminal over there—download everything the *Firedrake* has on Thrawn."

"Yes, sir," Ronan said, hurrying over to the terminal. "May I ask what this is all about?"

"You may," the director said sourly. "Apparently, Thrawn is the latest weapon Tarkin's picked to launch against me."

"*Weapon*, sir?"

"Weapon." The director dropped into a chair, deftly flapping his cape back with both hands to get it clear as he sat down. "As in, our dear grand moff's latest attempt to steal Stardust out from under me." He snorted. "And the Emperor just sat there and smiled. *Smiled.*"

Ronan felt a surge of contempt as he keyed the computer terminal. Typical. Instead of providing actual leadership, the kind of guidance Director Krennic gave his staff and workers on a daily basis, Emperor Palpatine chose to entertain himself by pitting his subordinates against each other and watching the resulting battles. "What do you want me to do?"

Director Krennic took a deep, calming breath. "Tarkin has maneuvered Thrawn into wagering the funds for his TIE Defender project against his ability to solve the gralloc problem our Kurost sector

shipment line is having. Thrawn has one week to get rid of the grallocs. If he fails, Stardust gets those funds."

"And Thrawn actually *accepted* those terms?"

"He did," the director said grimly. "Which puts us in an interesting
situation of our own. We want Thrawn to get rid of the grallocs; but
we want him to do it *after* his week is up."

Ronan thought about that. "That's certainly the best solution," he
said. "But what keeps him from simply stopping when his time runs
out?"

"In theory, nothing," Director Krennic conceded. "But in actual
practice, he strikes me as the stubborn sort. If he's close, I think he'll
keep at it." He gestured toward Ronan. "That's where you come in.
I've arranged for you to join Thrawn aboard the *Chimaera*, where
you'll watch the operation and send me reports on his progress.
You're to note any approach that looks even marginally promising
and send me the details."

"Yes, sir," Ronan said, peering at the display. Ah—there it was: The
navy's official file on Thrawn. The more unofficial files kept by many
of Imperial Center's hierarchy might be better, but Savit's private
files would be encrypted and he had no way of slicing into them. "So
if he *does* want to give up after his week . . . ?" he asked as he slid a
data card into the slot.

"Your job will be to see that he doesn't," the director said. "Failing
that, you're to collect whatever pieces he's found and bring them
back so that we can put them together into our own solution. Any
questions?"

"No, sir."

"Then you're dismissed," Director Krennic ordered. "Thrawn's expecting you; you're to meet him in the hangar bay." He pulled out a
data card and handed it to Ronan. "Here are the coordinates to the
transfer point for the *Chimaera* to use. Thrawn will know how to
decrypt it."

"Yes, sir," Ronan said. He tucked away the data card, nodded a
farewell, and turned toward the door.

"And Ronan?"

Ronan turned back. "Yes?"

"Watch him," the director said quietly. "Watch him carefully. He wouldn't be a grand admiral if he weren't smart, and there may be more to Tarkin's gambit than meets the eye."

"Not a problem, sir," Ronan promised. "Whatever Tarkin's planning, I'll be ready for it."

Savit had never met Thrawn before. But like Krennic, he'd heard stories of the man's exploits.

Now, face-to-face with him, he had to admit to a bit of disappointment.

Thrawn was visually impressive, certainly. The blue skin and glowing red eyes made a nice counterpoint to the grand admiral's white uniform and gold shoulder bars. There was an air of authority about him as well, a calmness and global awareness that contrasted greatly with so many officers, even senior ones, whom Savit had met and served with throughout his long career.

Even more telling, the fact that Thrawn's skin and eyes marked him as only near-human should have severely limited his rise through the ranks, if indeed he'd been permitted into the navy at all. The fact that he'd made it all the way to the very top was proof of his strategic and tactical abilities.

But he had one huge, glaring, fatal flaw. Clearly, he had absolutely no competence in the realm of politics.

The way he'd responded to Krennic and Tarkin proved that beyond any doubt. Brilliant tactician or not, favorite of the Emperor or not, he'd looked like a ratling caught in a floodlight sweep in there.

In fact, Savit would bet large sums of money that Thrawn *still* didn't know what all that had been about.

Easy enough to check. "Interesting, wasn't it?" he asked casually as he and Thrawn walked down the passageway toward the *Firedrake*'s hangar. "Their little dance."

"Excuse me?" Thrawn asked.

Savit mentally shook his head. He'd called it, all right. "The dance between Krennic and Tarkin," he said. "Krennic runs Stardust. Tarkin wants very badly to take it away from him. And so he brings you into play."

For a couple of steps, Thrawn seemed to digest that. "Does he think I will support him in his confrontation?"

"He might," Savit said. "But it's probably more a matter of him trying to show he's a better administrator than Krennic. Krennic has a problem; Tarkin is the one who's smart enough to bring in the expert to solve it. That expert being you, of course."

Another two steps' worth of silence. "So you're saying that, rather than being a problem solver, I'm merely a weapon?"

"Exactly," Savit said, his estimation of the man beside him rising a notch.

But only one. After all, Savit had had to lay it out for him. And even then, Thrawn had had to convert it to military terms before he was able to grasp the concept involved.

"And don't have any illusions," he continued. "Now that Tarkin has brought you onto the field of battle, both sides are going to try to use you. Tarkin will try to bludgeon Krennic with you, and Krennic will try to use Tarkin's association with you to diminish Tarkin's own standing with the Emperor."

"Only if I fail."

"Trust me," Savit said, snorting out a laugh. "If Governor Haveland couldn't get rid of the cursed things in three years of trying, you aren't going to do it in a week."

"We shall see," Thrawn said. "Have you the gralloc data the Emperor asked you to deliver to me?"

The man had confidence in himself. Savit had to give him that. "Right here," he said, pulling a data card from his pocket and handing it over. "How exactly do—?"

"Admiral?" a voice came from behind them.

Savit turned. A middle-aged man was striding toward them, his white tunic with its prominent colonel's rank plaque glittering in the *Firedrake*'s lights.

And behind the tunic, a thigh-length white cape fluttering along behind him.

Mentally, Savit shook his head. He knew of Krennic's pompous affectation regarding that long cape of his. He hadn't realized the director had foisted the same nonsense onto his senior staff.

"I was hoping to catch you, Admiral Thrawn, before you returned to the *Chimaera*," the stranger said. Despite his apparent haste, Savit noticed, the man didn't seem to be making much of an effort to hurry. In his daily life, apparently, the flowing cape automatically commanded the kind of respect that allowed him to save his own time at the expense of others'.

Maybe that was the case on Stardust. Not on a grand admiral's flagship. "Then you'd best hurry," Savit said. Turning his back on the other, he resumed walking.

He got three steps before he realized that Thrawn hadn't followed.

He stopped and again turned around. Thrawn was still standing where Savit had left him, waiting patiently for the man in the cape to catch up.

Savit shook his head, this time not even bothering to hide his annoyance. He'd just explained to Thrawn that he was Tarkin's weapon—and now he couldn't even stand up against the smallest move from Krennic's side?

Hopeless. The only question was whether Krennic or Tarkin would make the best use of him before tossing him aside.

The newcomer made his leisurely way to the others. He was perhaps younger than middle-aged, Savit saw now, at least in overall appearance.

But that was his skin and posture. His eyes, Savit noted, still looked old.

"I'm Assistant Director Brierly Ronan," he said, as if either of the grand admirals might not have already figured that out. "Director Krennic has instructed me to observe your operation, Admiral Thrawn."

"You are welcome aboard the *Chimaera*," Thrawn said. He turned to Savit. "You were saying, Admiral Savit?"

It took Savit a second to remember what Thrawn was talking about. "I was going to ask how exactly you were planning to proceed."

"From the beginning, of course," Thrawn said, inclining his head. "Thank you for your time and advice, Admiral. I believe Assistant Director Ronan and I can find the rest of our way alone."

"Yes," Savit said. "Good luck, Admiral."

"Thank you." Thrawn turned to Ronan and again inclined his head. "If you'll follow me, Assistant Director Ronan, I'm anxious to get started."

"I trust," Commodore Faro said as she unlocked the door to Ronan's new quarters and gestured him inside, "that this will be satisfactory."

Ronan stepped past her and looked around. As one of Director Krennic's senior associates, he'd seen the insides of any number of Star Destroyers. The suite Faro had assigned him wasn't the lowest someone of his rank could expect, but it wasn't the most luxurious the *Chimaera* had to offer, either. It certainly didn't match the suite Savit had given the director and his staff. Clearly, Faro and her commanding officer were hedging their bets, giving Ronan something that would keep him placid while at the same time making sure they had something better to offer someone of higher position, should that become necessary. Tarkin, perhaps, or even Director Krennic himself.

Typical. Politics, maneuvering, covering their backfills, trying to make everyone happy while looking for advantage wherever they could. Everyone did it, from that old fool of an Emperor down to the lowliest bureaucrat.

Ronan was just glad he didn't have to put up with that nonsense. Director Krennic's sheer brilliance, competence, and ability meant he didn't have to play those stupid games.

"Quite satisfactory," he told Faro, resisting the urge to point out that the *Chimaera* had better quarters available. Whenever possible, he preferred to rise above politics, too. "I trust in turn that he'll run the decryption on the data card as quickly as possible so that we can get under way?"

"Quite quickly," Faro assured him. "Though I confess to some perplexity as to why a hand-delivered data card needed to be encrypted in the first place."

"Director Krennic's orders," Ronan said. "Even aboard an Imperial vessel there might be spies, and even a trusted courier can be waylaid and information stolen. This way, even so brazen a thief would still come up empty."

"I see," Faro said. The words were polite, but Ronan could sense the word *paranoid* lurking beneath them.

Not that the opinions of others bothered him, of course. Precautions such as this were logical and creative, and were precisely why Stardust had remained hidden from prying eyes and sticky fingers all these years.

"Fortunately, decryption won't add that much time to our journey," Faro continued. "Admiral Thrawn had already determined our goal would be no more than three hours away, and most likely only two."

Ronan felt his eyes narrow. The location of the current transfer station was indeed only an hour and a half from here at Star Destroyer speeds. But that information was supposed to be a dark secret. "May I ask how he learned that?" he asked, putting some demand into his tone.

"The admiral assumed Director Krennic would have made one final attempt at solving the problem before confronting Governor Tarkin," Faro said, the barest slightest hint of amusement dancing in her eyes at Ronan's obvious discomfiture. "Admiral Savit's command area defines a specific section of this region, and Governor Tarkin's presence at the recent trade conference on Charra defines his own probable travel vector. For Admiral Thrawn, it was a simple calculation."

"Indeed," Ronan said, studying Faro's face. He'd assumed Thrawn was another political appointee, like most of the other eleven grand admirals, though in Thrawn's case it would be the Emperor playing the politics and not Thrawn himself. Clearly, this grand admiral had more than a modicum of native intelligence.

Which was not necessarily a good thing. Getting the gralloc problem solved *after* the deadline was the key to making sure none of Stardust's funds were drained off into Thrawn's shortsighted TIE Defender project. In Ronan's book, half a victory was still half a defeat.

Still, if Governor Haveland and Grand Admiral Savit hadn't been able to obliterate the grallocs after years of effort, there was no way a newcomer could accomplish that task in a week, no matter how clever he was. All Ronan needed to do was make sure that after Thrawn failed, he left behind enough pieces for Director Krennic to solve the problem.

"It will be interesting to see if the grand admiral's deduction is correct," he told Faro. Even now, he had no intention of giving her any more information—or private amusement—than necessary. "Please have someone alert me when we arrive."

CHAPTER 2

The transfer system was a breathtaking beehive of activity, with hundreds of ships of various sizes floating in clumps and queues, or jumping in and out of hyperspace near the edges. The focal points for most of the activity seemed to be a dozen large bulk freighters, spread out through the area, each running an innocuous civilian ID mark. Groups of smaller ships clustered around each of the freighters, waiting their turn to dock and transfer their cargoes. A handful of midsized warships patrolled the perimeter while sentry patterns of TIE fighters swept around and past them.

Faro had seen a similar scene once when she visited a system where a newly commissioned Star Destroyer was being provisioned and crewed. But never had she witnessed anything this elaborate.

The system, she also noted with a small sense of gloating, was also exactly an hour and thirty-two minutes from the *Firedrake* meeting point, putting it well within Thrawn's estimate of two hours or less. She wondered if Ronan would be impressed by the grand admiral's accuracy.

From the stony look on his face as he arrived on the *Chimaera*'s bridge, apparently not.

"Assistant Director Ronan," Thrawn said in greeting as he approached along the command walkway. "Or do you prefer to be addressed as *Colonel*?"

"Either is acceptable," Ronan said.

"But which do you *prefer*?" Thrawn asked again. "I assume the military rank is largely honorary."

A muscle in Ronan's cheek twitched. "Honorary, perhaps, but quite necessary to my work. You'd be surprised how many in the Imperial military refuse to take civilians and civilian orders seriously."

"I doubt I would be surprised at all," Thrawn said. He gestured toward the forward viewport. "Explain this to me."

Ronan's lip twitched disdainfully. "It's really not that difficult," he said, and Faro could hear a hint of condescension creeping into the arrogance. "Shipments of supplies come in from all over the local sectors. They're transferred to larger freighters, which will fly them to Stardust's location. That way, only carefully selected and screened pilots need to know the final destination."

"That much is of course obvious," Thrawn said mildly. "I was asking that you supply the details."

"What details?"

"I wish to know which ships are arriving from which systems in which sectors," Thrawn said. "I wish a list of the captains and crews, the individual cargo manifests, and which companies supplied those cargoes."

"What does any of that have to do with anything?" Ronan asked, frowning. "You're here to get rid of the grallocs."

"We are here to solve the problem," Thrawn corrected. "To that end, I need to know everything related to it."

"It's a question of security," Ronan said. "If it were relevant to your task, maybe. But it's not."

"I disagree," Thrawn said. "Shall we ask Director Krennic for his opinion? Or perhaps we should request a ruling from the Emperor."

Ronan's lips compressed, and he turned his head to glare out the viewport. He held that pose a moment, then gave a small sniff.

"There'll be a harbormaster aboard one of the ships," he said reluctantly. "I can probably get him to release the listings to me."

"Senior Lieutenant Lomar is our chief communications officer," Thrawn said, gesturing to the crew pit comm station. "He can assist you in sending your message." He shifted the pointing finger toward the viewport. "In the meantime, is *that* one of the grallocs?"

Ronan gave a little snort. "Yes."

Faro leaned a little farther forward. Barely visible against the lights of all those drifting ships, something dark was gliding or fluttering or flapping—it was hard to tell which—past one of the nearest of the maneuvering ships. Its batlike wings, slender body, and large, tendriled suckermouth branded it instantly as a mynock relative.

A *big* relative. Whereas mynocks seldom grew larger than a couple of meters, the creature moving around out there was at least five meters long and had a wingspan to match. That alone was probably enough to raise it from nuisance to serious threat. "Pretty fast," she commented. "I didn't think mynocks could maneuver that well, either."

"As Director Krennic said, they're a serious problem," Ronan said. "Did it land? I've lost it."

"I believe it attached itself to that VCX-200 freighter," Thrawn said, pointing at the ship the gralloc had been sweeping toward. "Lieutenant Pyrondi?"

"Sir?" the chief weapons officer replied.

"Opinion, Lieutenant," Thrawn said. "If we wish to take that creature, how do you recommend we do it?"

"Turbolasers would be quickest," Pyrondi said. "But with all these ships around, a miss could cause serious collateral damage."

"As well as a direct hit leaving little for us to study," Thrawn said.

"Yes, sir, that's the other problem with it," Pyrondi agreed. "If we instead used one of the laser cannons—"

"What do you need to study it for?" Ronan interrupted. "I thought Savit already gave you all of Governor Haveland's information."

"He did," Thrawn confirmed. "I find it useful to collect my own data."

Ronan started to say something else, seemed to think better of it, and waved a hand as if in apology. "Of course. Carry on."

"Thank you," Thrawn said. "You were saying, Lieutenant?"

"Laser cannons would be safer for bystanders," Pyrondi said. "But we'd have to get in closer to use them. Tractor beams are another possibility, and they've got more range than the laser cannons. But I'm not sure we can focus them tightly enough to grab something that small, especially something flitting around as much as these things are."

"What about the ion cannons?" Faro asked.

"I doubt they'd be effective, Commodore," Pyrondi said. "Given the grallocs' environment, they likely have a high resistance to ionic bursts of every sort."

"They seem also able to tack against solar wind," Thrawn said. "Your overall assessment seems valid, Lieutenant. But the first step in assessing any theory is to compare it with reality. We will begin with the ion cannons, and see what happens."

What happened was basically nothing.

The first problem was getting the *Chimaera* into position to shoot at one of the grallocs in the first place. On the one hand, Faro saw as they moved in closer, there were plenty of targets to choose from: hundreds of the dark-gray creatures, swooping in and out in search of power cables or improperly shielded sensor clusters, or already attached and feeding. But on the other hand, as Pyrondi had surmised, they moved so erratically that targeting them was next to impossible. After nearly an hour of trying to get into firing range, Thrawn ordered Pyrondi to find one that was already attached to a freighter and shoot it.

It was a waste of effort. As Pyrondi had also predicted, the gralloc flapped its way out of the ion burst without any apparent damage. The freighter itself wasn't so lucky, and once its captain got his comm system back up he threatened to call everyone from Krennic to Tarkin to the Emperor himself and have the stupid Star Destroyer commander disciplined for his action.

Thrawn didn't seem fazed by the complaints. Ronan did, though, and Faro found it fascinating to watch the play of expressions across his face. At one point, she thought he was going to march over to the bridge comm station and call Krennic himself.

Luckily for him, he decided to stay out of it.

Which he probably regretted when Thrawn then proceeded to order attacks on three more sitting grallocs and their associated freighters.

"Interesting," the grand admiral commented calmly when the last of the verbal firestorms from those freighters finally faded away. "Commodore, did you note the grallocs' vectors as they escaped our ion bursts?"

Faro frowned, searching her memory. As far as she'd been able to see, the grallocs simply shoved off the hulls and fluttered away to safety. Obviously, Thrawn had seen something more. "No, sir, not really," she admitted. "Once the attack failed, I was focused on assessing potential damage to the ships."

"Commander Hammerly, put the sensor recordings on the monitor," Thrawn ordered. "Let us have another look."

Faro watched the repeats closely. On the third attack, she thought she saw the pattern.

On the fourth she was sure of it.

"The gralloc follows the ion splash pattern as it runs away," she said.

"Very good," Thrawn said. "Commander: Replay the recordings. Commodore: Speculation?"

Faro frowned at the display as Hammerly ran the recordings again. "I can't tell, sir," she admitted. "It could be that the burst is confusing it, like the way some insects track along a bright glow rod thinking it's a planetary moon. Or it could be feeding on the ions themselves."

"Assistant Director?" Thrawn invited, turning to Ronan. "Have you any thoughts?"

"My thought is that this is your problem, not mine," Ronan said tartly. "My other thought is that you're wasting time." He stopped, and again it seemed to Faro that he was forcing a shift in mental gears. "But it's your mission, and your time," he continued in a calmer tone. "If you want to spend it advancing the cause of Imperial knowledge instead of flat-out killing the things, that's your business."

"I appreciate your indulgence," Thrawn said. "Lieutenant Pyrondi, have your crews prepare targeting solutions for the laser cannons. Assistant Director Ronan would like to see what it takes to kill one."

Hitting a freighter with an ion cannon burst would put the ship out of commission for anything from a few minutes to a couple of hours, but it rarely caused permanent damage. Not so the blast from a laser cannon. As a result, the parameters Thrawn set for the *Chimaera*'s firing crews severely limited where they could shoot, how rapidly they could shoot, and at what power settings they could shoot.

The result was even less helpful than the ion tests. In two hours, the *Chimaera* was able to find only three grallocs sufficiently in the clear for a shot, and the creatures' erratic flight patterns caused all three of those shots to miss.

"Shall we switch to turbolasers now?" Ronan asked with an air of strained patience as the last targeted gralloc ducked out of sight and range behind a YT-2400 freighter. "Putting in a wider blast profile might at least enable you to singe a wing."

"Admiral!" Hammerly called urgently. "Allanar N3 freighter bearing two forty-seven by thirty-three—erratic maneuvering, hyperdrive spinning up. I make four to six grallocs attached to its hull."

"They've scrambled its power and control cables," Ronan bit out. "If it jumps now—"

"Ion cannons," Thrawn snapped. "Target Allanar N3 and fire."

But it was too late. Even as the *Chimaera* sent a cluster of ion bursts toward the stricken ship, there was a flicker of pseudomotion and the Allanar vanished into hyperspace.

Ronan swore under his breath. "And one more lost. Probably before it even off-loaded its cargo."

Faro felt her eyes narrow. "Its *cargo*?" she asked, turning to face Ronan. "Is that all you care about? Its *cargo*?"

"And its crew, too, of course," Ronan said stiffly, sending her glare straight back at her. "I'm not a monster."

"No, of course not," Faro said, pitching her tone to be just shy of insubordination.

"How many ships have been lost this way?" Thrawn asked.

"I don't know," Ronan said, turning his glare on Thrawn. "Too many. What does it matter?"

"And they always disappear?"

"What kind of question is that?" Ronan demanded. "Of course they disappear. The cursed grallocs continue chewing through the power and control cables until the hyperdrive fails and they're lost in interstellar space."

"That seems counterproductive for the grallocs," Thrawn commented. "Attacking a part of the ship that will strand themselves as well as their food source."

"In case you hadn't noticed, grallocs are not exactly an intelligent species."

"Perhaps," Thrawn said. "But I believe you were suggesting a shift to turbolaser fire?"

"A shift to—?" Ronan's nose twitched, and Faro felt a flicker of malicious amusement. Thrawn was better at revisiting the thread of an interrupted conversation than most people expected, often to their confusion. "Oh. No, actually, I was being facetious."

"Ah," Thrawn said. "But you're right. It's time to switch to a new strategy." He raised his voice. "Captain Dobbs? Have you been observing?"

"Yes, sir," The senior TIE Defender pilot's voice came over the bridge speakers.

Faro frowned. She'd completely missed the point where Thrawn had called Dobbs into the conversation.

"Your opinion?" Thrawn asked.

"It'll be tricky, sir," Dobbs said. "They're pretty fast and way more maneuverable than any starfighter I've ever seen. But I think I can get one for you."

"Very good, Captain," Thrawn said. "Launch when ready. We'll find you a target."

"Yes, sir."

"What are you doing?" Ronan asked. "Who's Captain Dobbs?"

"Captain Benj Dobbs is the current commander of my TIE Defender squadron," Thrawn said.

Faro winced to herself. The *current* commander, replacing Captain Vult Skerris, whose innate arrogance had gotten him killed in the recent starfighter battle over Lothal.

Unfortunately, Skerris's arrogance had been matched by superb combat skill. Neither Dobbs nor any of the other Defender pilots were anywhere near that level.

And that could be a problem. Once Thrawn solved this gralloc problem and got clear of Tarkin's and Krennic's little spitting contest, the *Chimaera* would almost certainly be going back into combat.

Faro could only hope Dobbs and his pilots would rise to whatever level was required.

Ronan had seen demonstrations of Thrawn's prized TIE Defenders once or twice before. He hadn't been impressed.

He was even less impressed now.

The pilot—Dobbs—was competent enough, swooping around and through the mass of drifting ships, rather like an oversized gralloc himself, only with the Defenders' trademark three wings instead of the grallocs' two. Every time Thrawn's sensor officer fed him coordinates, he was on it, chasing after the target with steady focus and an almost grim determination.

But focus and determination were poor substitutes for success. After two hours of trying, Dobbs was no closer to that goal than he'd been when he launched.

Meanwhile, the grand admiral himself had apparently lost interest in the whole thing. He'd wandered off barely ten minutes into the proceedings, conferring with Commodore Faro down in one of the crew pits, abandoning Ronan to watch the pointless exercise alone.

Top-level naval commanders. Stuffed-uniform-useless, every single one of them.

Ronan took a deep breath. Every instinct within him was screaming at the inefficiency of this operation, from Thrawn's fascination with gralloc minutiae, to the wasted efforts with the ion cannons, to the failure of the Defender pilot to bring down his quarry. Efficiency was what Director Krennic demanded of his people, and Ronan had spent years honing his own abilities in that area.

But that wasn't his purpose aboard the *Chimaera*. Yes, he wanted Thrawn to solve the gralloc problem; but *not* in the quickest and most effective way possible. The longer the grand admiral dragged out these preliminaries, the better the chance he would run down the clock on Director Krennic's conditions.

At which point, those badly needed Defender funds would go safely and securely back to their proper home at Stardust.

"Your opinion, Assistant Director?"

Ronan jerked. With his eyes on Dobbs and his thoughts on the general incompetence that pressed in on Stardust from all sides, he hadn't noticed Thrawn come up behind him. "As I said two hours ago, this is a waste of time," he said. "Even your fancy Defender can't catch them."

"I agree," Thrawn said. "But that is largely because the grallocs wish to avoid him."

Ronan snorted. "Of course they wish to avoid him. They see him as a threat."

"And therein lies the key," Thrawn said again. "Commodore?"

"Lieutenant Fentaugh signals ready, Admiral," Faro called from the crew pit.

"Launch."

Ronan frowned. *Launch?* He looked back out the forward viewport.

Sure enough, a few seconds later a second TIE Defender streaked into view from the hangar bay in the *Chimaera*'s belly. It shot past the Star Destroyer's bow and headed out into the cluster of ships. "What's this for?" he asked. "Are you trying to corral one of the grallocs? Because I can tell you right now that chasing it with two ships won't do you any more good than chasing it with one."

"I agree," Thrawn said. "But Lieutenant Fentaugh's Defender isn't intended for pursuit."

"Then what's it for?"

Out of the corner of Ronan's eye he saw a small smile appear on Thrawn's face. "Bait," the grand admiral said. "Lieutenant Hammerly: Full sensor readout on Defender Two."

"Yes, sir." On the tactical display a sensor image of a TIE Defender appeared.

Ronan leaned a little closer to the display. Everything about the fighter looked completely normal . . . except that on one of the wings there was a blazing loop of high-voltage current.

"I had a bypass installed to feed the current normally meant for the number six laser cannon into an external loop cable," Thrawn continued. "Let us see what kind of interest it generates."

The blazing current generated interest, all right. Fentaugh's Defender had barely reached the nearest freighter before three grallocs abandoned the ships they were feeding on and headed at high speed toward it.

"Even faster than I realized," Faro murmured.

"Indeed," Thrawn said. "It will be interesting to see how they achieve such speeds. Captain Dobbs, I believe your target awaits you."

"On it, sir," Dobbs said briskly. "Do you want it dead or alive?"

"We'll begin with dead," Thrawn said. "If necessary, we can go back and capture a live one. I suggest the third gralloc of the group now pacing Lieutenant Fentaugh—do you see it?"

"The one lagging behind the others? Yes, sir."

"I presume from its relative lack of interest that it has recently fed," Thrawn said. "Take it."

"Yes, sir. Fentaugh, angle up-left twenty degrees and hold vector."

"Acknowledged."

It was, Ronan had to admit, about as neat and precise a maneuver as he'd ever witnessed. As Fentaugh's fighter held a steady course, Dobbs came up behind the group, nudging close behind the gralloc Thrawn had indicated. A quick, tight burst of laserfire, and the gralloc's flapping became a sort of reflexive fluttering and then went completely still.

There was, of course, still the matter of securing the carcass for transport to the *Chimaera*. Ronan expected Thrawn to order out a shuttle for that task, but Dobbs was already on it. Moving in close to the dead gralloc, he maneuvered the carcass between the forward points of one of his angled wings, then gave his fighter a quick spin, throwing the gralloc outward and wedging it solidly in place between the points. Then, with Fentaugh flying wingmate, he made a leisurely turn and headed home.

"Excellent," Thrawn said. "Commodore, go to medbay and confirm that the examination room and droids are prepared to receive the subject."

"Yes, sir." Faro climbed the stairs out of the crew pit and headed toward the aft bridge and the turbolift there.

"You have droids that can dissect a carcass?" Ronan asked.

"After a fashion," Thrawn said. "Imperial warships do not carry trained exobiologists unless the mission anticipates a need for them. However, the *Chimaera*'s library does include an exobio programming package. Two of our 2-1B medical droids have been reprogrammed, and should suffice for our purposes."

"I didn't realize the navy was that thorough."

"In general, it is not," Thrawn agreed. "I prefer to be prepared for as many contingencies as possible."

Ronan nodded to himself. In other words, Thrawn had spotted a gap in the navy's resources and taken it upon himself to make sure that gap was filled.

Once again, his opinion of this man reluctantly rose a notch.

"Come," Thrawn said, gesturing toward the aft bridge. "Let us see what we can learn about Director Krennic's adversaries."

CHAPTER 3

Most of the moffs and governors Grand Admiral Savit had dealt with over the years favored the use of holoprojectors for communication with other high-ranking civilian and military leaders. Part of that was probably the slightly lower resolution such images presented, which made their expressions and the thoughts behind them harder for adversaries and potential adversaries to read.

Mostly, though—he privately suspected—it was because the Emperor nearly always used holoprojectors, and for moffs like Haveland imitation was the most cynical form of flattery.

Still, today at least, the first part of that logic had failed. The expression on Haveland's flickering holoprojection was quite clear, and about as angry and frustrated as Savit had ever seen it.

"I've just received word," the moff bit out, "that yet *another* of my freighters has been taken and destroyed by these thrice-damned grallocs."

"So I've also heard," Savit confirmed. "The *Chimaera* reports that freighter AL6-KM44 was prematurely driven into hyperspace by a gralloc attack and presumably lost. It was an Allanar N3 light fr—"

"I know what kind of ship it was," Haveland cut in harshly. "I thought you said this blue-skinned Thrawn person was going to fix this problem."

"*Grand Admiral* Thrawn has barely begun his work," Savit said, putting the full weight of his rank and experience into his voice. Whatever he might think of Thrawn personally, the man was a fellow grand admiral and was *not* to be so casually insulted by a civilian, no matter how important Haveland thought she was. "I understand he's killed one of the grallocs and is doing some studies on it."

"*One* gralloc? What does he think he's going to do, deal with them one at a time?"

"I don't know what his plan is," Savit said. "Let me just remind you that you've had this thorn in your side for years without making any headway against it. Thrawn's supposed to be good at this sort of thing. I suggest you sit back and give him a chance."

"You suggest that, do you?" Haveland growled. "Well, let me tell you something about your precious hero. From what *I've* heard, much of his so-called success was due to a single man, someone he kept hidden in his shadow: unnoticed, uncredited, and unpromoted."

"Really," Savit said. "You've heard that, have you?"

"I have," Haveland said darkly. "Furthermore, once this secret adviser became so well known to the High Command that the scam was about to collapse, he conveniently and permanently disappeared. To this day, Thrawn refuses to tell anyone what happened to him."

"Intriguing," Savit said. "I don't suppose you have an actual name for this unsung genius."

A hint of uncertainty touched the edge of Haveland's indignation. "There are several possibles," she said. "Commander Alfren Cheno, Commander Eli Vanto, Admiral Plor Wiskovis—"

"And therein lies the unraveling," Savit said. "Multiple names and widely variant details are the hallmarks of unfounded rumors."

"An unfounded rumor is merely a fact that hasn't yet been confirmed."

"Or a soap bubble that continues to float until it bursts," Savit said. "I suggest you spend less time listening to idle gossip and more time focusing on ways to protect your ships from grallocs and other dangers."

"I suggest that *you* spend less time lecturing your betters and more time finding a way to get rid of these vermin," Haveland shot back.

"It's out of my hands," Savit said. "We'll both just have to hope that Tarkin and Krennic made the right decision in sending in Thrawn. Good day, Governor Haveland."

Haveland might have had a final word or two or twenty to deliver. Savit keyed off the holoprojector before she had the chance.

For a long moment, he gazed through the space where Haveland's image had been floating. Theoretically, of course, he could still go to the transfer point and either offer the *Chimaera* his help or at least see what kind of progress Thrawn was making. It was quite possible that that kind of teamwork was what Tarkin had been hinting at with his suggestion that Savit weigh in on Thrawn's side.

But politics was driving all of this, and both sides would be watching it unfold with the unblinking attention of hungry predators. Savit needed to choose the right moment to make his move, and even then it needed to be as invisible as possible. Until then, Thrawn was welcome to take all the heat his opponents could generate.

And yet . . .

Savit frowned. He'd heard the rumors Haveland had brought up. Unlike her, though, he'd taken the time to track down all the names the various stories listed as Thrawn's supposed captive genius. All the likely subjects were present and accounted for, either still in military service or else retired under perfectly reasonable circumstances.

All of them except one. And that one anomaly made Savit's instincts tingle uncomfortably.

Where *was* Commander Eli Vanto, anyway?

It had all started out well enough, Lieutenant Eli Vanto thought as he paged through yet another data listing filled with delicate Chiss script. Thrawn had told him that the Chiss Ascendancy had vital need of his talents and abilities, and that he'd arranged for Eli to be quietly released from his current duty aboard the *Chimaera*. Eli had accepted the new assignment and left Imperial space, arriving at the rendezvous point Thrawn had sent him to full of hope and expectation, with the excitement of the unknown tingling through him.

I am Admiral Ar'alani of the Chiss Defense Fleet, the blue-skinned woman had greeted him from the bridge of her ship. *Are you he?*

I am he, Eli had confirmed, making sure to fill his voice with the mix of confidence and respect that had served him well during his years in the Imperial fleet. *I am Eli Vanto. I bring greetings to you from Mitth'raw'nuruodo. He believes I can be of some use to the Chiss Ascendancy.*

Welcome, Eli Vanto, she'd replied. *Let us learn together if he was correct.*

That had been over a year ago. In retrospect, Eli thought a little sourly, he should have realized from Ar'alani's neutral words and tone that she wasn't impressed.

His first act aboard the *Steadfast* was to receive demotion from Imperial commander to Chiss Defense Fleet lieutenant. No real surprise there—different militaries would hardly have equivalent rank systems. His second act was to be dropped into an intensive course in Cheunh, the main Chiss language. Again, no surprise—though many aboard spoke the Sy Bisti trade language Eli was fluent in, it was certainly unreasonable to expect everyone to bend to the needs of a single crew member. Especially a newcomer *and* an alien.

But in and through all of that, Eli had expected to be put onto some kind of leadership or command track. Instead, he'd been dumped down here in the analysis department, sifting data, looking for patterns, and making predictions.

It was something he was very good at. Even Thrawn, with all his tactical and strategic genius, had recognized Eli's superiority at such things, and had utilized his skills to their fullest. In retrospect, it wasn't all that surprising that he'd passed that information on to Ar'alani.

The problem was that as far as Eli could tell, none of the data he'd been tasked to analyze meant anything at all.

They weren't listings of ship movements or cargo or smuggling manifests. They weren't groups of personnel, or alien troops, or alien operations. They weren't even anything internal to the *Steadfast,* patterns of power usage or data flow or something else designed to spot flaws in ship's functions or to predict imminent system failures.

To be honest, the whole thing felt like busywork. Eli had always hated busywork.

Still, Ar'alani struck him as a subtle sort of person. Maybe this was a test of his patience, or his willingness to enthusiastically obey even orders that seemed to make no sense. He'd certainly gone through a lot of such scenarios with Thrawn.

And really, it wasn't like the tour had been *all* routine. There'd been a seriously nasty skirmish with the Grysks and some of their allies near the Imperial edge of the Unknown Regions, which had made for a very interesting couple of days. After the excitement subsided, he'd hoped things might pick up a little.

To his disappointment, they hadn't. In fact, in many ways they'd actually slowed down.

Which wasn't to say the *Steadfast* wasn't in danger. On the contrary, it was in about as much danger right now as it had ever been.

The intercom at his station gave a little three-tone warble. "Lieutenant Ivant, report to the bridge immediately," First Officer Khresh's voice came over the speaker.

"Acknowledged," Eli called back, mentally rolling his eyes. The vast majority of Chiss names were composed of multiple syllables in three distinct parts, the first of which identified the person's family, the second of which was the given name, and the third of which reflected some social factor Eli hadn't yet figured out. Since using multisyllable titles all the time could seriously bog down conversations—and worse, timely military orders—the normal convention was to use core names for everything except in the most formal situations.

But there were a few exceptions to the norm. Admiral Ar'alani herself, for one, apparently had only a two-part name and no core name at all. The ship's navigators, the young Chiss girls gifted with Third Sight who used their ability to guide the *Steadfast* through hyperspace, also followed that pattern. Eli also hadn't figured out why they got the same naming convention as senior flag officers.

Early on, Ar'alani had explained to her officers and crew that Eli was another such exception, and that he should be addressed as *Lieutenant Vanto* or *Lieutenant Eli'van'to*. But for most of them the explanation didn't seem to have taken. Someone had taken Ar'alani's conversion of *Eli Vanto* into a standard three-part Chiss name, then created a core name out of the middle of it, and the name had stuck.

At first, Eli had wondered if it was a subtle insult, either to him or to the admiral who'd brought this alien into their midst. But Ar'alani hadn't taken offense at the flouting of her order, at least not in public, and eventually Eli decided to treat it as their way of accepting him as one of their own.

And it could have been worse. If he'd been unwise enough to tell them his middle initial—*N*—the name might have become *Invant*, which was way too close to *Infant* for comfort.

He was halfway to the bridge, passing the standard green- and blue-rimmed compartment doors, when the double-red-rimmed door to the navigation ready room a dozen meters in front of him slid open. One of the navigators stepped out into the corridor and turned toward the bridge.

Normally, seeing the back of a navigator's head wouldn't have given Eli a clue as to who she was. All of the *Steadfast*'s navigators were girls, nearly all of them between the ages of seven and fourteen, when Third Sight was at its strongest. On top of that, they tended to keep to themselves, and in all his time aboard he'd only met three of the five.

Vah'nya was the exception to all the rules. She was twenty-two years old, and unlike the children who shared her job she felt perfectly comfortable mixing with the rest of the adults aboard. Eli had seen and talked with her on a number of occasions, and had found her congenial company.

"Navigator Vah'nya," he called.

She turned to face him, a small smile touching her lips as she saw who it was. "Hello, Lieutenant Eli," she said. "What brings you to this part of the ship?"

"I've been ordered to the bridge," he said, eyeing her closely. Not just good company, but also highly intriguing. Though her Third Sight was slowly fading, as it did with all navigators, even at twenty-two she still had greater skill than all but one or two of the younger girls.

He'd looked into it a bit, and as far as he could tell no one knew why her ability had lasted this long. But then, with the whole Chiss navigation system a deep, black secret, it wasn't surprising that it hadn't been very well studied.

On top of all of Vah'nya's other interesting qualities, she was the only person aboard he'd been able to persuade to call him by his real name. That alone would have earned her high marks in his book.

"Ah," she said. "So you were not merely coming to see me?"

"No, not at all," Eli said, feeling his face warming. He wasn't entirely sure of the protocol regarding fraternization among the officers and crew, and he had no intention of learning about it the hard way.

"Too sad," Vah'nya said, in a tone that could have been mild sarcasm or complete sincerity. "Did Junior Commander Velbb say what it was about?" she added as the two of them continued forward.

"Actually, it wasn't Commander Velbb," Eli told her. "The order came from Senior Captain Khresh."

"Really?" she said, frowning. "That *is* unusual."

"I know." Eli gestured to her. "What about you? Are you coming on watch?"

"Yes," she said. "Though I feel I'm unlikely to be needed."

Eli wrinkled his nose. She had that right. Barely three hours after the *Steadfast* arrived in this system, Ar'alani had ordered a hard shutdown of the entire ship, a stage below even dark stealth mode, cutting unnecessary power use and all emissions, including active sensors. She'd given the ship one final burst from the drive, and from that moment on they'd been drifting, dark and silent, through the loose asteroid belt three hundred million kilometers from the system's sun.

That had been nearly a week ago. Eli had checked the ship's position, and studied the passive sensor reports, and he still had no idea what they were doing here. His best guess was that they were still following the ship they'd been tracking ever since leaving the Unknown Regions and that Ar'alani was afraid of spooking it.

As well she might. They were a long way from Chiss space and the various vague threats arrayed against them. This was a system deep within the Galactic Empire.

And the threats here were anything but vague.

"Still, if the unusual has happened to you, it could also happen to me," Vah'nya continued. "By the way, I understand you've become something of a disappointment to Senior Commander Cinsar."

"How so?" Eli asked, bracing himself. Cinsar had been assigned to guide the newcomer through the process of orienting to the *Steadfast,* its procedures, and its crew. It had been clear from the start that he didn't exactly relish the job, but he'd always treated Eli with at least an arm's-length respect.

"I'm told your Cheunh grammar and pronunciation are no longer amusing enough for him to share with his fellow officers," Vah'nya said, gazing down the corridor with a perfectly straight face. "Your procedural knowledge is likewise useless as a source of entertainment."

"I'm sorry for his loss," Eli said, giving her a hard look. "And how exactly would you, a simple navigator, be privy to the inner workings of Officer Country?"

"Please," she protested, a mischievous smile finally breaking through the carefully engineered calm. "I may be a simple navigator, but I *do* know my way around the ship. After all, I've been aboard for a long time. I should also say that Commander Cinsar also believes the speed of your progress is largely due to the competence of his teaching."

"And I wouldn't argue that point in the slightest," Eli said. "He's been an excellent and amazingly patient teacher. I owe him a lot." He pursed his lips. "I owe all of you a lot."

"I'm sure that in the future you'll repay the Ascendancy multifold," Vah'nya assured him. "In the meantime, it'll be interesting to see why you've been summoned."

"Yes," Eli said, gazing at the single red rim of the bridge door looming ahead of them. "It will indeed."

The *Steadfast's* bridge was smaller than the *Chimaera's*, with only a single deck instead of the walkway-and-crew-pit arrangement common in Imperial capital ships. Admiral Ar'alani's command chair was in the center of the double ring of consoles, but at the moment she was across the room by the sensor monitor station, her pure-white uniform standing out against the black garb of the rest of the officers and crew. She looked over her shoulder as the door slid open, caught Eli's eye, and beckoned him over.

"Good luck," Vah'nya said softly, her fingertips brushing across his shoulder as she headed toward the combined helm and navigation stations.

Eli worked his way through the close-packed consoles and reached Ar'alani. "Lieutenant Eli'van'to," she greeted him, gesturing him to the chair Sensor Officer Tanik had just vacated and was now standing beside. "Sit down. Tell me what you see."

"Yes, Admiral," Eli said as he lowered himself into the chair. Tanik touched a switch, and the monitor lit up with a view of a cluster of asteroids a few degrees off the *Steadfast*'s starboard bow.

For a moment the scene remained unchanged, with only the flowing time stamp showing that the recording hadn't been paused. Eli leaned a little closer in anticipation . . .

And then a speck of something flickered into view. Two seconds later there was a muted double flash from a nearby point, the flashes briefly lighting up the speck. The speck seemed to move, possibly to rotate, and a second double flash lit up the scene. The flash faded, the speck seemed to go a little darker, and the image returned to its original state.

"That event was observed approximately thirty minutes ago," Ar'alani said from beside him as the recording went into repeat mode. "There's been no further activity."

Eli nodded. No further activity that they'd been able to see, anyway. With the active sensors shut down, the *Steadfast* was flying half blind. "The incoming object was probably a ship," he said. "Most likely civilian, possibly a private yacht, more probably a freighter."

"Your reasoning?" Ar'alani asked.

"There was no indication of deflectors," Eli said. "The first shot might have caught them by surprise, but there was enough time between that salvo and the second one for the ship to have raised them. Those *were* shots, I assume?"

"Commander Tanik?" Ar'alani invited.

"Here's the initial analysis," Tanik said, touching a key and bringing up a data list on a second display. "The energy profile is definitely consistent with that of an energy weapon."

"My question for *you*, Lieutenant," Ar'alani said, "is whether it fits the profile of an Imperial weapon."

Eli peered at the display, running the numbers and mentally fitting them into known patterns, remembering that Ar'alani preferred accuracy over speed. He took his time studying the numbers, waited until he was sure, and then shook his head. "I don't believe it's something used by the Empire," he said. "However, it *does* share certain characteristics with Grysk weapons."

Out of the corner of his eye, he saw Ar'alani and Tanik exchange glances. Apparently, that was something they'd already guessed. "*Was* it a Grysk weapon?" Ar'alani asked.

"I don't think so," Eli said. "At least, not like the ones they've already used against us. But I could see this weapon as something, oh, a generation or two behind those. This armor-piercing spectrum isn't quite as focused or refined as the ones we've seen, which makes it less efficient."

"You said that the target might be a civilian craft or a freighter," Ar'alani said. "You didn't suggest the far more obvious possibility: an asteroid miner."

Eli frowned. Now that she'd mentioned it, why *hadn't* he suggested that? He focused again on the recording, watched the ship arrive and be attacked.

"It's not a miner," he said. "For one thing, it tried to get away. A normal mining ship would probably have lost its entire drive and maneuvering system with that first double shot."

"Unless the attacker was incompetent," Tanik said.

"I don't think so," Eli said. "The speed of his attack shows he was waiting for the ship and ready to fire. And that's the other thing. A miner wouldn't have come out of hyperspace into the middle of an asteroid cluster. Too much risk of running into something. Normal procedure is to come in above or below the ecliptic."

"Only this one came directly into the cluster," Ar'alani said. "*And* landed solidly in the attacker's primary targeting zone."

Eli nodded. "All of which strongly suggests that the ship didn't come out of hyperspace at that point on purpose. At least, not on its own captain's purpose."

"A mass shadow," Tanik murmured.

"Yes," Eli said, wincing. The Empire had such technology, built into massive *Interdictor*-class Star Destroyers, projectors that permitted an Imperial commander to either prevent an enemy ship from escaping or pluck a passing craft out of hyperspace and back into realspace.

But there was nothing the size of an Interdictor lurking nearby. Even at this distance, the *Steadfast* would have no trouble seeing it. If the attacker had used mass-shadow technology, it was far more compact than anything the Empire possessed.

Or else it was designed to cover only a small area. As if the attacker had known the precise vector his victim would be arriving along.

Something was happening out there. Something bad . . . and the *Steadfast* was still too far away to do anything about it.

Unless Ar'alani decided to break cover and move in. But it would take more than a wounded freighter to make her do that.

"Thank you, Lieutenant Eli'van'to," the admiral said, her voice quiet and thoughtful. "Return to your station. Mid Commander Tanik will send you everything we have on this incident, both the raw data and the tactical department's initial analysis. I expect that you'll see things others have missed—"

Eli felt a small swelling of pride. Maybe he was more useful to Ar'alani and the Chiss than he'd thought.

"—if only because of your greater familiarity with the Empire and its technology," Ar'alani finished.

The pride evaporated. "Yes, Admiral," Eli said.

He'd hoped Vah'nya might be looking in his direction as he left the bridge—she was too far away for him to say goodbye, but they might at least be able to exchange nods. But she was embroiled in conversation with the pilot and the navigator about to go off duty, her back to him.

He eyed the three of them. A full-grown Chiss man, a Chiss girl who came to about his elbow, and Vah'nya. Once again, Eli was struck by the oddness of it all.

But there was no time to think about any of that now. Ar'alani was right. Something was happening out there, and the knot in his gut told him that it was something nasty.

Ar'alani preferred accuracy to speed. In this case, Eli knew, he'd damn well better deliver both.

CHAPTER 4

Faro hadn't observed an actual dissection since that one semester at the Academy when they'd been taught how to use physiological cues to assess a nonhuman opponent's weaknesses. At the time, she'd found the whole procedure rather revolting, though she'd been intrigued by the tactical implications.

Here, as she, Thrawn, and Ronan watched from behind the safety partition the two medical droids take the gralloc apart, she found it just as distasteful. But she also found it much more interesting than she'd expected.

The secret of the creatures' speed and maneuverability was the first surprise. She'd expected it was something to do with the solar wind, using a sailcraft's tacking technique amplified or vectored by selective magnetic tissue, as was the case with their smaller mynock cousins.

But the grallocs had added a twist. The creatures had a set of tiny electrically charged intakes through which they drew in the thin interplanetary medium, ran it up to thruster speeds through organic superconducting conduits inside their bodies, and expelled it out other orifices as small but efficient jets. With the intakes and outflows clustered in spots all around the gralloc's body surface and wing supports, the creature wasn't restricted to simple forward movement, but could angle and dodge and even reverse direction at an instant's notice.

And the second surprise . . .

"You *do* realize this is a waste of time, don't you?" Ronan muttered from Thrawn's other side. "Governor Haveland's people have dissected dozens of these things. The data card I gave you has everything you need."

"Does it?" Thrawn asked.

Faro smiled tightly to herself. She'd already spotted the discrepancy between Haveland's data and their own, as she knew Thrawn had. Ronan, clearly, hadn't.

"Of course," Ronan said. "I can see you're interested in the organic propulsion system, but there's really nothing new there. The ionized solar wind gets drawn in—"

"Along with the Clouzon-36?"

"—and then—" Ronan broke off. "The *what*?"

"The Clouzon-36," Thrawn repeated, offering Ronan his datapad. "There, in both the intakes and the outflow."

Ronan took the datapad, and for a few seconds he gazed at it in silence. Then, with a small shrug, he handed it back. "Probably nicked a gas conduit while it was feeding on some power line," he said. "Means nothing."

"On the contrary," Thrawn said. "You'll recall that I suggested this creature's relative sluggishness implied it had recently fed. Clouzon-36 conduits are generally well armored precisely to prevent leakage. Have you obtained the ship and manifest listing I asked for?"

There was half a second's delay as Ronan shifted mental gears. "Yes, the full record came in about half an hour ago," he said. He looked like he wanted to say something else—probably, Faro speculated, something along the line of how much effort getting the list had cost him—but seemed to think better of it. "It's in my personal file on the main computer."

"Very good," Thrawn said. "You'll release it to Commodore Faro. Commodore, you and the tactical analysis group will correlate the gralloc's movements and identify the vessels it may have been feeding on just prior to the point at which it joined the pursuit of Lieutenant Fentaugh's Defender."

"Just a minute," Ronan said tartly. "This information is highly confidential, Admiral. It cannot and will not be handed off to random people."

"The *Chimaera*'s analysis group is completely trustworthy."

"I don't care," Ronan said. "*You* can have it." He shot a look at Faro, and his lip twitched. "Commodore Faro can have it," he added grudgingly. "No one else."

Thrawn considered, then inclined his head. "Very well. Commodore, you will take Assistant Director Ronan to your office, transfer the data to your file, and begin your analysis."

Faro suppressed a grimace. All by herself. Terrific. "Yes, sir," she said. "Assistant Director?"

A minute later she and Ronan were striding together down the corridor. "You disagree with my security measures," Ronan commented as they stepped into a turbolift car.

"Yes, I do," Faro said. "As I understand it, Stardust's big secret is where the ships go from here, not where they came from or what they're carrying. I don't see how including a select group of Imperial officers in this work would compromise your security."

"I don't suppose you do," Ronan said. "You take everything Grand Admiral Thrawn says as words carved in stone, don't you?"

"Hardly," Faro said. "I've disagreed with him on more than one occasion."

"And yet I imagine you always let him get his way?"

"He's my superior officer," Faro said stiffly. "There's not a *his* way and a *my* way, and I don't *let* him do anything. He gives the orders. I follow them."

"And he's always right?"

"No, of course not," Faro said. "No one is. But when he's wrong, it's usually because he has insufficient or faulty information, and he's always quick to correct any false steps."

"I see," Ronan said. "So if I told you Thrawn was the one standing in the way of your new assignment, you'd still say he was always right?"

Faro frowned. "What are you talking about?"

"I'm talking about your imminent appointment as commander of Task Force 231," Ronan said, a new touch of malicious amusement in his voice. "According to standard procedure, you should have been pulled off the *Chimaera* by now. Or had that little detail slipped your mind?"

Faro forced her face to remain neutral. Yes, that little detail had damn well *not* slipped her mind. She should have been called back to Coruscant the minute the *Chimaera* returned from Batuu and the Grysk mission and put into pre-command orientation.

On the other hand, that summons was only a few weeks late. Any number of things might have come up to delay it.

Still, High Command was normally very rigid about timing and protocol. This kind of delay was usually accompanied by a message resetting the orientation or the assignment.

There'd been no such communication. In fact, Faro had already taken the initiative, sending a quiet inquiry a week ago. So far, there'd been no reply. "Admiral Thrawn has assured me the assignment is solid," she told Ronan.

"And not only is he never wrong, but he never lies?" Ronan countered. "If you forgive my impertinence, Commodore, you're far too old to be this naïve. As it happens, I did some digging on my own. The details are a bit murky, but there's no doubt that Thrawn is the one who has blocked your reassignment."

"If you'll forgive *my* impertinence, Assistant Director, you're either wrong or lying," Faro said. "That's not how Admiral Thrawn does things."

"Believe what you will," Ronan said with a shrug that was entirely too casual. "Just remember that I have no reason to lie to you. I just thought you should know where you stand. Where you *really* stand."

Ten minutes later, with a copy of Ronan's shipping data safely locked in her computer, Faro settled down to work.

Or at least tried to settle down.

Thrawn wouldn't lie to her. Surely not to his flagship's commander. Certainly not without a good reason.

But if he *had* a good reason?

Ridiculous. Thrawn was totally committed to making the Imperial fleet as strong as it could possibly be. He'd shared her excitement—or at least had come as close to excitement as he ever did—when she'd first received word of her promotion and reassignment. At the time, he'd told her she would make an excellent flotilla commander, and congratulated her on her success.

But that was then. This was now. And if Ronan wasn't blowing smoke, Thrawn had apparently changed his mind.

But why? Had she done something at Batuu or Mokivj to undermine his confidence in her? Had she irritated Lord Vader, or someone else with connections to the highest ranks of Coruscant power, and the right amount of quiet pressure had been applied?

Surely it couldn't be simply that Thrawn didn't want to lose the *Chimaera*'s commander. Could it?

No. Thrawn didn't behave that way to his officers. He also didn't have the political finesse even to notice subtle pressures, let alone bow to them.

And despite Ronan's statement to the contrary, the assistant director had every reason in the Empire to lie to her. He clearly didn't think much of Thrawn—though to be fair, Faro had the feeling he didn't think much of *anyone*—and anyone who'd worked his way that high up in Krennic's staff was bound to be adept at political games. Thrawn had a single week to solve the gralloc problem and secure funding for his TIE Defenders, and anything Ronan could do to isolate the admiral from his officers would be make the challenge that much more difficult.

So Faro would assume Ronan was lying, and that there was some perfectly reasonable explanation as to what was going on with her assignment. She had a job to do, and she was damn well going to do it.

Besides, the faster she dug out the information Thrawn wanted, the better the chance that whatever she might have done would be forgiven.

She'd been digging at the shipping list for an hour when her intercom pinged. "Report on your analysis, Commodore," Thrawn said.

"I've hardly just begun, sir," Faro admitted. "There's a lot of material here."

"Understood," Thrawn said. "Secure your work and report to the bridge."

"Yes, sir," Faro said. "Shall I bring my preliminary findings?"

"That can wait," he said. "Right now we're going to take a small trip."

Thrawn and Ronan were waiting on the command walkway when she arrived. "Commodore," Thrawn said in greeting.

"Admiral," Faro said in turn, running a quick eye over Ronan. The assistant director was looking even more annoyed than usual. "May I ask where we're going?"

"On a ghost hunt," Ronan muttered.

"We've analyzed the vector the Allanar N3 was on when it jumped to lightspeed," Thrawn said, ignoring Ronan's comment. "There are two likely star systems along that path. I wish to see if the freighter might possibly have come out in one of them."

"I see," Faro said carefully, looking over at the nav display. The two systems Thrawn had designated were eight and twenty-two light-years away, respectively. If the Allanar *hadn't* made it to one of them, there was an awful lot of empty space between here and there for it to have lost itself in.

"I realize it's perhaps something of a long shot," Thrawn continued, again casually reading her thoughts and doubts. "But we must start somewhere."

"What we *must* do is clear out the logjam *here*," Ronan growled.

"We shall," Thrawn assured him. "The dissection and analysis of the gralloc continues. Until those results suggest a useful approach, we can do little except wait. I believe that our time would be better spent searching for the Allanar and its lost crew." He raised his voice. "Lieutenant Hammerly? Has your group made any progress on the question I posed?"

"Yes, sir, some," Hammerly said. "I'm afraid there's no way for our sensors to directly identify a Clouzon-36 spill, not at this distance."

Faro felt her eyebrow twitch. So the Clouzon-36 thing Thrawn had latched onto wasn't just some passing thought. Clearly, he thought there was something there worth pursuing.

"And the occultation approach?" Thrawn asked.

"Still working on that part, sir, but there are definitely some possibilities," Hammerly said. "We're running some tests and tracking through the physics."

"Excellent," Thrawn said. "Keep me informed."

He turned back to the viewport, his hands clasped behind his back, his posture one that Faro recognized as thoughtful meditation. With another glance at Ronan's sour expression, she walked to the edge of the walkway closest to the sensor station and crouched down. "What's the occultation approach?" she asked quietly.

"One of the admiral's clever little ideas," Hammerly said, just as softly. "He thinks that if we can get the source of a leak between us and the system sun, or even a bright star, the light scattering and diffraction pattern through the gas can identify whether the leakage is Clouzon-36. If he's right, it could give us a way to spot the stuff at much greater distances than standard scanning methods."

"Nice," Faro said. And not just the fuel from a leaky freighter, but also gas deposits in asteroid belts and other sources. That would be immensely useful for miners hunting down the rare fuel.

"Agreed," Hammerly said.

There was a breath of moving air, and Faro turned to see Thrawn walk up behind her. "A question, Commodore," he said quietly. "Have you looked at the cargo list from the Allanar N3 yet?"

"Yes, sir, first thing," Faro said.

"Anything unusual about it?"

"Well . . . not on the surface," she hedged. "It was mostly replacement parts, with a few packages of foodstuffs thrown in. Nothing I saw that shouldn't be there."

"Anything unusual about the foodstuffs? Something species-specific, perhaps?"

"There was a package of blosphi extract," Faro said. How in *hell* did

Thrawn always get ahead of her this way? "It's mostly sold as low-cost rations for Wookiees."

"It's also considered a delicacy by a few other species," Thrawn said. "What about the replacement parts? Did you cross-check the types of equipment they're used for?"

"No, sir, not yet," Faro said, wincing a little. Sometimes she was able to anticipate what the admiral wanted. This time, she'd apparently missed completely. "I thought I should first organize the entire combined inventory."

"Quite right," Thrawn assured her. "Can you separate out the Allanar's inventory and send it to me?"

"Certainly, sir," Faro said, pulling out her datapad. She found the file and keyed it over to him.

"Thank you." With a final nod, Thrawn walked casually back across the command walkway.

"What was *that* all about?" Hammerly asked.

"No idea," Faro admitted. "He might just be poking around, or he might have a specific idea he's chasing down."

Hammerly gave a little grunt. "Either way, I'm guessing there'll be trouble at the end of it."

Faro nodded, thinking about what Thrawn had told her about this insane agreement Krennic and Tarkin had dropped in his lap. To link a vital starfighter program to what was essentially a bet was just ridiculous. "Agreed," she told Hammerly. "Let's just hope it's not Thrawn who gets the short stick."

"Or us," Hammerly said.

Faro felt her throat tighten. The short stick. Such as being denied a promised appointment to command a navy flotilla. "Or us," she agreed.

"Commodore?"

Faro turned. Thrawn had rejoined Ronan and had turned again to face her. "Is my ship ready?"

Faro ran her eye over the status boards, her momentary brooding over lost opportunities vanishing into the shiver that was suddenly running up her back. Officially, that was merely the fleet's standard pre-jump question from a ship's commander to his bridge crew.

But Thrawn seldom used it except when the *Chimaera* was heading into battle.

What exactly was he expecting to find out there?

"It is, sir," she said, glancing at the tactical. He'd put the ship at mid-level readiness, she saw, one step down from battle stations. "Do you wish full combat readiness?"

"*Combat* readiness?" Ronan demanded, his voice somewhere between stunned and outraged. "Thrawn—"

"*Admiral* Thrawn," Faro shot back.

Ronan glared at her. Faro held his glare and sent back one of her own. "*Admiral* Thrawn," he said grudgingly, turning away from her. "Putting your ship and crew at battle stations is a complete waste of time and effort."

"Hardly, Assistant Director," Thrawn said calmly. "Additional readiness drills are never a waste of effort. As to the TIE pilots you no doubt noticed are standing ready in their fighters, it may be we'll arrive to find ourselves in a search-and-rescue mission. Mid-level readiness will suffice for now, Commodore. You may make the jump to hyperspace when ready."

"Yes, sir. Helm: Activate hyperdrive."

Out the viewport, the stars stretched into starlines and then faded into the mottled sky of hyperspace. "Arrival in three point seven minutes, Admiral," Faro said.

"Thank you, Commodore."

The seconds ticked by. Faro split her time double-checking the status boards, looking over the officers and crew at their stations, and studying what she could see of Thrawn's face. Ronan she ignored completely.

The hyperspace sky switched back to starlines, then to stars, and they were there. "Full scan," Faro ordered. "Energy concentrations, power usage, sensor emissions."

"Scanning," Hammerly confirmed.

More minutes ticked by. Ronan, Faro saw uneasily, was getting more and more agitated, though trying hard not to show it. Thrawn, in contrast, stood silent and motionless and glacially calm.

"Contact," Hammerly said suddenly. "Artificial object—refined metal—no power or sensor emissions. Too far away for life-form readings. Bearing three-five-three by twenty-two. About six hundred thousand kilometers, right at the edge of sensor range."

"Can we make a microjump?" Thrawn asked.

"Yes, sir," Lieutenant Agral confirmed from the helm. "It's a bit short, but we can do it."

"How close can you bring us in?"

"As close as you want, sir."

"Excellent," Thrawn said. "Bring us in two kilometers from the object."

"Two kilometers, yes, sir," Agral said. "Computing now."

"Incredible," Ronan said, a note of surprise in his tone momentarily eclipsing his usual antagonism. "How did you know? There wasn't any pattern to the lost ships' vectors. I know—Director Krennic checked."

"You are correct," Thrawn said. "What the previous analysis failed to note was that over two-thirds of the missing ships' vectors—specifically, twenty-eight of forty-one lost ships—pointed toward nearby systems."

"So they jumped toward star systems," Ronan said, still sounding puzzled. "So what? There are star systems everywhere."

"You miss the point," Thrawn said. "Not just star systems. *Nearby* star systems. The odds of such a thing happening with that many random jumps are vanishingly small. It followed that those particular vectors were not, in fact, random."

Faro felt her breath catch in her throat. "The ships weren't lost," she murmured. "They were stolen."

Ronan shot her a startled look. "*What?* No—impossible. The crews of these ships—" He broke off.

"The crews of the ships leaving the transfer point are carefully chosen," Thrawn said, finishing the thought for him. "The crews bringing in the supplies are not."

"Who?" Ronan demanded, his voice suddenly like crushed ice. "Who's doing this?"

"As yet, that is unknown." Thrawn nodded toward the viewport. "But I expect we shall find some clues."

"Ready to make microjump, Admiral," Agral called.

Thrawn nodded. "Do so."

The starlines flared, but this time the sky had no time to change further before the lines collapsed again.

And there it was. Not the Allanar, as Faro had assumed, but a compact mobile way station, hyperdrive- and thruster-equipped. A pair of docking collars on opposite sides allowed for expedited off-loading of cargo from one ship and transfer to another, with sorting and re-packaging facilities aboard the station itself. It was the sort of thing Faro had seen used by smugglers, pirates, rebels, and contraband dealers.

Only this one would never be used again. The laser gashes and torpedo pits that had all but demolished the hull made that very clear.

Faro was the first to say what they were all thinking. "It was attacked," she said quietly.

"TIEs: Launch," Thrawn ordered calmly. "Secure the perimeter; search outward to two thousand kilometers. Sensors and point defenses on full alert. Commodore Faro, have Major Carvia deploy a spacetrooper patrol to examine the hull for traps and residual danger, and prepare a survey team to go inside once the spacetroopers have finished their examination."

"Acknowledged," Faro said, pulling out her comlink and keying for the *Chimaera*'s stormtrooper commander.

"And bring us around to starboard," Thrawn added. "I want a closer look at those docking collars."

There were no traps on the wrecked station or inside it. What *was* inside was more destruction.

And bodies. Lots of bodies. Eighteen of them, torn up as badly as the station itself.

"Shredding projectile weapons," Faro murmured as the visual feed from the survey crew paused on one of the bodies.

Ronan nodded silently from his seat at the conference room table, trying very hard not to be sick. He'd seen dead bodies before, certainly—the very size of the Stardust project inevitably meant a comparably large number of accidents. There'd also been at least three civilian or pirate vessels that had wandered into the wrong place at the wrong time, and had had to be dealt with.

But these weren't the victims of a slipped crane or welder tank gone critical, or even the cleaner and more sanitary deaths from stormtrooper blasterfire. These bodies looked like they'd been dropped into a threshing machine, with blood and torn flesh and muscle everywhere.

He tried to remind himself that these men had been thieves who'd stolen from Stardust and the Empire, and that they deserved punishment. The rationalization didn't help.

"Are you certain there are no more bodies?" Thrawn asked.

"Very certain, Admiral," the survey leader assured him. "We've been into every compartment, and looked everywhere else that someone could have been squeezed. These eighteen are all there are."

"Interesting," Thrawn said thoughtfully. "At one point there were more of them aboard."

"How do you know?" Ronan asked.

"Food and oxygen usage records," Thrawn said, tapping a key on his console. In the corner of the survey team's video, a set of numbers appeared. "I estimate there were twelve others."

"The missing freighter's crew?" Faro asked.

"Unlikely," Thrawn said. "The degree of battle damage inside the docking collars indicates both were unoccupied at the time of the attack. At any rate, the usual complement for an Allanar N3 is between four and seven. Even if all but one stayed on the station while the remaining crew member flew it away, the numbers still come up short."

"So where did they go?" Ronan asked.

"The twelve?" Thrawn asked, turning those unsettling glowing red eyes toward him. "The likely explanation is that they were taken by the attackers. Possibly dead, more likely alive."

"That makes no sense," Ronan protested. "Pirates stealing from other pirates don't take prisoners. The last thing they want is extra mouths to feed."

"*If* the attackers were, indeed, pirates," Thrawn said. "Consider the timeline."

He tapped another key, and another listing appeared on the display. "Twenty-eight ships disappeared, allegedly due to gralloc damage. All disappeared on unique vectors. However."

He touched a control, and the list turned into a schematic with multiple vectors angling out from the center. "Observe the following pattern," he continued as three of the lines brightened. "Numbers one, two, and three leave on these vectors an average of fourteen hours apart. Note that not only are the vectors grouped in the same octant, but that the systems that are the likely end points are also relatively close together."

"Clever," Faro said, nodding. "So the first freighter arrives, transfers its cargo to the station and from there to another ship, and the freighter is sent off to vanish into deep space."

"Possibly with its crew still aboard," Ronan murmured.

"Perhaps," Thrawn said. "That would depend on how closely the organizer of this theft wishes to keep the secret of his activities. Continue, Commodore."

"Then the station relocates to the second system and waits until the second freighter pretends it's been attacked by grallocs and flits off with its cargo," Faro said. "Repeat as often as you can keep everyone thinking it's all just random accidents."

"And all the blame falls on the grallocs," Thrawn said. "Your thoughts, Assistant Director?"

Ronan gazed at the schematic. What could he say? The station, the vectors, the timing—it couldn't possibly all be just a terrible coincidence.

But if it wasn't coincidence, why hadn't anyone else noticed all the pieces and put them together?

Because the only one smart enough to do so was Director Krennic himself, of course, and he was far too busy with the overall project to have time for such minutiae.

Thrawn was smart, too. But he wasn't that smart. More to the point, he'd completely skipped over one very important piece to his puzzle.

"An interesting theory, Admiral," he said. "But you left one small fact dangling. If the Allanar isn't here, where is it?"

"A fair question," Thrawn said, "and one we should now address. Commodore, you brought us here on the same vector the Allanar disappeared along, did you not?"

Faro started to speak, then paused. Ronan saw a small frown crease her forehead, and her posture stiffened a bit.

Mentally, he shook his head. He'd never cared for commanders who liked to entrap their subordinates, trying to catch them in mistakes and humiliate them front of their fellow officers and crew.

Sadly, more and more people seemed to play that game these days, from the sadistic Emperor and his cackling manipulation, through Tarkin and his cultured viciousness, all the way down to minor warship captains who would never amount to anything and knew it. Even Lord Vader pulled such stunts on occasion, generally with people like Director Krennic who'd risen to position and power solely through ability and hard work.

And from the look on Faro's face, she was used to this kind of abuse from Thrawn. He was smart, all right, but there was a hidden gloating nastiness beneath the surface.

Thrawn, Tarkin, Vader, the Emperor—they all deserved one another. Fortunately for the Empire, there were a handful of men like Director Krennic who could stand up to them.

There was another flicker as Faro's expression changed. "No, sir, I didn't," she said, a quiet confidence in her voice. "We left the transfer point on that vector; but we were farther out on the edge than the Allanar. We arrived in the same system, but didn't travel through exactly the same space."

Thrawn inclined his head. "Very good, Commodore," he said.

And smiled.

Ronan frowned. He *smiled*? But smiling wasn't part of the game. The object was humiliation, and Faro had escaped the trap. Thrawn should have scowled, or at the very least hidden his disappointment behind a neutral expression.

But he'd *smiled*.

"So let us backtrack along the vector—the *precise* vector this time—and see what we find."

"Yes, sir." Faro's eyes lowered to her own console—

And to Ronan's surprise, she snapped her head up again. "Admiral?" she asked, her voice studiously neutral. "Are you suggesting . . . ?"

"The possibility exists," Thrawn said, his voice gone a shade darker. "Compute the vector."

"Yes, sir," Faro repeated, and again lowered her gaze.

"And *now*, Commodore," Thrawn added quietly, "you may bring the *Chimaera* to full combat readiness."

CHAPTER 5

Admiral Ar'alani frowned on people running on her warship, unless there was a very good reason for it.

Given the message Eli had just received, he was pretty sure this qualified.

He reached the bridge slightly out of breath. "Admiral," he said, spotting her standing beside the comm console.

"Here, Lieutenant," she called, her voice grim. "*Now.*"

"Yes, ma'am," Eli said, hurrying between the consoles. The bridge was fully staffed, he noted, though most of the consoles were still shut down or on standby. "You're sure it's him?"

"Quite sure, Lieutenant," Ar'alani said, motioning the officer to vacate the comm station seat. "And if we don't hurry, he's going to ruin everything. You need to warn him off."

"Yes, ma'am," Eli said, keying the board. A focused comm laser had already been set up for him, he noted, pointed toward the distant mobile way station drifting along at the very edge of the *Steadfast*'s best passive optical sensors.

Even at this distance, the distinctive arrowhead shape of an Imperial Star Destroyer was unmistakable.

And if that was indeed the *Chimaera* out there . . .

He keyed for the Imperial encryption he'd added to the *Steadfast*'s comm system, a code he knew Thrawn would instantly recognize and could quickly decipher. It came up, and he started to encrypt a brief note, starting with his name, and adding a warning to desist.

And then suddenly it was too late. Even as the distance and the time lag showed the Star Destroyer still floating beside the station, there was a flicker from much closer and the Imperial ship popped back into realspace at the same spot where the Allanar N3 freighter had appeared a few hours ago. "Admiral—"

"I see it, Lieutenant," Ar'alani said, hissing a curse between her teeth. "Of course he would blunder in."

"What do we do?" Eli asked.

"We hold back and see what happens," Ar'alani said. "With luck, we may still be able to salvage this operation."

"And if he's attacked?"

"Then your former shipmates may be in serious trouble," Ar'alani said. "As will be Mitth'raw'nuruodo himself."

With the transfer point eight light-years away, the *Chimaera*'s next trip wasn't supposed to have been another microjump. But as the starlines flared briefly and then collapsed Faro knew that it had become exactly that.

And as the stars reappeared, she felt a horrible tingle of déjà vu.

It was the Grysks again. It had to be. This was the same compact, cloak-and-interdictor trick the *Chimaera* had run into near the planet Batuu as the would-be conquerors experimented with ways of isolating Imperial worlds and blocking access to the Unknown Regions.

Only that experiment had been out near the border between Wild Space and the Unknown Regions. What were they doing *here*, nearly the entire way across the Empire?

"Contact!" Hammerly called, her voice tight. "Ship debris bearing zero-one-eight by twelve; distance, two kilometers. Material and design consistent with an Allanar N3 light freighter."

"Lieutenant Pyrondi: Ion cannons," Thrawn ordered. His voice was its usual calm, but Faro could hear the edge beneath it. He recognized the implications of running into a Grysk-style interdictor cylinder this deep in the Empire as well as she did. "Saturate the area midway between us and the debris."

"What's going on?" Ronan demanded, a slight quaver in his voice as the *Chimaera*'s ion cannons began spitting out a barrage. "What happened?"

"Commodore?" Thrawn invited.

"It's a device we tangled with out in Wild Space," Faro told him. "It generates a gravity well like the one from an Interdictor Star Destroyer, only smaller and with a more limited range."

"I see," Ronan said, staring out the viewport as the Star Destroyer's attack continued. "No, actually, I *don't* see. Where is it?"

"Somewhere between us and the debris," Faro said. "It also has a cloaking device that operates except when the gravity generator is activated."

"A cloaking field? Just how big is this thing?"

"Not very," Faro said. "But we should be able to find it. The Allanar hit the edge of the field coming from the transfer point; we hit it coming from the opposite direction. That gives us the approximate size of the gravity field as well as the approximate point of origin."

"Assuming the debris has not moved significantly since the Allanar was attacked, and that the gravity field is reasonably symmetric," Thrawn added. "We shall know soon enough. Lieutenant, widen your aim a bit. Commander Hammerly, watch for a splash pattern."

The last time they'd done this, it had taken a considerable amount of time and effort to track down the generator. This time, knowing the field's size and approximate center, the operation went much more quickly. Pyrondi had just opened up her targeting contour when there was a barely seen splash and a flicker of light, and the interdictor cylinder popped into sight.

And it was indeed the size and shape and design that Faro remembered.

The Grysks were here.

Ronan bit out a startled curse. "What in the name—?"

"Cease fire," Thrawn ordered. "Sensors and weapons on full alert. There will be a hidden ship or observation post somewhere nearby."

"No, that can't be," Ronan muttered, the words coming out mechanically as he stared at the cylinder. "You can't create a gravity well and a cloaking field at the same time."

"Like I said, except when the gravity well is running," Faro reminded him, her eyes flicking between the viewport and the sensor displays. With all the rocks and gravel floating out there scattering their sensor sweeps, this was going to be a challenge. "Now be quiet—we have work to do."

"Perhaps not as much as you fear, Commodore," Thrawn said calmly. "The debris field will impede sensors, certainly. But its very presence will also . . . ?"

Faro smiled. Indeed. For once, maybe, the Grysks had outsmarted themselves. "The debris will also show the subtle gravitational effects caused by an invisible mass nearby," she said. "Hammerly?"

"On it," Hammerly said briskly. "Mapping, analyzing—Admiral! Behind us!"

Faro twisted her head around to the rear display. One of the larger asteroids had seemingly exploded, sending a cloud of rock in all directions.

Only it wasn't an asteroid, and the debris was nothing more than the remains of a camouflage shell.

And appearing now through the dispersing rock cloud were the dual hulls and multiple-breaking-wave design of a Grysk warship.

"Admiral, we're under attack!" Ronan yelped, jabbing a finger at the ship moving toward them.

"Not yet," Thrawn said, his voice still calm. "We still have a few more moments before they're in range. Commander Hammerly, continue your sweep."

"Continue your *sweep*?" Ronan demanded. "What are you talking about? It's *there*, Thrawn—it's right *there*."

"Calm yourself, Assistant Director," Thrawn said. "That vessel is a warship. We seek an observation or research post. *That* is where we will find our answers."

"You mean if they don't blow us out of space before that?" Ronan snarled. "You haven't even turned to face them."

"There's time for that," Thrawn assured him. "Commander?"

"A moment, sir," Hammerly said, peering closely at her displays. "I think we've almost—got it, sir. Bearing—"

"I see it," Thrawn said. "Lieutenant Pyrondi, on my mark fire a full ion salvo at Commander Hammerly's location. The moment the salvo is away, Lieutenant Agral, you will swing the *Chimaera* around toward the approaching ship, dropping the bow as we turn to present our dorsal surface to them."

Faro smiled. She saw where he was going now.

"At that moment, Commodore," Thrawn continued, "you will launch the Defenders and two squadrons of TIE fighters in a Marg Sabl maneuver. As they reach their outward apsis and begin to close on the enemy, Lieutenant Pyrondi, you will deliver full salvos of turbolaser fire to their ship."

He looked at Ronan, a small smile on his lips. "Let us see how well they can stand against an Imperial Star Destroyer."

Of the eight to ten words Admiral Ar'alani spat out, Eli only knew three.

The gist, however, was pretty clear.

Two weeks' worth of work and tens of thousands of light-years' worth of travel, all of it down the drain.

She turned to Eli, her eyes seeming to glow extra hot, and he braced himself for the coming blast. But she merely held the glare a fraction of a second and then turned to the command console. "Full activation," she ordered. "All systems. I want weapons up in fifteen seconds."

Eli felt his eyes widen. Fifteen *seconds*? He'd been on Imperial warships coming from dead cold to full combat readiness, and the process had never taken less than nine or ten minutes.

But to his amazement, the Chiss pulled it off. Status grids that had been showing perhaps two or three ACTIVE lights amid a sea of

STANDBYS and INACTIVES changed to full ACTIVE as if a wave of col-
ored paint had been thrown over them. Displays that had been blank
lit up with data and graphics showing weapons status and tactical
data. Officers and crew who'd been sitting quiet and unmoving began
murmuring rapid commands into headsets and keying spin-up and
targeting orders on their boards.

    And with two of Ar'alani's fifteen seconds to spare, the *Steadfast*
was poised for battle.

    "Plasma spheres: Full portside salvo," the admiral ordered. *"Fire."*

    The distant *thud* from the portside capacitors barked, half heard,
half felt through the bridge, and the brilliant yellow globes arrowed
away from the *Steadfast*'s launchers.

    The Grysk warship reacted instantly, a barrage of laser blasts
erupting from its point defenses.

    But plasma spheres weren't solid objects that could be destroyed
so easily. The lasers flicked uselessly through their surfaces, creating
momentary distortions before their self-focusing electromagnetic
fields could restore their proper shape. There was a flash from the
Grysk, a brief flicker of hazy white glow around it—

    "Electrostatic barrier," someone called sharply.

    Eli winced. And those barriers *could* stop plasma spheres.

    Sure enough, the spheres reached the glow and burst like soap
bubbles, expending their energy and ionization bursts just short of
the warship's hull. The Grysk's lasers again lanced out, this time targeting the *Steadfast,* and the low hum from the ship's deflectors rose
into a screech.

    "Roll ship," Ar'alani ordered. If she was worried that the deflectors
might overload, it didn't show in her voice. "Starboard spectrum lasers: Full salvo on the electrostatic generators. Sensors will feed you
the node locations. Follow with starboard plasma sphere salvo. Prepare Breachers in case we get an opening."

    The *Steadfast* was still in mid-roll, and the Grysk warship's lasers
were still trying to carve open its deflectors, when the *Chimaera*
joined the battle.

    The first attack was a full turbolaser volley, multiple green bolts sweeping across the Grysk warship's surface. "Damage?" Ar'alani called.

"None detected," Tanik called from the sensor station, and Eli could hear a hint of contempt in his voice. "They fired too soon. At that distance, the barrier diffuses the blasts enough to make them useless."

"An odd mistake," Ar'alani murmured, just loudly enough for Eli to hear. "Perhaps Thrawn is no longer in command."

"He's in command, all right, Admiral," Eli assured her. "And that wasn't a mistake. The volley wasn't intended to cause damage. He just wanted to draw their attention to the *Chimaera* for a few seconds."

"To draw their attention from *us*?"

"No." Eli pointed to the tactical display, and the barely seen specks now converging on the Grysk. "From his TIE fighters."

Ar'alani hissed between her teeth. "Belay starboard lasers," she called. "Lieutenant Vanto, are the *Chimaera*'s sensors good enough to have spotted the electrostatic loci?"

"Yes, ma'am," Eli said. "And I know Grand Admiral Thrawn is good enough to have noted the effects of our attack."

"Let's see if that's the case," Ar'alani said. "Belay plasma spheres. Prepare Breachers."

A second later the Grysk seemed to suddenly notice the fighters closing in on it. A dozen more lasers blazed out, slashing frantically at the attackers.

But it was too little too late. Two of the lasers found their targets, but the attack was being led by Thrawn's TIE Defenders and their shields were more than adequate to shrug off the glancing attacks. Before the laser gunners could adjust their aim the TIEs were on them, pouring fire into the electrostatic generator nodes and the point-defense lasers themselves. The TIEs finished their strafing run and scattered away as the hazy white glow flickered and then disappeared—

"Over to us," Ar'alani said matter-of-factly. "Breachers: Laser sites, full salvo. *Fire.*"

The *Steadfast* jerked as the six missiles blasted out of their tubes. Eli turned to the tactical, holding his breath as the Breachers burned toward the warship. On the enemy's flank, the *Chimaera* was moving forward toward the common enemy and was once again raking the warship's hull with fire.

But now, with the diminished distance and the loss of the electrostatic barrier, the turbolasers were doing real damage. More Grysk lasers lanced out, but the sheer number of weapons available to them had been diminished by the combined Chiss and Imperial attack. The TIEs reached another apsis and circled around, staying clear of the *Steadfast*'s and *Chimaera*'s weapons and watching for another opening.

Two of the Breachers disintegrated under enemy fire, but the other four made it through. They slammed into the hull and exploded, bursting into sticky acid globs that began eating through the metal and ceramic and leaving blackened pits that would even more easily absorb the energy of the self-tuning Chiss spectrum lasers.

"Enemy hyperdrive spinning up," someone called in warning. "Looks like they've had enough."

"Too bad," Ar'alani said. "If we pull around, can we get in position to target it before they can escape?"

"No need," Eli said, pointing at the tactical. "The TIEs are on it."

"I see them," Ar'alani said. "Cease fire, all weapons. Let's give the Imperials a clear shot."

One shot was all they needed. Again led by the shield-equipped Defenders, the fighters swooped across the rear of the warship's hull, spitting laserfire at the hyperdrive and thrusters. The fighters disappeared from the *Steadfast*'s sight around the edge of the Grysk's hull . . .

"Hyperdrive disabled," came the confirmation. "Thrusters down to eighty-seven percent."

"Very good," Ar'alani said. "Move closer and target remaining weapons ports with plasma spheres. Lieutenant Vanto, contact the *Chimaera* and suggest to Admiral Thrawn that he switch to ion cannons. The more intact it is when we capture it, the more we'll be able to learn."

Apparently, the Grysk commander agreed with her assessment. Two seconds later, with the *Steadfast*'s last salvo of plasma spheres already on the way, the warship exploded.

The bridge fell silent. For once, even Ar'alani didn't seem to have anything to say.

The ping from the comm station in front of Eli startled him out of his paralysis. He glanced at the message—"Admiral?" he said tentatively. "Admiral Thrawn sends his greetings, and would be honored if you'd join him aboard the *Chimaera* for a consultation."

"Would be?" Ar'alani said, again turning those burning eyes on Eli. "Thank him for his invitation, Lieutenant, and inform him that I'll be over at my convenience."

"Yes, ma'am," Eli said. Clearly, she was still angry at Thrawn for barging into the Chiss operation. Apparently, her response was to make him wait.

In the Empire, no one but the Emperor himself would dare suggest that their time was more valuable than a grand admiral's. But Ar'alani wasn't an Imperial. She was a Chiss, and she was angry.

Fly on the wall. The old adage flicked briefly through Eli's mind before common sense intervened. The upcoming meeting between the two admirals was likely to be memorable, and not in a remotely pleasant way. Better to stay here safely out of the confrontation's blast radius.

"Secure to Second Preparedness," Ar'alani continued. "I want a survey team to the wreckage immediately. Every piece of debris is to be collected, sifted, and analyzed."

She leveled a finger at Eli. "And while they do that, Lieutenant Vanto, *you* will have my shuttle prepared. You and I are going to go and have a talk with your former commander."

"Yes, Admiral," Eli said, suppressing a sigh. *Be careful what you wish for,* the other old adage whispered.

Even when you weren't at all wishing for it.

Despite Ar'alani's implied threat of foot-dragging, she actually didn't linger aboard the *Steadfast* for long. Eli had barely received confirma-

tion that the shuttle was prepped and crewed when the admiral finished her string of commands to the bridge officers and ordered him
to accompany her to the hangar bay.

It was with decidedly mixed feelings that Eli watched the *Chimaera* growing steadily to fill the shuttle's viewport. Back in his cadet
days, he'd been thrown together with Thrawn completely against his
will, and for a long time he'd resented the disruption in his life. Gradually that attitude had changed, largely keeping pace with how his
view of Thrawn had changed from obstruction to interesting anomaly to the best thing that could have happened to Eli's own career.
Before Thrawn offered this abrupt change in the course of Eli's life,
Eli had dared to see his commander as almost a friend.

What he didn't know—what he'd never known—was how Thrawn
saw *him*.

Did Thrawn have friends? Eli or anyone else? Had he had friends
when he was growing up in the Chiss Ascendancy, or had he always
been different, the oddness of his mind leaving his young peers bewildered or resentful?

It wasn't just a general Chiss quality. Admiral Ar'alani was an excellent commander, and smart enough in her own way, but there was
a spark that Thrawn had that she didn't. She didn't have the same
knack for observing and analyzing the universe around her, nor did
any of the others Eli had met aboard the *Steadfast*.

How unique *was* Thrawn?

It wasn't something Eli needed to know. It wasn't something he
deserved to know. But it was something he very much *wanted* to
know.

Though he probably never would.

Thrawn was waiting for them in the hangar bay, a helmet tucked
under one arm, his white uniform partially concealed by an armored
chest plate. Standing in watchful flanking positions on either side
were four death troopers, their black armor somehow looking extra
ominous in the hangar bay's lowered light. "Admiral Ar'alani,"
Thrawn greeted Ar'alani gravely in Cheunh as she and Eli walked up
to him. "It's good to see you again."

"And you, Admiral Mitth'raw'nuruodo," Ar'alani said, nodding. Her voice, Eli noted, was studiously neutral. "I trust you are well?"

"I am," Thrawn assured her. "The Empire appreciates your assistance in defeating the Grysk warship."

"The Ascendancy was pleased to do so. I trust you suffered no casualties?"

"None," Thrawn said. "And you?"

"The same," Ar'alani said.

Thrawn nodded; and finally, his eyes turned to Eli.

Reflexively, Eli stiffened to attention. Over a year since he'd left the Empire. Over a year since he'd spoken to his onetime commander and mentor. Over a year of feeling like he didn't belong, without any genuine purpose to his life. Thrawn's encouragement right now was just what he needed—

"Good day, Lieutenant Vanto," Thrawn said, nodding once and then turning back to Ar'alani. "We need to go to the observation post," he said, beckoning to her and Eli as he started toward his own waiting shuttle. "The boarding party has done its initial sweep. We should join them as quickly as possible."

Eli froze, his own readied greeting freezing in his throat. That was *it*? *Good day, Lieutenant Vanto*? All the long months since their last meeting, and that was all the greeting he got?

"Of course," Ar'alani said, turning to follow. "Come, Lieutenant."

"Yes, Admiral," Eli said, the whole sense of unreality still digging at him. *Good day, Lieutenant Vanto* . . .

He started as the death troopers silently closed in around them, feeling his growing bewilderment and resentment disappear into understanding. Of course—Thrawn was merely being formal here because of the urgency of the situation and because there were strangers present. Once they got someplace more private, that stiff and proper exterior would surely open up.

Thrawn's portrayal of the structure as an observation post had given Eli the mental picture of something fixed in orbit, able to move only under the system's composite gravitational pull. But as they approached, he saw it was more like the kind of portable survey labs the

Republic had used during the height of its expansion phase. He could see sampling nozzles, sensor clusters, drive flares, and the telltale vents and power cables of a hyperdrive. Most of the station was dark—clearly, the *Chimaera* had hit it with a massive ion burst—but even as they approached, some of the external lights were starting to return. Around the back of the post, he could see the edge of a heavily damaged Allanar N3 light freighter secured to the hull, presumably the ship the *Steadfast* had seen being yanked out of hyperspace.

"Interesting design," Ar'alani commented. "Not one I've seen before."

"Nor I," Thrawn said. "I believe this was created by one of the Grysk client species."

"Perhaps *they* can give us some insights regarding our enemy."

Thrawn shook his head. "Unfortunately, they won't."

"You're certain?"

"Yes," Thrawn said, his voice dark. "All of them are dead."

"Murdered."

Major Carvia and four of his stormtroopers are waiting in the command center. With them, their limbs double-shackled, are two Grysks. "Chiss," the left one said. *His nose flattens, the wrinkles around his eyes deepen, the muscles around his mouth tighten. Perhaps anger, perhaps surprise, perhaps gloating.* "I suppose we should have expected you." *His Meese Caulf speech holds some fluency, but it also holds an accent. There are some mispronunciations.*

"I suppose you should have," Ar'alani said. *Her voice and body stance hold interest and controlled anger. Her Meese Caulf is far more fluent.* "Did you tell them, Mitth'raw'nuruodo?"

"Not yet. I thought you would like to have the pleasure."

Ar'alani inclines her head. Her expression holds anticipation and mild gratitude at the gesture. "Thank you. I thought you would like to know that your backup defense ship is gone," she said. "Destroyed."

The Grysks' expressions change, their torsos tensing and drawing back briefly before relaxing again. "To what exactly do you refer?" the left one asked.

"The warship that was hiding beneath a pile of rock," Ar'alani said. "The warship waiting for trouble. The warship that found that trouble, and paid the price of overconfidence."

The right Grysk starts to turn his head toward his fellow, but breaks off the motion before it is completed. Perhaps surprise, perhaps disbelief. "If you speak in bluff, you make a poor job of it," the left Grysk said. *His tone is deeper, the words coming out with more deliberation. Perhaps caution, perhaps disbelief.*

"No bluff," Ar'alani said. "Perhaps you would like to see an image of its current state?"

The right Grysk's expression remains unaltered, but the left Grysk's body stance returns to its original position. Perhaps he has now accepted the warship's destruction.

Ar'alani has seen the shifts in body stance, too. Her expression holds sudden understanding. "Or didn't you realize there was anyone else out there?" she asked.

The left Grysk's expression changes again. It now perhaps holds anger or betrayal. "There wouldn't be much use in having a guardian if we didn't know about it, now, would there?" he said.

"Tell us what happened here."

The left Grysk makes a sound like a wet whistle. "Figure it out for yourself."

"I wasn't speaking to you. I was speaking to my troop commander."

The Grysk's expression changes. This time it almost certainly holds anger and contempt. "You ask a mere hireling for his thoughts?"

"A human hireling is more to be respected than a Grysk slave."

The anger deepens. "You dare call *me* a slave? I am Lifeholder and Deathbringer. I am Seeker of Conquest."

"Commander?"

"It looks like they went through the post and killed everyone, sir." *Major Carvia's voice holds contempt and disgust.* "Five humans and eighteen beings of a species we couldn't identify, all of them stabbed multiple times. The humans were in what looked like examination or confinement rooms. The others were in various places around the ship." *He hesitates, his body stance holding reluctance.* "I'm afraid we also found a Chiss. A young girl. She wasn't slaughtered like the others, though." *The new words come out in a rush, his tone holding regret, the words designed to offer a small consolation.* "I think she might already have died before the killings."

Ar'alani's body stance stiffens. Her narrowed eyes hold a sudden hope. "Where is she?"

"No."

Ar'alani turns. Her expression holds disbelief and growing anger. "What did you say?" *Her voice holds threat.*

"You seek vengeance. I understand. But these are *my* prisoners, and I cannot yet allow you to vent your rage upon them."

Ar'alani stands motionless. Her body stance holds confusion and anger, but she remains silent. Her expression changes, now holding understanding. "We'll speak of this later, Mitth'raw'nuruodo," she said. *Her voice holds careful neutrality.* "You will now allow me to see the fallen."

"Certainly. Major Carvia?"

"Yes, sir." *Major Carvia's voice holds recognition that something has happened, but no understanding of the balance or details.* "This way, Admiral," he said. *He leads the way out into the corridor. Two death troopers join him. Ar'alani moves to walk beside Thrawn, with Lieutenant Vanto behind them. The remaining death troopers follow.*

"Thank you," Ar'alani said in Cheunh. *Her voice is low, holding understanding and acceptance, but also some anger.* "That said, don't ever speak to me that way again in front of my officers or crew."

"Was it not necessary? Lieutenant Vanto, did you see disrespect to your admiral?"

"So it perhaps appeared on the surface, Admiral," Vanto said. *His voice holds hesitation, but also understanding. His Cheunh speech is still imperfect but quite acceptable.* "I'm assuming that's what the Grysks saw, too."

"Then you saw my words as an effort to create an imaginary wedge between Admiral Ar'alani and me that they may hope to exploit?"

"Yes, sir," Vanto said.

"Very good, Lieutenant," Ar'alani said. "But you missed one crucial part. I had a surge of hope, and Admiral Mitth'raw'nuruodo didn't want the prisoners to see or recognize that. So he made it appear as if I was angry in order to confuse them." *She gestures toward the comlink on Vanto's belt.* "Call to the *Steadfast* and order Navigator Vah'nya brought here."

"Does Navigator Vah'nya have Second Sight?"

"She does." *Ar'alani's tone is firm, her body stance holding understanding and anticipation of what awaits them. It likewise holds fear that her hope is in vain.*

"Yes, Admiral." *Vanto's voice now holds confusion. While he is certainly familiar with Third Sight, he has doubtless never heard of Second Sight. But his hand is quick and sure, holding no hesitation or questioning as he draws out his comlink to obey the order.* "You said . . . hope?"

"Hope, Lieutenant," Ar'alani confirmed. *Her expression now holds grim amusement.* "For I believe there is every chance that Major Carvia's dead navigator is in fact very much alive."

CHAPTER 6

Grand Admiral Savit was sifting through the reports from the Third Fleet's latest pirate cleansing operation when the call came through from Director Krennic.

"Admiral Savit," Krennic said tersely. Even with the limitations of the flickering holoimage, Savit could see the man wasn't happy. "I need you to go find out what Thrawn is up to."

Savit raised his eyebrows a millimeter. "Excuse me, Director?"

"I've just received word that Thrawn has engaged in a battle somewhere near my transfer point," Krennic said. "I need you to find out what's going on, and who's involved, and then stop it."

"A moment," Savit said, sitting up straighter in his seat. A *battle*? "What kind of battle? How big? Who was he fighting?"

"Weren't you listening?" Krennic bit out. "I don't know the details. Assistant Director Ronan sent a quick report—he sounded rather frantic, actually—but apparently hasn't been able to provide a follow-up. That's why I need you to go there. If Thrawn's decided to go pirate hunting, and I have to move the transfer point—again—the whole Stardust schedule will be dangerously compromised."

"I was under the impression it already was."

"You know what I mean."

"No, actually, I don't," Savit said. "Because you haven't given me any real information. You need Ronan to send you more details."

"I've already asked," Krennic said. "As I said, he hasn't responded."

"Well, then, I don't suppose it can be *too* serious."

"Unless he's being interfered with," Krennic shot back. "He's hardly a free agent, you know. The whole *Chimaera* is rotten with people who are fanatically loyal to Thrawn. There's only so much they'll let Ronan do."

"Which should tell you something right there," Savit said. "When a ship is that devoted to its commander, it's because he's earned their trust and respect. I suggest you stop worrying about Thrawn and worry about getting Stardust back on track."

Krennic's eyes hardened. "Interesting suggestion, Admiral. So I shouldn't worry about whatever insanity Thrawn's perpetrating near my operation and go back to my own business? Is that what you're saying?"

"What do you suggest I do, Director?" Savit asked, keeping his own voice and expression calm. Experience had taught him that the best way to push an angry person into making mistakes was to refuse to join in that anger. "I have my own duties and responsibilities. I can't simply rush off at your request to deal with a problem you haven't even proved exists."

For a long moment Krennic just stared at him. "You like Thrawn, don't you, Admiral?" he said at last.

"Thrawn is a fellow grand admiral," Savit said, watching the director's face closely. An odd question, especially coming from Krennic. Where exactly was he going with this? "Likes and dislikes don't enter into it."

"No, but you really do like him," Krennic said. "Cultured types, both of you, him with his art and you with your music. Did I ever tell you I was at one of your mother's cultural galas some years back when your *To the Stars* was just a work for solo performer?"

"No, you didn't," Savit said. "I don't know how that relates to—"

"Unusual combination, you know, gifted composer *and* gifted performer," Krennic said. "And it was sheer genius that you subsequently worked that piece into a full opera. Did you know at the time how much Chancellor Palpatine and Governor Grazlos liked operas?" He waved a hand. "Doesn't matter, does it? The point is that you attracted the right kind of attention and made the right kind of contacts and ended up with your commission." He smiled genially. "In fact, I don't think it would be overstating the case to suggest that that opera and your subsequent works, along with the associated favors each new piece gained you from the never-satisfied Coruscant elite, might well have had a hand in your promotion to grand admiral."

Savit smiled back. So that's where he was taking this. The fool. "You may be right," he said. "It's been said that Coruscant's cultural life is the suede glove covering the granite fist that is the true Imperial power. Tell me, Director: Are you threatening me, or are you threatening my family?"

Krennic's eyebrows rose. "I?" he asked innocently. "I don't threaten, Admiral. I merely point out that what is favored among the elite today can be lost among the discarded dregs tomorrow."

"Then you really don't understand the elite," Savit said. "One moment, Director: I have a priority transmission coming through."

"Admiral—"

Krennic's voice broke off in mid-sentence, his image likewise freezing in mid-outrage. Savit keyed his personal comm system and punched in Grand Moff Tarkin's private number. "This is Grand Admiral Savit," he said to the screener droid. "I need to know if Governor Tarkin has received any information from his source aboard the *Chimaera* about an alleged battle near the Stardust transfer point."

He smiled to himself as he keyed off and switched back to Krennic. "—*dare* leave me hanging—" the director was snarling.

"Apologies, Director," Savit said. "I believe we were talking about the elite and veiled threats?"

"We were talking about Thrawn and the way his actions are threatening Stardust," Krennic bit out.

"Ah," Savit said. "Forgive me, Director, but it seems to me that you've lost sight of a key fact. If Thrawn gets distracted by other matters and fails to meet your deadline, he forfeits the Defender funding that you so desperately want to keep."

"And *you*, Admiral, seem to have lost sight of the fact that if he fails completely the grallocs continue to harass my cargoes and wreck my schedule," Krennic said. His voice was calm again, his attitude back on balance. "Or perhaps you haven't. I understand you're another of the Defender's secret supporters."

"Hardly a secret one," Savit said. "But yes, I think the Empire would benefit more from a few million advanced starfighters than from your precious Death Star." He paused, enjoying the flicker of shock that crossed Krennic's face. The true name of Stardust's end product was a deep, dark secret, and Savit wasn't supposed to be among the handful of top people who knew it. "I'm sorry—was that supposed to be a secret?" he added genially.

"I believe you know the answer to that," Krennic said. His voice was still calm, but the texture had darkened considerably. "As for Thrawn's deadline, I wouldn't worry about that. Ronan is there, and he'll ensure Thrawn doesn't achieve his goal in time. Eventually, he'll find a way to destroy the grallocs, which will be most helpful. But I'll also keep the Defender funding."

There was another ping from the comm. Tarkin, right on schedule. "In that case, Director Krennic, I may need to reconsider my earlier decision," Savit said, keying Tarkin into the audio part of the conversation but keeping his holo invisible to Krennic. "If I can help Thrawn fulfill the agreement, the Defender project will continue, and that would be a good thing." He keyed Tarkin's hologram into the loop. "Wouldn't you agree, Governor Tarkin?"

"Indeed I would," Tarkin said calmly. "Good day, Director Krennic."

Savit held his breath, watching both holograms closely. Here was where his blade-edge gamble could turn against him. He'd basically blindsided both Tarkin and Krennic into this confrontation, and if either of them chose to respond by making a full-blown, enemies-forever issue of it, Savit could find himself in trouble.

But for right now, such potential reprisals seemed to have been left for the future. Tarkin's expression was calmly malicious, showing that he'd quickly grasped what was going on and almost certainly deduced Savit's part in it. Krennic's face, after a brief moment of surprise and outrage, had also settled into his standard combat expression as he faced his more immediate enemy.

"Good day, Governor," Krennic said, matching Tarkin's tone. "I didn't realize you'd been brought into this conversation."

"Admiral Savit asked if I'd received any information about Grand Admiral Thrawn's battle an hour ago," Tarkin said. "My source says that his TIE Defender squadron played a pivotal role in the victory."

"I see," Krennic said, a bit of fresh strain invading his calm. "I didn't know the battle was that extensive. Can you tell me who exactly the *Chimaera* was fighting?"

Savit leaned a little closer to the display. That was indeed the crucial question.

But for the moment, at least, it was going to remain a mystery. "My source didn't have that data," Tarkin said. "Apparently, it involved two other ships, non-Imperials, possibly engaged in a private dispute of their own."

"Rival pirates?" Krennic pressed. "Pirates and rebels?"

"As already stated, I don't know," Tarkin said, a hint of amusement touching his eyes at Krennic's obvious agitation. "But I've sent a request to my source. If I should obtain that information, I will of course share it with you."

"Of course," Krennic said. His eyes turned back to Savit. "Under the circumstances, Governor, perhaps you'd be good enough to join me in requesting that Admiral Savit investigate the situation."

"I'm certain Grand Admiral Thrawn has it under control," Tarkin said. "But if he requests aid, I shall certainly reconsider your request."

And that, Savit knew, was that. Krennic was caught between two rocks, with the pressing need for Thrawn to clear up the transfer point mess pressing up against the need for him to not clear it up too quickly. Tarkin, for his part, had everything to gain by letting Thrawn work without interference and solve the gralloc problem on his own terms and timing. The fact that he got to see Krennic squirm was just an added bonus.

And of course, with their private agreement for Savit to cooperate with Thrawn should assistance be needed, Tarkin held one final card.

As for Savit himself, the best thing he could do was stay completely out of it until and unless that card needed to be played. The more invisible he could remain, the better.

"Then I believe my part of this is finished," he said. "Governor Tarkin, I'll likewise be interested in learning more about the situation, should you receive further information."

Tarkin inclined his head. "I'll be certain to pass it on to you," he promised.

"Thank you," Savit said. "And thank you, too, for your interest, Director Krennic. Perhaps I'll see you someday at one of my mother's cultural galas."

Krennic offered only a slight smile in return. But it was clear he'd gotten the message. Threats against Savit's family, even off-edge, veiled ones, were unacceptable. "Good day, then," Savit said, and keyed off.

And as the two holos vanished, Savit permitted himself a smile of his own.

"And *that*," he murmured to the universe, "is how a grand admiral deals with things."

He keyed for the bridge. "Signal for the *Misthunter*," he ordered the comm officer. "Captain Rasdel has spoken of a contact he claims to have inside Governor Tarkin's office. Tell him he's to activate that contact and feed me anything pertaining to Stardust within our patrol area."

He smiled to himself. Tarkin could promise all he wanted that he would pass on information. Savit preferred a bit more of a sure thing.

And with that accomplished, it was time to put this ridiculous political infighting nonsense behind him and get back to work. "And then send a transmission to the *Harbinger*," he continued. "Tell Captain Pellaeon I want him and his first officer to meet me here in one hour to discuss his next pirate-hunting mission."

———

Major Carvia was clearly uncomfortable allowing Thrawn and the others to enter the observation post medcenter without him. Thrawn's death trooper escort was even more reluctant. It took a direct order to make the three of them wait out in the passageway.

Some of it, Eli knew, was the presence of Ar'alani, an admiral from an unknown and unevaluated alien fleet who might pose a threat to the stormtroopers' commander. But most of it, he suspected, was because of him. A man who'd once worn the uniform of the Imperial Navy, but now wore the black of the Chiss Defense Fleet.

Eli didn't know what Thrawn was going to say about him to the stormtroopers, or to Commodore Faro, or to anyone else. Actually, he didn't know if the grand admiral would say anything at all. For all he knew, Thrawn might send him back to the Ascendancy still carrying the burden of shame and suspicion.

He didn't mind for himself. Thrawn had said he might be of use to the Chiss, and Ar'alani seemed satisfied with his work, and for right now that was enough.

It was his parents who had to bear the brunt of the stigma, and his former friends in the fleet who had to see his name forever draped with contempt.

Which made Thrawn's aloofness toward him so puzzling. Didn't he realize what Eli had gone through? What he'd given up for him?

Maybe before this was over he could get Thrawn alone, even if only for a minute, and find out what his former commander was thinking.

If he couldn't, he could only hope that whatever it was Ar'alani had in mind for him, it would be worth it.

Carvia had identified the room as the observation post's medcenter. To Eli's eyes, it looked more like a disturbing mix of treatment bay, torture chamber, and dissection room. A human body was slumped in a sort of exam chair, his arms and legs strapped down, apparently stabbed to death right where he sat. Three bodies of a species Eli didn't recognize were crumpled on the floor, two near a console in the center of the room, the other near the dead human, all of them lying in pools of a pale-pink blood.

The Chiss girl, in contrast, seemed completely untouched. She was lying on her back on a treatment table at the rear of the room, her arms at her sides with the hands tucked beneath her legs, a double fold of black cloth draped across her face and upper torso. There was no blood, but as far as Eli could tell she looked very much dead.

Ar'alani apparently thought otherwise. Before the door had even closed behind them she was striding quickly across the room toward the table. "Somnia?" Thrawn asked as he and Eli followed.

"A variant of the technique, yes," Ar'alani said over her shoulder. "You'd already left before this one was developed. I'll need the lights lowered."

"Yes." Thrawn glanced around and headed toward the control console at the center of the room. "Lieutenant Vanto, a towel soaked in hot water, if you please."

"Yes, sir," Eli said, heading in the opposite direction toward a wide double sink. "May I ask . . . ?"

"Some navigators, especially the younger ones, occasionally experience a sort of sensory overload," Ar'alani said. "It's accompanied by such symptoms as headaches, body aches, sparkle-vision, and vertigo."

"The prescribed treatment is sensory deprivation and a mental regimen called somnia," Thrawn added. He reached the console, glanced over it, and turned one of the controls. In response the room's lights faded to a barely visible glow. "The effect is to lower the metabolism in such a way as to diminish the physical symptoms, while the sensory suppression speeds the mental recovery."

Eli nodded, looking at the girl with new eyes as Ar'alani removed the cloth covering her face and torso. The hands pressed under the girl's legs would muffle touch stimulus from the fingers, while the cloth would partially block sight, hearing, and smell.

Aboard a Chiss ship, there were presumably facilities specifically dedicated to the process, probably hidden back in the navigators' section out of sight of the rest of the crew. Here, the girl had had to improvise. "So the Grysks didn't realize she was still alive?"

"An interesting question," Thrawn said. "The answer will carry some equally profound implications. But we'll get to that shortly. Ar'alani?"

"She's alive," Ar'alani said, and there was no mistaking the relief in her voice. "Lieutenant Vanto?"

"Here," Eli said, hurrying over and handing her the wet towel. "What do you want me to do?"

"Stand back," Ar'alani said as she folded the towel and laid it on the girl's forehead. "I don't want the first face she sees to be human."

Eli grimaced. But the admiral was right. After what the girl had undoubtedly been through here, she needed to wake up to some un-ambiguously friendly faces. "How long will it take?" he asked as he backed away.

Without warning, the girl's body twitched violently, her back arching for a moment before she collapsed back onto the table. She cried out, a wordless half scream, half whimper—

"Come back!" Ar'alani said sharply. "Navigator of the Chiss Ascendancy, come back!"

The girl's eyes snapped open. For a moment she just stared at the woman leaning over her. Then, abruptly, she lunged up from the table and wrapped her arms tightly around Ar'alani's neck, squeezing as if her grip were all that kept her from sliding off to her death.

And as if a dam had shattered, she burst into tears.

Out of the corner of his eye, Eli saw Thrawn motion him back toward the door. Watching with a sense of strangeness as the hard, cold, stiff Chiss admiral he'd come to know murmured soothing words to the terrified girl, Eli backed silently away.

Thrawn was waiting when he reached the door. "Analysis, Lieutenant?" Thrawn asked quietly.

"I think the dead aliens were in charge of the mission," Eli said. "They seem to have been the ones interrogating the human when he was killed. I assume he and the other humans were from the Allanar N3 freighter we saw being attacked a few hours ago?"

"Most likely," Thrawn said. "Further analysis should give us that answer. Continue."

"The aliens were running the show, but they had a pair of Grysk overseers," Eli said. The girl seemed to be calming down some, he noted, though she still had Ar'alani in a death grip. "But the over-seers weren't part of the day-to-day operations."

"Why do you say that?"

"Because they didn't realize the girl was still alive," Eli said. "I'm assuming this had happened before, and that the aliens knew all about it. The fact that she was in here instead of her quarters suggests they wanted to keep an eye on her."

"Very good," Thrawn said. "What happened then?"

Eli pursed his lips, savoring the warm glow from Thrawn's compli-ment. "There must have been some falling-out," he said. "When you attacked, maybe when you disabled the post, the aliens revolted and the Grysks killed them in reprisal."

"No," Thrawn said.

The warm glow disappeared. "It wasn't a revolt?"

"Observe the locations of the bodies," Thrawn said. "Observe also the equipment cabinet on the wall near the treatment tables."

"I see it," Eli said. The cabinet was as much display case as actual cabinet, with an array of medical tools visible through the transpar-ent doors.

"Note the presence of several large scalpels and other cutting tools," Thrawn said. "None is missing. If the aliens were in revolt, these three would surely have armed themselves with whatever weapons they could find."

"Yes, I see," Eli said, grimacing. He should have spotted that.

"Furthermore, none of their bodies were inside or near the com-mand center," Thrawn said. "Nor were there any blood marks to indi-cate that there might have once been bodies that had been subsequently removed. The only blood on the command center floor were traces tracked in by the Grysks as they returned to await our arrival."

"Understood," Eli said. Okay, so he'd missed one. *Learn, let the embarrassment or chagrin go, and move on.* "So once the post was disabled they knew we'd capture it and didn't want us interrogating anyone. Since you'd fried their electronics, they couldn't initiate their self-destruct, so they had to go through the ship and kill every-one manually."

"What makes you think they had a self-destruct?"

"Because the warship had one."

"Excellent," Thrawn said, nodding. "Death before capture, particularly in a clandestine operation such as this one."

"And yet, the two Grysks are still alive," Eli pointed out. "Did the stormtroopers get to them before they could suicide?"

"I'll confirm with Major Carvia, but I don't believe that was the case," Thrawn said. "More likely they chose to wait in order to learn what we know about them and this operation. Did you notice anything else about them?"

Eli searched his memory. "There was something odd when you were talking about their backup ship. I think they were surprised to hear that you'd destroyed it."

"Not entirely correct," Thrawn said. "I believe they were unaware the ship was here at all." He cocked his head. "Which brings us to you, Ar'alani, and the *Steadfast*. What exactly brought you to this system?"

Eli looked over at the other two Chiss. The girl had stopped crying but was still holding tightly to Ar'alani. The older woman was now holding her with one hand and gently stroking her hair with the other. "I think the admiral should be the one to tell you that," he said.

"The admiral is otherwise engaged, and time may be critical," Thrawn said sternly. "I'm therefore asking you."

"Yes, sir." A deserter and a traitor to the Empire . . . and yet here he was, about to tell Chiss secrets to his former Imperial commander. Did that offer a degree of redemption? Or did it simply make him twice a traitor? "The *Steadfast* was sent out to investigate reports that Grysk or Grysk clients might have infiltrated this part of the Empire. We tracked a ship to this system, but we were pretty far behind it and it vanished somewhere out here in this asteroid cluster."

"Cloaked," Thrawn murmured.

"Yes," Eli confirmed. "But Grysk cloaking devices are notorious for limiting sensor readings outward almost as much as they do inward, and she thought there was a good chance we could sneak up on them. She gave the *Steadfast* a controlled thruster burn, then went dark and let us coast in. We were nearly in range for some serious work when we saw them take the freighter."

"Yes," Thrawn said thoughtfully. "And then the *Chimaera* arrived and interfered with her plan."

Eli hesitated. But there was no way around it. "I believe that's how she sees it, yes."

"No doubt," Thrawn said. "This ship you were following. What information were you able to glean about it?"

"Hardly anything, really," Eli admitted. "The drive emissions were definitely Grysk, but we've seen some of their client species use the same thrusters, so that didn't tell us anything one way or the other about its origin."

"I'm more interested in size," Thrawn said. "Specifically, was it the size of this observation post or the warship, or was it possibly something else."

Eli caught his breath as it suddenly clicked. "You're saying that neither this ship nor the ship we destroyed is the one we were following? That there's a *third* cloaked Grysk ship out there?"

"So I conclude," Thrawn said. "I presume it was a supply ship, here to restock the observation post."

"But it arrived over a day ago," Eli pointed out. "Are they that slow at transferring supplies?"

"Possibly," Thrawn said. "It's also possible that its continued presence may indicate that it was being prepared to take the captives from the Allanar N3 for relocation to another Grysk ship or base."

"We have to warn the *Steadfast*," Eli said, pulling out his comlink. "And the *Chimaera*—"

"No," Thrawn said, putting a restraining hand on his arm. "Pause and consider. If the hidden ship is monitoring our communications, we don't want them to know we're aware of their presence."

"They won't know what we're saying," Eli said. "Our encryption is secure."

"Never assume any message is secure," Thrawn said. "I suspect that our communications are already compromised. Who's to say yours aren't as well?"

"But—"

"Don't worry about the *Steadfast*," Thrawn said. "Admiral Ar'alani has likely already deduced the presence of the third ship and has left the *Steadfast* on full alert."

Across the room, Ar'alani had extricated herself from the girl's grip, though her arm remained protectively around the girl's shoulders. The girl herself was staring at Thrawn and Eli, blinking through the darkness and the remnants of her tears. "Come," Ar'alani called. "She's ready to talk."

Thrawn and Eli headed back across the room, Thrawn taking a moment to turn the lights back up as they passed the control console. "Good day, Navigator of the Chiss," he said gravely as they reached the others. "I am Grand Admiral Mitth'raw'nuruodo, currently in service to the Galactic Empire. This is Lieutenant Eli Vanto, former officer of the Empire, now in service to the Chiss Ascendancy. What's your name?"

"I'm Un'hee," she said, her voice low. "I was . . ." Her throat worked. "I was taken from my home by the Grysks two years ago. I've served them ever since."

"She was five when she was taken," Ar'alani said. "And she may prove to be the Grysks' greatest mistake."

"How so?" Thrawn asked.

"She's navigated Grysk ships through a large part of their hegemony," Ar'alani said. "If she can reproduce or parallel the pathways she opened for them, we may be able to lift some of the veil of secrecy they've worked so hard to construct."

"Interesting," Thrawn said. "And so the rest becomes clear."

"Which parts were unclear?" Ar'alani asked.

"Why the aliens didn't tell the Grysks that Un'hee was still alive," Thrawn said. "Presumably they were unwilling clients, as may have been much of their species, and they chose to protect Un'hee's life as their last act of defiance against their overlords."

"I thought the Grysks subverted entire populations," Eli said.

"That's their preferred method," Ar'alani said. "But it's sometimes

easier and faster to bend just the government to their will and purpose."

"Especially in cultures where the people follow their leaders
blindly," Thrawn said. "It appears in this case that this particular
group were not as obedient to their government's direction as the
Grysks thought."

"Or else the time they'd spent under Grysk command gave them
new insights," Ar'alani said, cocking her head. "And you deduced all
this from afar?"

"Hardly," Thrawn said. "I was merely investigating the disappear-
ance of Imperial supply ships. I had no indication that the Grysks
were involved in the thefts until we were attacked." He inclined his
head to Ar'alani. "My apologies for interfering with your operation."

"Apology accepted but unnecessary," Ar'alani said. "So we know
now why Un'hee was kept alive. That also suggests a reason the two
Grysks chose to remain alive to await us."

"They wanted confirmation of Un'hee's death before they died,"
Thrawn said, nodding. "Perhaps they realized that they should have
checked that for themselves instead of accepting their slaves' word."

"But realized it too late," Ar'alani said. "You were indeed correct to
hide my hope from them." She wrapped her arm a little tighter around
Un'hee's shoulders. "And now that hope hangs by a thread."

"The hidden supply ship," Thrawn said, nodding. "Our two Grysk
prisoners must have a way of communicating with it even while
shackled. If they suspect Un'hee still lives, they will certainly call in a
strike against this post."

"A post that is still recovering from your ion attack," Ar'alani said.
"Whatever defenses it has cannot be assumed to be functional."

"And the danger's about to double," Eli said. "Vah'nya's on her
way. If the Grysks decide to take out the post, they'll get two navigators for the price of one."

"One of whom also possesses Second Sight," Ar'alani said grimly
as she pulled out her own comlink.

"No," Thrawn said. "If they see you wave her off, they may suspect
something."

"They won't fire," Ar'alani insisted. "Launching an attack will reveal their position, allowing them only a single shot before the *Stead-fast* destroys them. That single shot can be toward the observation post or Vah'nya's shuttle, and they don't know which would be the better target."

"Agreed," Thrawn said. "But they know Un'hee is here, alive or dead, and they don't know whether the approaching ship has any value at all. If their attention is drawn by an abrupt change of the shuttle's course, their wisest move would be to make sure the more likely threat is neutralized."

Eli checked his chrono. "Besides, if the shuttle's on schedule, it may be close enough for an attack against the post to take it out, too."

Ar'alani glared at him. Eli tensed, but the glare instantly softened. "That may be true," she conceded. "But right now, at least, there's a chance. Once Vah'nya is aboard, it really *will* be two navigators for the price of one."

"Or possibly more," Thrawn said. "Un'hee, are there other Chiss aboard this group of Grysk ships?"

"No," Un'hee said. "They use others as their navigators. Other peoples, some trained by the Attendants. I was the only Chiss. I was—" A wave of pain and fear swept across her face. "A gift."

"I see," Thrawn said, his voice grim. "Good. That means we may fire on the Grysks without concern for Chiss lives."

"That still leaves both Un'hee and Vah'nya in danger," Ar'alani said. "We need to find a way to carry both to safety."

"We will," Thrawn confirmed. "A properly tailored story to our captive Grysks should accomplish that. We need only—" He broke off at the sound of a soft chime and pulled out his comlink. "Yes?"

Eli couldn't hear the answer. But suddenly Thrawn's expression went rigid. "No," he said flatly. "You will not . . ." A short pause . . . "Understood," Thrawn said. "Very well. Send him in."

"Send whom in?" Ar'alani asked suspiciously.

"A person of trouble," Thrawn said. "Prepare yourself, Lieutenant Vanto. This is likely to be unpleasant."

CHAPTER 7

Ronan had asked Thrawn to let him accompany the grand admiral to the alien observation post. Thrawn had refused. Ronan had demanded Commodore Faro let him take a second shuttle and catch up with the party. Faro had also refused, and with a veiled satisfaction at that snub that bordered on insubordination.

But Director Krennic's whole life was an example of not giving up, and Ronan had learned from the best. Eventually, he worked his way down the chain of command until he found a crack in Thrawn's close-knit officer corps. She was the chief hangar master, a senior lieutenant named Xoxtin with no love for either Thrawn or Faro and a properly respectful attitude toward the Empire's elite.

Ronan himself wasn't part of that elite. But Director Krennic was, and in those circles Ronan's connection to that name carried considerable weight. The flowing white cape probably didn't hurt, either.

There were three main docking ports on the structure. Thrawn's shuttle occupied one of them, while the second was blocked by an unfamiliar vessel maneuvering its way to a landing—a vessel, he noted, that had the same vaguely reptilian shape and carried the same multi-circle sigil as the still-unidentified ship now floating in the distance off the *Chimaera*'s portside flank.

So apparently even as Thrawn was denying a high-ranking Imperial official like Ronan access to the observation post and its technology, he had no problem bringing a group of aliens aboard. Glowering, he docked his shuttle at the third port, talked his way past the stormtrooper who wanted to ask Thrawn's permission before letting him aboard, and headed in the direction the stormtrooper pointed him.

After all this effort, he thought grimly to himself, as he strode down the silent corridors, the trip had better be worth it.

It was.

The stormtrooper commander and the two death troopers standing guard were obvious indicators as to which room Thrawn and his party had holed up in. Unlike the earlier stormtrooper, though, these three weren't so easily bullied by Ronan's name and rank. One of them went silent as he called it in, and for a long moment Ronan could only stand there and glare while the grand admiral made a decision. Finally—reluctantly, Ronan thought—the three guards stepped aside and let him through.

The stormtrooper had called it a medical bay, though it seemed to Ronan less like a treatment room and more like an interrogation center. But that was all peripheral. His full attention was on the four people standing across the room beside a padded treatment table.

Grand Admiral Thrawn.

A female with Thrawn's same blue skin and glowing red eyes wearing a white uniform of unfamiliar cut.

A girl, maybe six or seven, also with blue skin and red eyes, wearing a simple jumpsuit, sitting on the table.

The fact that Thrawn's people had apparently been one side of that brief battle out there raised a number of highly important questions, questions Ronan would definitely be asking somewhere down the line. But for the moment, all of that paled in the sudden glare of the fourth person of the group.

Commander Eli Vanto. Deserter from the Imperial fleet. Apparent collusionist with an alien government.

Traitor.

"I asked that you remain aboard the *Chimaera*," Thrawn said. His tone was even, but Ronan could hear the edge beneath it.

"You should have known that order had no power," Ronan countered, his eyes on Vanto. So many things had now suddenly come clear. "Director Krennic and Governor Tarkin made very precise lines as to where your authority over me ends."

"Aboard an Imperial warship, the commander is the ultimate authority," Thrawn said.

"But I see now why you were so anxious to keep me out," Ronan continued. "Hello, Commander Vanto. Or did your desertion gain you a new rank? Something to go along with your new friends and allies?"

"It's Lieutenant Vanto now, Assistant Director," Thrawn said. "And his departure from the Empire wasn't desertion. On the contrary, it was personally authorized by the Emperor himself."

"Was it, now," Ronan said, feeling a rush of cynicism. A common defense in this kind of situation: One party would invoke a big name, and the second party would counter with an even bigger name. Ronan had brought up Tarkin and Director Krennic, leaving Thrawn nowhere to go but to name the Emperor.

A common defense, but a foolish and ultimately self-defeating one. Out here, far from Imperial Center and civilization, Thrawn might get away with such a claim for a time. But ultimately the words would have to be backed up, and then it would fall apart.

And if the Emperor roused himself from his doddering long enough to actually pay attention, Thrawn's career might also fall apart. As might Thrawn himself. "And of course you have documentation proving that?" he asked, not bothering to hide his cynicism.

"There is no documentation," Thrawn said. "But that will be a discussion for another day. Time is short, and we need to utilize it to the fullest."

Behind Ronan, the door slid open. He turned, taking a step to the side, fully expecting to see the death troopers enter in a belated and futile attempt to detain him.

Instead he found himself facing yet another blue-skinned face, this one attached to a young woman in a black uniform. "Who are you?" he demanded.

The woman's eyes flicked past Ronan to the group at the table. "This is Vah'nya," Thrawn identified her. "She doesn't speak Basic."

"Of course not," Ronan growled, glaring as Vah'nya sidled carefully around him and joined the others. "So is this how it is? You bring in your people in the hope of subverting Stardust?" He narrowed his eyes. "Or do you think you can steal it entirely? Because if you even try—"

"Calm yourself, Assistant Director," Thrawn cut in sharply. "No one is threatening your project. But we are in grave danger here, and must act quickly if we're to escape unharmed."

Ronan felt his lip twist. Another common defense and deflection.

But as he gazed into the grand admiral's eyes, and into the eyes of the others lined up alongside him, he had the eerie feeling that this time, at least, Thrawn was telling the truth. "Explain," he said.

"There is another enemy ship out there," Thrawn said. "Cloaked and waiting."

"For what?"

"For news as to whether she is alive or dead," Thrawn said, gesturing to the girl sitting on the table. "We must assume that the two Grysks under restraint in the control room have a way of talking to that ship. We need to find that line of communication and either shut it down or in some other way put their minds at rest."

"Or?" Ronan asked.

"Or they destroy this observation post," Thrawn said. "And us along with it."

Ronan focused on the girl. Her face was tight and tearstained, fear and exhaustion filling her eyes. Surely she didn't have any useful talents or expertise. Not a child that young.

The obvious conclusion was that she knew something. Something vital, something the ship out there didn't want anyone else to know.

What in the Empire could she know that was *that* important?

"So what are you going to do?" he asked.

"As I said, we need to put their minds at rest," Thrawn said.

"Or," Vanto said thoughtfully, "we need to give them what they want."

"In what way?" Thrawn asked.

"We now have two docked Imperial shuttles," Vanto said. "We could send one of them back empty and try to get the Grysks to shoot at it."

"Absurd," Ronan scoffed. "They'll surely be able to detect whether there are any life-forms aboard."

"Then we sweeten the pot," Vanto said. "We put the two Grysks aboard and send a message to the *Chimaera* warning that a pair of valuable prisoners are on their way. We don't let them fly it, of course," he added quickly, "but strap them in."

"Then who *does* fly it?" Ronan asked. "You?"

"No one flies it," Vanto said. "The *Chimaera* reels it in with a tractor beam."

Ronan snorted. Maybe losing this idiot to Thrawn's people hadn't been such a disaster for the Empire after all. "And so after all that, we just let them blow up the prisoners and our best chance of finding out what's going on?"

"The prisoners are hardly our best chance," Thrawn said. "They'll already have prepared themselves for death precisely to forestall any such interrogation." He smiled faintly. "However, that being said, I don't believe we have to make that choice."

"You're expecting the other ship to have to make it?" Ronan shook his head. "Ridiculous. If you're going to bait them, you'll need to send a clear-language message, and they're surely not stupid enough to fall for that."

"I never said the message would be clear-language," Thrawn said softly. "On the contrary, I have a code I fully expect them to be able to decipher."

Ronan frowned. There'd been an odd edge of darkness to that comment. "An *Imperial* code?"

"Indeed," Thrawn said. "Yes, Lieutenant Vanto's plan should work quite well." He pursed his lips slightly. "With, I believe, a few more small refinements."

He turned to the white-clad woman and began jabbering in an unknown language. She replied, and he said something else. The woman turned to the girl and spoke, got an answer in return, then spoke to Vah'nya, who also replied. For a moment Vah'nya and the girl spoke, and then the white-clad woman joined in.

Vanto looked over at Ronan, looked back at the group of jabbering blue-skins, then silently crossed over to him. "They're working out a battle plan," he said quietly. "Basically a flush-and-trap setup—"

"Are you talking to *me*, traitor?" Ronan cut him off tartly.

Vanto's eyebrow twitched. "Apparently not," he said. "My apologies." Inclining his head, he began backing away.

Ronan clenched his hand into a fist. Stalemate. "Stop," he ordered. "I'm . . . sorry." He forced out the word. "Tell me what they're saying."

Vanto eyed him another second, then again inclined his head. "As I said, a flush-and-trap," he said. "They want to draw the cloaked ship out of hiding and then let it lead us to its base."

"What makes you think it has a base?"

"The Grysks need to have a comm center for an operation this far from their territory," Vanto said. "They can't use the HoloNet for long-range communications—the Empire can tap into those messages— so they'll be using something called a triad. If we can find the triad and the associated base—"

The white-clad woman said something in a sharp tone. Vanto broke off and turned to face her, and for another moment she jabbered at him. He replied with a couple of words in the same language and an inclined head.

Thrawn said something. The woman turned to him, and Ronan had a sense it was less a discussion now and more of an argument. "What are they saying?" he asked.

"Admiral Ar'alani says this operation is none of your business," Vanto said.

Ronan bristled. "Oh, she does, does she?"

"Admiral Thrawn disagrees," Vanto continued. "He believes that the presence of Grysks here suggests they're more prepared to move against the Empire than he'd anticipated."

A shiver ran up Ronan's back. He'd already wondered about Thrawn's people being here. The thought of an unknown alien species poised to move against the Empire was even more ominous.

Especially if that action included an attack on Stardust.

"Admiral Thrawn's telling her you're a senior official in a project called Stardust," Vanto said. "He suggests that if the Grysks are preparing a move, Stardust could be of great value to the Imperial defense."

Ronan felt his eyes narrow. Thrawn had better not be suggesting that Director Krennic would simply hand it over to him.

The woman—Ar'alani—snapped something again at Vanto. He turned back and answered, and Ar'alani again said something sharp. This time, Thrawn didn't intervene.

And when Vanto turned back to Ronan, he had a carefully controlled expression on his face. "Admiral Thrawn and Admiral Ar'alani request that I act as your liaison and translator for the moment," he said.

Ronan felt his skin tingle. To deal with a traitor—to listen to him and, worse, to *talk* to him?

And worst of all, to *rely* on him?

No. That was absolutely crossing a line. "Tell your admiral to forget it," he said firmly. "Your presence is an affront to everything I believe in."

"Then you will be returned to the *Chimaera*," Thrawn said, "and will remain in your quarters until the current operation is ended."

"You have no such authority," Ronan shot back.

"On the contrary," Thrawn said coolly. "As I said, a ship's commander is the ultimate authority for what can and cannot be done. Furthermore, the *Chimaera* may be going into battle, and standing orders specifically require me to protect high-ranking passengers, in any way I deem fit."

Ronan felt his eyes narrow. There was no way Thrawn could make that stick. Ronan could send a message to Director Krennic detailing everything that had happened, including Thrawn's collusion with a possible alien invasion force and his association with the traitor Eli Vanto. Once the director got such a message, there was every chance Thrawn would find himself on the next prisoner transport to Imperial Center.

But of course that assumed Thrawn wouldn't cut off his access to the *Chimaera*'s comm system. If the admiral could invoke battle rules to lock Ronan in his quarters, he could probably do that, too.

And there was no chance in the Empire that Ronan was just going to sit by while Thrawn took an Imperial ship into danger. Even if he could just be a voice of reason, it was his duty to maintain a presence in Thrawn's upcoming deliberations and actions.

"Fine," he growled. "Vanto can play translator. What now?"

"We shall offer the bait," Thrawn said. "And then see if the enemy will take it."

"We shall be sending Assistant Director Ronan's shuttle back to the *Chimaera*, Commodore," Thrawn's voice came over the speaker. "Two Grysk prisoners will be aboard. They're to be treated as both highly valuable and highly dangerous."

"Understood, Admiral," Faro said, frowning at the comm display. Thrawn had specified the G77 encryption, a code that was in the ship's archives but one they'd never used.

Still, she'd long since learned that whenever Thrawn did something without a good reason, it was usually because there was a *very* good reason lurking beneath the surface.

"For security purposes we'll be sending it without a command crew," Thrawn continued. "You'll arrange for a tractor beam to bring it in. I also want Captain Dobbs to run a full-wrap escort."

Faro smiled as the veil of confusion began to part. Captain Dobbs and his Defender squadron, fighters whose full capabilities this particular group of Grysks might well be unfamiliar with.

Apparently, the *Chimaera*'s admiral was baiting a trap.

"Understood, sir," Faro said. "I'll recall Dobbs and his squadron immediately from patrol."

"Thank you, Commodore," Thrawn said. "Let me know when you're ready. Once we have the prisoners aboard, I fully expect that our enemies' plans, now shrouded in mystery, will be laid bare before us."

Faro felt her lip twitch. *Shrouded in mystery.* There it was: confirmation of the conclusion she'd already come to.

Somewhere out there was another cloaked Grysk ship.

"And those plans will soon see the light of day?" Faro suggested.

"Not immediately," Thrawn said. "But all that is dark will eventually be made light if one shows the proper persistence."

"Understood, sir," Faro said again. "We'll be ready when you need us."

"Thank you, Commodore. Admiral out."

The transmission cut off, and Faro crossed to the weapons console. "You get all that?" she asked.

"Yes, ma'am," Pyrondi said grimly. "So we've got another lurker. Wonderful."

"It could be worse," Faro said. "The fact that it didn't join the battle when its companion was fighting for its life—"

"And losing."

"—and definitely losing," Faro agreed, "suggests it doesn't have a lot of firepower. Probably a scout or resupply ship that got caught at the wrong place and time."

"I guess we'll find out soon enough." Pyrondi tapped thoughtfully at her lip. "Could be a little tricky if it decides to hit and run. Aside from stumbling around a little blind, I don't think there's anything that prevents a cloaked ship from flying."

"There are the drive emissions that will stream outside the cloak," Faro reminded her. "Looks like we're supposed to follow it."

"Not going to get far if they jump to lightspeed."

"True." Faro nodded in the direction of the Chiss ship, lying off the *Chimaera*'s bow a few kilometers away. "Maybe the Chiss have ways of tracking ships through hyperspace that we don't."

"I guess we'll find out," Faro said.

"I liked your line about their plans seeing the light of day," Pyrondi added. "There's nothing like concentrated turbolaser fire to brighten up a dark night. Too bad Thrawn said no."

"I don't think he said *no*," Faro said. "Just *not yet*. So stop pouting, Senior Lieutenant, and get your crews ready."

She looked out the viewport. "The universe is about to get interesting again."

The plans were made, the relevant information had been relayed to the *Chimaera* and *Steadfast,* and the players were in position.

And now came the waiting. For Eli, that was always the hardest part.

The fact that Assistant Director Ronan was glowering beside him wasn't helping any, either. The two of them were a few paces behind Thrawn and his death trooper guard—the troopers, Eli noted with private amusement, having formed a box around the grand admiral, pointedly blocking Ronan from approaching him—all of them gazing out the Grysk observation post's main viewport. The shuttle that was about to be the focus of everyone's attention wasn't visible from where they stood, but Eli could see the *Chimaera* holding position a few kilometers away. Beyond it, partially blocked from view, was the *Steadfast*. Both ships, he knew, were at full alert and ready for combat.

At least Eli hoped they were. The problem was that Grysk forces were often supplemented by some of their client species, and each of those clients possessed a slightly different palette of tech and weaponry. That meant there was always the chance for a surprise, possibly even a lethal one.

"This is insane," Ronan muttered. "Thrawn's going to get all of us killed."

"I think the idea is to not get *any* of us killed," Eli said. "Regardless, I'm sure he would be open to better suggestions."

Ronan snorted. "Maybe from you or Ar'alani. Not from me. So where are they?"

"Who?"

"You know who," Ronan ground out. "Ar'alani, Vah'nya, and the little girl. If you want to assume I don't have a brain, at least recognize that I have eyes."

"Sorry," Eli said, putting as much apology into the word as he could. He'd hoped Ronan wouldn't notice the absence of the three Chiss for at least a little while longer. "I believe Admiral Ar'alani is consulting with the others."

"Consulting about what?"

"I don't know," Eli said. For once, it was the truth—he really *didn't* know what the three of them were up to. It had to have something to do with the Second Sight that Thrawn and Ar'alani had mentioned, but he was completely in the dark as to what that was.

"Does it have to do with whatever the girl knows?" Ronan pressed. "It must be something she knows—she certainly can't have any talents or training these Grysks might want. Not at her age."

"I really don't know what they're doing," Eli said again, suppressing a grimace. Ronan had hit way too close to the mark on that one. "I'm sure we'll be told whenever the others feel we need to know."

"*Need to know* is a slippery term," Ronan growled. "Doesn't matter. If they want me to intervene with Director Krennic on their behalf, they're going to have to learn they have to tell me whatever I want to know whenever I want to know it."

"The Emperor might think otherwise."

Ronan snorted quietly. "The Emperor," he said scornfully. "You and Thrawn keep invoking his name as if it's a magic spell that can be used against me. Trust me: The Emperor fully supports Director Krennic, which means he fully supports me. Furthermore, once Stardust is operational, the rest of the political structure on Imperial Center will be completely irrelevant. Director Krennic and the Emperor will be the only ones that matter."

Eli thought back to his one and only meeting with the Emperor, when Thrawn had been brought to Coruscant from his exile near the Unknown Regions. The Emperor's voice . . . his presence . . . his eyes . . .

Especially his eyes. "Or it'll be *just* the Emperor," he said.

"Trust me—the director will be there as long as Palpatine is," Ronan said. "Right now, I'd be more concerned with your own future. I have three-quarters of a notion right now to drag you back to the *Chimaera,* order you locked up, and send a message for ISB to come arrest you for desertion."

"I think Admiral Thrawn would have something to say about that," Eli said, resisting the urge to point out that the navy, not the Imperial Security Bureau, handled desertion issues.

"You really don't understand who I am, do you?" Ronan said. "Fine. Neither does Thrawn, really."

Eli shifted his attention to Thrawn as the grand admiral pulled out his comlink. There was a brief, inaudible conversation, and then he half turned. "Assistant Director, Lieutenant Vanto," he called, beckoning to them. "The operation begins. Please; join me."

And as the death trooper guard reluctantly parted for them, Eli felt his heart pick up its pace.

Time, indeed, to see if the enemy would take the bait.

"Go." Admiral Thrawn's voice came across the bridge speakers.

Faro straightened a little. "Defenders, take up formation. Tractor control, lock on and bring it in."

There were a pair of acknowledgments, and she felt the subtle shift of the command walkway under her feet as the *Chimaera*'s tractor beam lanced out, locked onto the shuttle, and began reeling it in. On the tactical display, the six TIE Defenders of Captain Dobbs's task force had settled into position, flying close escort around the larger craft.

And everyone else aboard the *Chimaera*—and presumably aboard the *Steadfast* as well—was staring at the asteroid cluster for signs of the hidden enemy.

Faro rubbed her fingertips restlessly on the seam of her uniform trousers, painfully aware that Thrawn's plan could fall apart in any of a dozen different ways. He was probably right about the hidden

Grysks having only one shot, and knowing they had only one shot. But there was no way to truly predict where they would take it. If they decided their compatriots aboard the shuttle were as good as dead anyway, they might still decide to take out the observation post instead. If they did, and if the *Chimaera* couldn't counterattack fast enough, both the Imperial and the Chiss ships might suddenly find themselves bereft of their commanders.

Faro had no idea what the Chiss authorities would say or do in such a case. She knew *exactly* what Imperial High Command would say and do to *her*.

The shuttle was picking up speed now as the tractor beam overcame the vessel's initial inertia and as the distance between the two ships diminished. Faro watched its progress, aware of the delicate balance she needed to strike: too fast and the Grysks might not have time to take their shot, too slow and they might suspect a trap. The shuttle had covered a third of the distance now . . .

And abruptly a barrage of laserfire exploded from an empty spot beside one of the larger asteroids. The salvo skimmed past the top of the observation post and slammed full-power into the Defender escort—

And dissipated like ocean waves against basalt sea-stack rocks, the fury of their energy ricocheting harmlessly into space.

As Thrawn had expected, and as Faro had hoped, this particular group of enemies apparently hadn't heard that the Empire now had TIE fighters with shields.

"Turbolasers: Lock onto target," Faro snapped, mentally crossing her fingers. She understood that Thrawn had had to couch this part of his order in vague terms to prevent the eavesdropping Grysks from catching on, but right now the big question was whether Faro herself had correctly deciphered his wishes. "Fire low power to center, higher power to edges."

"Pattern acknowledged," Pyrondi called back. "Turbolasers firing . . . no hit. Repeat, no hit."

Faro swore under her breath. Still under the protection of their cloaking device, the Grysks were running. "Hammerly, find their drive emissions. TIE patrols, move in with full saturation spread. *Find* them, people."

"Drive emissions detected and plotted," Hammerly said as a line projection appeared on the tactical. "Short burn—could have used maneuvering jets to veer off vector."

"But they're coasting now?"

"Yes, Commodore. No fresh emissions detected."

Faro eyed the tactical. Most ship maneuvering jets used compressed gases, which were safer to use near docking ports and other ships, and at this range Hammerly's sensors couldn't detect such cold emissions.

On the plus side, maneuvering jets weren't very powerful. If the cloaked ship had started on Hammerly's vector, and then veered off it, there was no way it could invisibly come back around for another crack at the shuttle. "Dobbs, join the search," she ordered. "Low-power shots—right now we just want to find them."

"Acknowledged," Dobbs said briskly, and a quick glance back at the shuttle showed the Defenders breaking escort formation and joining the other TIEs in their sweep.

"Tractor control, full power," Faro ordered. With the hidden enemy flushed out, there was no longer any point in delaying the shuttle's arrival. If Thrawn was right, the two prisoners had already ingested enough poison to ensure they wouldn't be alive to give up any secrets. But that didn't mean the medical team Faro had standing by in the hangar bay shouldn't try.

"There!" Agral snapped.

"I see them," Faro said. The Grysk ship had become visible just past the far edge of the asteroid cluster. "Helm—"

With a flicker of pseudomotion, the Grysk made the jump to light-speed.

"Chiss ship is on the move," Hammerly warned.

"Helm, pull aside and give them room," Faro ordered Agral. If the Chiss had a way of tracking the Grysk ship through hyperspace, they might still pull this off. The *Steadfast* gave a flicker of its own—

And abruptly stopped. "What the *hell*?" someone said.

Faro hissed out a curse. "And they were kind enough to leave us a little farewell gift," she said. "Admiral Thrawn?"

"I'm here, Commodore." Thrawn's voice again came over the speaker. "Well done."

Faro blinked. Well *done*? "Sir, the Grysk ship escaped," she said carefully. Could he have somehow missed that fact?

"I fully expected it would do that," Thrawn assured her. "The first phase of battle is over. We now enter the next phase. Captain Dobbs?"

"Yes, sir," Dobbs's voice joined in.

"Would you be so good as to locate that gravity-well generator for us?"

"Yes, sir."

As Faro watched, Dobbs broke his Defender away from the rest of the fighters that had been engaged in the pursuit. There was a flicker as he jumped to lightspeed, and Faro started a mental countdown. Five seconds to get some distance; another three to come around in a tight circle; four or five more to come back to the asteroid field . . .

Abruptly, a fat cylinder flickered into sight a kilometer in front of the Chiss ship. Even as Dobbs's Defender popped out of hyperspace, the cylinder again vanished as the gravity-well generator turned off and the cloaking device turned back on.

"Do you have it?" Thrawn asked.

"Yes, sir," Faro confirmed. "Looks like they've fine-turned the system so that the generator stays cloaked until it detects something approaching in hyperspace. Makes it a lot harder to find."

"It also suggests the Grysks have developed a more sophisticated hyperspace sensor system," Thrawn said.

"Or one of their clients has," Faro said. "Do you want me to retrieve it?"

"I believe Admiral Ar'alani's people are planning to do that," Thrawn said. "We shall content ourselves with studying the one from the observation post that we disabled earlier."

"Yes, sir," Faro said, wincing. She was pretty sure Coruscant would not be happy about Thrawn giving away Grysk tech. But she also had no intention of arguing with him about it.

Especially not with a Chiss warship floating off the *Chimaera*'s flank.

"In the meantime, Commodore," Thrawn said, "you're to prepare the *Chimaera* for flight. When I return, we shall journey to the Grysk forward base and communications center."

Faro felt her eyes widen. But the ship that might have led them to that base had gotten away. Hadn't it? "You know where it is, sir?"

"I will soon," Thrawn said. "Prepare my ship, Commodore. For flight, and for combat."

CHAPTER 8

"It got away," Ronan said. "It got *away*."

It was probably not the right thing to say to a grand admiral, a small voice warned from the back of his mind. Not the proper words, and certainly not the proper tone.

But right now he didn't care. The alien ship had come out of hiding, gotten a free and open shot at the prisoners—an attack that had failed only by the sheer luck that the TIE Defenders Thrawn had assigned to escort duty happened to have their shields up—and then escaped right from under the *Chimaera*'s nose.

Thrawn could pretend all he wanted that this was part of his plan. Ronan had seen any number of other people sputter that same excuse to Director Krennic. But the fact was that Thrawn's turbolaser crews had had a clear shot at the fleeing enemy, and had failed to take it down.

Or maybe it hadn't been the *Chimaera*'s crews. Maybe it had been interference from Ar'alani's ship that had fouled things up. Ronan hadn't had a clear view from their position on the observation post, but it was obvious that Ar'alani's ship had been moving forward when the Grysk attacker fled into hyperspace.

If that was the case, Thrawn's position was even more precarious. Instead of covering for a failed command crew, he was covering for people—and worse, *working* with people—who weren't even part of the Empire. People who could very well be present or future enemies.

How much did the Emperor really know about Thrawn and his people? Or if he knew, how much did he actually care?

"Calm yourself, Assistant Director," Thrawn said evenly. "Were you not listening to my conversation with Commodore Faro a moment ago? This is merely the first phase of the battle. The second phase will soon commence."

"How?" Ronan demanded. "The ship is gone. Are you going to invoke some old Jedi magic spell to haul it back here? Or are you expecting the ship to come back on its own?"

"That particular ship?" Thrawn shook his head. "No. Others . . . perhaps. We shall see. Regardless, for the moment your part in this has ended. Major Carvia and his stormtroopers will escort you back to the *Chimaera*."

"I don't think so," Ronan said evenly. "Ar'alani's still here, and I get the feeling you and Vanto haven't finished with her. Until she heads back to her own ship, I'm not going anywhere."

"The admiral gave you an order," Carvia said, taking a step toward him.

"Yes, I heard it," Ronan said, glaring back at him. "And we've already been through this. I have a mandate from Director Krennic and Governor Tarkin. Admiral Thrawn cannot order me to go somewhere unless I agree to go."

"At ease, Major," Thrawn said, holding up a hand as Carvia took another step forward. "Assistant Director Ronan is more than welcome to stay. You and your stormtroopers may instead escort Lieutenant Vanto to the shuttle."

"Hold it," Ronan said, shooting a look at Vanto. The younger man was standing silently to the side. "He can't go aboard an Imperial ship. Not with a charge of desertion hanging over him."

"Consider him to be on loan from Admiral Ar'alani," Thrawn said. "I need his expertise with numbers and data."

"What numbers?"

"The ones you gave me," Thrawn said. "I need him to sort and track through the cargoes and personnel from the missing ships."

"Absolutely not," Ronan said flatly, a surge of anger and betrayal flooding through him. "I categorically forbid you to allow him access."

"I have a deadline—" Thrawn said.

"I don't care."

"—as do you and Director Krennic," Thrawn continued as if Ronan hadn't spoken. "The Emperor's patience is not unlimited, and Stardust remains dangerously behind schedule."

"I don't care," Ronan repeated. "I will *not* see sensitive Imperial data put into the hands of a—" He looked again at Vanto, who seemed to be making a valiant effort to stay as invisible and unobtrusive as possible. "—of a traitor."

"Then you are a fool," Thrawn said.

Ronan snapped his glare back to the grand admiral. "What did you call me?"

"I called you a fool," Thrawn repeated. For the first time, there was a fleeting glimpse of actual anger in his voice. "A stolen ship masquerading as an accidental misfire has carried its cargo to a secret way station. Not a lost ship, as Director Krennic imagined, but a stolen one. An enemy force has attacked and destroyed that way station and intercepted that ship and its cargo. Humans are missing from the station, and those from the ship have been murdered."

"Thieves and pirates," Ronan said contemptuously.

But he could hear the hesitation in his own voice. Thrawn was right, curse him. Someone had found a way to steal supplies and equipment from Stardust, and these Grysk aliens had found their own way to tap into those thefts.

And if they knew about this particular supply line and transfer point, what next? Were they planning a full-fledged attack on it? The thieves *or* the Grysks?

Or could they even know about the other transfer points, the ones bringing in some of the more vital equipment?

Were they planning an attack on the Death Star itself?

And *that* was the truly terrifying possibility. Until the battle station was fully operational, it was vulnerable to attack.

No pirate gang was big enough to hit it. Not that any of them had enough time and energy to spare, not with Grand Admiral Savit systematically taking down all such criminal groups in the region. But the Grysks might conceivably be able to mount an effective attack.

So, for that matter, might Admiral Ar'alani.

Ronan didn't trust Thrawn. Not with Ar'alani and a ship full of his own people on the scene.

The Emperor might have made him a grand admiral. He might even trust him. But that was hardly a ringing endorsement as far as Ronan was concerned. He'd also made Tarkin a grand moff, and that smooth-talking manipulator was as slippery and evil as they came.

No, Ronan didn't trust Thrawn. But at this point, all alone on an alien observation post, his best chance was to pretend that he did.

"You make your point," he said. "Fine. Vanto can work through the data. But only with Commodore Faro supervising."

"Thank you," Thrawn said. As if Ronan had had any real choice. "Lieutenant Vanto, you'll head back immediately with Major Carvia. Assistant Director Ronan and I will join you presently."

"Admiral Thrawn will, anyway," Ronan said, recognizing the double ploy Thrawn had just performed. If Vanto wasn't here, and therefore no longer available to translate, there was no point in Ronan staying, either. "I might as well return with you, too."

"As you choose," Thrawn said. "I'll have Commodore Faro meet you in the hangar bay and escort Lieutenant Vanto to a place where he can work."

"Actually, I think we'll just set him up in the commodore's office," Ronan said.

For once, Thrawn seemed to actually be taken by surprise. "The commodore may have objections to that."

"That's too bad," Ronan said calmly. "You've already agreed that the data needs to be kept secure. What better way to do that than to handle the analysis directly from Faro's computer?"

"What better way, indeed," Thrawn said, on balance again. "I shall inform the commodore to meet you and prepare her aft bridge office for Lieutenant Vanto's use."

"Good," Ronan said. "I trust we'll see you aboard soon?"

"You shall," Thrawn promised.

No, there was nothing more Ronan could do here, he told himself as he, Vanto, and the stormtroopers headed toward the docking port. But there was plenty he could do aboard the *Chimaera*.

Specifically, he could send an urgent message to Director Krennic detailing exactly what was going on out here.

Once that was accomplished, he decided, it might be instructive for him to join Vanto in Faro's office and watch over the traitor's shoulder as he sifted through the transfer point ship numbers. If Vanto had his own plans for that data—or if Thrawn had given him private instructions about them—Ronan would be able to figure it out.

And if they had something treasonous up their sleeves, even invoking the Emperor's name wouldn't save them. *Either* of them.

Un'hee remains seated on the examination table. Vah'nya sits beside her. Both are hunched forward, as if carrying weights on their upper shoulders. Their hands are clasped together, the fingers white-edged from the strength of their mutual grip. Their facial temperature is elevated. Their eyes are tightly closed. The muscles in Vah'nya's face are tightened, the muscles in her throat working. Her expression and body language hold severe strain and concentration. They also hold perhaps fear, perhaps reluctance.

Un'hee's expression is distant, as of one nearing sleep. It holds hints of fear and despair.

"They near the end," Ar'alani said.

She stands beside the door. Her hand rests on her concealed sidearm. Her stance holds alertness. Her expression holds fear. "Do you fear Vah'nya will be unable to draw out the necessary information?"

Ar'alani's expression shifts, now suggesting a degree of annoyance. "It's not fear, Mitth'raw'nuruodo," she said. *Her voice holds the same annoyance, but to a lesser degree than her expression.* "I hope you realize how disconcerting your mind-reading tricks are, even when they don't work."

"I don't read minds, Ar'alani. Only faces. If not fear, then what?"

Ar'alani is silent for two and a half seconds. "What do you know of the Second Sight?" *She speaks more softly now. The annoyance is gone, but her voice still holds fear.*

"Very little. I'm not privy to the deepest secrets of the Ascendancy."

"Nor should you be." *Her voice now holds a degree of contempt.* "You were sent to the Empire to learn about it, not to join it."

"I took advantage of the tactical situation presented to me. What is it about this situation that most concerns you?"

"I cannot tell you."

"Then you rob us of our best hope of victory. Partial information is of no use to me."

Ar'alani is silent another two seconds. "You should not know this," she said. *Her voice holds resignation, but also stubbornness.* "The Council will be furious if my words leave this room."

"They will not."

"Not even to your Emperor?"

"He commands only the loyalty of my actions, not the loyalty of my heart and mind. The deepest secrets of the Chiss will always remain secrets."

"I can only hope that's true." *Ar'alani's voice holds renewed concern.* "There are tales of his powers. Unlike you, it is rumored that he *can* read minds."

"The secret will remain safe. What do you fear?"

"Third Sight is the sight from without," Ar'alani said. *Her voice lowers again in volume. Her tone holds fresh awareness that she is about to speak that which she fears will be compromised.* "Second Sight is the sight from within."

"Within what?"

"Within *whom*," Ar'alani corrected. "Even now, Vah'nya's mind delves deeply into Un'hee's, seeking information about Un'hee's use of Third Sight to navigate Grysk ships to this place."

"Does this delving endanger Un'hee?"

"Under normal conditions, no," Ar'alani said. "Vah'nya will find the information and thus be able to duplicate the paths that will take us to the Grysk forward base."

"What if the conditions aren't normal?"

"The danger comes if Un'hee also possesses Second Sight." *Ar'alani's face warms, her facial muscles stiffening. Her fingers tighten on her weapon, as if preparing to ward off an attack.* "In that situation, there is a danger that she and Vah'nya will become lost within each other's souls."

"Is there no record of Un'hee's abilities?"

"Second Sight normally doesn't manifest until the age of ten or eleven," Ar'alani said. "Un'hee is only seven."

"But the effect may still occur?"

"It may," Ar'alani said. "Or it may not. In my reading I've not heard mention of such an event between two such unusual navigators." *She gestures toward the two girls still sitting closely together. Her fingers are stiff, the rigidity of the movement holding uncertainty and dread.* "Un'hee, by all precedent too young to know if she has Second Sight. Vah'nya, by all precedent too old to retain Third Sight. The one defies history. Perhaps the other does, too."

"It's Vah'nya you fear for most, isn't it?"

"I fear for both," Ar'alani said. "But yes, Vah'nya is the one who most tightly holds hope for our future. Learning how she's been able to extend Third Sight beyond the normal age is the key to a defense force the like of which the Chiss have never known."

"I'm sorry to hear that."

Ar'alani turns. Her face holds sudden suspicion and wariness. "Why so?"

"Because if Vah'nya is able to learn the path to the Grysk base, I'll need her to guide the *Chimaera* there."

"No." *Ar'alani's voice holds complete refusal. Her body stance holds defiance and sudden anger. Her hand tightens harder on her weapon.* "She stays with the *Steadfast*."

"I need her to guide me to our enemies."

"You have your own navigational system."

"I cannot translate Un'hee's memories into numbers within a nav computer."

"You will not take her into danger."

"I must. The Grysk base may be within observation range of Imperial ships or worlds. Furthermore, the enemy may still hold living prisoners we can rescue. You and the *Steadfast* must not be seen by any of them."

"I don't fear either the Grysks or your Empire." *Ar'alani's expression holds defiance and contempt.*

"Then fear for me. Even now Assistant Director Ronan decides what to report to Director Krennic, and beyond him to the Emperor. Chiss military activity within sight of Imperial forces could end my career. Possibly my life."

Ar'alani is silent for seven seconds. Her expression shifts, now holding frustration and resignation. Her fingers tighten one last time around her weapon, then reluctantly relax. "Either result would be less than useful for the Ascendancy, I suppose," she said. *Her voice holds a degree of dark humor and irony.* "Very well. When Vah'nya returns from the entwinement, I'll inform her of her new duties. I warn you that she'll most likely be unwilling and fearful."

"Vanto will be with her at the beginning. Unfortunately, he won't be with us for long."

"Will his departure be because of Ronan?"

"That may ultimately be the case. Ronan and his actions remain unpredictable."

"He's a threat." *Ar'alani's expression holds no hesitation or uncertainty.* "I trust you have a plan to eliminate him?"

"I have a plan to eliminate the threat."

"Be certain that you do." *Ar'alani's expression and tone now hold grim resolve.* "As I said, your place with the Empire is important to the Ascendancy. If you don't eliminate Ronan, then I will."

There is the sound of a muffled gasp. Vah'nya and Un'hee jerk upright from their hunched positions, their torsos arching a few degrees backward before straightening again into proper vertical postures. The motions of both navigators are in close synchronization. Vah'nya's eyes open, followed half a second later by Un'hee's. Vah'nya turns her head to look across the room, Un'hee's eyes remain lowered, ending their earlier movement synchronization.

"They've separated," Ar'alani said. *Her voice holds relief.* "The danger has passed." *She takes a step forward.* "Navigator Vah'nya, are you all right?"

Vah'nya's expression holds weariness and a slowly fading fear. "I am. That was . . . difficult."

"I'm certain it was," Ar'alani said. "Do you have the path?"

"I do." *Vah'nya's voice continues to hold weariness, but also resolve.* "I can take you to the Grysk forward base."

"Excellent." *Ar'alani's voice holds wariness. Her expression holds close focus.* "But for the next few hours you won't be aboard the *Steadfast*. Grand Admiral Mitth'raw'nuruodo has asked for your assistance in taking the battle to our common enemy, and I have granted his request."

Vah'nya's facial muscles tighten. Her eyes go back and forth, then focus on Ar'alani's face. "Will someone from the *Steadfast* be with me?" she asked. *Her voice holds anxiety and dread.* "Lieutenant Eli, perhaps. Will he at least be there?"

"He will be present when you come aboard. Unfortunately I have another mission for him."

"A mission more important than protecting Navigator Vah'nya?" Ar'alani asked. *Her voice holds challenge.*

"Yes."

"No," Vah'nya said. *The anxiety in her voice deepens.* "I can't go alone. Please don't make me go alone among strangers."

"There is no one else," Ar'alani said.

"What about you?"

Ar'alani turns, her widened eyes holding total surprise. "I? Impossible. I command the *Steadfast*. I must remain with my ship."

"Your ship and crew will be quite safe here for the brief time that our mission requires."

"The Grysks might return."

"Not yet. Perhaps eventually, but not yet. At any rate, the first task of your people here is to search this observation post and draw out all of its secrets. Your presence is hardly required for that task."

"I am the commander," Ar'alani said. *Her voice holds insistence.*

"And Vah'nya is a vital resource of the Chiss Ascendancy. For the next hours, she needs you more than the *Steadfast* does."

"I would feel better if you were along," Vah'nya said. *Her voice holds hesitation and fear, as well as a growing unhappiness.* "Please, Admiral?"

"The Command Articles permit it."

"Kindly don't lecture me on what the Command Articles do or do not permit." *Ar'alani's tone holds irritation. But it no longer holds hesitation or indecisiveness.* "Very well. For the sake of Navigator Vah'nya and the future of the Chiss Ascendancy, I'll accompany you." *Her expression holds a brief moment of anger.* "I do *not* do it for your sake."

"I ask no more. Let us travel to the *Chimaera* and prepare. The sooner this second part of the battle is over, the sooner the third and final part may begin."

CHAPTER 9

"There," Vanto said, pointing to a pair of lines he'd marked on Faro's office computer display. "Those two right there. Do you see them?"

"Of course I see them," Ronan growled. Not that they told him a single damn thing.

Not that *any* of it told him anything. He'd been sitting here for nearly two hours while Vanto went back and forth through the data, then up and down, then sideways and inverted, then who knew what else. During that whole time Vanto hadn't spoken at all, except for an occasional grunt or soft, tuneless whistle under his breath.

Faro had dropped in twice, apparently just to check on his progress. She'd looked over Vanto's shoulder, nodded silently at Ronan, and left.

Maybe this was how Vanto always did things. Faro had worked with him when he was still one of the *Chimaera*'s officers. Maybe she was used to it.

Or maybe they were just playing games with the observer Director Krennic had foisted off on them, and whom none of them wanted around.

Either way, Ronan was sick of it. If there was anything in there to find—and Ronan still didn't believe the data held any of the dark secrets Thrawn seemed to think were there—it was clear Vanto wasn't going to succeed in his digging.

But then, Ronan had already written this off as a waste of time. Someone who was actually good at this kind of analysis wouldn't have had to desert the Empire and go running off to Thrawn's people.

To Ronan's left, the door leading to the aft bridge slid open. He looked over, expecting to see Faro stick her nose in again—

"Any progress, Lieutenant?" Thrawn asked as he stepped inside.

"Yes, sir," Vanto said. "I was just about to show Assistant Director Ronan." He tapped another pair of keys.

Abruptly, the lines of numbers reshuffled themselves into four color-coded groups in the corners of the display. "Here are the key elements," Vanto said. "First, as you pointed out, Admiral, twenty-eight of the forty-one missing ships vanished along suspicious vectors. Those twenty-eight were most likely stolen. Second point: While the stolen ships' cargoes were reasonably diverse, I was able to make several connections among them. Three of them carried foodstuffs, mainly human, but also an unusual amount of blosphi extract."

"Wookiee food, right?" Ronan asked, frowning. A large number of Wookiees had been pressed into service in Stardust's early days, but he'd thought their contribution had largely ended.

"In a way," Vanto said, "Wookiees don't particularly like it, but it's a cheap alternative to their usual diet and provides enough nutrition to keep them going. More likely it was for someone else—some species find it a delicacy. The more interesting connection was the specific types of machine parts that were stolen. Each ship carried certain specific parts, though no more than seven percent of its total cargo."

"Buried among the other, more prominent items," Thrawn said.

"Yes, sir," Vanto said. "Presumably so as not to draw attention to them. But here's the interesting part. The items include TRL-44 cylinders, Klymtra spark collimators, Boorian synchronization grids, thorilide shock absorbers—"

"Wait a minute," Ronan interrupted, a sudden icy feeling jabbing into the pit of his stomach. "Thorilide shock absorbers are—no. You're wrong."

"Do you recognize those elements, Assistant Director?" Thrawn asked calmly.

Ronan glared at him. He recognized them, all right. And he was pretty damn sure Thrawn did, too. "They're components for point-defense turbolaser batteries," he growled. "But that's impossible. Turbolaser components are transported on special freighters, under special security." He gestured. "Especially these. They're a brand-new design, barely two months off the testing line."

"Lieutenant Vanto?" Thrawn prompted.

Ronan looked over in time to see Vanto's lip twitch. "Together, the stolen ships carried the necessary components for eight complete turbolasers," Vanto said. "Not the armored outer casings, of course, or the Tibanna gas to drive them. But all the crucial internal parts are here."

Ronan looked at Thrawn. He was looking back, an infuriating calmness in those glowing red eyes. "Fine," Ronan bit out. "Assume you're right. Assume this isn't some false pattern or mistake."

"You can see for yourself the pattern is genuine."

"Assume it's not a false pattern," Ronan repeated, chewing out each word. "How could it have happened? Those shipping manifests are carefully controlled and monitored. No pirate gang could have altered them to include these components or to give the proper clearances to these freighters."

"I agree," Thrawn said. "The only reasonable conclusion is that the changes were made at the source."

"Someone in Stardust?" Ronan shook his head. "No."

"Then someone further down the pipeline," Vanto said. "Someone in Esaga sector."

"Esaga sector?"

"The stolen ships all originated from three worlds in that sector," Vanto said, pointing at one of the corners of his display. "Equipment was brought in from other sources, repackaged aboard those particular ships, and sent to the transfer point."

Ronan stared at the display, the ice in his stomach digging in a little deeper. Esaga. Governor Haveland's sector.

Governor Haveland, who'd made such a strong case to Director Krennic as to why Stardust should funnel as many of its supply chains as possible through her territory.

Ronan hadn't been in on that decision or most of those discussions. But he remembered the director commenting on how eager Haveland had been, and wishing other moffs and governors would embrace Stardust's needs with equal enthusiasm.

Privately, especially over the past couple of years, Ronan had suspected that much of Haveland's enthusiasm was the hope that an influx of Stardust funds and personnel would finally give her the resources to eradicate the grallocs that had plagued so many of her systems for so long. Indeed, even as the Stardust equipment supervisors had been forced to periodically change the transfer points in an ongoing attempt to shake off the pests, Ronan had further suspected Haveland was perhaps quietly sweetening the deal with those supervisors in order to keep Stardust from abandoning her territory entirely.

But the supplies had mostly gotten through, and the rest of Stardust was proceeding mostly on schedule, and in the press of other matters the question of Haveland and her grallocs had been set aside and largely forgotten.

"An interesting plan," Thrawn murmured thoughtfully. "Allow a small number of freighters to be lost to gralloc interference in order to accustom Stardust's overseers to such losses. Once that pattern has been established, special ships with special cargoes can disappear under supposedly identical circumstances and no one will think to look into it further."

Ronan grimaced. No one, that is, except Thrawn himself. Even Director Krennic had seen the grand admiral's current task as nothing more than dealing with the grallocs.

"But time is short," Thrawn continued. "We must move quickly if we're to find the truth. Lieutenant, you said you had identified the relevant systems?"

"Yes, sir," Vanto said. "I don't yet know which port the ships are from, though. The connections were designed to be difficult to read."

"No doubt. Can you do it?"

"Yes, sir," Vanto confirmed. "But it'll take another couple of hours at least."

"You can work en route." Thrawn turned to Ronan. "The shuttle will depart in thirty minutes, Assistant Director. I trust you can be ready to go by then."

"Go?" Ronan asked, frowning. "Go where?"

"The Aloxor system," Thrawn said. "It's the closest of Lieutenant Vanto's three suspect worlds. We must obtain evidence before the conspirators realize their plot has been uncovered."

"So call ISB and turn it over to them," Ronan said. "I understand Colonel Wullf Yularen is a personal friend of yours. I'm sure he can find an agent somewhere who can dig into this."

"I have, in fact, already been in contact with Colonel Yularen," Thrawn said. "But if someone in Governor Haveland's administration is involved, that person will surely have private contacts within ISB. If we report this on any official channel, the conspirators will learn of it and destroy all traces of their activity before it can be uncovered."

Ronan glared at him. But he was right. The network of quiet and undeclared contacts among the Empire's elite rivaled even the Holo-Net for speed and accuracy of information transfer. "Fine," he said. "So send Vanto. There's no need for me to personally see any of it."

"On the contrary," Thrawn said. "You are the one and only voice Director Krennic will listen to. You must be a direct witness to the plot."

Ronan shot a look at Vanto. Clearly, the traitor was also hearing about this plan for the first time. Just as clearly, he wasn't any happier about it than Ronan was.

"The shuttle is being prepared, and I have assigned two of my men to escort you," Thrawn continued, pointedly looking Ronan up and down. "I trust you have some civilian clothing you can use?"

"I wear this uniform proudly, Admiral," Ronan said stiffly. "I've worn nothing else in public in years."

"I assume that is a *no*," Thrawn said. "I'll instruct the quartermaster to fabricate local clothing in your size." His eyes shifted to Vanto. "In *both* your sizes," he added. "It will be waiting in the shuttle bay. Lieutenant Vanto, I'll need you on the command walkway for a moment before you go. Good hunting to you." Nodding to each of them in turn, he turned and strode out of the office.

Again, Ronan looked at Vanto, to find the other also looking back at him. "You're a deserter and a turncoat," Ronan said flatly. "I despise both."

"I know," Vanto said, his voice even.

"But I despise traitors and thieves even more," Ronan continued. "So as long as we're working on this, we work together. No official or unofficial consequences. Afterward . . . let's just see where we end up."

"Understood." A smile twitched at the corners of Vanto's mouth. "I should point out that dropping veiled threats before heading off into danger isn't the wisest thing a person can do."

"What, you mean you might take a shot at me?" Ronan scoffed. "Don't be ridiculous. I'm a high-ranking Imperial dignitary. It's worth your life if anything happens to me. Besides, Thrawn's precious Defender project depends totally on me and my support."

"I didn't make any threats," Vanto said calmly. "I simply thought I'd point it out." He stood up. "If you'll excuse me, I need to meet the admiral on the bridge."

"A question," Ronan said as Vanto reached the door. "Why does Thrawn even have templates for civilian clothing aboard?"

"Because it's sometimes easier to get information when people don't know who you really are," Vanto said.

"I'm an Imperial officer," Ronan countered. "That should be enough to get us what we want."

"Agreed," Vanto said. "But as I said, sometimes it's easier. I'll see you in thirty minutes."

Ronan waited until the door had closed behind him. Then, muttering under his breath, he went to the desk chair and sat down.

He'd seen those numbers before, of course. He'd spent over an hour looking at them and sifting through them after he'd handed over the data to Thrawn and Faro. He hadn't seen a single thing of interest there.

Vanto, in less than two hours, had uncovered a complete conspiracy.

It was all there, too, right out in the open. Ronan could see that now. But it had taken someone with Vanto's abilities, and someone with Thrawn's conviction that there was something in there worth hunting for, to see it.

Ronan scowled. His working assumption had always been that people in positions of power and authority were lazy or incompetent or both, Director Krennic being the sole exception. Now Governor Haveland had added *felonious* to that list.

There would be a certain satisfaction in turning Vanto over to the navy. But there would be far greater satisfaction in watching ISB haul Haveland off in binders.

He snorted and blanked the display, sending the data back to Faro's secure folder. Time to sort all that out later. Standing up, he crossed to the door and walked out into the aft bridge.

And stopped short just outside the office door, his breath freezing in his throat. The bridge and aft bridge were bustling with activity—apparently, the *Chimaera* was preparing for action of some sort. Standing on the command walkway, a circle of calm in the middle of the commotion, wcre Thrawn and Vanto.

Standing beside them in the midst of that calm were Ar'alani and the girl Vah'nya.

The frozen breath inside Ronan turned instantly to boiling blood. This was an *Imperial Star Destroyer*, the very symbol of the Empire's strength and determination. Thrawn had no business—he had no *right*—to bring outsiders to the heart of that power.

To hell with Vanto's treason. To hell even with Haveland's. In a single stroke, Thrawn had outdone them both. Ronan took a step toward them, glancing around for troopers or stormtroopers he could commandeer to put the insubordinate grand admiral under arrest—

Abruptly, the girl Vah'nya twitched.

It wasn't something violent or deliberate, like a medical condition or the prelude to an attack, but more like she'd been startled by something. Ronan frowned—

And then, a few meters behind the girl, someone coming up from the portside crew pit tripped on the top step and fell forward, slamming both hands palms down on the metal deck to break his fall.

The double slap echoed loudly across the bridge, sending twitches and jumps through everyone in earshot, including Ar'alani and Vanto.

But not the girl. The girl had twitched first. Before it happened.

Ronan's boiling blood froze back into ice. The girl wasn't just an alien. She wasn't just an outsider. She was a Force-sensitive.

She was a Jedi.

He stared at her, his half-formed plan to confront Thrawn evaporating into uncertainty. This was no longer something clear-cut and obvious.

A Jedi.

What could Thrawn be planning?

Or was he in fact planning anything at all? Could he be unaware of who this girl was? Was the scheme Ar'alani's, not Thrawn's?

It was insane. The Emperor had demolished the Jedi Order and forbidden any resurgence of their ancient religion. Someone with Thrawn's insight surely couldn't have been taken in so completely by someone's scheme. Not Ar'alani's or anyone else's.

But that would imply that Thrawn himself was a part of it. How could he defy the Emperor this way?

Unless it *wasn't* defiance.

Ronan gazed at the four of them, watching Thrawn's lips moving as he gave inaudible instructions to the others. Could this whole thing be a carefully orchestrated scheme by Thrawn and the Emperor—with Director Krennic's advice, no doubt—to seek out and destroy the Jedi among Thrawn's people?

Yes. Surely that had to be it. It would also explain why the director had sent him out here in the first place. Thrawn knew exactly what was going on, and was playing Ar'alani along in the hope of finding, defeating, and destroying this new threat to the Empire.

In which case, Ronan's best option was to pretend he hadn't seen anything and let the scheme play out.

He could be wrong, of course. It could still be that Thrawn was up to his neck in treason here. But right now, Ronan had bigger fish to spear. Thrawn might be a traitor; Governor Haveland was *definitely* one. All Ronan needed was proof, and with luck he and Vanto would soon have that in hand. He turned and headed for the turbolift to grab what he'd need for a couple of days off the *Chimaera*.

At least he'd had a chance to send word back to the transfer point for the shipmaster to lock things down. Governor Haveland wouldn't get her hands on a single additional ship or cargo.

And if Thrawn was, in fact, a traitor?

Not a problem. Ronan could always denounce him to Director Krennic after he got back.

Eli took a careful breath. "Death troopers," he echoed, just to make sure he'd heard Thrawn correctly.

"Is there a problem?" Thrawn asked.

Eli looked away from him at the preparations going on all around the bridge. What could he say? That death troopers were the elite of the elite, in both competence and fanaticism? That they hated traitors and renegades even more than Ronan did?

Or that Eli himself was exactly the kind of person that men like that would normally shoot on sight without a second thought?

"Perhaps a change in personnel should be considered," Ar'alani suggested into the silence, her own eyes on Eli. "Lieutenant Eli'van'to seems uncomfortable with your choice of guardians."

"Then he had best become comfortable with it," Thrawn said, his tone hardening a little. "The spaceport he and Assistant Director Ronan will be traveling through will likely present many dangers, not only from criminals and suborned Imperials, but also from loyal officials and guards seeking to interrupt his inquiries. Only death troopers will have the credentials and authority to circumvent such actions, should that become necessary."

"Ronan also has high-ranking credentials," Eli pointed out.

"Credentials that officials at a small spaceport may have never seen, for a project they've likely never heard of," Thrawn countered.

"Since you mentioned danger," Ar'alani put in, "I presume these death troopers are combat-capable even without their armor and heavy weapons?"

"They are," Thrawn said. "Moreover, I'm sure you've also noticed that highly trained warriors such as these carry an aura of hidden danger about them, a sense that many criminals will recognize and avoid. It's very likely that their very presence will make combat unnecessary."

"Understood," Eli said with a sigh. Out of the corner of his eye he saw Vah'nya twitch suddenly. The girl hadn't said a word since this conversation began, and Eli wondered why she was even here. Probably because Thrawn had wanted Ar'alani in on their chat and Vah'nya was sticking close to her commander. "I trust you've also made it clear—"

He broke off as a muffled double slap echoed across the bridge. Eli twitched in response, looking toward the sound to see a clearly embarrassed ensign pick himself up off the deck at the top of the portside crew pit stairway. "I trust you made it clear," he began again, "that turning me in to the authorities would be counterproductive to the mission?"

A small smile touched the corners of Thrawn's lips. "That point has been made very clear," he promised.

"You trust them that far?" Ar'alani asked.

"I do," Thrawn said. "Their loyalty to me will guarantee protection for those under their care." He lifted a finger. "However, I wish you to keep their true identity a secret from Assistant Director Ronan. Should he choose to bring charges against me in the future, I wish for them to maintain their anonymity."

Eli winced. Consorting with possible enemies of the Empire; unsanctioned and unreported military actions; failing to report contact with unknown and unidentified forces—he could think of a dozen charges right off the top of his head that Ronan might choose to raise. Serious charges that could derail a career, or worse.

Yet even in the midst of that, Thrawn was thinking about how his actions might affect his subordinates.

Surely that level of consideration meant that he hadn't simply sent Eli off without a second thought. Didn't it?

But that conversation was still for the future. Right now he had a job to do. "Understood, sir," he said briskly. "We won't let you down."

"I know," Thrawn said. "Go now and find the evidence we need, Lieutenant. And warrior's fortune be with you."

The demands were coming again. Though this time, at least, they were coming from Director Krennic and not Governor Haveland.

Not that it really mattered. Regardless of the source, Grand Admiral Savit was getting roundly tired of them.

Especially when they were demanding he do something that was not only foolish but also completely counterproductive.

"You don't understand, Admiral," Krennic said, his eyes boring into Savit's. At least this time the director had opted for a normal video transmission instead of Haveland's overblown and self-indulgent hologram communication. "Assistant Director Ronan was *very* clear that there's immediate danger to the Kurost transfer point. Governor Haveland has managed to scatter the local Imperial forces across her sector on a dozen insurgency-suppression missions, and even if she called them back immediately I doubt they could disengage and respond in a sufficiently timely matter. Your fleet is the only sizable force within range."

"Perhaps it's *you* who doesn't understand, Director," Savit said, fighting to keep his voice calm. "We're currently engaged in a running battle with a large and highly dangerous pirate gang, one that I'm convinced also has ties to the rebels threatening the Empire's stability. Breaking off now could be disastrous."

"Not protecting the transfer point could be even more so," Krennic countered.

"The pirates are fighting for their lives," Savit said. "The last thing they have time for is preying on your precious foodstuffs, kitchen supplies, and recreational equipment. Don't look at me that way—I know the cargoes that go through Kurost. I also know that all the genuinely valuable cargo is shipped through other channels."

"It's not pirates Ronan's worried about," Krennic gritted out. "He says there are at least two alien factions showing interest in the transfer point."

"Really," Savit said, eyeing Krennic closely. "And what does Ronan say Grand Admiral Thrawn is doing about it?"

For the first time in the conversation, Savit detected a note of hesitation. "Ronan was somewhat vague on that," Krennic conceded. "But I have the impression Thrawn could use your assistance."

"Really," Savit said, permitting himself a small smile. If Krennic only knew that he and Tarkin were finally on the same page on something. "*My* source says Thrawn has the situation well under control." It wasn't actually *his* source, of course, but Captain Rasdel's man inside Governor Tarkin's office, reporting on the information Tarkin had received from his contact aboard the *Chimaera*. But Krennic didn't need to know that. "May I suggest that Assistant Director Ronan is jumping at shadows?"

Krennic's face darkened. But Savit could tell he'd hit a nerve. "Ronan doesn't jump at shadows, Admiral," the director said stiffly. "Unlike certain other people, he always has the best interests of the Empire at heart."

"Whatever you say," Savit said. "At any rate, moving ships to your transfer point would be of little advantage. Your own Imperial detachment already has a sizable force guarding the freighters. More important, simple logic suggests that if there *are* pirates targeting your supply lines, they're likely moving their operations back a step to raid the freighters as they come out of the assembly systems in Esaga sector. Certainly there's been an increase in pirate and smuggler presence there."

"And if that's the case, what do you intend to do about it?"

"If it meets with your approval," Savit said, not bothering to disguise his sarcasm, "I thought I'd send a ship to each of your Esaga staging areas and see if we can catch them. That *does* meet with your approval, I trust?"

"It does indeed," Krennic said, his tone and expression making it clear he recognized the mockery but dismissed it as being beneath his notice. "I trust you, in turn, will keep me informed as to your progress."

"Of course," Savit said. "As you will, no doubt, continue to keep me apprised as to Assistant Director Ronan's assessments from the *Chimaera*."

"Of course," Krennic said.

"Excellent," Savit said. "I'll be in touch, Director."

Krennic inclined his head, and the display blanked.

Savit gazed at the empty screen, feeling his lip curl. As if either of them had the slightest intention of doing what they'd just promised.

Politics, he'd heard someone say once, would ultimately be the death of the Empire. Politics between men like Krennic and Tarkin; politics all the way up to Palpatine himself. Infighting, jockeying for position, backstabbing with a smile, all the while ignoring the *real* threats. Threats from without . . . and from within.

Not if Savit could help it.

In the meantime, there were pirates and other more immediate matters to deal with. Pulling up the listing of the Third Fleet's ships, he began choosing which ones to send to Krennic's precious assembly systems.

CHAPTER 10

Thrawn had done this same trick once before, just a few short weeks ago. Then, in deference to Lord Vader's desire for privacy—as well as the fact that Vader could probably kill everyone aboard the *Chimaera* without batting whatever soulless eyes were hidden behind that mask—Thrawn had sent Faro and everyone else off the bridge.

Faro hadn't been happy about that. Not because she had any interest in seeing how Vader pulled off this mysterious navigation trick Thrawn had come up with, but because flying into possible danger with an unstaffed bridge was a laser-etched invitation to trouble.

This time, in deference to Faro's concerns, she'd been invited to stay.

Which meant this time it was Admiral Ar'alani's turn to be unhappy.

For a long minute she and Thrawn went at it in the Chiss language, Ar'alani's voice stiff and angry and determined, Thrawn's calm and equally determined.

Faro stood silently by, hardly daring to breathe lest she draw unwelcome attention to herself, wishing she knew what they were saying, wondering how it was going to end. Every so often she shot a sideways glance at the girl, Vah'nya, who was also standing silent and motionless.

Once, one of those glances happened to catch Vah'nya looking back at her, and in the girl's face Faro could see a hint of Faro's own concern and anxiety. They were about to enter a serious situation, the outcome of which neither Faro nor Vah'nya could entirely predict, a situation that could tax the *Chimaera*'s resources to the limit. Bad enough that they had to leap into the unknown without Thrawn and Ar'alani dragging out the anticipation more than necessary.

Finally, with one last exchange, Ar'alani turned away, her eyes narrowed and clearly still unhappy. Thrawn looked at her another moment, then shifted his eyes to Faro. "Admiral Ar'alani has agreed to allow you to stay," he said, his voice still calm. "Her one condition is that you take up position at the weapons station, where you'll be ready to initiate combat should our arrival be less circumspect than we anticipate."

"Understood, sir," Faro said, glancing again at Vah'nya. Unlike Ar'alani, the girl seemed merely relieved to be getting on with it, with happiness or unhappiness apparently nowhere in her personal equation. "Actually, that was also going to be my suggestion. Are you ready for me to clear the bridge?"

A hint of a smile touched Thrawn's lips. Silent approval for her anticipation of his next order? "I am," he said.

Faro took a deep breath. "Clear the bridge!" she called. "Rig for stealth; all consoles except Weapons locked into standby, reroute control to secondary command. Weapons, leave your consoles hot; Senior Lieutenant Pyrondi, report to secondary command as backup controller. I say again: Rig for stealth, and clear the bridge."

There was a scattering of acknowledgments, and the officers set about obeying her orders. Faro sent her gaze slowly around the bridge, watching for any fumbling or lingering, trying to assess the overall mood of her people as they were being ordered out and the Chiss visitors weren't.

Not surprisingly, Faro could sense some confusion as they finished their lockdown procedures and headed for the turbolift. But there was no real suspicion, certainly no overt resistance to the order. Most of these men and women had served under Thrawn long enough to trust him.

Most had also served under Faro, as well, and also trusted her. Possibly not as much as they trusted Thrawn, but they certainly obeyed her orders with a similar degree of confidence.

So why didn't Thrawn think she was ready to command Task Force 231?

"Your service record indicates you speak Sy Bisti," Thrawn said.

Faro dragged her mind away from that question. Going into a dangerous situation was no time for brooding. "Yes, sir, a little," she said, turning back to him. Thrawn's eyebrows rose, just fractionally— "Though I understand it better than I speak it," she hastened to add.

"Very good," Thrawn said. "From now on we shall use that language whenever we are with Admiral Ar'alani and Navigator Vah'nya."

"Yes, sir," Faro said. The last of the officers disappeared into the turbolift, leaving Faro alone with the three Chiss.

"Commodore, please escort Navigator Vah'nya to the helm and instruct her in its operation," Thrawn said, switching to the Sy Bisti trade language.

Faro's first impulse was to remind Thrawn that he spoke the girl's native language and was therefore far and away the better person for such tutoring. But as she looked at Thrawn, and at Ar'alani standing stiffly beside him, she recognized what this was really all about.

Trust.

Ar'alani didn't trust Faro. Not with the details of this apparently top-secret navigational technique the Chiss had worked out; certainly not with Vah'nya herself. By sending Faro and Vah'nya off together, Thrawn was stating for the other Chiss that he himself *did* completely trust the commander of his flagship.

Or at least he trusted her enough not to mess this up.

Not that Ar'alani seemed to have gotten the message. Faro could feel the Chiss admiral's eyes on her the whole way down into the crew pit.

Faro had worried that her only marginal expertise with Sy Bisti would make it difficult to give Vah'nya the instruction she needed.

But the young woman was smart, and the helm controls were relatively intuitive, and after a couple of minutes Vah'nya pronounced herself ready to go.

Midway through the procedure, Ar'alani joined them, standing close enough behind Faro that she could feel the Chiss's breath on the back of her neck. It didn't make the procedure any easier.

Thrawn was waiting at the starboard alcove weapons station when Faro emerged from the crew pit. "Is she ready?" the admiral asked.

"She says she is, sir," Faro answered.

"You have doubts?"

Faro hesitated. "She seems . . . troubled, sir. Not just nervous or even frightened, but . . . I'm not sure. Like there's a struggle going on inside her."

"Indeed there is," Thrawn said quietly. "But the battle isn't with herself. Rather, it's with the memories of the place we're about to travel to. Memories that are not hers, but have been filtered through the mind and emotions of a seven-year-old girl."

"I see," Faro said, wishing she did. This was the first she'd heard of a seven-year-old girl being involved in any of this. Had she been aboard the observation post and been sent back to the Chiss ship?

But then, it was also the first she'd heard about shared memories. Were the Chiss able to actually transfer thoughts from one to another? Or did Thrawn simply mean that the seven-year-old had given a verbal or written report that had been exceptionally detailed?

"I shall be at the defense station," Thrawn continued. "I am hoping to catch them unawares, so do not attack unless I give that order."

"Even if we're attacked first?"

"Even then," Thrawn confirmed. "There are certain goals we must achieve before we destroy our enemies."

He turned and crossed the bridge toward the defense console in the portside alcove. As he passed the crew pit, he looked down at Ar'alani and nodded. "She may proceed," he said.

Ar'alani nodded acknowledgment and turned to Vah'nya. A moment later the stars blazing through the viewports stretched into starlines, and the *Chimaera* was once again in hyperspace.

The last time, with Vader at the helm, the *Chimaera*'s passage had seemed a bit jerky. Now, with Vah'nya navigating, there was no doubt about it. Faro had been on a watercraft once, and the ship's movement reminded her of how every small wavelet the boat had encountered had translated into a small bounce or skid or hesitation. It was a far cry from the precise, mathematically determined jumps driven by nav-computer calculations, and it struck her as both discomfiting and unstable.

Still, Thrawn seemed unworried as he stood at the defense console. Faro could only see the top of Ar'alani's head, but there was no indication that she was concerned, either. Perhaps the difference was due to Vah'nya's relative youth, or perhaps the information from the younger girl hadn't been completely clear.

And speaking of information . . .

Surreptitiously, Faro looked across at Thrawn, studying the admiral's profile. The fleet rules were quite clear: Contact with an enemy force needed to be reported at once to the High Command. That went double for unknown enemies, and triple if the contact involved combat.

Yet to the best of Faro's knowledge, Thrawn hadn't filed any reports. Not with Coruscant or anyone else.

Which could pose a serious problem down the line. Especially since Ronan was sending his own undoubtedly slanted messages back to Director Krennic.

Faro probably should have found a way to cut off Ronan's access to the HoloNet after the *Chimaera*'s first run-in with the Grysks. Now, with Ronan and Eli apparently off on some mission of their own, it was too late.

"TIE Squadrons Two and Three: Report to your fighters," Thrawn called into the intercom. "TIE Defenders: Report to your fighters in fifteen minutes."

Faro frowned. So Thrawn wasn't going to lead off with the Defenders? Not his usual strategy.

Out of the corner of her eye, she saw him coming toward her. She gave her instruments and displays a quick look, confirmed everything was ready. "Weapons systems prepped and ready, Admiral," she said briskly as he reached her side. "Senior Lieutenant Pyrondi confirms all systems and crews standing by."

"Excellent." Thrawn paused. "You seem disturbed, Commodore."

"Sir?" Faro asked, suppressing a sigh. Of course he'd seen her looking sideways at him earlier, and of course he'd sensed the concern in her face and body language.

Hopefully, he'd interpreted it as stress related purely to the upcoming action.

"An exercise, Commodore," he said. "I will tell you the past of our current operation, much of which you do not yet know. You will then tell me the present." He smiled faintly. "After that, we shall endeavor together to tell the future."

Another of the admiral's famous brain-twister tests. Wonderful. "Yes, sir."

Thrawn paused a moment as if gathering or organizing his thoughts. "Director Krennic arranged with Moff Haveland to bring a number of his Fifth Priority shipments through Esaga sector," he said. "At that time, or perhaps somewhat later, someone else decided to steal some of those cargoes."

"I see," Faro said. No, she hadn't known any of that. "I wouldn't have thought Fifth Priority cargoes were worth that much effort."

"Normally, they're not," Thrawn said. "But our thief was somewhat more ambitious. He found a way to shuffle some of the cargoes around at an intermediary point in such a way that more valuable components were swapped out for some of the lower-level ones. Specifically, he obtained components for point-defense turbolaser batteries."

Faro felt her eyes widen. "How many?"

"We believe eight full sets have been stolen. If the thief is also working other supply lines, he may have obtained more."

Faro nodded. Point-defense turbolasers weren't as powerful as the *Chimaera*'s main weaponry, but they were a vital component of a ship's or battle platform's defense against missiles, enemy starfighters, or even just wayward meteors.

That also explained the high-level encryption they'd used earlier when baiting their trap, as well as why the Grysks had fallen for the ruse. Apparently, the thief had contacts in the Empire's highest echelons, and the Grysks had obtained both those contacts and the encryption.

"The thief of course needed an excuse for the ships to vanish without tipping his hand," Thrawn continued. "His chosen method was to create a way to draw grallocs to the transfer point and the ships gathered there. Once the chaos created by the creatures was established, the chosen ships and crews could pretend they'd been damaged, make the jump to hyperspace, and reemerge at another point to transfer their cargoes to the thief's ships."

"The mobile way station."

"Correct," Thrawn said. "At some point, however, an unexpected complication disrupted the thieves' calculations. The Grysks and one of their client species moved into the area and discovered their plan."

"That's the part that most worries me," Faro said. "We left the Grysks in the Unknown Regions, out past Mokivj and Batuu. What in space are they doing this deep in the Empire?"

"On that point I can only speculate," Thrawn said. "But the established Grysk strategy seems to be to learn what is most precious to a species and then use that weakness to subvert either key leaders or possibly the entire populace to the Grysk will and purpose. I assume they made their start on Batuu, learning only then that the humans of that world were far below the level of Imperial personnel. For whatever reason they chose this region, and set about basing the next stage of their conquest here."

A shiver ran up Faro's back. *Their conquest.* Not a single shot fired, at least not by anyone besides Thrawn and the *Chimaera,* and not a single admiral or moff even aware that the Empire was under attack.

Yet the Grysk conquest had already begun.

Or maybe it was farther along than even Thrawn realized. There was a growing unrest in the fringes of the Empire, an increasing number of systems and peoples hostile to Imperial rule. How many of those systems and species were quiet or unwitting allies of the Grysks?

For that matter, how much of the growing Rebellion was being driven by that same unseen enemy?

"The thieves had set up a system whereby the stolen ships would enter hyperspace on different vectors, with the way station moving in advance to the new rendezvous point. The Grysks were able to decipher the instructions and encryptions and attack the way station, killing or capturing its occupants."

"And knowing that another freighter was on its way," Faro said, "they moved an observation post and one of their gravity-well generators along that vector, but out in the asteroid cluster where they assumed they wouldn't be disturbed. The Allanar N3 we chased showed up, got caught, and its crew taken and murdered."

"Very good," Thrawn said. "That is indeed what happened."

"And then we crashed the party," Faro said, looking over at Ar'alani. "I gather the Chiss were already on the case and were tracking the Grysks from the other direction?"

"They were actually tracking the supply ship."

"The supply ship that we allowed to escape?"

"Correct," Thrawn said. "I don't believe that at the time Admiral Ar'alani knew the full depth of the Grysk involvement." He raised his eyebrows. "We arrive now at the present. Your analysis of the situation?"

Faro pursed her lips. Thrawn always provided the clues and the logical path in these mental challenge games. The trick was to find that path and follow it. "There were only two Grysks on the observation post, overseeing several of their clients," she said slowly. "That suggests the clients were the ones with the necessary expertise for this job, and the Grysks were just making sure they kept working. You said there were several people missing from the way station, which suggests the Grysks took them elsewhere for interrogation or testing."

"Who is likely doing the testing?"

"Again, probably the clients," Faro said. "So . . . you let the supply ship go—"

"A supply ship crewed by whom?"

"Also probably the clients," Faro said. "I'm guessing the Grysks are trying to keep their footprint here as small as possible, in case something like this happens."

"That is also my assumption," Thrawn said. "We also know that the two Grysks on the observation post had orders to die rather than be captured."

Faro grimaced. Which they had, unfortunately, right after their shuttle reached the *Chimaera*. The medical droids were still trying to identify the poison they'd used on themselves, but at this point the question was mostly academic.

Only . . .

"Only they didn't die before the supply ship jumped to lightspeed," she said. "That means . . ."

"Yes?" Thrawn said, an encouraging note to his voice.

"The girl," Faro said. The pieces were starting to fall together now. "The seven-year-old. I assume she was a kidnapped navigator like Vah'nya?"

"Yes."

"Did the Grysks know she's alive?"

Another smile, slightly bigger this time. "No."

"So we're heading for a Grysk forward base consisting of another ship or group of ships," Faro said. "As far as they know, the only way we could have found them is by interrogating the two Grysks we took from the observation post." She raised her eyebrows. "And if the prisoners lasted long enough for us to get the base's location, their friends will have to assume they're still alive."

"Exactly," Thrawn said. "And *that*, I believe, is what they fear most. The Grysks running this project are not merely soldiers, following orders with no useful knowledge of their own. They are high-ranking personnel with important information about their operations against the Empire. The Grysks cannot afford for that data to fall into our hands."

"So you let the supply ship go to give them warning," Faro said. "A warning that's vague enough that they presumably won't run."

"Vague or otherwise, they dare not run," Thrawn said. "Leaving with nothing but uncertainties is the worst outcome of all for them. So they will wait for us, hoping we will not appear, fearing that we will. And then?"

Faro looked at Ar'alani again. "We let them send one more message before we destroy them," she said. "A message that will bring the rest of the Grysks in this area down on us to sterilize the area." She looked back at Thrawn. "By destroying us."

"Very good, Commodore," Thrawn said, inclining his head. "Very good indeed. But don't look so concerned. They will bring as powerful a force as they can, certainly, but that force will not be overly large. As you said, they wish to minimize their presence here."

"Understood," Faro said. It sounded easy enough.

But it wasn't.

Because by failing to call in the earlier battles to the High Command, Thrawn had effectively cut the *Chimaera* off from other Imperial assistance. It was up to him, along with maybe the *Steadfast*, to deal with this.

Unfortunately, the fleeing supply ship had seen the Chiss before it jumped to lightspeed. Thrawn knew how to use surprises like that with great effectiveness against an enemy, even one holding overwhelming odds. Too late to think about that now.

Or had Thrawn already thought about it? Could he have already put Ar'alani's presence into his calculations?

"We should arrive soon," Thrawn said into her thoughts. "Think about what we are likely to face, and consider the available options."

"Yes, sir, I will," Faro promised.

Which wasn't to say, she thought darkly as she watched him return to the defense console, that she wouldn't mind if he, too, did some thinking along those lines.

Hopefully, a *lot* of thinking.

CHAPTER 11

The starlines collapsed, and Eli found himself gazing out the shuttle's forward viewport at a half-lit planet of green and blue swirls mixed into large swaths of dark brown.

Lots of desert. That was never good.

"We're here," Pik announced in a clipped voice from the pilot's seat. "I need a city or a port."

"Right," Eli said, fighting back the reflexive urge to add a *sir*. Pik and Waffle might have the tone and boldness that often came with command, but as death troopers the only ones they actually could give orders to were other stormtroopers.

He made a face. *Pik* and *Waffle*. Ridiculous names for any adults, let alone a pair of men who'd been specially trained to deal out death and destruction and to leave nothing but scorched ground behind them. His best guess was that they were nicknames like the ones TIE pilots sometimes gave each other.

Though in the death troopers' case, it was probably intended more as a way to obscure their true names. Either way, there were probably some interesting stories behind the nicknames.

Eli had no intention of asking about those stories.

"We want a place called Tiquwe," he told Pik. "It's in the southern hemisphere, about midway between—"

"Understood," Waffle interrupted, peering at the nav display. "Heading in."

"Thank you," Eli murmured.

They didn't like him, of course. The only thing that kept them obeying him—and offering the barest level of courtesy—was their respect and loyalty to their admiral. Thrawn had ordered them to guard Eli during his mission, and that was what they were going to do.

They could also be upset because they'd had to wear civilian clothing on this trip instead of their distinctive black armor. Whether it was the prestige or the advantages of the equipment itself, Eli had long noted the stormtrooper aversion to showing their faces in public.

Especially when they were faces like these.

It wasn't that Pik and Waffle were ugly or disfigured in any way. On the contrary. There was a symmetry and chiseled dignity about their faces that Eli had rarely seen in other human beings. Add to that their bigger-than-average size, their lean but well-defined musculature, and an unusual sheen to their neatly trimmed hair and they would be ideal candidates for Imperial recruitment displays.

But only if those displays didn't show their eyes.

Eli shivered as he remembered his first clear look at those eyes. Cold and piercing, seeing everything, evaluating everything, dismissing everything. They held a touch of passion, a touch of pride, and far more than a touch of muted craziness.

Back when he'd been serving aboard the *Chimaera,* he'd heard whispered rumors that death troopers had been medically augmented beyond even stormtrooper training, becoming in the process something that was more, and less, than human.

Having now seen these two, Eli would never again doubt those rumors.

"I hope it's a place where this wreck will fit in," Ronan muttered from the passenger seat beside Eli.

"It is," Eli said, feeling the shuttle cabin shrink a little tighter around him. During the time he and Thrawn had been working their way up through the ranks of the navy, there'd been plenty of occasions when it seemed like everyone around them had nothing but distrust, hostility, or outright contempt. This shuttle, and the three other people aboard it, left all those others in the dust. "Grand Admiral Thrawn inherited it from a smuggler who wasn't going to need it anymore. He'd use it whenever he needed to go someplace where Imperial forces or officials weren't welcome."

"I'm sure he found a *lot* of places like that," Ronan growled. "He could at least have upgraded the interior to something civilized."

"Ineffective and ill advised," Pik said over his shoulder. "If someone saw an interior that didn't match the exterior, the illusion would fall apart."

"So you don't *let* anyone see it," Ronan countered. "Easy enough. So what is this Tiquwe place that we'll so wonderfully fit into?"

"It's a scum town," Waffle said flatly. "Section of decent port, smaller section of Imperial port, larger section of smuggler and pirate port. Populace either helps out or hides, dead-end Imperial officials and troopers do likewise. There won't be any assistance here we can trust."

"But we won't need any," Pik said. "We'll find a ship headed for the Stardust transfer point, prove it's been sabotaged, and we'll be done."

"You make it sound simple," Ronan said. "I assume we'll be landing in the better part of the port instead of the smuggler section?"

"Are you thinking of identifying yourself to a local official and asking for assistance?" Pik countered. "In that case, I assume you weren't paying attention a moment ago. A place like this runs on bribes and extortion. Unless you know for a fact that the official you're approaching hasn't been corrupted, you'll probably die."

"Translation: Leave your fancy whites in your carrybag and stick to not looking at strangers," Waffle added.

"I don't have my uniform—" Ronan broke off.

"Don't lie," Pik said sternly. "I know officials like you. You want to be ready to suit up and pull rank on someone if you think it'll get you what you want."

"If you know men like me, you should also know you're required to show deference," Ronan countered.

"We show deference to our Primary, and to others who've earned it," Pik said. "We have a mission, and we'll fulfill it. Don't expect any more."

"Or any less," Waffle said. "Vanto: I trust you have no problem landing in the bad part of the port if that's where Control sends us?"

"None at all," Eli assured him, shivering a little. *Deference to those who've earned it.* That wasn't the way the Imperial hierarchy normally worked, and he couldn't decide whether the death troopers' attitude toward Ronan was refreshing or frightening. "I assume you have weapons that will also fit into the location?"

"Yes," Pik said. "Just remember that if there's killing to be done, *we'll* do it. You just stay out of the way."

"Understood," Eli said. *Frightening,* he decided. "We will."

Eli had wondered if there would be any trouble landing in the smuggler section of the port. Not that he was worried about codes and clearances, but the locals might require something along the line of passwords or trusted names.

But there were no such requirements or associated complications. Maybe names changed so frequently around here that no one cared about them as long as the visitor had money.

"Wonderful," Ronan said under his breath as Pik locked down the ship and the four of them headed out into a winding street crowded with vendor carts, small shopping kiosks, faded storefront businesses, and a steady stream of shady-looking pedestrians and the occasional small vehicle all jostling one another as they made their individual ways through it all. "I don't suppose it occurred to you that requesting a docking bay closer to the main port would have cut down considerably on the amount of time we're going to waste getting through this mess."

"You don't make requests in a place like this," Pik said. "You go where they send you, or eyebrows get raised."

"Eyebrows *and* blasters," Waffle said. "If there's any talking to be done, you let us do it."

"Unless it's with spaceport officials," Ronan said. "In that case—"

"You let *us* do it," Pik repeated. "You don't know how to talk to people like this."

"Listen—" Ronan began.

"No, *you* listen," Eli cut him off, suddenly tired of the man. Ronan reminded him of some of the officials he'd met when he was in the Imperial Navy, and not in a good way. "This is *their* element. Not yours, not mine; *theirs.* They were sent along to watch over us, so let them do their job."

Ronan was probably coming up with a withering retort when Pik abruptly lunged to the side. Eli jerked reflexively, twisting around to see what was going on.

He was just in time to see the death trooper pluck a credit stick from a young man's hand and give the boy a contemptuous shove back into the milling crowd. "Pickpockets," he growled, holding the stick up for Eli's view before sliding it back into his pocket.

The hand was still in his pocket when two more men jumped him, grabbing his arms and twisting him around to try to break his balance and bring him to the ground.

As a military man, Eli found himself impressed by the layered diversion/attack strategy of pickpocket and muggers. As a potential victim, he found himself flinching back from the sudden flurry of activity, feeling helpless without a weapon or the warning deterrent of a uniform.

As a bystander, he found himself oddly entertained.

Instead of fighting against his attackers, Pik went along with their motion, letting himself be swung around. The two men, clearly expecting resistance instead of cooperation from their victim, fumbled briefly with their own balance as they tried to keep their feet under them. At the moment of greatest speed and greatest distraction Pik lifted his feet, and as all three men started to tumble together to the ground he set his feet back down and shoved upward, only then twisting his shoulders back in the opposite direction.

The combination worked. With his assailants' grips on his arms already weakened, Pik was able to break completely free. One of the men almost regained his balance before a pair of quick punches to neck and stomach sent him back to the ground. The other never even rose again to punching position before slamming into the pavement. He was trying to get his hands under him when a deceptively gentle-looking kick dropped him back flat again.

Someone nearby swore, and suddenly there was a blaster pointed at Pik's face. "Freeze, you son of—"

The rest of the warning turned into a yelp as Pik's hands moved in a blur to snatch the blaster out of the man's hand and deliver two gut punches that sent him to join his friends on the ground.

"He told you to freeze, gutterspawn."

Eli turned to look. A dirty-faced woman was behind him, standing well back from Pik, pointing a blaster at him. "I guess the lesson is not to get too close, huh?" she said. "All of you, back up—"

That was all she got out before a small object shot across Eli's view from Waffle's direction. It slammed into the back of her gun hand, shoving the weapon aside. Even as she tried to bring it back onto target, a similar object, this one coming from Pik, smashed into her forehead, snapping her head back and sending her staggering a couple of steps. Before she could recover Pik was on top of her, twisting the blaster out of her hand and sweeping his foot across her ankles to knock her legs out from under her and drop her to join the increasing number of people on the ground.

"Interesting," Ronan said calmly from Eli's side. "Not something I've seen done with comms before."

"Probably not on the manufacturers' recommended usage lists, either," Eli said as Pik, tucking one of his two captured blasters under his arm, picked up the two objects he and Waffle had used against the woman.

"Specially reinforced," Waffle explained as Pik handed him back his comm.

"I guess the *real* lesson is not to go in one at a time," a new voice came from behind Eli. "Turn around, please. Slowly, of course."

Making sure to keep his hands visible, Eli obeyed.

This man, at least, had taken his own advice. The crowd that had been back there a minute ago, moving along on errands or else watching the brief fight, had magically pulled back to both sides. In the newly formed gap, standing in a line across the middle of the street, were four hard-looking men and an equally hard-looking woman, their hands resting on holstered blasters.

"Five at a time works, too, if you want to give it a go," Pik offered.

"Easy, stranger," the man in the middle cautioned. "Another demonstration like that, and you'll have gone a long way toward proving you're exactly the kind of people we don't like around here."

"Which are?" Pik asked.

"The kind that are bad for business," the man said.

"You mean the Imperials?" Ronan asked.

"The Imperials? The *Imperials*?" The man spat. "The *Imperials* aren't the problem, fancy man. The *Imperials* take their money and scamper off someplace to spend it. It's Grand Admiral Spit-Face Savit who's the problem."

"You really think a grand admiral would take the slightest interest in this dirtball?" Waffle scoffed.

"Do these look like our joking faces?" the woman countered.

"What's Admiral Savit doing?" Ronan asked.

"Like he said, being bad for business," the woman said. "Sending in agents. Spying on everything we're doing. Shutting us down." Her voice dropped ominously. "Killing us."

"And we're looking for a chance to return the favor," the man said. "You four, f'rinstance. You got the clothes and the ship fine, but you don't have the faces."

"Or the attitude," the woman added. "Arrogant. Not furtive enough."

"Or frosty enough," the man said.

"Try drawing those blasters and see how frosty we can be," Waffle challenged.

"See, that's kind of the right attitude," the man said. "Usually don't see an Imperial with a blaster bother getting his hands dirty. They usually just shoot everything in sight."

"That *is* a point in your favor," the woman added. "Actually, it's probably the only point still keeping you alive."

"So here's what's going to happen," the man said. "Sisay and I are going to take you inside and have a little chat. She's really good at that sort of thing."

"We're going to ask you a few things," the woman—Sisay—said. "Like who you work with, who you might have met along the way here, what your business is on Aloxor, why you're in Tiquwe—well, you get the idea."

"If we don't like what we hear—if we think you're not our kind of people . . . well, you get the idea there, too," the man said. "We'll also go through your clothes, gear, and carrybags."

Eli felt a fist close around his heart. Despite Pik's warning, Ronan had stubbornly insisted on bringing his assistant director's uniform with him in the carrybag slung over his shoulder.

"You'd be surprised how many ISB agents are careless enough to stash Imperial-issue weapons in their bags," Sisay said.

"How about we instead say that our business is none of yours and that we're moving on?" Waffle suggested. "It'll be simpler and won't leave so many bodies lying around."

"You assume it'll be *our* bodies and not yours littering the streets," Sisay said, drawing her blaster. "Maybe Skulk wasn't completely clear that it won't be just the two of us doing the interrogating. Or even just the five of us."

Eli looked sideways at the crowd gathered around them. Most of them were simply watching, but there were a handful who also had their hands on their blasters. Too many, and too far away, even for a pair of death troopers.

Unfortunately, the death troopers didn't seem to have done the same math. Eli could see them starting to subtly change positions, easing toward a back-to-back combat stance.

And if Eli didn't do something fast, they were going to get all of them killed.

He lifted a hand as if giving a silent order. "Fine," he said, biting out the word like it was coming out under duress and only because a group of idiots had pushed him into it. "Let's have that talk, right now, before you do something you'll regret. But in private. You five; no one else."

Skulk and Sisay exchanged looks. Waffle threw a frown at Eli that was half annoyance, half thoughtful speculation. Eli kept his eyes on Skulk, trying to look as dead-faced as the two death troopers beside him.

"Fine," Sisay said at last. "You don't mind if we put binders on you, do you?"

"Actually, we mind a lot," Eli said. "We also aren't being traipsed around the whole town." He looked at the shop beside them. "This looks like a good place. You seem to know the people in this neighborhood. Invite the owner to take a walk."

Again, Sisay and Skulk exchanged looks. "All right, we'll play along," Sisay said. "Skulk, you heard the man. Go tell Jeffrie he could use some exercise."

With a final look at Eli, Skulk walked through the crowd and disappeared into the shop.

Ronan took a step closer to Eli. "What are you *doing*?" he whispered.

"Hopefully, saving our necks," Eli whispered back. "If not, lowering the odds."

Skulk reappeared in the doorway. "Come on," he called.

"After you," Sisay added.

Eli nodded to her and walked through the crowd. Skulk moved aside to let him through, drawing his blaster as he did so.

Sisay, in contrast, holstered her weapon as Eli and the others passed and held out her hands in silent command. Glowering and clearly reluctant, Pik nevertheless obeyed and handed over his captured blasters.

A minute later they were all inside. It was a chocolate shop, Eli noted distantly, heavy with an aroma he would have found pleasantly enticing under other circumstances. "Let's hear it," Sisay said.

"Sure," Eli said, looking around as if checking for listening devices or eavesdroppers. "You ever hear of a man called *Nightswan*?"

Sisay's face changed, just enough. "I heard he was out of business," Skulk said.

"He is," Eli said. "I'm his replacement."

"Describe him," Sisay said, her voice stiff and wary. "Describe everything."

"Dark hair," Eli said. "Dark eyes. The textured skin of a man who's spent a lot of time in the sunlight. Miners' hands, scarred and callused. Slim body, but a full face. Never killed anyone unless he absolutely had to."

He ran down the complete description, everything he remembered about the man who'd called himself Nightswan: how he looked, the sound of his voice, the way he did business, details about some of the man's operations that Thrawn had thwarted over the years. The others listened in silence, their expressions not giving anything away.

Finally, he ran out. "Satisfied?" he asked.

"You met him, I'll give you that," Sisay said. Her lip twitched. "Probably worked with him some, too," she conceded reluctantly. "So what's the story?"

"The story—which I didn't know myself until recently," Eli said, "is that Nightswan made a deal with the Hutts."

This time, there was a definite reaction. "What kind of deal?" Skulk asked.

"The kind you don't want to make," Eli said, putting some bitterness into his tone. "*Or* inherit. The point is that the Hutts are collecting on the debt. Part of their price is that we deal with your friend Savit."

"Really," Sisay said, a cynical smile touching her lips. "The Hutts aim high, I'll give them that. And how exactly do you intend to accomplish this lofty goal?"

"Through him," Eli said, nodding at Ronan. "There's an assistant director on one of the Emperor's big projects—guy by the name of Ronan. He's a big enough wheel that if he asks Savit for an audience, Savit is likely to give it to him."

"And *he's* going to be your Director Ronan?" Skulk asked, eyeing Ronan dubiously.

"He's not perfect," Eli conceded. "But he looks enough like Ronan to pass anything but a full bioscan. Yeah, I know—it's crazy. But it's that or let the Hutts take it out of our hide some other way."

Sisay snorted. "Hard to believe Nightswan would get himself entangled that way."

"I didn't believe it, either," Eli said, watching them carefully. So far they seemed to be buying the story. "I'm guessing the details are interesting. But Nightswan's gone, the Hutts didn't give me the history, and I'm not stupid enough to ask."

"So what exactly is the plan?" Skulk asked, still looking Ronan up and down.

"The Hutts say there are some ships connected to this project that load up here in Tiquwe," Eli said. "We find one of them, get Snick here aboard—"

"*Ronan,*" Ronan cut in, his voice sonorous and severe and heavy with reproof. "I am Assistant Director Ronan." He drew himself up. "There is no one here named *Snick.*"

"Sorry, *Assistant Director,*" Eli apologized, ducking his head and mentally throwing Ronan a salute. His biggest fear—aside from the probability that Sisay's gang wouldn't buy it—was that one of his own group would sabotage the effort before it even got started.

Instead Ronan had watched Eli's play and joined in at exactly the right moment.

"You should be." Ronan took a deep breath.

And to Eli's astonishment, his face and body seemed to sag a little as the pompousness and scorn went out of him. As if he'd become an entirely different person.

It was an impressive performance. And as Eli looked back at Sisay and Skulk, he saw their lingering doubts fade away.

"Nice," Skulk said. "You got the attitude down cold. So where is this ship, and how are you going to get aboard?"

"We start by getting to the fancy part of the spaceport, preferably without having to knife or blast anyone," Eli said. "If you want to open a path, great—we'd appreciate the help as long as you keep a low profile. If you'd rather sit it out, that's fine, too. Just stay out of our way."

"I think we'll tag along," Sisay said. "At least for the moment. It's a dangerous part of town, and there are a few Imperials out there who no one's bought. Yet."

"Well, maybe today we'll find a bargain," Eli said. "Let's get moving before we attract any more attention we don't want."

"Sure," Sisay said. "We'll just take those bags . . . ?"

Eli hesitated. But there was nothing for it. Silently, he slipped his carrybag off his shoulder and handed it to one of the men as Ronan did the same.

"Great," Sisay said, her tone almost cheerful. "Okay. Follow me."

CHAPTER 12

Traveling by normal hyperdrive, with coordinates established via a normal nav computer, a ship's captain always knew where and when the ship would arrive.

With a Chiss navigator at the helm, all of that went straight out the viewport. Faro had no idea where they were going or what the target system would be like, and had only the vaguest idea of when they would arrive.

But she'd always been good at playing things off the sleeve, and during her time aboard the *Chimaera* she'd had the opportunity to hone that innate skill to a fine art.

And so when the starlines collapsed, an hour into the trip and barely ten seconds after Ar'alani's abrupt warning, she was ready.

"All bridge personnel, return to stations," she called, running her eyes over the status boards and tactical displays. A movement caught the edge of her eye, and she looked over to see Ar'alani help an unsteady Vah'nya out of the crew pit and lead her toward the temporary quarters Thrawn had had set up for them in his aft bridge office suite. Briefly, Faro wondered if she should offer assistance, decided that

Ar'alani would almost certainly refuse, and returned her attention to the tacticals.

The data was starting to flow in now, and she took a moment to note the overall geography: single sun, eight uninhabitable planets and an assortment of equally barren moons, no fueling depots or orbiting habitats or way stations of any sort. Other ships . . .

She felt her lips compress into a thin line. There it was, two hundred kilometers almost directly ahead, floating dark and quiet with just the smallest glint of reflected light from the distant sun marking its place. The Grysk ship that Thrawn had hoped to find.

Vah'nya had come through.

There was a brush of air as Thrawn appeared at her side. "Report, Commodore?"

"We have it, sir," Faro said, tapping the spot on the tactical and peering at the fine-tune data beginning to scroll across the sensor display. "Or *them*, rather—it looks to be a pair of ships conjoined by short pylons or umbilical tubes."

"What do you make of the configuration?"

Faro keyed for the highest magnification, wishing she could use the active sensors. But Thrawn had ordered the *Chimaera* rigged for stealth, and for the moment the passives were all she had. "Looks like . . . they're tied up alongside each other, lying bow-to-stern?"

"That was my conclusion, as well," Thrawn said. "A highly vulnerable position, is it not?"

"It is indeed, sir," Faro agreed. Two ships tied together bow-to-bow had their thrusters pointed in the same direction, and in an emergency could charge off together while they closed off their umbilicals and disengaged their connection in a safe and orderly fashion. Tied bow-to-stern, on the other hand, meant lighting up their engines would do nothing but spin them in tail-chasing circles until the umbilicals were ripped apart.

"Your conclusion?"

Faro smiled grimly. "It's bait," she said. "The Grysks want us to think that they're helpless and we can just move in."

"And who is aboard?"

Faro's first impulse was to give the obvious answer: the Grysks and the client species the *Chimaera* had run into at the observation post. But even as she opened her mouth she realized that it wasn't quite that simple. "Just the clients," she said. "The Grysks had time to pull out, and they did."

"Where have they gone?"

"Back to their base, I assume—no," she interrupted herself. Once again, it wasn't that easy. "They're still here," she said slowly, looking at the tactical display with new eyes. Still nothing showing but the conjoined ships. "As you said earlier, uncertainty is their biggest dread. They want to watch what happens. But at the same time, they don't want to be in the center of our targeting ring if we *do* show up."

So: a stealthed ship. She looked again at the tactical.

And made a face. No. Damn. Not *stealthed.*

Cloaked.

"So they will be watching from a cloaked ship," Thrawn repeated her unspoken conclusion back at her. "How would you set about deducing their location?"

The first group of bridge crew had arrived and was crossing the aft bridge toward their stations. Ar'alani and Vah'nya, Faro noted, had already disappeared. "If the ship out there is the bait, there's presumably also a trap," she said. "It's possible that they've brought in a major warship, but I'm guessing not. They haven't had much time, and as you also said they don't want to open themselves too much to observation and possible capture."

"So if not a warship . . . ?"

"A booby trap," Faro said, wrinkling her nose. "Probably packed the conjoined ships with all the explosives they could find, waiting for us to stroll confidently into range."

"It would no doubt be a satisfying sight," Thrawn said, a bit drily. "Assuming, of course, that they could see it."

Faro frowned. Why wouldn't they be able to see it? Blocked by the debris? There certainly weren't any meteor clumps that might get in the way.

Nothing except their own cloaking field.

"They're within a spherical shell centered on the conjoined ships," she said. "Bounded on the inner edge by the safe distance from the booby trap they've set up, and on the outer edge by the limit their cloaking field puts on their sensor range."

"Excellent," Thrawn said. He raised his datapad and tapped a key. "Here is my estimate and interpretation of those boundary conditions, using likely explosive availability figures for the first and Admiral Ar'alani's knowledge of Grysk cloaking fields for the second."

The double sphere appeared on Faro's tactical display, centered on the distant conjoined ships, with Thrawn's search zone shaded in red. Faro studied it, noting the relative closeness of the two spheres and the odd fact that the sections currently in front of the *Chimaera* and at the far side of the zone had been eliminated from consideration. "May I ask why these two sections have been blanked?" she asked.

"If we arrive, we will most likely arrive from this direction," Thrawn said. "They would hardly wish to be in our line of fire if we choose to simply destroy the conjoined ships without investigation."

"Or on the far side where they might catch any misfires," Faro said, nodding. "Not nearly as much territory in there to search as I was afraid we'd have to deal with."

"Agreed," Thrawn said. "Still, there is more than can be resolved with a few ion bursts. So we begin by gathering more information."

Faro looked at the status boards. "TIE Squadrons Two and Three indicate ready."

"Excellent." Thrawn looked back over his shoulder at the next group of officers streaming from the turbolift. "I believe Senior Lieutenant Pyrondi has arrived."

A moment later the other woman joined them. "Senior Lieutenant Pyrondi reporting for duty, ma'am," she said formally. "Admiral," she added, stiffening briefly to attention.

"Lieutenant, how many of your Class A–rated tractor beam operators are currently on duty?" Thrawn asked.

Pyrondi keyed her datapad. "Three of the five, sir."

"Excellent," Thrawn said. "Loop those three and two others of your choice into the following conversation. I wish to instruct them in a new maneuver called a *slingshot*."

Ar'alani had rejoined Thrawn and Faro on the bridge by the time the tractor operators were ready. The Chiss started to say something— "Sy Bisti, Admiral, if you please," Thrawn said in that trade language.

Ar'alani sent an annoyed look at Faro—"We have found them?"

"We're about to tighten the search," Thrawn said. He switched back to Basic. "Lieutenant Pyrondi?"

"Ready, Admiral."

"Launch Squadron Two, and engage tractor beams."

"Acknowledged. Squadron Two: *Launch*."

Faro looked at the displays, watching with fascination. As far as she knew, this maneuver had never been tried before.

Of course, in all fairness to the tactical planners on Coruscant, it was only this very specific combination of circumstances that made the maneuver useful in the first place.

The TIE fighters appeared, twelve marks on the tactical. Unlike the usual launch pattern, though, they didn't come screaming out of their drop racks at full power, roaring around the rim of the hangar bay and charging to the kill. Instead they simply drifted lazily into view, their engines cold, their sensors and targeting computers on low power. The initial momentum given them by the racks sent them drifting clear of the bay's edge and out beneath the ship.

Pyrondi was gazing at the display, watching the fighters drift away. Faro looked sideways at Thrawn, wondering if he would intervene, knowing he wouldn't. He'd explained all the nuances of the maneuver to Pyrondi and had handed over control of the operation to her. Now he would stand back and quietly assess how his senior weapons officer handled the task. Faro counted out five more seconds . . .

"Forward tractors: *Engage*," Pyrondi ordered.

Abruptly, six of the TIEs jerked forward as the ventral tractor beams caught them, showing up as milky white lines on the tactical connecting the fighters to the very tip of the *Chimaera*'s bow. The TIEs picked up speed as they were reeled in toward the bow . . .

"Disengage," Pyrondi called. "Helm, pitch five degrees positive."

The white lines vanished, leaving the TIEs with the speed and direction the tractor beams had given them. They were nearly to an impact with the *Chimaera*'s bow when the ship pitched upward the five degrees Pyrondi had ordered, clearing the path for the TIEs to sweep safely past.

Faro shifted her attention to the forward viewport, watching as the darkened fighters swept past and outward, heading toward the conjoined Grysk ships.

Thrawn remained silent as Pyrondi repeated the process with the remaining TIEs. "Excellent work, Lieutenant," he said as the fighters faded into the starscape ahead. "Tell me, who were the operators on Tractors Three and Five?"

Pyrondi consulted her datapad. "Matavuli on Three, Nasmyth on Five."

"Make a note of those names, Commodore," Thrawn instructed. "Matavuli's aim is tentative and his overall procedure weak. He requires additional training."

"Yes, sir," Faro said, making a note on her datapad. "And Nasmyth?"

"He should be considered for Class A status," Thrawn said. "Find a convenient opportunity to administer the test."

He turned to Ar'alani and switched back to Sy Bisti. "The fighters are on their way to a closer inspection of the conjoined ships," he said. "With only low power usage and no sensor emanations, they should remain invisible to the cloaked Grysk ship."

"I see little importance in the joined ships," Ar'alani said dismissively. "The Grysk will surely have already destroyed any useful data aboard."

"They certainly will have tried," Thrawn said. "Yet the most dangerous data remains: members of their client species who might be persuaded to give up their secrets."

"*If* there are any still aboard."

"There are." Thrawn gestured to Faro. "The evidence, Commodore?"

"Infrared analysis suggests that there are ten to twenty life-forms aboard," Faro said, fighting through the awkward Sy Bisti words. At least the language's grammar was relatively easy.

"Grysk clients?" Ar'alani asked.

"Or Grysk clients and all or some of the twelve missing members of the pirates' mobile way station," Faro said.

"Whom we hope to rescue if such is possible," Thrawn added.

For a moment Ar'alani gazed out the forward viewport. "The joined ships are the bait of a trap," she said. "The cloaked ship is the true enemy and therefore our primary target."

"*One* of our primary targets," Thrawn corrected. "There is a second equally valuable target. Possibly of even higher priority than the ship itself."

"You speak of the triad?" Ar'alani asked.

"Yes."

Faro nodded to herself. The Grysks could hardly use the HoloNet for long-range contact with their main base, not with the Empire routinely monitoring all transmissions that went through that system. The solution was a communications triad, a technique used in the Unknown Regions, Wild Space, and at the Empire's own fringes.

The problem was that a triad needed space—a *lot* of space—to set up the three poles of the transceiver.

She looked back at the system's geographic plot. Eight planets, five of them gas giants, the other three a minimum of eight light-minutes away. The former didn't have any solid ground in which to plant the triad, while the latter would require communications lasers to punch signals that far, in both directions, not counting the awkward and potentially dangerous built-in time lag. Four of the gas giants' moons were within a light-minute of the conjoined ships, but that would still require either a laser or a finely columnated maser transmitter at both ends to exchange messages. Unless the triad was cold or on standby, such massive power emissions should be clearly visible to the *Chimaera*'s sensors.

And under the circumstances, the Grysks lurking behind their cloaking device surely wouldn't want to be out of contact with their main base during the crucial minutes it would take to bring up their comm system. "Admiral, how big do these triad poles have to be?" she asked.

"Not overly large, though they are quite massive," Thrawn said. "One would fit within the *Chimaera*'s bridge."

"Or within one of the conjoined ships?"

"Easily," Thrawn said. "The separation between the poles is the crucial factor. Admiral?"

"The distance can vary," Ar'alani said. "Grysk triad poles typically run—" She paused, and Faro had the sense she was converting units in her head—"five to ten kilometers apart."

"The one on Batuu used a six-kilometer separation," Thrawn added. "The key factor is that the separation must be strictly maintained among all three. That argues against the poles merely floating in orbit, as small perturbations would quickly distort the separation and make them useless."

"There are no asteroids or meteors nearby that are sufficiently large," Ar'alani said. "The triad must therefore have been established on one of the planetary moons."

Faro gazed at the displays. Except that, as she'd already noted, none of the moons was closer than a light-minute away. Would the Grysks really put themselves that far from the triad?

Especially since there was no reason why that gap should even have been necessary. As far as she could tell, the conjoined ships didn't have to be this far out from anything else in the system. If they had a triad planted on a moon, why hadn't they set up shop in orbit around that moon, or at least around the moon's primary?

"What is your intent with the fighter craft?" Ar'alani asked.

"Their mission is threefold," Thrawn said. "First, to gather information the *Chimaera* cannot obtain at this range without the active sensors. Second, to possibly provoke a reaction from the cloaked ship that would reveal its location."

Faro felt her stomach tighten. In other words, Thrawn had sent out some bait of his own.

She understood that there was sometimes a need for such things.

But putting her people in that kind of deliberate danger was never something that came easy.

"And third," Thrawn finished, "to be in position for a strike against the conjoined ships should I choose to launch one."

"You said you wished to capture alien prisoners and rescue the Grysks' captives," Ar'alani reminded him.

"If possible," Thrawn said. "As always, the safety of the *Chimaera* and the goals and good of the Empire stand paramount."

Ar'alani looked pointedly at Faro. "A moment, Commodore Faro."

"Of course, Admiral," Faro said, nodding.

She'd assumed Ar'alani would lead Thrawn to a quieter part of the bridge for a private talk. But of course, that wasn't necessary. Turning back to Thrawn, she launched into a quiet but clearly impassioned speech in the Chiss language.

Faro turned away from them. Hardly necessary under the circumstances, but it seemed the polite thing to do. Besides, she'd learned enough about expression, vocal tone, and body language from Thrawn that even just standing there watching them might be considered a form of eavesdropping. Better to busy herself with the *Chimaera*'s business and let Ar'alani have her moment.

She stepped back to the weapons station, studying the displays over Pyrondi's shoulder. The lead wave of TIEs was making its leisurely way toward the conjoined ships, with the second wave about half a minute behind them. The fighters were sending back the readouts from their targeting sensors via tight-beam lasers, but all of them were still too far for their equipment to pick up anything the *Chimaera*'s own passive sensors hadn't already spotted.

"I just got Lomar's last comm sweep data, ma'am," Pyrondi said quietly, her eyes flicking over Faro's shoulder to the Chiss conversation behind her. "He's still not getting any transmissions from anywhere."

"Could they be using comm lasers?" Faro asked.

"Possibly," Pyrondi said. "The dust level out here is low enough that it's unlikely a particle would drift into a laser beam and reflect strongly enough for us to spot it."

"Hammerly's got people watching for that, I assume?"

"Yes, ma'am."

"What if the laser was punching a signal to one of the closest moons?" Faro asked. "Never mind the dust—would it be powerful enough to ionize any of the solar wind particles?"

"I don't know," Pyrondi said thoughtfully. "That would probably be a question for Hammerly or Lomar."

"I'll ask them," Faro said. She glowered at the displays one final time and turned away.

And frowned. There'd been something there . . .

She turned back, her eyes flitting back and forth among the various displays. Something had caught her eye.

But what? Everything seemed exactly the same as it had been. The TIEs were making their silent way toward the conjoined ships. The ships themselves were still unmoving and equally silent, the distant sunlight glinting off their hulls. There were no indications of energy output from comms, drives, or weaponry from anywhere within sensor range.

Faro stiffened. *The sunlight glinting off the conjoined ships' hulls.*

She spun around. "Admiral Thrawn?" she called.

He broke off whatever he was saying to Ar'alani and walked toward her, his pace measured but with a sense of strong interest behind it. "Yes, Commodore?"

"The conjoined ships, sir," Faro said, pointing to the display and mentally crossing her fingers. Ar'alani, coming up now behind Thrawn, had the kind of look that warned that Faro had better have a damn good reason for interrupting their conversation. "I saw the sunlight reflected off their hulls, and I remembered—"

"They've moved," Thrawn murmured.

"Yes, sir," Faro said, feeling a surge of relief. So it *wasn't* just her imagination. He saw it, too. "We'll have better data when the TIEs get closer, but I'm guessing it's a slow rotation around their common center of gravity."

Thrawn half turned toward the crew pits. "Commander Hammerly? Any indication of thruster or maneuvering jet usage from the target?"

"No, sir," Hammerly called back.

"Were you able to get the occultation program running?"

"Yes, sir, at least partially," Hammerly confirmed. "We're using it on the target, and so far haven't seen any indication of cold-gas discharge."

"Thank you." Thrawn turned back. "If the rotation is not new, it must have been present before we entered the system."

"Possibly a sensor-sweep technique," Ar'alani suggested in Sy Bisti. The annoyance Faro had seen in her face a moment ago was gone, replaced by a growing interest. "If they have collimated or shield-focused sensors, a slow rotation would allow them to see farther without risking active sensor emanations."

Thrawn shook his head. "The rotation is too slow. I estimate an hour or more for a complete circuit."

"Which would make it useless in any active situation," Ar'alani conceded. "Any thoughts as to its purpose?"

"It may not have one," Thrawn said. "It may simply be residual motion from the last shuttle launch."

"I wouldn't want to rely on such a conclusion," Ar'alani warned.

"Nor would I," Thrawn said. "I would also hesitate to create elaborate theories based on insufficient information. Another half hour, and the lead TIEs will be close enough to gather more data."

He turned to Faro, inclining his head in silent acknowledgment of her observation. "I'll be in my office until then, Commodore, should you need me."

"Yes, sir," Faro said.

"Admiral," he said, nodding to Ar'alani. Turning, he strode toward the aft bridge.

"His artwork?" Ar'alani asked quietly.

Faro nodded. "I don't think he's got anything that was created by the Grysks themselves," she said. "But he has holo copies of art from some of their victims."

Ar'alani made a sound in the back of her throat.

"You disapprove of his ability?" Faro asked.

"That word is meaningless," Ar'alani said with a touch of scorn.

"My opinions, whether approval or disapproval, are irrelevant to reality."

"Then what is your problem with it?"

Ar'alani looked sharply at her. Faro held her gaze, forcing herself not to flinch. Ar'alani might be an admiral and therefore outrank her, but Faro was a commodore, and furthermore the commander of the ship they were currently standing in.

To her surprise, Ar'alani's glare softened, and something that might have been a smile touched her face. "Very good, Commodore," she said. "You're strong and confident. Mitth'raw'nuruodo chose well."

"Thank you," Faro said. "Though in all fairness, my appointment to the *Chimaera* came from the Imperial Navy High Command, not Admiral Thrawn himself."

"I wasn't referring to your position," Ar'alani said, "but rather to his choice of protégée. I have nothing but respect for Mitth'raw'nuruodo's abilities. I disagree with his choice of position." Another half smile. "Unlike yours, he *has* chosen his."

"You mean his service with the Empire?"

"Yes." Ar'alani half turned to gaze out the forward viewport. "There are grave threats facing the Ascendancy. The Grysks and their clients, predominantly, but others as well. We need him to lend his name and his history to our cause. But so far he refuses." She turned back to Faro. "Is his life here truly so much better?"

Faro thought about Batonn, and the mission the Emperor had sent him on with Lord Vader, and his position in the current power struggle between Grand Moff Tarkin and Director Krennic. "His life here is precarious," she told Ar'alani. "But this is apparently where he thinks he can best serve all of us. Including the Ascendancy."

Ar'alani made the throat sound again. "That statement is nonsensical."

"Is it?" Faro countered. "Consider. The Grysks have clearly set their sights on the Empire. Their presence here proves that. Ask yourself what would happen to the Ascendancy if they should succeed in taking over the Empire, or even a significant percentage of the Empire's resources. Is *that* what you want coming against your people?"

For a moment Ar'alani was silent. Then she turned again to the viewport. "There are other ways," she murmured.

"Perhaps," Faro said. "If so, I'm sure the admiral would be more than willing to hear about them." She gestured toward the viewport. "But for the moment, *this* is the battle Admiral Thrawn has chosen.

"And I, for one, intend to help him win it."

CHAPTER 13

As the group had prepared to leave Jeffrie's place, Eli had noticed through the window that there were still a few gawkers loitering outside the storefront, apparently waiting to see which of the people who went in came out again under their own power. The fact that all of them were going to do so, he suspected uneasily, might raise as much curiosity as one or more of them being carried out in a body bag.

Fortunately, Sisay had apparently had the same thought. She avoided the whole issue by slipping them out the back, through a narrow alley filled with trash bins and ragged-looking people sifting through them, and beneath a pair of lifter droids that were waiting patiently for the scavengers to finish. Another back door, a trip through and out the front of a café, and they were on their way.

Eli had expected the trip to be short, with Sisay's group based somewhere close to where Pik had landed their shuttle. But as they continued on through the noisy streets, it became clear that that wasn't the case. Apparently Sisay had been outside their territory on other business and had just happened to pick up on the odd newcomers.

Or perhaps more likely, Admiral Savit's pressure had the local pirate gangs enough on edge that they were *all* patrolling the spaceport on the lookout for the grand admiral's agents.

A casual study of the people they passed along the way bolstered that theory. Eli had seen this sort of town before, back in the Wild Space systems where his family's shipping business operated, and he knew how the unwritten status rules were structured and maintained. At the beginning of their walk, fewer than 10 percent of the people they passed seemed to recognize either Sisay or Skulk, and their subtle reactions suggested that about half of that number recognized them positively and the other half negatively.

But as they moved along, the recognition factor rose steadily. Half an hour after leaving the shop, it seemed like everyone they passed knew the gang.

On the downside, the percentages that looked at them favorably or unfavorably still hovered around 50 each. Unfortunately, an ambivalent status like that inevitably transferred to anyone in their company, which put him, Ronan, and the death troopers in that same precarious social position.

Thrawn had suggested that the death troopers' aura of imminent danger would ward off unwanted trouble. With Savit's sweep of the area, it looked like that plan had unfortunately backfired.

Finally, with the walls of the commercial part of the spaceport visible in the distance—the *decent* part, as Waffle had called it—they arrived at a somewhat decrepit building. Sisay led them through a faded lobby—the place had apparently once been a hotel—to a wide staircase leading to the second floor. They passed two men lounging lazily at the top of the stairs, their alert and penetrating eyes in sharp contrast with their feigned lethargy, and into a suite of rooms midway down the hallway.

"So why exactly are we here?" Eli asked as Sisay gestured them to chairs arranged in a conversation circle in front of a battered desk.

"Did you forget?" Skulk asked, crossing to a liquor shelf behind the desk and selecting two of the bottles. "We need to take a look at your gear."

"I thought we were past that," Eli said, wincing as the sound of carrybag sealing strips being undone came from behind him.

"You thought wrong," Skulk said, turning to face them and holding up the bottles for their inspection. "I've got seagrape brandy and Chopkic wine. Who wants which?"

"We don't want a drink," Waffle said. "We want to get on with our job."

"And it's getting late," Eli added, feeling a thin layer of sweat breaking out on the back of his neck. He'd thought that Sisay and the others had bought his story back at Jeffrie's place. Now, it seemed, they still had doubts.

And with the questioning having now been relocated to Sisay's stronghold, the lopsided odds Eli had hoped to avoid had instead gotten worse.

Pik and Waffle recognized that, too. Eli could see the tension stiffening their necks and cheek muscles even as they tried to feign nonchalance.

"Relax," Sisay said, looking at each of the Imperials in turn as she walked around to the other side of the desk. It seemed to Eli that her gaze lingered for a moment on the two death troopers. "The guard shift change is when you want to move, and that's not for another three hours. We've got time."

"We're not worried about the guards," Eli said. "We have all the right codes and passes. The problem is maybe missing the ship we need to take to get to Savit."

"Yeah, let's talk about those passes," Sisay said, sitting down behind the desk and leaning back into the chair. "Brackis, you see them in there?"

"Yeah, here they are," someone said from behind Eli. One of the men who'd been with them at Jeffrie's came around the conversation circle and tossed the four data cards from the carrybags onto Sisay's desk. "Outer etching looks pretty good."

"Thanks," Sisay said. She held Eli's gaze another second, then lowered her eyes to the data cards. "Does indeed. Looks *very* good. You mind telling me who the artist was?"

"I don't know," Eli said. "All of our stuff came from the Hutts."

"Sure is nice to have a handy excuse like that, don't you think?" Skulk commented as he set a glass of brandy on the desk in front of Sisay. "The Hutts this, the Hutts that."

"What do you want me to say?" Eli countered. "If you'd ever worked with the Hutts, you'd know they don't exactly take you into their confidence."

"See, that's the thing," Sisay said, her voice suddenly going hard. "We *have* worked with the Hutts. And this story of yours just doesn't etch out."

Out of the corner of his eye, Eli saw Ronan shift position slightly. *Keep it together,* he thought urgently toward the older man. *We can do this. Just keep it together.* "Really," he said, putting some scorn into his voice. "In what way, exactly?"

"The Hutts don't hire nobodies to do their dirty work," Sisay said. "They all have their own stables of smugglers, pirates, and hired guns."

"Who says we're nobodies?"

"*I* say you're nobodies," Sisay said. "And no Hutt would hire you when we're already here."

"You're missing the obvious point," Ronan put in. "They couldn't hire you, because you don't have *me.*"

"And he's the one who gets us close to Savit," Eli said. "So whatever jealousy you've got going here, ramp it down."

"This isn't about jealousy," Skulk said. "It's about the blowback if you scorch the job."

"Or the even nastier blowback if you aren't who you say you are," Sisay said, her voice going even darker. "Like if you're more ISB plants trying to dig us out."

"That makes no sense," Eli protested. "*You* accosted *us.* We didn't try to recruit you or dig out all your wonderful secrets."

"We're here to do a job," Pik said. "Get in, do it, and get out."

"Yeah," Sisay said. "About that." She lifted a finger—

And from behind Eli came the sound of blasters being drawn from their holsters.

"You're making a big mistake," he said, trying one last time. "You mess up our mission, and you'll be *very* sorry the Hutts know who you are."

"We'll see," Sisay said calmly. "I think we'll start with the simple stuff: electrodes, flash-pows, drifties. The stuff that doesn't do any real damage, or at least nothing permanent. Lots of places to go from there if we need to. Each of you in different rooms, of course—can't have you running stories off each other."

"If we miss that ship—" Eli began.

"We'll be very, very sorry," Sisay cut him off. "Yeah, we got it. So. Anyone want to tell me anything before we get started?"

Eli took a careful breath. It wasn't over, he told himself firmly. Not by a long shot. Even if Sisay suspected they were ISB infiltrators, she and her people would hardly be prepared to deal with a pair of death troopers. Surely either Pik or Waffle would find an opening; and once one of them was free, he should be able to grab the others and get out of here.

Of course, that would still leave them in a building and a neighborhood dominated by Sisay's gang. But they would cross that ramp when they reached it.

"Just that you're wasting everyone's time," he said. "But I can see you don't care."

"That's right, we don't," Sisay said. "Okay, let's see. The man with the mouth can go in room one. Snick—sorry; *Ronan*—he can go in room two—"

She broke off as a soft tap came from outside. The door opened and one of the men who'd been lounging by the stairs stuck his head in. "Sorry, boss," he said apologetically. "But Mole's here. He says—"

"Who?" Sisay interrupted.

"Mole," the man repeated. "He's Parpa's new slicer."

"I know who he is," Skulk said. "Parpa says he's the greatest thing since tomo ribenes. What does he want?"

"He says he can't find Parpa and needs to talk to him right away. He thought you might know where he is."

"Who does he think we are, the Smuggler Information Bureau?" Skulk growled. "Tell him to get lost."

"No, wait," Sisay said, throwing a thoughtful look at Eli. "You say he's a slicer?"

"Slicer, repro—does lots of computer and droid stuff," Skulk said.

"Including data forgery?"

"Probably," Skulk said, looking at Eli, too, as sudden understanding came into his voice. "You think?"

"Why not?" Sisay gestured. "Send him in."

Eli looked at the passes lying on the desk, a hollow feeling in his stomach. A decent slicer would declare them to be excellent forgeries, all right.

Unfortunately, an *expert* slicer would recognize them as the genuine article.

He shifted his attention to Pik's profile. There was no indication that the death trooper had any idea of the trap that had opened up in front of them. Somehow, Eli had to alert him to be ready to take action.

The door opened wider, revealing a thin, nervous-looking man in a neat but slightly worn tunic, a datapad gripped in both hands in front of his chest. "Sorry to bother you, Ms. Sisay," he said, his voice as twitchy as his face. He shot a glance at Skulk standing behind her, an equally quick look at the four Imperials, and took a tentative step forward. "I need to talk to Mr. Parpa," he went on, the words coming out in a tangled rush. "He wanted me to reroute some shipping idents, but he wasn't clear about two of them, and I really need to talk to him, only I can't find him—he's always doing this to me—and I hoped you'd know—"

"Okay, okay—hold it," Sisay cut him off. "First: I don't know where Parpa is."

"Oh," Mole said, hunching his shoulders. "Right. I'm so sorry—"

"Second," Sisay went on, raising her voice over his, "I'm sure he'll be back before you need to know about those other shipments."

"Oh, no, Ms. Sisay, you don't know Mr. Parpa," Mole said. "He's always doing this to me—running off without full explanations—"

"Third," Sisay said, beckoning him forward, "I've got a little job of my own for you."

"I—" Mole broke off, blinking. "A job? But I—I don't work for you. And Mr. Parpa might not like it if—"

"It's five-minute job," Sisay again cut in, her voice starting to sound a little strained. "Parpa will never know, and you'll make a little extra money for the week."

"I—I don't know," Mole said, starting to stammer. "Parpa—he knows everything. If he catches me . . ." He looked at the Imperials, then started to look back at Sisay.

And Eli saw his gaze catch on the data cards lying on the desk. "What are those?" he asked, craning his neck a little. "Are those *Imperial* ident data cards?"

"That's what we want you to tell us," Sisay said. "That's the job. Still not interested?"

"Oh. Well. I . . ." Mole looked at the Imperials again. His eyes shifted to something behind Eli—"Whoa!" he gasped. "Is that—? Whoa!"

Eli looked over his shoulder. The searchers had dug Ronan's uniform out of his carrybag and laid it out over the edge of a side table.

"Is it *real*?" Mole asked as Eli turned back again. "It looks real. It's not real, is it?"

"You can check it out later if you want," Sisay said, picking up one of the data cards and holding it out. "This first."

"Oh," Mole said. "Right." Stepping to the desk, shying away from Waffle's stare as he passed the death trooper, he took the card from her and plugged it into his datapad.

Eli braced himself. If Mole was good enough, here was where he and the others were going to have to make their move.

He tried to catch Pik's eye, hoping to alert him. But Pik's full attention was on Mole. Eli could only hope he'd already figured it out.

Casually, he looked around. When Pik made his move, he decided, he would jump up, spin around, and throw his chair at the men still behind him.

Assuming, of course, that he could even lift the chair. It had seemed pretty solid when he first sat in it, and it might turn out to be too heavy to be a good weapon. He eased backward a couple of centimeters, leaning against the chair's back. Definitely solidly built, but he couldn't get a real feel for the weight.

He hated not having all the information he needed, an attitude he'd no doubt picked up while serving with Thrawn. Thrawn made up for any gaps in his data by being good at improvisation, a talent Eli sorely lacked.

He didn't know if the chair would work. But with nothing else close at hand, he would just have to risk it.

Still, he couldn't help wondering if Thrawn would have come to that same conclusion and decision, or if he'd have come up with some other plan.

Eli felt a wry smile twitch his lips. Of course Thrawn would have another plan. His plan would have been to never get himself into a situation like this in the first place.

"What's so funny?" Sisay demanded.

Eli started. He hadn't realized his smile had been that visible. "I was just thinking about what the Hutts will say if you mess up our mission."

"If you even *know* the Hutts," she said.

"Oh, he knows the Hutts," Mole said, looking up at last from the datapad. "Or maybe he knows someone who knows someone who knows the Hutts. Anyway." He pulled out the data card and wiggled it between his fingers. "It's good work. It's *really* good work."

"Did the Hutts make it?" Skulk asked.

Mole blinked at him. "How did you know that? I just figured it out myself."

"Because you just told us," Sisay said.

"Oh." Mole blinked again, then frowned at the data card. "Well, I mean it *might* be Huttese. They don't exactly sign their work. No one does, really, except a forger I knew once named Hollander. He had a strange—"

"Is it a forgery?" Skulk bellowed.

"Yes," Mole said hastily, cringing back. "Yes. A very good one. It should pass just fine."

"Thank you," Sisay said icily. "You can go now. Brackis, walk him out. Get him a hundred-credit chit on the way."

"Oh," Mole said. "Yes. Thank you." He stepped forward and laid the data card carefully back on the desk. "You've got the new entry pass for him, too, right?"

"What entry pass?" Sisay asked.

"The new entry pass," Mole repeated, frowning. "The one Governor What's-Her-Name set up."

"Governor Haveland?" Eli asked.

"Yeah, that's the one," Mole said. "No one gets into the Imperial part of the spaceport without one." He waved a hand in dismissal. "Doesn't matter. A guy who can make idents like this will breeze right through it."

"Except the guy who made the ident isn't here," Eli growled. "When exactly did this new pass go into effect?"

"I—" Mole looked at Sisay, then Skulk, then back at Eli. "I don't know. A few hours ago. A day. Maybe two. But like I said . . . oh. He's not here?"

"No," Eli ground out. *Damn.* Was this just some crazy coincidence of rotten timing?

Or was Haveland onto them? Could someone have tipped her off that her hand had been spotted inside the Stardust goodie jar?

But that was impossible. The only people who knew Thrawn had cracked this thing were on the *Chimaera*.

Or were right here in this room.

He shifted his gaze to Ronan . . . to find that Ronan was likewise looking at him.

"Well, okay, no big deal," Mole rattled on. "You need a pass? I can make you one."

"I thought they were special," Sisay said.

"Well, sure," Mole said. "But there's special and there's *special.* Anyway, what I heard was that they're changing them out every couple of days, so they don't have to be really *too* great."

"Every couple of *days*?" Eli echoed. "Do you know when they'll change them again?"

"In a couple of days, I suppose," Mole said. "I mean, I suppose I could look it up. Or I could just make him one?" he added, looking questioningly at Sisay.

"How long would it take?" Sisay asked.

"For one?" Mole shrugged. "A couple of—"

"For four," Pik corrected.

Mole blinked. "*Four?* Oh. Well, now you're talking five or six hours."

"Fine," Sisay said. "I want a few more hours with them anyway. Go get whatever you need and bring it over."

"Wait, wait, wait," Mole protested. "I can't work here. Mr. Parpa said—"

"I don't care what Parpa said," Sisay cut him off. "You go get your stuff. I'll square it with Parpa."

Mole huffed out a sigh. "Okay," he said reluctantly. "But it'll take an hour to pack up and a couple of porter droids to get it over here. It'll be easier if we take them to Parpa's and I do it all there."

"You'll do it here," Sisay said in a voice that left no room for further argument.

For a wonder, Mole got the message. "Okay," he said again. "So do they want to be visiting the harbormaster or the dock manager or someone else?"

"Does it matter?" Skulk asked.

"Of course," Mole said, as if it were obvious. "The passes are personalized. They have to be validated by the right person."

"We don't want to see anyone in particular," Eli said. "All we really want is to get to one of the Imperial cargo ships that'll be heading out soon."

"Really?" Mole said, brightening. "That's all? Great. In that case, why don't I just take you into the Imperial section through the back door?"

"What back door?" Sisay asked, frowning.

"The back door," Mole repeated, frowning in turn. "*The* back door."

"Yes, we heard you the first time," Skulk growled. "There's no back door into the Imperial docking area."

"Well, not an *official* one," Mole said. "And it's, y'know." He held his hands a dozen centimeters apart. "Narrow. People can get through, but no cargo. No big droids, either. I heard of a guy who tried to get a B2 super battle droid through, and—"

"How come I've never heard about this?" Sisay demanded, an ominous edge to her voice.

"How should I know?" Mole said, cringing back a little from her stare. "You want me to take you there? I can take you there." He sent a jerking glance around the room. "I can take all of you."

"How about you just take *us*?" Eli said, feeling a faint whisper of cautious hope. Whether or not Mole was right about a secret entrance, this might be their best chance to lose Sisay and the others. "If that's okay with *you*," he added acerbically to Sisay.

"Nice of you to ask," Sisay said. "Brackis, get their stuff back in their bags. You, Grimkle, and Porff will go with them."

Eli suppressed a curse. So much for getting clear of the gang. "Thanks for the offer, but we don't need to make a parade out of this," he said.

"Did I say anything to suggest that it was optional?" Sisay asked mildly. "You know, on second thought, I think Skulk and I will join you, too. Everyone loves a good parade." She got to her feet. "Hurry it up, Brackis."

"Finished," Brackis said, resealing the carrybags. "All set."

"Great." Sisay stood up, scooping up the IDs and dropping her hand to rest on the butt of her blaster. "Mole, lead the way. Brackis behind him." She gestured toward the door. "Gentlemen?"

Eli had hoped that the walk this time would be as long as the last one, giving them time to find a way to ditch Sisay and the others and make their own, more private way to the proper part of the spaceport.

It wasn't going to be easy. As soon as they left the building, Sisay had re-formed the group into a sort of moving double ring, with Eli, Ronan, and the two death troopers in the center and Sisay and her men hemming them in around the edges. Mole walked in front, completely oblivious to the tension behind him.

Still, if the trip was long enough, the others' vigilance might waver. Eli kept an eye on their captors as they walked, as well as watching the pedestrians, carts, and kiosks. If the opportunity presented itself, he had to be ready to move.

But they'd only been walking for about three minutes when Sisay moved up beside Mole. "How much farther?" she asked.

"Not very," he said. "Couple of blocks."

Eli mouthed a curse. They'd seen the wall to the commercial section of the port from Sisay's place, but he'd assumed Mole's back door would lead through the wall that isolated the Imperial part from the rest. Apparently, the route was through the commercial section instead.

"See, there's the perimeter wall up there—see it?" Mole continued, pointing. "That wall with the sensor wire and percher guard droids—"

"Yes, I see it," Sisay said. "Where's this secret back door?"

"It's supposed to be in a condemned building running along—"

"*Supposed* to be? You mean you haven't seen it?"

"Of course not," Mole said, sounding bewildered. "Why would I need to go to the spaceport?"

"Right." Shaking her head, Sisay fell back to the main group.

But instead of rejoining them, she drifted farther back, losing herself in the crowd. Eli glanced over his shoulder a couple of times but wasn't able to spot her.

He was starting to wonder if she'd ditched them when she reappeared on the other side of the ring. "Trouble?" Skulk asked.

She shook her head. "Thought I saw something. False alarm."

Skulk nodded and gestured down the street. "It's that blue house up ahead," he said. "Mole just pointed it out."

"Okay," she said. "You go in with him; I'll bring up the rear. Blasters out as soon as we're inside."

The door to the blue house, not surprisingly, was locked. Fortunately, Mole had brought something that was able to quickly pop it open. "It should be in the back," he said over his shoulder as he walked in. "Hurry up before someone sees us."

"Yeah, because there can't be more than a hundred people out here," Sisay muttered under her breath as she took Eli's arm and gave him a shove through the doorway.

A minute later they were inside a spacious, high-ceilinged foyer decorated with faded geometric shapes. "Should be back here," Mole said, pointing toward a long hallway ahead. "The back butts up against the wall, and—"

"Don't bother," Sisay said. Her blaster was out now and pointed at Eli. "We're not going any farther."

"We're not?" Mole asked, blinking at her. "Then why are we here?"

"Because I figured this would be easier than having to lug a bunch of bodies out of my office," Sisay said.

"What the *hell*?" Eli demanded as the other pirates stepped back from the four Imperials, their weapons already out and ready. "I thought we had a deal."

"You thought wrong," Sisay said. "Where's your mark?"

"My what?"

"Your mark," Sisay repeated. "People who work for the Hutts are always given a mark." She held her left hand out toward him, spreading it open to reveal a small black spot in the skin between the middle and ring fingers. "Here's mine. Where's yours?"

Eli clenched his teeth. He'd never even heard of that. "Not all the Hutts do that," he hedged.

"*All* of them do it," Sisay retorted. She closed her hand and lowered it to her side. "If you don't have a mark, that means you lied about the Hutt connection. If you lied about that, you probably lied about everything else." She lifted the blaster a little higher. "I don't like people who lie to me."

"You're making a mistake," Eli insisted, trying desperately to think. Sisay's men were lined up in front of them, far enough back that he'd never make it to any of their weapons before they could shoot. There was nothing nearby to throw, nothing they could hide behind, and with their backs to the foyer wall there was nowhere any of them could run.

"Not nearly as big as yours," Sisay said. "You see, a few minutes ago I got a call. Seems an Imperial Star Destroyer has suddenly arrived and taken up position over our lovely little town."

Eli felt his mouth drop open. A Star Destroyer? *Here?*

His first fleeting hope was that it might be Thrawn, come in the nick of time to rescue them. But an instant later he knew that was impossible. There were pirates and Grysks out there, and Thrawn wouldn't allow himself be distracted by anything else until he'd finished dealing with them.

But if not Thrawn, then who?

"What does that have to do with us?" he asked. "Anyway, you told us that Savit is cleaning out the pirate nests. Tiquwe is probably just next on his list."

"Or maybe he got nervous when your little group disappeared off his sensors," Sisay countered. "Hmm?"

"We're not with Savit," Eli insisted. "Or with any other Imperials."

"Sure," Sisay said. "But there's a Star Destroyer overhead, and we need to get back to tweak our records before the stormtroopers arrive, so we're out of time. You want to tell me who you are? Or are you going to make me wonder for the rest of my life who it was we killed today?"

"Whoa, whoa, whoa," Mole breathed, holding his hands up palms out. "Ms. Sisay—I don't—you can't—Mr. Parpa—"

"Oh, relax, Mole," Sisay said in a tone of strained patience. "We're not killing *you*. You want to run back to Parpa, go ahead. We don't need you anymore."

"Oh. Okay. Thanks. Uh . . ." Mole licked his lips. "There was—you said something about a hundred credits. Right? I mean, you said if I read the data card—"

"Oh, for—" Sisay clamped her teeth around the rest of the sentence. "Brackis, give him his damn hundred credits. And then you get the hell out of here."

"Yes, yes. Sure." Mole sidled quickly to Brackis, wincing away from the other's blaster as the man dug a coin from his pocket. He slapped it into Mole's hand—

And in a single smooth motion, Mole grabbed the hand, yanked Brackis off balance toward him, and twisted the blaster out of his other hand.

Before Eli could do anything more than gape in disbelief, Mole slammed the blaster across Brackis's throat, then swiveled around on one foot and snapped the edge of his other foot in quick succession into Grimkle's knee, ribs, and head. Grimkle was still collapsing from the triple blow when Mole leaned toward him, snatched his blaster from his now slack grip, and sent it spinning squarely into Skulk's face, knocking him backward. Another snap kick into Porff's stomach and a backhand smash with Brackis's blaster into the other man's face, and he spun around to level his blaster at Sisay. "Drop it," he ordered.

For a frozen second Eli thought she was going to obey. Her blaster was still pointed at Eli, and she must have known that there was no way she could turn it toward Mole in time.

But with the rest of her team sprawled unconscious or twitching in pain at her feet, she also must have known that it was over. And for some people, taking a few of the other side with them at the end was worth the effort. Eli saw her finger start to tighten on the trigger—

And with a screeching scream that sounded incredibly loud in the foyer's confines Mole's blaster bolt slashed through her.

Her body collapsed to the floor, and for a long moment the only sound Eli could hear was the echo of the shot in his memory. "Too bad," Mole said, lowering the blaster.

Only it wasn't Mole. Not anymore. Not the Mole they'd met in Sisay's office, anyway. There was no twitchiness or nervousness in his voice. His stance was straight and confident, his shoulders un-rounded, his eyes cool and calm and measuring.

He measured each of them in turn—long, perceptive looks that took no more than a quarter second each—and then his gaze re-turned to Eli. "You must be Vanto," he said, lowering the blaster but keeping it ready. "Which would make you Assistant Director Ronan," he added, giving Ronan a microscopic nod.

"Yes," Ronan breathed, clearly struggling to take it all in stride and not quite succeeding. "And you?"

"Call me Dayja," he said. "Imperial Security Bureau. Colonel Yularen called and said Grand Admiral Thrawn had asked for one of his agents to drop by and keep an eye on you. I was already on the scene, so I got the job."

"But you were here undercover?" Ronan said. "Isn't that . . . gone now?"

"Yeah." Dayja shrugged. "No big deal. It was really just a favor to Grand Admiral Savit. He's on a campaign against the pirate gangs in this sector and wanted ISB to help him figure out the best places to dig. So what do you want to see Savit about, anyway?"

"We don't," Eli said. "What we want is to get into the Imperial part of the port and check on a certain freighter."

"There *is* really a back door, isn't there?" Ronan added.

"There are always back doors," Dayja assured him. "This freighter got a name?"

"The *Brylan Ross.*"

"Okay," Dayja said. "Let's get you inside, and see what was worth burning a cover identity for."

"It doesn't have to be burned," Pik pointed out. "These are the only ones who know. Four more shots, and you can go back with any story you want."

Dayja regarded him thoughtfully. "Let me guess. Death troopers?"

Pik inclined his head slightly. "And just so you know, we were going to take them down as soon as you were out of our way."

Ronan's eyes went wide. "You're *death troopers*?"

"You have a problem with that?" Pik asked, looking darkly at him.

"No, I just thought—no," Ronan finished, his voice trailing off.

Pik shifted the glower to Dayja. "How about you?"

"No problem," Dayja said calmly. "But as for your suggestion, we're not tanking them in cold blood. I don't work that way. We'll tag them and leave them here for Savit's people to pick up."

"Whatever you want," Pik said. "They're your prisoners. But they're pirates, and they deserve to die."

"I prefer to think of it as ISB's interrogators deserving some interesting work," Dayja said coolly. "Give me a minute to tag 'em, and we'll hit the road." He pulled a small pack of tracking needles from inside his jacket lapel and set to work.

Eli turned to Ronan. "By the way, that was a pretty amazing performance back at Sisay's place. Going from Assistant Director Ronan to, well, to nobody."

"Thank you," Ronan said stiffly. His lips puckered, and some of the attitude faded away. "I wasn't *always* an Imperial bureaucrat, you know. Not exactly a nobody, but pretty close."

"All set," Dayja said, standing up and putting the needle case away. He cocked an eye at Eli—"Oh, and by the way, Vanto, the Hutts don't mark their operatives. She put that mark on herself when she dropped behind everyone. Probably figured she could get one last shot at tripping you up. Next time you go undercover, try to research your role a little better."

"I'll do that," Eli promised, smiling to himself. Earlier, he'd wondered how Thrawn would have handled this kind of situation. Now he knew.

Thrawn still would have walked into the trap. He simply would have made sure there was backup waiting.

CHAPTER 14

There is no Grysk art available. That lack creates limitations, perhaps fatal ones. Perhaps Grysks do not create in that way.

But there is art from their victims. It will have to suffice.

The curves and lines are well remembered. The abandonments and hesitations are likewise so. Much of the art points to their creators, but there are commonalities that may point to Grysk characteristics.

There is the sound of movement from the resting part of the office suite. A shadow appears and shifts position.

"Admiral Mitth'raw'nuruodo?" Vah'nya asked. *Her voice holds weariness and some fear.*

"Yes. Did I wake you?"

"No." *She takes two steps through the doorway from the resting area and stops. Her eyes move around the group of holograms, lingering on one before moving on.* "Admiral Ar'alani says you like art."

"I study it. Do you like art?"

"A little." *Her voice still holds weariness, but now also holds interest.* "I like music better." *Her eyes return to the sculpture they focused on a moment ago.*

"Music is seldom of use to me. Do you like this sculpture?"

"No," Vah'nya said. "But it reminds me of something."

"Something you've seen? Or perhaps something from Un'hee's memories?"

Vah'nya hesitates. Her expression and body stance hold confusion. The confusion fades away. "Yes," she said. *Her voice holds discomfort.* "Un'hee saw something similar in her Scratchling master's quarters."

"The Grysk client species is called Scratchling?"

"She doesn't know their true name." *The discomfort held in her voice is joined by a deepening dread.* "She thinks of them as Scratchlings because of the sound of their voices. Are you going to send me away? Admiral Ar'alani said she would take me back to the *Steadfast* aboard a shuttle when I was finished guiding your ship."

"So she also said to me. She fears for your safety. Do you wish to go?"

"No."

"Do *you* not fear for your safety?"

She hesitates. Her expression holds concern and the uncertainty, perhaps the apprehension, of the risks taken by lying to a command officer. The uncertainty fades. "Yes, very much."

"Then why do you wish to stay?"

Her expression stiffens. The muscles of her throat and shoulders hold a mix of fear and determination. "Un'hee feared and hated the Scratchlings and their Grysk masters. She has nightmares about them." *Her eyes narrow. Her expression now holds sympathy and quiet rage.* "I want to remain so that I may watch you destroy them."

The art flows with meaning. It carries hidden clues, subtle hints. It speaks of the Grysks, reflecting arrogance, confidence, and cunning.

"And so you shall. Come with me, Navigator Vah'nya. You shall face the enemy.

"And we shall destroy them together."

The first wave of TIEs was nearly to optimal viewing position when Thrawn returned. Navigator Vah'nya, to Faro's surprise, was trailing along behind him.

And as Faro watched the pair approaching, she thought she could detect a new confidence in Thrawn's step, a focus and direction that had been missing when he retreated to his office to think and meditate.

He was onto something.

Faro met them at the aft end of the command walkway. "Admiral," she said, stiffening to attention. "Orders, sir?"

"Orders indeed, Commodore," he said, his eyes sweeping the bridge. "Prepare my ship for combat."

"Yes, sir," Faro said, hiding her surprise. The original plan had called for the *Chimaera* to first gather data from the fighters' recon before bringing the ship to combat mode. "May I remind the admiral that bringing us to full battle readiness will require us to abandon stealth mode?"

"It will indeed," Thrawn agreed. He looked past her shoulder to where Ar'alani was gazing out the forward viewport. "We must give our enemies a reason to communicate with their superiors. Commander Hammerly, status of our target?"

"No change, sir."

"Its rotational speed is unchanged?"

"Yes, sir."

"Lieutenant Agral, take over monitoring of target rotation," Thrawn ordered, tapping his datapad. "Here is an algorithm to add to your navigational sensor analyzers. Use it to find the locations I've designated as Points One and Two. When the target changes rotation, use it to recalibrate."

"Yes, sir," Agral said, clearly surprised at being handed part of Hammerly's sensor duty, but taking it in stride.

"Commander Hammerly, switch your full attention to the occultation programs," Thrawn continued. "The Grysk warship is somewhere along a line thirty kilometers directly above and thirty kilometers directly below the joined ships. When you locate it, feed the coordinates to Senior Lieutenant Pyrondi and her turbolaser gunners."

"Yes, sir."

"The Grysk ship is *above* the conjoined ships, sir?" Faro asked, frowning.

"Or below it," Thrawn said, gesturing forward. "Come."

He continued forward along the walkway toward Ar'alani. Faro dropped into step beside him, noting as she did so that Vah'nya was still behind them.

Ar'alani was waiting when they reached her. Her glowing red eyes flicked behind Thrawn and Faro to Vah'nya, hardening noticeably as they then shifted to focus on Thrawn. "You were going to return us to the *Steadfast* before entering battle," she said darkly in Sy Bisti.

"Navigator Vah'nya wishes a memory of this day," Thrawn said. "One she will then be able to share with Navigator Un'hee."

Ar'alani looked back at Vah'nya. Whatever she saw in the girl's face was apparently enough for her to drop the subject. "You have a combat strategy?" she asked instead.

"I do. You'll recall our unanswered question about the communications triad?"

"The question was hardly unanswered," Ar'alani said. "We concluded it could only be on one of the nearby planetary moons."

"No," Thrawn said. "What we concluded was that the distances between the poles had to remain stable, which would preclude simply placing them in individual orbits." He raised his eyebrows slightly. "But if they weren't in simple orbits . . . ?" He paused expectantly.

Faro frowned, trying to think. Not in simple orbits. Rotational algorithms. The ship directly above the conjoined ships . . .

And then she got it. "The conjoined ships don't just have *one* of the triad poles," she said. "They have *two* of them. The poles are outside the ships, anchored on long tethers stretching to both sides."

"With the joined ships doing a slow rotation to ensure that the tethers remain taut," Ar'alani said, nodding. "Thus maintaining the required distance." She flashed a look at Faro. "The third pole must then be aboard the warship."

"Exactly," Thrawn said. "The poles will be a considerable distance from the conjoined ships and thus difficult to see."

"Especially since an enemy's attention would be focused mainly on the ships themselves," Faro said. "Leaving the poles unnoticed and ignored unless someone was specifically looking for them."

"As Lieutenant Agral is doing now," Thrawn agreed.

"Not a particularly clever arrangement," Ar'alani said. "If the warship is away, or even just out of position, long-range communication is impossible."

"You believe it foolish because you aren't accustomed to working with slaves," Thrawn said, a dark edge to his voice. "On a forward base such as this, where Grysk overseers are undoubtedly outnumbered, a successful revolt would still leave the slaves helpless, unable to either escape or call for assistance."

"They can't leave because of the conjoined ships' bow-to-stern configuration," Faro said, nodding to herself. "Which the Grysks needed in order to get the triad poles rotating properly in the first place. Keeping the ships from leaving in a crisis was just an extra bonus."

"We assumed the configuration was for our benefit, a way to make their bait more attractive," Thrawn said. "Warriors rarely make such elaborate arrangements purely for the sake of their enemies. Their plans will always first and foremost benefit their own interests and goals."

"Yes, sir," Faro said. "I'll remember that."

"As should we all." Thrawn raised his voice and switched back to Basic. "Lieutenant Agral?"

"A moment, sir . . . yes! *Got* them, sir!"

"Excellent," Thrawn said.

Faro suppressed a smile. Agral was the youngest of the senior bridge crew, and sometimes his youthful enthusiasm bumped into the more sedate official protocol.

Fortunately for him, Thrawn appreciated enthusiasm from his subordinates. "Put it on the tactical," Faro ordered.

Two new marks appeared on the displays: the triad poles tracing out their distant circles in harmony with the conjoined ships' rotation.

Faro checked the scale. Five kilometers each from the ships, putting them ten kilometers apart. "Commander Hammerly, your target is—" She ran the triangle calculation in her head. "—approximately eight point seven kilometers above or below the conjoined ships."

"Yes, ma'am."

"Not so hasty, Commodore," Thrawn said thoughtfully. "Consider that the Grysks are certainly aware that their outrider poles might be discovered, and that the purpose might be recognized, and the location of the third pole might therefore be easily deduced."

And also consider that the Grysks aren't fools, Faro added silently to Thrawn's list. "So they won't just be sitting where an enemy would know to shoot at them," she said. "At the same time, they won't want to be too far out of communication. So they'll be close to that nine-kilometer spot, but far enough away that a targeted spread will miss them."

"Very good," Thrawn said. "I believe I have also detected a hitherto unrecognized trait hidden in the artwork that has been created around their species. They are interested observers, wishing to see all, and especially eager to see and savor moments of their own triumph."

"Yes, sir," Faro said, his earlier comment finally clicking. "So we give them something that's not just exciting to see, but also worth sharing with their superiors."

"Indeed," Thrawn said. "Commander Hammerly, what data from the TIE fighters?"

"They're just entering passive sensor range, sir," Hammerly said. "Do you want me to signal them to bring active sensors online?"

"Not yet," Thrawn said. "We'll use ours. Commodore Faro: Bring the *Chimaera* to full battle status."

"Secure from stealth mode," Faro called. "Battle readiness."

All around them, the bridge came to life as systems that had been off or on standby were run back up to active status. "Commander Hammerly, active sensors," Thrawn called.

"Sensors active," Hammerly confirmed. "Reading three weapons clusters on each of the conjoined ships, energy weapons and torpedoes both, and the nodes of an electrostatic barrier generator."

"Sir, Major Quach asks if you want his TIEs to go active," Pyrondi called.

"Negative, Lieutenant," Thrawn said. "Leave them dark for the moment. Lieutenant Lomar: open a hailing channel. No encryption."

"Channel open, sir."

"Unidentified ships, this is Grand Admiral Thrawn of the Galactic Empire," Thrawn called. "You are trespassing in Imperial space. I order you to power down all weapons and defenses and surrender for inspection."

There was no response. Thrawn signaled, and Lomar muted the comm. "Are you genuinely expecting an answer?" Ar'alani asked, a bit drily.

"Of course," Thrawn replied. "Though not an immediate one. We will hope they were surprised by our sudden appearance and are even now deciding exactly how to respond."

"Such response possibly including an attack on the *Chimaera* from their cloaked warship?"

"Not yet," Thrawn said. "Not at this distance. And so we offer added incentive. Commodore, move us toward the conjoined ships."

"Helm: ahead, one-quarter speed," Faro ordered. "Be aware of the TIEs and the outriding triad poles."

"Yes, ma'am," Agral acknowledged. "Quarter power."

Thrawn signaled again. "Comm open," Lomar said.

"This is Grand Admiral Thrawn," Thrawn called. "If you do not answer in the next thirty seconds, we will launch a boarding party to take your ships by force of arms."

He signaled again. "Major Carvia, are your stormtroopers ready?"

"They are, Admiral," Carvia's voice came over the bridge speaker.

"Launch shuttle," Thrawn ordered.

"Shuttle launched," the hangar master confirmed.

"Commander Hammerly, watch closely," Thrawn said. "The chance to destroy a group of Imperial stormtroopers should add extra incentive to our bait."

Faro gazed at the tactical, watching as the shuttle and, still lagging behind it, the *Chimaera* itself moved closer to the conjoined ships. An extra prize like that should indeed lure the Grysks into action.

She felt her stomach tighten. More human bait. And if the Grysks decided to take them out, all those lives would be lost.

Only the Grysks weren't playing Thrawn's game. Hammerly's

scanners still showed nothing: no diffuse ion path from low-level thrusters, no occultation from cold-gas maneuvering jets, no radar or laser emissions from comms or targeting systems.

Could the Grysks be asleep? Could they all have fled before the *Chimaera* even entered the system, leaving only the conjoined ships and a group of slaves and prisoners behind?

The stormtrooper shuttle had entered the tactical's inner sphere, the distance Thrawn had estimated would be within the blast radius from the destruction of the conjoined ships. Were the Grysks merely waiting until the shuttle was closer and the stormtroopers' destruction was assured?

Or was the bait just not quite good enough?

"Lomar: Signal to the shuttle," she said, trying to remember the code they'd already proved that the Grysks had cracked. Right: G77. "Encryption G77," she added. Out of the corner of her eye she saw Thrawn turn a frown on her—

"G77," Lomar confirmed. "Ready."

Faro braced herself. "Shuttle commander, this is Commodore Faro," she called. "Hold position off target; repeat, hold position off target. I'm coming to take personal command of the boarding force."

"Shuttle command, acknowledged," Carvia replied. "What's your ETA?"

"I'm prepping my shuttle now," Faro said. "I'll be there in ten."

She signaled Lomar, and the transmission cut off. Bracing herself, she turned to face Thrawn.

Ar'alani got in the first word. "That was insubordinate," she said coldly.

"I agree, and I apologize," Faro said. "But there was no time for a consultation. I needed to stop the shuttle before it moved any deeper into killing range."

"Explain," Thrawn said, the calm in his voice in sharp contrast to the antagonism in Ar'alani's.

"You said they needed a good reason to call their base, sir," she reminded him. "It was looking like even a ship full of stormtroopers might not be an image worth sending home."

"So you offer them an Imperial flag officer."

"Yes, sir."

For a long moment, Thrawn eyed her thoughtfully. Then he inclined his head. "Your shuttle will be ready when you reach the hangar bay."

"Thank you, sir," Faro said. She stiffened to attention, then turned and headed toward the turbolift.

And as she walked, she noticed the bridge seemed have gone unusually quiet.

She'd expected to find an empty shuttle waiting for her. To her surprise, Major Carvia was already strapped into the pilot's seat. "What are you doing here?" she asked, strapping in beside him.

"Admiral Thrawn told me what you were doing, Commodore," he said, dropping the shuttle out of the bay without waiting for her to completely finish the strap-in process. "I figured if my stormtroopers *and* my commander were going to be in harm's way, I might as well join them."

"That wasn't necessary."

Carvia shrugged. "No offense, ma'am, but my pilot's rating is higher than yours. Figured that if things went top-heavy, I might be able to scrape you out of something you couldn't scrape out of by yourself."

"I appreciate the thought," Faro said. "On the other hand, it could just mean that we'll *both* die."

"Nah." Carvia flashed her a tight smile. "Not with Grand Admiral Thrawn calling the shots from the bridge. He'll get us through this." He tapped the transmitter key. "*Chimaera,* this is Carvia. Commodore Faro is aboard; shuttle is away and headed in. ETA, four minutes."

"Acknowledged, shuttle," Lomar's voice came from the speaker. "Standing by."

Faro gazed out the shuttle's viewport as the conjoined ships grew steadily larger. They were Grysks, all right, she could see now, with their distinctive breaking-wave design. The first stormtrooper shuttle was visible in front of them; a quick check of the tactical showed they'd already passed the still-dark groups of TIE fighters. She watched as they crossed the invisible line into the killing zone . . . caught up with the stormtrooper shuttle and continued on in convoy with it . . . watched as the conjoined ships began to completely fill the viewport . . .

What the *hell* were the Grysks waiting for?

Or *were* they waiting? In her mind's eye she saw the Grysk commander gloating aloud as he twitched the maneuvering jet controls, sending brief bursts out into the vacuum of space, drifting toward the point where the triad would become active. Could the puffs of gas perhaps be too diffuse for Hammerly to pick up on?

Worse, could they all be on the warship's far side, where they wouldn't even be visible from the *Chimaera*'s position?

"They're speeding up," Carvia said suddenly.

Faro snapped out of her speculations. "What are?"

"The conjoined ships," he said, pointing to the shuttle's sensor display. "They're rotating faster."

Faro frowned at the display. Their angular momentum had picked up, all right. Not much, only a few percent, but the ships were definitely moving faster.

But the sensors were picking up no indication of thruster or maneuvering jet usage. Even with the shuttle's limited sensor package, she and Carvia were close enough to detect something like that.

But if the thrusters weren't firing . . .

Damn. "They're reeling in the triad poles," she breathed.

"They're *what*? Oh, *hell.*"

Faro nodded, a sudden tightness in her gut. *Don't raise the bridge, lower the river.* The old engineering-class joking maxim came back to her.

The Grysk warship was indeed sitting on the line Thrawn had specified . . . only it wasn't the full 8.7 kilometers above the conjoined ships that Faro had assumed. It was, instead, much closer to them. All the commander needed to do was bring in the other two poles to the proper distance, and the triad would become active without the warship ever needing to move.

Faro's finger twitched toward the comm's transmitter key. She had to tell Thrawn. Had to warn him that the plan he'd set up wasn't going to work.

The finger froze a centimeter away from the key. Of course Thrawn would see the ships' rotation and come to the right conclusion. Surely he would.

Only maybe he hadn't. The murmur of bridge conversation still coming from the shuttle's speaker showed no signs of sudden revelation, or heightened activity, or anything else. Could Thrawn have missed it?

But if he had, what should Faro do? What *could* she do? Calling back to the *Chimaera* now might simply alert the Grysks that their subterfuge had been spotted. In that case, the enemy might opt for destroying the shuttle and conjoined ships even without being able to send a live view of the triumph to their base.

"Ship rotation stabilizing," Carvia said. "Settling into its new angular speed."

Faro no longer had a choice. Even if it precipitated a premature attack, she had to let Thrawn know what was happening. She reached for the transmit key—

"*Chimaera*'s rolling!" Carvia snapped. "Ninety degrees, up on its side—"

And from the shuttle speaker came a clear female voice—Vah'nya's voice—speaking a single accented but completely understandable Basic word.

"*Fire!*"

And from behind the shuttle, blazing past its canopy, came a firestorm of turbolaser bolts as the *Chimaera* opened up with a full double broadside: a starboard salvo converging on a point six kilometers above the conjoined ships, a portside salvo blasting with equal fury at the same spot beneath the ships. The portside bolts continued on their way unhindered, fading into the darkness of interplanetary space. The starboard salvo vanished for an instant above the ships.

And then the entire area erupted in fire and shattered metal as the cloaked Grysk warship abruptly became visible, its hull crackling and blackening under the *Chimaera*'s withering assault.

The turbolaser fire was still pounding at the enemy when the shuttle's comm erupted into pure static.

"What the—?" Carvia barked.

"It's all right," Faro said quickly. *This* part, at least, she'd figured out right away. "The *Chimaera* is jamming all frequencies and all signals so that the warship can't trigger whatever doomsday explosives are on the conjoined ships."

The words were barely out of her mouth when the dark TIE fighters they'd left behind them came to full power and screamed past, laser cannons adding their own rain of destruction to the Star Destroyer's bombardment.

The Grysk warship was beginning to return fire now. But starting from the low power levels that had been necessary for maintaining a proper cloaking field, they were at a huge disadvantage. The *Chimaera* continued to hammer away, raking the Grysk with general fire while the TIEs slipped in and out, blasting at more specific targets. Midway through the assault, the warship seemed to break apart, and only as the broken section angled off at high speed did she realize she was seeing the supply ship that Thrawn had chased away from the Grysk observation post.

The freighter made it nearly ten kilometers before a pair of TIEs dropped into pursuit and blew it to dust.

"Come on," Faro said, motioning to the shuttle controls. "I think the admiral's got this part in hand."

"Where are we going?"

"Where we're supposed to," Faro said. "Let's find these prisoners we came here to rescue."

CHAPTER 15

We do not struggle against flesh and blood—the old Clone Wars–era saying whispered through Faro's mind—*but against ideas and fears, against hopelessness and manipulation.*

They certainly weren't fighting against flesh and blood on the conjoined ships. Here, the enemy was all in the form of booby traps.

It started with the docking hatches themselves, rigged to explode if an unidentified ship came too close. Fortunately, by the time Faro's transport arrived, the commander of the first shuttle had sent a pair of spacetroopers to investigate and had discovered the trap. With the *Chimaera* having lifted its jamming, Carvia had a short conversation with the TIE commander, and a couple of directed salvos later the hatches had been harmlessly detonated. The spacetroopers rigged a pair of boarding tubes, and they were in.

The TIEs had spotted several large caches of explosives on the hulls, presumably prepped for a signal from the warship. With the warship now reduced to debris and glowing plasma, those were no longer a threat.

But the corridors and hatchways were riddled with smaller traps,

some designed for a single unwary intruder, others apparently intended to clear entire passageways. Fortunately, the Grysks hadn't
had a lot of time to prepare their gauntlet, and most of the traps were
fairly obvious and relatively easy to detonate from a safe distance.

At Carvia's insistence, Faro stayed near the back of the boarding
party as the stormtroopers painstakingly cleared the way. They'd
made it nearly to the center of the ship, and were approaching a large,
open hatchway, when the lead stormtrooper abruptly held up a hand.

"Life-forms ahead," Carvia murmured. "Let's just hang back a little, Commodore, if you don't mind." The lead stormtrooper eased an
eye around the hatchway—

"Found them," he said. Pulling away from the edge, he took a long
step into the center of the opening, his E-11 blaster rifle held up in
covering position. Two stormtroopers slipped past his left into the
compartment, two more disappeared inside past his right, and two
more passed him and took up guard positions aiming farther down
the corridor, just in case the compartment was a diversion.

"Report," Thrawn said over Faro's headset.

"Eight humans and a beat-up Dashade grouped together in a corner of the room, sir," one of the stormtroopers said. "Actually, none of
them looks in very good shape. Six nonhumans, unknown species,
grouped together in the center. Three of them have blasters, two of
them pointed at the prisoners. The third—well, sort of aimed in our
direction, but mostly pointed at the deck. No immediate threat."

From the room, and echoed faintly through Faro's headset, came
a series of sounds like an animal's claws scratching against metal
sheets. "I think they're trying to talk, sir," the stormtrooper added.

"Let me try Sy Bisti on him," Faro suggested. "Can you hook me to
your external speaker?"

"Yes, Commodore . . . okay, you're on."

"Do you speak Sy Bisti?" Faro called in that language.

More of the scratching. "Admiral, if they're from the Unknown
Regions, they might understand the Chiss language," she suggested.

"Doubtful," Thrawn said. "But I'll try Meese Caulf." He spoke a
few words.

Abruptly, the scratching broke off. A moment of silence, and a different voice spoke up, the words still scratchy but now sounding like actual words.

"One of the others seems to understand, sir," the stormtrooper confirmed.

"Yes," Thrawn said. He spoke again, and there was another answer, this one much longer. Another exchange—"Commodore, he claims to fear for his life and the lives of his companions," Thrawn translated. "I've given him my word, but he claims to need a face-to-face guarantee or he will kill the human prisoners."

"If he's been working under the Grysks, I'm not surprised he's a little paranoid," Faro said, starting forward. "Let me see if I can defuse the situation."

"A moment," Thrawn said. "Your visual monitor appears to be off."

Faro felt her face warm as she peered down at her chestplate. She'd switched off the tiny cam on the flight into the combat zone, not wanting to have even so small a transmission running lest the Grysks pick it up, and she'd forgotten to turn it back on when they reached the ship. "Sorry, sir," she apologized as she switched it on.

"No apology necessary, Commodore. We have the signal now. Proceed, but with caution. I will continue to translate for you."

Faro nodded. Walking past the stormtroopers, she slipped through the hatchway.

The compartment was laid out exactly as it had been described. The humans and a lone Dashade sat on the deck in one corner, the Dashade's olive-skinned reptilian bulk towering over his fellow prisoners. The six unidentified nonhumans huddled together in a standing clump in the center. Faro eyed the Dashade with interest—they'd turned up on the list of species that particularly liked the blosphi extract Thrawn had noted in the stolen supply ships.

She shifted her attention back to the six unknown beings in the middle of the compartment. Two of them had their backs to her, their blasters pointed at the prisoners, while the third held his loosely in his hand, the muzzle pointed at the deck a meter in front of him. His facial skin above the high collar of his tunic was a wrinkled mess of dark red and dirty white, with a lipless slit of a mouth tucked away amid the folds. But the black eyes staring out at Faro were bright and clear and oddly tense. He gestured, and the being to his left spoke—

"'Are you the guarantor of our safety?'" Thrawn translated.

"Yes," Faro said. "I'm Commodore Karyn Faro, commander of the Imperial Star Destroyer *Chimaera*. Surrender your weapons, and I will promise you your lives and safety."

Thrawn translated her statement. Faro tensed . . .

With a sigh that seemed to collapse his whole body, the armed being bowed his head to his chest. He let his blaster drop to the deck—

"Kill him," Thrawn snapped.

Faro felt her eyes widen. What the *hell*?

Before she could speak the two stormtroopers flanking her opened fire, raking the being's torso with blaster bolts. The creature jerked violently backward.

And as he collapsed, a small cylinder Faro hadn't noticed flew out of his other hand.

He was still falling when the other beings leapt into motion, the nearest grabbing for the bouncing cylinder, the others opening fire on the prisoners. Each of them got a single shot off before they, too, were sent sprawling by stormtrooper blasterfire. The being diving for the cylinder stretched out his hand—

"Kill them all," Thrawn ordered, raising his voice to be audible above the noise.

Five seconds later, it was over.

Faro swallowed hard, shaking with reaction and adrenaline. What in hell's name had just happened?

"Major, are there any injuries?" Thrawn asked.

"Two of the prisoners were hit, sir," Carvia reported as four of the stormtroopers hurried over to the corner. "We're checking on them now."

"Also check them for booby traps."

"Absolutely," Carvia said grimly. "All our people are unhurt."

"And Commodore Faro?"

"Safe, sir," Carvia said, his voice going grim. "Is that cylinder what I think it is?"

"I believe so," Thrawn said. "Take care when handling it. The explosives it was set to trigger are most likely still within range and active."

A cold chill ran up Faro's back. Basically the very same thought that had led her to coming aboard the enemy ship in the first place.

Only instead of the hidden warship wanting to lure in and destroy a high-value target from combat distance, here it had been intended to be up close and very, very personal.

"They must have been desperate to keep the Grysks' goodwill to agree to sacrifice themselves this way," Thrawn continued, his voice calm again. "Commodore, are you all right?"

"Yes, sir," Faro managed. Enemies of the Empire took shots at her all the time, but usually she had shields and turbolasers and officers and crew and an entire ship protecting her. Here on the ground, the experience was considerably different.

"Good," Thrawn said. "My apologies for allowing you to walk into danger that way. But while I suspected there would be a final attempt, the remaining Grysk clients had to be offered a chance to turn back from that path."

"Understood, sir," Faro said. "And I completely agree."

"Good," Thrawn said again. "A medical team is on the way to treat the injured. A detailed sensor scan indicates there are no other beings aboard either ship, so I believe the need for your presence there has ended. Once the stormtroopers have finished clearing out any further traps and brought the survivors to the *Chimaera,* an analysis group will go aboard and search for data the Grysks may have been careless enough to leave us."

"They may also be worried about information carried by surviving prisoners," Faro pointed out. "Because whoever they sent their last message to doesn't *know* their suicide team didn't have second thoughts."

"A fact and concern I hope to use against them," Thrawn agreed. "I do not know if the Grysks did indeed send a message before we destroyed the warship, but the triad was certainly active at the time."

"With any luck, the last image they sent was that of their own destruction."

"That would certainly provoke a reaction," Thrawn said. "I had thought that the Grysk response would be to the observation post. Now I believe this will be the location of our final confrontation with them. Major Carvia, escort Commodore Faro back to your shuttle and return her to the *Chimaera.*"

"Yes, sir," Carvia said.

"And I trust, Commodore," Thrawn added, "that this has been a learning experience for you."

"Yes, sir," Faro said grimly.

And it had.

The *Chimaera* had faced the Grysks in combat before, and while they were formidable opponents, they weren't any worse than other enemies the Empire had fought and defeated.

Now, for the first time, she truly understood why Thrawn was so deeply concerned about this particular threat. An enemy who could enslave the hearts and minds of their captive species so thoroughly that they were willing to die on the Grysks' behalf—even when their masters were gone, even when those masters would never know whether those slaves had fulfilled their final orders—posed a terrible threat to the galaxy. With an enemy like that pulling the strings, one could never be certain if an ally was still an ally, or a subservient species still subservient. The Grysks could wear a thousand faces, and could wield a thousand weapons.

They might not be able to destroy the Empire from without. But they might well be able to subvert and destroy it from within.

"Good," Thrawn said. "We will speak further once we have examined the prisoners. Perhaps they will have useful information to give us."

"I don't know what I can tell you," the man who called himself Bleary said. His voice was tired and anxious and nervous, Faro noted, the voice of a man who's been pulled out of one laser cooker only to be dropped into another. Rescued from the Grysks, he and his companions were now facing charges of piracy and theft of Imperial property. "They would sit us down for hours, asking us everything about the Empire, threatening our lives, our families, our clan totems—whatever the hell those are—and on and on."

"Did they utilize body scanners or other measurement devices?" Thrawn asked.

"I don't think so," Bleary said. "I suppose there might have been something in the chairs, but I don't think so. Anyway, they didn't need anything. Those things—well, you saw them. Screechy voices, long fingers, crazy eyes. They'd have two or three of those things standing behind us the whole time, those fingers wrapped around our heads and the back of our necks. Creepiest thing I ever saw. They'd ask questions, and the screechers would just stand there hanging on to us. Then, after it was all over, they'd all sit down together and talk about the whole thing."

"How do you know they were talking about the interrogations?" Faro asked.

Bleary gave her a nervously scornful look. "What, you think they were talking about the weather? What else could they have been talking about?"

"Perhaps the stolen cargo that was in your transfer station," Thrawn suggested.

Bleary flinched back in his chair. "Yeah. I . . ." He trailed off.

"Tell us about it," Thrawn said. "Who gave you your orders?"

"I don't know," Bleary said. "Maliss and Sorath—they were the bosses—they're the ones who hired us for the job."

"How?" Thrawn asked.

"What do you mean *how*?" Bleary asked. "We were a . . . well, we weren't pirates, exactly. More like backstage assistants. Anyway, we'd worked with a couple of pirate groups, and I guess Sorath remembered us. I mean, we might even have worked with him directly—Dashades all look alike to me. Anyway, he called us in and hired us to run the way station, collect cargoes from the freighters that would be coming, then switch the stuff and the crews to new freighters and dump the original ones. We had a schedule for moving the station to different places, and the freighters kept coming in, and everyone was happy."

"Maliss and Sorath both knew the organizer?"

"I don't know," Bleary said. "Maliss was always the one who gave us the tweaks or revised schedules. Sorath might have known, too, but you're never going to get anything out of him."

"We shall see," Thrawn said calmly. "Tell us of the coming of the Grysks."

Bleary's face scrunched up. "I don't know how they found us," he said, his voice shaking slightly. "Maybe they followed one of the freighters. Maybe it was just luck. But we were shifting cargo around to get ready for the incoming ship and suddenly they were there. Big ship, lots of firepower."

"They fired on you?"

"Oh, yeah," Bleary said bitterly. "Though they didn't really need to. We didn't even know the ship was there until it blew open one of the outer hatches." He shivered. "And then *they* came aboard."

"The Grysks?" Thrawn asked.

"Yeah, if that's what they're called," Bleary said, hunching his shoulders. "Not the screechers, the ones who were running the ship. The ones with blasters." He waved a hand. "Maliss and Sorath charged straight in—you know Dashades—but they weren't ready for a real fight. Maliss got killed in the first wave. Sorath took over and tried to push back."

He swallowed hard. "We weren't fighters. None of us except Sorath. He let them whittle us down to twelve before he finally surrendered. I don't know—I guess he figured they just wanted the cargo and maybe we could do a deal with them."

"Apparently not," Faro said.

Bleary snorted. "They didn't seem to care about the cargo. Matter of fact, I don't think they even looked at it. They were more interested in us. Who we were, what we liked, what we were afraid of. The stuff I already told you."

Faro nodded, giving a little shiver of her own. Searching for the handles and levers they could use to turn a given group of humans to their side.

"How many cargoes have you transferred?" Thrawn asked.

Bleary looked down at the table. "Eighteen," he muttered. He looked back up. "But handling stolen merchandise isn't as bad as stealing it. Right?"

"That will be for the prosecutors to decide," Thrawn said. "Thank you. You will now be taken to another compartment for questioning in more detail, both about your crimes and about your time in captivity." He motioned, and the navy troopers flanking the door stepped forward.

"All right," Bleary said, standing up, holding his arms awkwardly with the binders around them. "But look. I mean . . . they were getting to some of us. They really were. Creepy as hell. Westerli and Yimmer especially—you could see that they were starting to think that we should be working for the Grysks instead of Sorath. Or maybe they'd been so scared or dug into that they were thinking that. I don't know. All I know is that you need to keep real close watch on them."

"We are," Thrawn said. "We are keeping close watch on all of you."

Bleary seemed to sink into himself. "Yeah. I . . . So what happens to me after you're done asking questions?"

"That will depend on how cooperative you are," Thrawn said quietly. "And perhaps how much the Grysks got to you, as well." He gestured, and the troopers took the prisoner's arms and walked him out of the conference room.

"So that's it," Faro said when the hatch was once again closed behind them. "Looks like there won't be anything tying this back to Governor Haveland."

"I'm not surprised," Thrawn said. "Still, we haven't yet talked with Sorath. He may have information he's willing to give us."

"Maybe in exchange for some blosphi extract?"

"Very good," Thrawn said, giving her a small smile. "I wondered if you would pick up on the thought that that particular delicacy had been added to the stolen cargoes specifically for him. No, I doubt we shall gain much more from them. But I'm certain Colonel Yularen's interrogators will welcome the challenge."

"Yes, sir," Faro said, eyeing him closely. The piracy and the disruption of Krennic's supply chain were the reason the *Chimaera* was out here, and solving the crime was what would make or break Thrawn's TIE Defender program. But she could see that that wasn't where his thoughts were right now. "What are we going to do about the Grysks?" she asked. "You've closed down their observation and probe operation and demolished their forward base. What's next?"

"What's next is the main command center, the force that was coordinating this effort," Thrawn said, his eyes narrowing. "It will be somewhere within a few hours' travel, supporting this operation and possibly others as well."

"Well, I think we've delivered a pretty strong message," Faro said.

"We have indeed," Thrawn said. "And now that the conjoined ships have been cleared of traps, I shall go across and see what I may glean from what they left behind."

"So that we can deliver an even stronger message?"

"No, Commodore," Thrawn said. "Not a message. Not even a warning.

"I intend to deliver complete and total destruction."

CHAPTER 16

Ronan hadn't paid much attention to the Tiquwe spaceport as they were coming in from space. But the place had already turned out to be bigger than he'd expected, and even as he squeezed through Dayja's secret door he was glumly anticipating the long walk still ahead of them.

Fortunately, Dayja was already on top of the situation. Ronan finished his passage through the wall to discover the ISB agent had gone off somewhere on his own. By the time Vanto and the death troopers made it through behind him, Dayja was back with a commandeered speeder truck.

Commandeered, or stolen. From what Ronan knew of the ISB, it could be either.

But at this point he didn't care. All that mattered was locating the freighter Vanto had identified and finding out whether or not Thrawn's theory was right.

Preferably before the stormtroopers from the Star Destroyer looming overhead caught up with them. Being forced to present his credentials out in the open in a place like this would be begging for some pirate or smuggler to take a shot at him.

Just as bad, he decided as he grimly hung on to the truck's safety bars, would be if Dayja's lunatic driving got them stopped by some low-level spaceport workers. If Sisay had been right about many of them being in the pay of criminal organizations, their reaction to having a high-ranking Stardust official in their midst might be even worse than a pirate's potshot.

Fortunately, Dayja seemed to know what he was doing. His crazily winding path through the spaceport's commercial section somehow managed to avoid inspectors, officials, port guards, watch droids, and everything else that might impede their progress. They reached the outer edge of the official Imperial section—whose wall and defenses, Ronan noted, were far more elaborate and forbidding than those of the commercial section—without incident. Abandoning the speeder truck, Dayja led them to a temporary work shelter that had been erected over a scorched freighter hulk clearly far beyond any chance of repair. Inside the wreck, he opened up the hatch to the lower cargo hold, opened the camouflaged hatch in the hold's deck, led them through a dank underground passage and up and out again into an abandoned dispatch office. Another commandeered vehicle, and they were off on yet another twisted ride.

And then—suddenly and somehow paradoxically before Ronan expected—they were there.

"There's your freighter," Dayja said, gesturing to the slightly dilapidated vessel crouched on its landing skids, the name *Brylan Ross* in faded letters on the underside. "You've got half an hour before the loaders and stock checkers get back."

"We've got *what*?" Ronan demanded. "What are you talking about?"

"I rescheduled all the people who are supposed to be crawling over this ship so you'd have a little privacy," Dayja said, his eyes narrowing a little. "You're welcome. I suggest you stow the attitude and get on with it before they all wander back."

Ronan glared at him. That kind of unwanted initiative wasn't exactly praised under Director Krennic's administration, especially when such thoughtless actions could jeopardize more important operations. In this case, moving everyone away from the *Brylan Ross* could draw attention to both the freighter and its data backtrail, which could open up access to the whole Stardust supply line.

But Dayja hadn't known that, and probably wouldn't have cared if he had. And at this point, it was too late to fix it. Ronan would just have to hope the port workers didn't have a sense of curiosity.

"So what's first?" Dayja asked.

"We know some of the cargoes were switched out of other ships," Vanto said. "I suggest you and Assistant Director Ronan start there. I'll take a look at the hull, see if I can find any signs of tampering."

"What kind of tampering?" Dayja asked.

"Tampering designed to draw in grallocs," Vanto said.

Dayja looked at Ronan. "He's kidding, right?"

"Unfortunately, he's not," Ronan growled. "Fine. I trust you can get us inside?"

Dayja gave a little snort. "What, a piece-of-junk freighter like *this*?"

"It happens to be under the auspices of the Stardust project," Ronan said stiffly. "As such—"

"Yeah, yeah," Dayja interrupted, turning and heading for the forward hatch. "Come on."

One of the conditions Director Krennic had insisted on when he first agreed to ship Death Star material through Esaga sector was that Governor Haveland provide the best security available, not just for the ports but also for the freighters themselves. Ronan had already seen the kind of back doors Tiquwe contained; now he discovered that Stardust's freighter security was equally sloppy. It took Dayja barely ten seconds to slice the hatch lock, and another ten to disable the supposedly undetectable and unbreachable backup alarm system.

Director Krennic, Ronan knew, would not be happy about the situation. But for now, the lack of decent security was working in their favor.

Assuming, of course, that Thrawn and Vanto were right about this ship.

"You have an inventory list to check against?" Dayja asked as he headed aft toward the main hold. "Or do you need me to pull one up for you?"

"I don't care what's supposed to be here," Ronan growled, dropping his carrybag by the hatch and following. "I only care about what's actually in the boxes."

"Okay," Dayja said. "Fine. Just lead the way, and tell me what you want me to do. I get paid no matter what."

Glowering, Ronan pushed past him in the narrow passageway and stomped into the hold. Probably nothing in there but food, clothing, and cooking supplies. Vanto had been the one who claimed there were turbolaser parts, and Ronan had just seen how glibly Vanto could lie when he wanted to.

In fact, this whole soap bubble was probably just Vanto trying to get in good with his former commander while making Ronan and Director Krennic look bad in the bargain. He'd probably never expected Thrawn would actually send him to Aloxor.

The crates were lined up neatly on both sides of the hold's center aisle, six high, crash-webbed in place. "Where do you want to start?" Dayja asked.

"Anywhere you want," Ronan said. The easiest ones to get to would be those on the top, he decided. He could grab one of the loadlifters racked underneath the tool bar at the back of the hold, move it to the top box, use something to carefully pry open the top—

He jerked as the sound of splintered plastic came from behind him. He spun around to find Dayja casually slicing into the front of one of the crates second up from the bottom with a fold-up knife. "What are you *doing*?" he demanded. "Stop that!"

"Top one's too obvious," Dayja said calmly, ignoring the order. "Lazy inspectors start there and work down a couple before they lose interest and pass on the rest."

"Dayja—" Ronan started toward him.

And stopped abruptly as Dayja lifted his knife away from the crate and waved it casually in Ronan's general direction. "Careful—flying splinters," he warned. "Clever inspectors sometimes start at the bottom and work their way up, but it takes so long to shift the crates that they usually only get through the bottom row before they run out of time."

He finished cutting into the crate and pulled off the front, revealing what looked like the parts of a disassembled laser cooker. "A really suspicious inspector might start at the middle, and a conscientious one will look at everything," he continued, peering at the cooker's pieces and carefully inserting the tip of his knife between two of them. "So I usually start with second or third up from the bottom. That's where smart people like to hide things."

"I don't suppose it occurred to you," Ronan said between clenched teeth, "that if it turns out there's nothing there, one look at that and the port inspectors will lock the ship down so fast it'll make the Emperor's head spin."

"Careful," Dayja warned. He leaned on the knife hilt, and a small radion tube popped out of the packing material. "In some quarters, that could be seen as treasonous talk. Anyway, *you're* the one who said there was contraband."

"*I* did not say that," Ronan insisted, wincing as the tube clattered onto the deck. "It was Vanto and Thrawn who said it."

"My mistake," Dayja said, flicking on the knife's tiny spotlight and peering into the opening. "I guess Vanto and Thrawn get all the credit, then."

"All the—*what*?"

"The credit," Dayja said, reaching into the opening and pulling out a heavy-looking double-flared cylinder, "for spotting this. I don't know what it is, but it's sure as hell not part of a laser cooker."

Ronan stepped forward, his frustration evaporating into sudden dread. "Does it have a part number?" he asked as he pulled out his datapad.

"Yeah," Dayja said, turning the cylinder over and angling his light. "It's a TRL-44. Serial number—"

"Never mind that," Ronan murmured, staring at the cylinder. Vanto had been right. Vanto and Thrawn both.

Stardust had been compromised.

"You want me to open any of the others?" Dayja asked. He was gazing at Ronan's face, his flippant tone gone.

"No," Ronan said. He looked at the rest of the crates, his stomach churning. How many others, he wondered, were hiding stolen turbolaser parts? "No, that's good enough."

"Hey!" A distant voice drifted back from the bow.

Ronan tensed, relaxed again as he recognized it as Waffle's. "Back here," he called.

"Come to portside," Waffle called. "Vanto wants to show you something."

Vanto and Pik were waiting beside the midships portside thruster when Ronan and Dayja arrived. The outer shielding sleeve had been taken off, and some of the wires had been pulled out of their cable trays. "We're here," Ronan said shortly. "What is it?"

"Take a look," Vanto said, pointing at the opening. "That's supposed to be compressed argon gas for the maneuvering jets."

Ronan looked in. There was a long cylinder nestled in just under where the sleeve would be, green with angled white lines. "I'll take your word for it," Ronan said. "Are you saying it isn't?"

"Closer," Vanto said, tapping the tank with a finger. "See those small grooves?"

"Look like normal seams to me."

"But they're too deep," Vanto said. "I know how maneuvering tanks are supposed to be laid out—my family runs a shipping business. A little extra heat from this coil—this one right here—and that seam would pop."

"So some argon leaks. So what?"

"It's not argon." Vanto shone a light at the underside of the tank, and Ronan saw that he'd scratched a line through the coating shell along the length of the cylinder. "The cylinder's been painted over. See the markings? Red, yellow, red, white, red. That's Clouzon-36, not argon."

Ronan looked at Dayja. "He's right," Dayja confirmed. "I know the markings—hijacked Clouzon-36 is on our permanent watch list." He ran a finger over the green coating. "You're not supposed to be able to paint over this kind of marking, though. Other coloration isn't supposed to stick. Interesting."

"Must be something new on the market," Pik said.

"Must be," Dayja agreed. "Pirates and smugglers always get the good stuff first."

"There's more," Vanto said, again pointing into the opening. "Here are the control and power cables from the hyperdrive, right alongside the Clouzon-36 tank. That's the theory on the missing ships, right? That the grallocs start digging into the power cables and trigger the hyperdrive by accident?"

"Yeah, I see," Dayja said, peering closer. "The cables have been reinforced with extra shielding."

"A *lot* of extra shielding, actually," Vanto agreed. "So at the proper time the crew fires up the heater and lets the Clouzon-36 leak out. A gralloc smells it, comes roaring in, and attaches itself to the hull so it can eat the gas. The crew goes into panic mode, screams that the gralloc is shorting out the hyperdrive control—"

"Yes, yes, I got it," Ronan snapped. *Damn* him.

Damn all of them, for that matter. Vanto and Thrawn and Tarkin and Haveland and everyone else. So Stardust's equipment had been stolen and the equipment managers made fools of. So everything Director Krennic had thought about the gralloc problem was wrong. That didn't mean Vanto had to rub Ronan's nose in it.

He forced back the reflexive anger. No, that wasn't fair. Director Krennic had challenged Thrawn to eliminate the gralloc threat. The fact that he'd uncovered a criminal conspiracy instead was hardly a reason to resent or hate him.

But it also wasn't like this was over. Far from it. Ronan was sitting on proof of subversion, theft, and treason, and unless he moved quickly he would likely find himself facing down people who desperately wanted to remove that proof from existence. Along, probably, with anyone who'd seen it.

He looked up. The Star Destroyer was still sitting up there, trolling for pirates and smugglers.

Or was it? Had Grand Admiral Savit sent it to clean out the Tiquwe spaceport, like Sisay had thought?

Because Ronan couldn't see any shuttles full of stormtroopers dropping from the hangar bay to cause havoc. Was that instead one of Governor Haveland's warships, sent to watch for trouble with her next to-be-stolen freighter?

Or could it be both? If Haveland and Savit were working together . . .

Mentally, he shook his head. *Paranoia,* he chided himself.

But the lesson was clear. There was no one he could trust. No one except Director Krennic. Certainly none of the men currently standing beside him.

That problem, at least, would be easy to solve. "All right, I've seen enough," he said. "Dayja, can you call someone from the port inspector's office? No, wait," he added, as if a new thought had just occurred to him. "Better not put this on the comm system. Go find someone with authority and get them over here. *Quietly.* Vanto, you and the others stay here and watch this part of the ship. We don't want someone wandering by and wondering why that sleeve has been taken off or, worse, taking a hammer and wrecking the proof."

"What about you?" Dayja asked.

"I'm going to take some holos of the contraband," Ronan said. "We'll need proof to show the inspector if we're going to get anyone to take this seriously."

"Will you be safe in there alone?" Vanto asked. "Maybe you should take Pik with you."

"I'd rather he watch things out here," Ronan said. "Don't worry—I'll lock the hatch behind me." He gestured to Dayja. "Well, don't just stand there. Go get someone before this thing blows up in our faces."

"Right," Dayja said. "Back in five. Make sure you lock that hatch."

A minute later Ronan was inside, the hatch securely locked behind him. A minute after that he was in the cockpit.

Ten seconds after that he had keyed the start-up sequence.

Vanto would be furious, he knew. So, probably, would Dayja.

Ronan didn't care. There was no one in the entire Aloxor system he could trust right now. The only way to keep this discovery and the evidence safe was to get the freighter to Scarif and Director Krennic.

"Going somewhere?"

Ronan twisted around in his seat. Dayja was standing at the cockpit hatchway, leaning against the wall with his arms folded across his chest. "What are you doing here?" Ronan demanded.

"Oh, come on," Dayja said scornfully. "You may be able to fool a kid and a couple of death troopers, but really?"

"It's the only way I can keep the evidence safe," Ronan said, trying desperately to think. He'd heard that freighter captains sometimes kept blasters in the cockpit in case the ship was attacked and boarded. But where it would be hidden on this one—

"I agree," Dayja said. Unfolding his arms, he continued into the cockpit, squeezed past Ronan, and dropped into the copilot's seat. "I'm thinking Coruscant and ISB headquarters."

"I'm not," Ronan said, eyeing him uncertainly. "What about Vanto?"

"I told him there was a secure comm in the data transfer node around the corner," Dayja said. "He's on his way to whistle up my partner."

"You have a partner?"

Dayja shrugged, a little too casually. "Not recently."

"What about the death troopers?"

"One's with Vanto, the other's watching the ship," Dayja said. "Don't worry about them—they're unarmed, and all the muscle and martial arts training in the world won't do much against a ship hull. I trust you know how to pilot this thing?"

Ronan snorted. "Of course."

The final red light winked green, and he eased in the repulsorlifts. A glance out the side viewport showed Waffle standing well back from the freighter, staring openmouthed as it rose into the sky. Ahead, Ronan caught a glimpse of Vanto and Pik charging around the corner toward him. Their expressions were too distant for him to make out, but he could guess the basics.

He looked back at the navigational board, feeling a sudden and unexpected twinge of guilt. Vanto might be a deserter, but abandoning him in the middle of a spaceport was still a pretty shoddy thing to do.

But he didn't dare take Vanto or the others along. Anyway, the shuttle they'd flown to Aloxor should still be okay. It would be a long walk back there, but the pirates had their own problems right now, and he doubted the death troopers would have any trouble clearing a path for the three of them.

As for Thrawn . . . well, Thrawn would be angry, too. But again, Ronan didn't care. Once the Death Star was up and running, there would be enough slack in the navy budget again to get his Defender project funded. That should keep him happy.

"So where *are* we going?" Dayja asked.

"For the moment, that's classified," Ronan said, wincing. It was a good question.

Because as far as he knew, Dayja wasn't cleared to know about Stardust or anything else that was happening at Scarif. If Ronan flew directly there, it was a good bet that Director Krennic would order Dayja put into detention on general principles until the Death Star was operational and off on its first mission. Maybe he'd hold on to him even longer.

Yularen wouldn't be happy about losing an agent's services that long. Dayja himself would no doubt be furious.

Ronan sighed to himself. He was making more enemies today than he'd probably accumulated in his entire career. But it didn't matter. Director Krennic would be pleased with what he'd accomplished, and his approval was all that mattered.

Still, there might be a way to keep Yularen and Dayja off that new-enemies list. Ronan could stop somewhere along the way to Scarif, drop Dayja, and then take off again. Someplace under strong enough Imperial rule that a lone ISB agent without a support system wouldn't be in any danger, but disconnected enough from Stardust that no one involved in this plot would be there. Ord Pardron, maybe, or Radnor. A quick swing by one of those—

"Freighter *Brylan Ross*, this is the ISD *Stormbird*," a harsh voice burst from the cockpit speaker. "Identify yourself and your crew."

"What in space are they picking on *us* for?" Dayja muttered. He reached for the mike key.

"No," Ronan snapped, slapping his hand away.

"What's the problem?" Dayja asked, his voice suddenly suspicious. "You've got all the ID you need, right? Assistant Director *Ronan*?"

"It's not that easy," Ronan said, visions of plotters with shadowed faces and small but deadly knives flashing through his mind. "I need to know who this *Stormbird* is assigned to."

"Why?" Dayja asked, pulling out his datapad.

"Because this rot goes all the way to the top," Ronan said, looking out the viewport. There were other ships in the air, coming from all sectors of the spaceport, apparently going about their business without interference or challenge. The Star Destroyer had definitely and specifically targeted the *Brylan Ross*. "Thrawn thinks Governor Haveland herself is involved. If that ship is part of Haveland's sector group, we need to get away from it."

"Good luck with that," Dayja said, punching keys. "It's really hard to outrun a tractor beam."

"*Brylan Ross* captain, identify yourself or prepare to be brought aboard for inspection," the voice said.

Ronan hunched his shoulders. Dayja was right. Tractor beams were hard to dodge and impossible to outrun.

But they *could* sometimes be distracted.

He did a second, more careful visual sweep of the area. The spaceport itself was fairly flat, but there were some tall buildings along the rim. If he could get into the shadow of one of them, maybe zigzag between two or three more, the tractor operators might lose him long enough for him to angle away and hide among the other ships streaming out into space. Resettling his fingers on the yoke, he keyed the thrusters to full power and angled toward the nearest of the tall buildings.

"*Brylan Ross,* you are ordered to hold station!"

Almost there. Ronan braced himself for the jerk that would mean the Star Destroyer had grabbed him—

Abruptly, the freighter jerked to the side. Ronan swore, twisting the yoke over, trying to break the pull.

No response. He yanked the other way.

Only then, as he glanced down, did he realize his side of the board had gone dark.

Dayja had taken over control.

"What the *hell*—?"

"You ever flown something this big?" Dayja cut him off. He spun the yoke the other direction, forcing Ronan to grab for his seat's armrests. "I didn't think so. You want to get out of this? Then sit back and let me handle it."

Another twist, and Ronan was yanked the other way as Dayja sent the freighter cutting in a tight circle around the building Ronan had been aiming for.

Only instead of weaving around it and then heading toward another building as Ronan had planned, he did a complete 360 and headed back over the spaceport. "What are you *doing*?" Ronan demanded.

"You go weaving around the city and the local patrollers will shoot you down like a grumf," Dayja said. "Three things you have to remember about tractor beams."

There was another jerk, and Ronan felt himself shoved toward the deck as the Star Destroyer's tractor grabbed at them. Another quick twist on the yoke from Dayja and the freighter settled down again.

"First: Over a spaceport or other inhabited region, they're going to use low power and tight focus," Dayja continued, his voice casual. "That makes the beams relatively easy to break clear of."

Another jolt, and another quick maneuver from Dayja that got them out of it. "Of course, that won't last," Dayja said, "especially if you're making a pain of yourself. So second thing to remember—"

This time the jerk was much stronger, pressing Ronan even deeper into his seat as the tractor beam grabbed the freighter and started yanking it upward.

"—is that tractors don't just freeze you in place," Dayja continued, still in a conversational tone. "The laws of motion still apply."

Ronan frowned out the viewport. The freighter was indeed still moving horizontally across the spaceport even as it was pulled up-ward.

Though how that could gain them anything he couldn't imagine. If Dayja managed to weave the freighter out of the range arc of this particular beam, one of the Star Destroyer's other operators would simply take over, and they'd still be caught.

"And the last thing to remember is that operators almost always lock the beam as soon as they've made contact," Dayja said.

They were moving higher and higher, still angling across the spaceport—

"So if the beam gets intercepted—"

A sudden shadow fell across the *Brylan Ross*'s cockpit. Ronan looked up, just in time to see the larger freighter as Dayja slid them neatly beneath it.

"—then so does the lock—"

He twisted the yoke hard over, and the *Brylan Ross* banked into a tight curve and shot back out at right angles to its original course.

"—and sometimes you can lose them," Dayja concluded.

An instant later Ronan was pushed back into his seat as Dayja ran the thrusters up to a power level Ronan had never guessed was even possible in this kind of commercial vehicle. They were driving across the landscape—shot over the far end of the spaceport—wove in and out of another pair of freighters, one of which got off a nervous shot at them that fortunately went wild—angled up toward the sky and the stars just starting to become visible—

And with a jolt that snapped Ronan's teeth together, the freighter was again grabbed.

Dayja twisted the yoke. The *Brylan Ross* jerked like a caught fish, but it stayed in the tractor's grip.

Dayja huffed out a breath and shrugged. "Well," he said, as he shut down the thrusters, "I *did* say *sometimes*."

Ronan let out a shuddering breath of his own. "What now?"

"You grab your bag and put on your fancy assistant director uni-form," Dayja said. "Cape, too. You *do* have one of Krennic's silly capes, right?"

"It was issued with the uniform," Ronan said stiffly. He was tense enough right now without having to listen to snide comments from an ISB flunky.

"Good," Dayja said. "People in authority love capes. That should give you enough credibility that they'll sit still for your explanation of all this. Just make it fast."

Ronan felt his eyes narrow. "How much of a hurry are we in?"

"Enough of one," Dayja said. "The *Stormbird*'s part of Savit's Third Fleet . . . but if they're here watching over the Stardust transports, it's because Governor Haveland asked them to. That means they'll be sending her a message as soon as they've gotten us aboard. If they haven't done that already."

"And then we'll be turned over to her?"

"If not her directly, then whichever one of her staff coordinates these shipments."

Ronan stared out the viewport at the last of the blue sky as it turned into starry black. Proof of treason, and the Stardust assistant director who'd found that proof . . . and no one with any rank or status knew Ronan was here. No one except Thrawn.

"We need to talk to Savit directly," he said. "Not one of his officers, but the grand admiral himself. We need to plead our case to someone who can't be intimidated or disappeared."

"Whoa," Dayja said. "It's not *we*, friend. It's *you*. You leave me out of this. My name, my position, my status—none of that gets mentioned. Clear? I'm just the guy Mole who you hired to fly this thing to Coruscant."

"Why?" Ronan demanded. "You're ISB, and you've seen the evidence of treason."

"And if Haveland finds out about that, I'll be disappeared a lot faster than you will," Dayja said grimly. "ISB hasn't exactly endeared itself to the Empire's power structure. As soon as Haveland finds out I haven't had a chance to check in with anyone, I'll be done."

Ronan looked at the comm section of the board, feeling a sudden stir of hope. If they could get a message to Thrawn—

"And Star Destroyer tractor beams usually have jamming fields folded into them," Dayja added. "So no, we can't call anyone."

Ronan hissed between his teeth. "So it's up to us?"

"Yep," Dayja said. "Us, and maybe Vanto and his death trooper guard, if they get clear and make it back to Thrawn in time."

"Of course," Ronan murmured. Eli Vanto. Deserter and traitor. A man Ronan had promised to his face to bring up on charges. "Yes. I'm sure we can count on him."

CHAPTER 17

Thrawn had been aboard the conjoined Grysk ships for nearly three hours when Hammerly called Faro over to her station.

"I'm not sure what it means, Commodore," the sensor officer said, "but one of my people just picked up a small occultation."

"How close was it?"

"Not very," Hammerly assured her. "About twelve hundred kilometers."

"Dust?"

"It didn't look like it, ma'am," Hammerly said. "Or like a clump of normal solar wind particles, either. It may not be anything, but it was . . . worrisome enough . . . that I thought I should tell you even though we don't have much data yet."

"Absolutely," Faro confirmed. "How long before we get an analysis?"

"It's running now," Hammerly said. "Do you think we should contact the admiral?"

"Not yet," Faro said. "You know how he gets when he's in deep analysis mode. Besides, communication with the Grysk ship's been spotty—lot of big heavy containers over there creating comm shadows. Let's wait until we have something solid to report before we bother him."

She looked out the side viewport. On the other hand . . .

"Helm, do you have Hammerly's anomaly on your board?" she called.

"Yes, ma'am," Agral called back.

"Bring the *Chimaera* around," Faro ordered. "Put us between the anomaly and the conjoined ships, bow toward the anomaly. Pyrondi, forward turbolaser crews on full alert. Hammerly, full active sensors. If there's something out there, I want to be ready for it."

"Acknowledged, Commodore."

The minutes ticked by. The *Chimaera* took up its new position, and the status boards confirmed that Pyrondi's weapons and crews were ready. Faro resumed her place on the command walkway, her eyes sweeping the sky. Imperial cloaking technology was limited, with several ways a good sensor operator could punch through it. Grysk tech, unfortunately, was proving a harder nut to crack. Maybe when the navy experts dissected the cloaked gravity-well generator the *Chimaera* had captured near the observation post, they'd find a weakness.

Or if Coruscant couldn't do it, maybe the Chiss could. Was that why Thrawn had let Ar'alani and the *Steadfast* take the second generator?

Or was it that he always put his own people first, as so many persistent rumors claimed?

Could that be why he'd blocked Faro's promotion to command Task Force 231? Had she unwittingly done something to annoy the Chiss?

"What is the matter?" a voice behind her demanded in Sy Bisti.

Faro scowled to herself. Speak of the devil . . .

She turned around to see Ar'alani striding up behind her. To her mild surprise, the admiral's face and posture weren't angry, as Faro had expected, but merely intense. Her eyes, too, were doing an orderly sweep of the sky in front of them. "I'm not sure yet, Admiral," Faro said. "Our sensors picked up a stellar occultation that might have been caused by a gas discharge in the distance."

"What kind of gas?"

"We're still analyzing that."

"Any objects nearby that might have caused the discharge?"

"None," Faro said. "Though a sufficiently large gas bubble might be able to hold together long enough to drift in front of a star."

"Not with this level of solar wind," Ar'alani said. "Have you informed Admiral Mitth'raw'nuruodo?"

"Not yet," Faro said. "We wanted to wait until—"

"Inform him now."

Faro nodded, her arguments about Thrawn's focus and availability evaporating in the heat of Ar'alani's stare. "Lieutenant Lomar, signal Admiral Thrawn," she said in Basic.

For another minute no one spoke. Faro shifted her attention back and forth between the viewport and Hammerly, hunched over her sensor console. That analysis better turn up pretty damn soon . . .

"Thrawn," the admiral's voice came over the speaker. "What is it, Commodore?"

"We've spotted an anomaly, sir," Faro replied, resisting the impulse to bring Ar'alani's name into this just in case Thrawn ended up being annoyed by the interruption. Faro had given the order, and that made the full responsibility hers. "An occultation caused by a small gas pocket or discharge—"

"Got it, ma'am," Hammerly spoke up suddenly. "It was nitrogen gas."

"How pure, Commander Hammerly?" Thrawn asked.

"Very pure, Admiral."

"It was nitrogen," Faro told Ar'alani in Sy Bisti.

Ar'alani spat out something vicious sounding. "Grysk," she snarled. "Grysk ships use nitrogen maneuvering jets. Commodore Faro, prepare a full spread of weapons fire—"

"Calm, Admiral," Thrawn said, his own voice glacial. "Commodore: Distance?"

"It was at twelve hundred kilometers when we spotted it, sir," Faro said. "But we don't know how fast it's going."

"Then let us find out," Thrawn said. He switched back to Basic. "Full turbolaser salvo along the vector between the anomaly and the joined ships, to be fired at my command."

"Yes, sir," Faro said, frowning, gesturing the order to Pyrondi. Twelve hundred kilometers was far beyond the turbolasers' normal combat range, at least for something carrying any decent armor. "Shall I also send TIEs to intercept?"

"You may send two if you wish, but keep them well clear of the vector," Thrawn said. "All ship's sensors and recorders are also to be focused along that line and set for full magnification."

"Yes, sir." Faro caught Hammerly's eye, got a brisk nod in return. That was Hammerly, always anticipating orders. "Major Quach?"

"I've diverted two TIEs from the outer sentry line, Commodore," Quach's voice came back with the odd tinny echo typical of TIE pilot helmets. Some TIE commanders Faro had known never left their shipboard command centers if they could possibly manage it. Quach, in contrast, climbed into a cockpit every chance he got. "Moving into position; weapons and sensors ready."

Faro nodded. "We're ready, Admiral."

"Very good, Commodore. Stand by . . . *fire*."

The sky out the forward viewport lit up as the brilliant-green bolts sizzled through the tenuous solar wind, the perspective making them seem to converge in the distance. A second salvo followed close behind them, then a third, and a fourth.

Nothing. "Widen your focus," Faro ordered. "Blanket the area two degrees off the vector."

"Acknowledged."

Faro threw a sideways look at Ar'alani. The Chiss stood unmoving, with no sign of the tension that was gripping Faro's own throat. The turbolaser blasts continued blazing across the sky—

"Got it, Commodore," Pyrondi snapped. "Looks like a cylinder—"

An instant later the blackness in front of the *Chimaera* erupted in the roiling yellow cloud of a distant violent fireball. "*Damn* it—sorry, ma'am," Pyrondi bit out. "It was *there*, and it didn't look that damaged."

"A self-destruct," Thrawn said calmly. "Triggered when the barrage disabled its cloaking field. Major Quach, were the TIEs able to get some readings?"

"Yes, sir, some pretty good ones," Quach said with grim satisfaction. "Transmitting to the *Chimaera* now."

"Commander Hammerly, start at once on a full analysis," Thrawn ordered. "Lieutenant Agral, use our two data points to calculate the speed of the projectile. Question: How soon would others coming from comparable distances at similar speeds arrive at the conjoined ships?"

Faro felt a sudden coldness run up her back. "Are you saying there are *more* of them, Admiral?"

"I believe there are, Commodore."

"A doomsday device," Ar'alani murmured in Sy Bisti. She looked at Faro—"The Grysks were prepared for their base to be captured. What they did not wish was for the base to be examined or looted."

"Indeed, Admiral," Thrawn said in the same language. "That's why I believe there are other such devices converging on us. The Grysks would not content themselves with only one such weapon." He switched back to Basic. "Lieutenant Agral?"

"Approximately four point three hours, Admiral," Agral said.

"Good," Thrawn said. "That should be sufficient time to arrange a defense."

"That assumes they're all scheduled to hit at the same time, sir," Faro warned. "Some of the bombs might arrive earlier."

"Unlikely," Thrawn said. "The point of the attack is to utterly destroy the conjoined ships and anyone examining them. A sequence of explosions, rather than a single massive blast, might leave sections intact. It would certainly warn off the investigators."

Faro shook her head. A group of cloaked bombs, presumably sent on their way by the warship before its destruction, and starting far enough back that the *Chimaera* hadn't detected the emissions from their thrusters. A leisurely attack, but one intended to be overwhelming. "I hope there's something over there worth that kind of effort."

"Oh, there is, Commodore," Thrawn said quietly. "There is indeed. They attempted to destroy all data before they fled, but such complete destruction is a difficult task even under the most optimal conditions. Unfortunately for them, the conditions here were rushed and apparently chaotic."

Faro looked at Ar'alani. "You've found a way to defeat them?"

"Patience, Commodore," Thrawn said, a hint of a lighter tone peeking through the darkness in his voice. "I have barely begun my investigation."

"Yes, sir," Faro said. An investigation that was going to be over way too soon if they didn't come up with a way to detect and stop the incoming bombs.

"I'll return at once to the *Chimaera*," Thrawn continued. "Convene a meeting of all senior officers. We have four hours to find a solution."

"Let me get this straight," Savit said, looking between the two flickering figures floating above his holopad. "You've captured a freighter that supposedly has proof of sabotage or theft, and a man who says he's a senior official of the Stardust project. And you can't tell me whether either of those claims is true?"

"It's . . . complicated, sir," Captain Lochry hedged.

"Not in the least," Governor Haveland insisted. "This man and this ship were apprehended in *my* jurisdiction. Captain Lochry's confusion is irrelevant: *I* get to decide what's done with them."

Savit kept his eyes on Lochry. "Complicated how, Captain?"

"This Assistant Director Ronan—"

"This *alleged* Assistant Director Ronan," Haveland cut in.

"Yes, let's address that first, shall we?" Savit said. "I trust you've been in contact with Stardust?"

"Yes, sir," Lochry said. "I tried to reach Director Krennic, but his office tells me he's in conference with the Emperor and can't be disturbed. The most senior official I could actually talk to said that Ronan is off on some special assignment."

Savit pursed his lips. How many other people, he wondered, knew that Ronan had indeed gone to oversee Thrawn's gralloc investigation?

Probably not many. Certainly not anyone else in this conversation.

Knowledge was power. Especially knowledge no one else had, and no one else knew you had. "Any confirmation of his claim that he was sent off with Grand Admiral Thrawn?" he asked.

"No one I spoke to knew anything about that."

"Did it happen to occur to you to try talking to Thrawn himself?" Haveland asked acidly.

"Yes, Governor, it did," Lochry said, his face hardening. "The *Chimaera* is apparently out of contact, probably in some deserted system where HoloNet access is weak or nonexistent."

"Not in *my* sector."

"In *anyone's* sector," Lochry shot back. "Uninhabited systems that no one travels to aren't worth the expense—"

He broke off, visibly gathering himself. Lochry had served in Esaga sector when Havelock's father had been governor, Savit knew, and some residual hard feelings apparently remained. "At any rate," Lochry continued in a calmer tone, "our *alleged* assistant director is asking to be delivered directly to *you*, Admiral, and not to Governor Haveland."

"Ridiculous," Haveland bit out. "Prisoners don't get to dictate the terms of their treatment."

"Did he say why?" Savit asked.

"He was impressively vague on that point," Lochry said. "But I got the impression that he feared for his safety."

Savit felt his lip twist. His safety, or perhaps the safety of his prize.

Hardly unreasonable. Haveland had worked hard to have one of Stardust's supply lines run through her sector. Suggestions that her people weren't doing their jobs would not be well received at the governor's mansion.

Actual solid proof of malfeasance would undoubtedly be met with something even stronger.

"Do you believe him?" Savit asked.

Lochry hunched his shoulders in an uncomfortable shrug. "I don't know, Admiral. His ID looks good, his face matches the records, and his uniform is the right one."

"All of which can be bought," Savit pointed out.

"Yes, sir, exactly," Lochry said. "But then there's the business at the spaceport. The expertise demonstrated during the *Brylan Ross*'s escape attempt was far outside the skill set one would expect of a high-level bureaucrat. He even knew about the boost level in the freighter's thrusters and how to access it."

"I thought you said he had a pilot."

Lochry snorted. "Right," he said scornfully. "A no-account drifter with a no-point history and no-hope future."

"You ran his ID?"

"Oh, yes, sir," Lochry said. "Name's Mole. About as checkered a past as you can get. Cross-checking with the Tiquwe records pinned him as currently working for one of the pirate groups in town, probably as a slicer or expendable bumper. Got a history of spice use, too. Fair chance Ronan had to wake him up and carry him bodily to the freighter."

"He wasn't the pilot, then?"

"I don't see how," Lochry said. "He was drifting in and out during his interrogation."

"Enough," Haveland said sternly. "I don't care about whatever dregs you've pulled out of the drain. What I care about is this impersonator, and since Esaga sector is my jurisdiction it's my decision. If Captain Lochry doesn't want to go to the trouble of delivering the prisoners, I'd be happy to send one of my ships to take them off his hands."

"I appreciate your thoughtfulness," Savit said. "But for now, I think we'll let Captain Lochry keep them. If we're able to contact either Director Krennic or Grand Admiral Thrawn, we may be able to clear this up without further bother on anyone's part."

"That's not even remotely a possibility, and you know it," Haveland growled. "The man is a criminal, a liar, and a saboteur. I demand that he be turned over to me immediately."

"Your request is so noted," Savit said coolly. "If you wish to appeal to the Emperor, you may do so. Until then, I stand by my decision." He reached for the comm switch. "Thank you, Governor Haveland. I'll be in touch."

"Admiral—"

Savit tapped the switch, and Haveland's image vanished.

"She is a pip, isn't she, sir?" Lochry growled, his holo finally letting loose with the contemptuous expression he'd so obviously been holding back while Haveland was still in the conversation.

"She's a woman who sees a threat to her little domain and is scrambling to protect it," Savit said. "Quite predictable, really. What do you think of her claim that your Ronan impersonator is a saboteur?"

Lochry's eyebrows went up a couple of millimeters. "You don't think he's really Ronan, either?"

"I've met Director Krennic," Savit said, letting out some disdain of his own. "I can't imagine for a minute he would send an administrator hunting for sabotage or theft or whatever he thought he was doing on Aloxor."

"I suppose," Lochry said. "As to the sabotage . . . I don't know that, either. He freely admits they pulled off the outer thruster sleeve, but as near as I can tell all he's proven is that someone was trying to use the *Brylan Ross* to smuggle an extra tank of Clouzon-36. There may be more of it stashed elsewhere, but if there's a crime here I don't want to go poking around and possibly contaminate the evidence."

"Quite right," Savit agreed. "Best to leave the freighter exactly as it is."

"Yes, sir," Lochry said, nodding. "I've got it cordoned off in a corner of the hangar bay with a squad of troopers guarding it."

"Good," Savit said. "Well. I admit I'm intrigued by all this. I think it's time to see this man for myself."

"Sir?" Lochry asked carefully. "I thought you'd agreed that I'd hold on to the prisoners for now."

"I've reconsidered," Savit said. "Whoever they are, it sounds like they're genuinely afraid of Haveland. That suggests that the prudent course would be to get them as far out of her reach as possible. Rendezvous with me—" He peered at his navigational chart. "Let's make it the Sev Tok system."

"Yes, sir," Lochry said, still sounding reluctant. "I'll set course immediately."

"Good," Savit said. "And as long as I'm taking the prisoners, I might as well take the freighter, too. The whole litter in one pen, as it were. Make sure it's prepped to be transferred over by the time I arrive."

"Of course, Admiral," Lochry said.

"And don't look so glum," Savit chided with a small smile. "The reason you were at Aloxor in the first place was that Haveland insisted that we watch over her cargo for her. It's only fair that whatever glory comes from catching this thief or saboteur should reflect on us, not a lazy moff who couldn't be bothered to handle her own security."

"I suppose so," Lochry said. "Especially if some of that glory comes in the form of not letting them get killed?"

"Indeed, Captain. Indeed."

CHAPTER 18

The walk back through the Tiquwe spaceport to the pirate and smuggler section was long and wearying. Fortunately, the pirates and smugglers infesting that part were too busy getting ready for the anticipated Imperial raid to bother with strangers.

Which was just as well for them. The mood Eli was in, he would have welcomed any excuse to turn the death troopers loose and slaughter every single one of them.

What the *hell* kind of game was Ronan playing at? Ditching Eli and the others, and flying off on his own?

Especially since he might not even have gotten away. It had been hard to tell from the ground, but it had sure looked like the *Brylan Ross* doing the tractor beam dance with that Star Destroyer overhead. Had Ronan tried to escape and botched the job?

Or was it something more sinister? All that jinking and maneuvering—Pik had said he spotted Dayja in the cockpit as the freighter was lifting off. Had that crazy flying been Ronan and Dayja fighting for control? Had one of them wanted to take the ship to the Star Destroyer while the other didn't?

And if so, which one of them had won the struggle?

Eli didn't know. But the only conclusion that made sense was that one of the two was secretly working with the thieves.

But again, which one? And why?

The flight off Aloxor was nerve racking. If Ronan was the one who'd surrendered the *Brylan Ross* to the Star Destroyer, then by now the Imperials knew all about the shuttle they had arrived in. If they wanted to make a clean sweep of it, it would be trivial to pluck the shuttle out of the sky.

But no challenges came. Pik joined with the rest of the traffic flow, right under the Star Destroyer's nose, and made the jump to light-speed without interference.

Leaving Eli still wondering what had happened.

The questions would probably have driven him crazy on the trip back to the Grysk observation post except for one thing. Thrawn was there, and Thrawn would be able to figure it out.

Only Thrawn wasn't there. Nor was the *Chimaera*.

"First Officer Khresh says the *Chimaera* left to go chase down the Grysk supply ship that got away from us," Eli told the death troopers after a short conversation with the *Steadfast*. "That was a few hours ago, and they haven't heard anything since."

"Really," Waffle growled, eyeing the Chiss ship.

"I don't like it," Pik said flatly. "Fair bet that other admiral—Ar'alani—sent him off on a fake chase."

"I doubt it," Eli said. "Khresh says she went with him."

Pik swiveled around in the pilot's seat to stare at him. "Ar'alani went *with* him?"

"That's what Khresh said," Eli confirmed. And not just Ar'alani, but also Vah'nya.

And *that* was the part that particularly worried Eli. Vah'nya was a one-of-a-kind navigator, and he knew how protective Ar'alani was of the young woman. The situation must have been extraordinary for the admiral to let her out from behind the *Steadfast*'s weapons and deflectors. Especially aboard a foreign ship.

The two death troopers were talking quietly together. "Is there a question?" Eli asked.

"We're deciding what to do next," Pik said. "Best course is to head back to Aloxor, contact the local governor, and get someone to send a ship to hunt down the *Chimaera*."

"We have a perfectly good ship right here," Eli reminded them, gesturing out the viewport at the *Steadfast*.

Waffle snorted. "No."

"We're death troopers, Vanto," Pik said. "We don't go aboard non-Imperial ships unless our Primary does."

"Okay, fine," Eli said. "You can wait here after you drop me off."

"Did you hear what I said about non-Imperial ships?" Pik asked.

"You don't have to go aboard."

"That includes non-Imperial hangar bays."

Eli glared at the back of his head. "Grand Admiral Thrawn is your Primary," he said tartly. "He assigned you to protect me. Unless you think dropping me near the *Steadfast* in a vac suit and letting me swim the rest of the way comes under that heading, you'll take me into the hangar bay as I asked. After that, if you want to go to Aloxor, that's fine with me. Or you can sit here by the observation post and wait for the *Chimaera* to return. Your choice."

The two men exchanged looks. "Fine," Pik growled. "But we're staying aboard the shuttle. You'll be on your own."

"That's fine," Eli said. "I'm sure they'd prefer you do that anyway."

"I'm sure they would," Pik said. "Call them and get clearance for us to dock."

"Thank you for seeing reason," Eli said. "And I already did."

First Officer Khresh was waiting as Eli left the shuttle and stepped into the hangar bay. "Welcome back, Lieutenant," Khresh said, the words and tone perfunctory. "We have a potential crisis that we need your assistance with."

"Admiral Ar'alani?" Eli asked.

"Yes," Khresh said. "She's been gone too long, and some of the crew are becoming uneasy."

Translation: Mid Commander Tanik was pushing at him to do

something, possibly stirring up members of his family and their allies to add their own pressure to the mix. That kind of political maneuvering and infighting was supposedly forbidden aboard military
vessels, but with the heightened tensions simmering back in the Ascendancy that policy was starting to show cracks. "I'm sorry, but I
don't know where they went," he told Khresh.

"Of course you don't," Khresh said impatiently. "But we know that
she and Mitth'raw'nuruodo went to find the Grysk forward base.
The only person aboard the *Steadfast* who knows how to find it is
Navigator Un'hee."

"Then all you need to do is ask—"

"She'll only talk to you."

Eli blinked. "To—*what*?"

"She says she'll only take the *Steadfast* to that place if you ask her,"
Khresh said, the frustration that had been lurking beneath the surface boiling over. "You are—" He muttered something Eli's Cheunh
lessons hadn't covered. "She'll only talk to you."

"I'll be happy to speak with her," Eli said. "Where is she, the navigators' section?"

"The admiral's office," Khresh said. "I thought the surroundings
there might spark thoughts of loyalty and duty."

Eli resisted the reflexive urge to ask if it had worked. Obviously, it
hadn't. "All right. Let's go."

The little girl was sitting in Ar'alani's contemplation chair, swiveled
to face the admiral's memory wall. She jerked a little as Eli and
Khresh came in and hastily turned the chair away from the wall. Her
eyes darted back and forth between them before settling on Eli. "Are
you Lieutenant Eli?" she asked tentatively.

"This is Lieutenant Eli'van'to," Khresh said, his voice stiff and formal. "He will speak with you." With a final unreadable look at Eli, he
turned and left the office.

Eli waited until the door had closed behind him. Then he took a
step forward, giving the girl his best smile. "Hello, Navigator Un'hee,"

he said. "As First Officer Khresh said, I'm Lieutenant Eli. I understand you wanted to talk to me?"

"Yes," the girl said, her voice soft and nervous. "Do they also call you Ivant?"

"That's my core name," Eli said. "Or it would be if I were a Chiss. Obviously, I'm not. In my culture, my friends and family would call me *Eli*."

"Eli," Un'hee said, frowning. "So just the first part?"

"Yes."

"Strange."

"Some of the things about us are strange," Eli conceded. "Of course, to us some of the ways of the Chiss are equally strange. But that's good. Learning about each other's ways and learning how we're alike despite our differences is a way to enrich our lives."

"Maybe," Un'hee said, her body seeming to hunch into itself again. "But differences aren't always good. There are bad differences among the Chiss. Some Chiss can't be trusted. Vah'nya showed me."

"She *showed* you? How?"

"Through Second Sight," Un'hee said, lowering her eyes as a shiver ran through her. "Our minds . . . entwined."

"I see," Eli said, nodding as it finally clicked. So Vah'nya had somehow touched Un'hee's mind through this Second Sight in order to find out how to locate the Grysk forward station from Un'hee. In the process, Un'hee had apparently gotten some of Vah'nya's thoughts and memories in return. "Did Vah'nya say you could trust me?"

"She told me you weren't Chiss," Un'hee said. "She said you don't stand on either edge, but act only for the whole Ascendancy."

"That's correct," Eli said, thinking about the various family-driven tensions aboard the *Steadfast*. "Admiral Ar'alani also acts only for the Ascendancy," he said. "As do you navigators."

"That's what Vah'nya said," Un'hee said. "But Admiral Ar'alani isn't here. Vah'nya said that if she wasn't here, I could trust you. Was she wrong?"

"No, not at all," Eli assured her. "You can absolutely trust me, just as I can trust you. But it's Admiral Ar'alani who needs you the most right now. She and the humans of the *Chimaera* have gone to destroy the Grysks who once enslaved you. But we don't know where they went, and some of the others are worried. You're the only one who can take us to her."

"Are *you* worried about her?"

Eli pursed his lips. "I'm worried, yes," he said. "But only in the sense of uncertainty. Without full knowledge, a person has to rely on trust and hope. Insufficient hope usually comes out as concern."

He nodded toward the memory wall, the collected trophies and mementos of Ar'alani's life and career. "But I'm not worried that Admiral Ar'alani's in overwhelming danger," he added. "I've watched her during the time that I've served aboard the *Steadfast,* and I know that she's smart, capable, and resourceful. More than that, she's in the company of one of the greatest military minds the Chiss culture has ever produced. Standing together, I don't believe there's a force in the universe that can defeat both Admiral Ar'alani and Grand Admiral Mitth'raw'nuruodo."

He raised his eyebrows. "I'd like to prove that to you. Would you help me prove it to you?"

"You want me to take the ship there?" Un'hee asked.

"Yes," Eli said. "Can you do that?"

The girl hesitated, and he saw her eyes drift to the memory wall. "All right," she said. "But only if you stand beside me."

Eli nodded. As soon as Un'hee went into the Navigator's Trance necessary to guide the ship, she would be essentially helpless, blind to anything else going on around her. If she was already nervous about who among the *Steadfast* she could trust, that situation could be overwhelming. "I'll stand beside you and protect you," he promised. "No one will approach or interfere. Not as long as I live."

She looked at him. Back at the memory wall . . . and when she turned back the final time, there was a new resolution in her eyes. "Navigator Vah'nya trusts you," she said, working her way to the edge of the chair and climbing down. "So does Admiral Ar'alani. I guess I can, too."

———

Khresh was pleased and relieved that Un'hee had agreed to lead them to Ar'alani and the Grysk forward base.

He was less pleased when Eli requested that he be allowed to wear a sidearm on the bridge during the flight.

For Khresh, it was a bending of standard protocol. For Eli, it was a non-negotiable obligation. Un'hee would only be able to function if she felt safe, he insisted, and only an armed protector could give her the proper sense of security.

It seemed to work. Eli's eyes were on Un'hee when Khresh finally gave in and called for a sidearm, and he could see some of the tension lines in her face smooth out. He walked with her to the helm; and as he stood beside her, the weapon strapped around his waist, she rested her hands on the controls, bowed her head, and slipped into her trance.

And the *Steadfast* was off.

"Did she say how soon?" Khresh asked quietly.

"She doesn't really know," Eli said, a bit surprised that the first officer's annoyance at him was already gone.

On the other hand, Khresh had gotten what he wanted. The *Steadfast* was on its way to find its commander, and Eli had noticed that for a lot of Chiss the path to reaching a goal was far less important than the goal itself.

That could be an admirable quality. It could also make for a very nasty kind of casual viciousness.

"Third Sight does seem to affect the time sense," Khresh said ruefully. "It makes proper preparation difficult." He looked sideways at Eli. "In some ways I envy your Empire's more well-defined navigational methods."

"It's not my Empire anymore," Eli said firmly. The idea that he was still loyal to the Empire instead of the Ascendancy was something he needed to push back against anywhere and everywhere it raised its head. It was the same battle, he'd long since realized, that Thrawn had been fighting throughout his life in the Empire.

The awkward question, and one Eli wasn't yet prepared to answer, was whether either of them had actually made the complete break they both claimed.

"Probably no more than an hour or two, though," he continued, deflecting the doubts back into a dark corner of his mind. "I'd go ahead and put the ship on full alert in half an hour or so."

"*Thank* you, Lieutenant," Khresh said drily. "I feel much better, resting now in the comfort of your wisdom and experience."

Eli gave a mental sigh. Apparently, some of the first officer's annoyance was still there.

"I'd also suggest you keep your recorders ready to go," he said, ignoring the sarcasm. "Whatever Admiral Ar'alani and Grand Admiral Mitth'raw'nuruodo are up to, I guarantee it'll be interesting."

The four hours Thrawn had allotted for planning and preparation were nearly gone. Now, with everything set, it all came down to waiting.

Faro hated waiting.

"Don't look so glum, Commodore," Ar'alani advised as she strode past Faro on her way to the forward viewport, where Thrawn stood motionless with his hands clasped behind his back. "It's simple physics. It will work."

Faro glowered at her back. The physics were hardly simple, but they were straightforward enough.

But like every good magic trick, the crucial part was in the timing.

For his next trick, Grand Admiral Thrawn will make a Grysk base disappear.

Ar'alani reached Thrawn and handed him the datapad she'd brought from Hammerly. Thrawn gave it a quick look, and for another moment the two Chiss held an inaudible conversation.

Faro watched them for a moment, wondering if she should walk over and join them. But Thrawn knew she was back here, and he would call if he wanted her. Shifting her gaze, she looked past them at the conjoined ships sitting just visible in the distance, still doing their slow rotation, poised for their part of the trick.

Ar'alani had wanted Thrawn to station humans aboard to handle the operation, arguing that Thrawn's own calculations offered a better than 85 percent chance that anyone aboard would make it through unscathed. Thrawn had countered with a reminder of the other 15 percent, and the point that there was no sense in risking the Grysk forward base *and* valued members of the *Chimaera*'s crew as well. The remote triggers, he had assured her, would be more than adequate to the test.

At the time, Faro had agreed with the decision. After all, they were her crew, too. But now, staring at the conjoined ships floating all alone and vulnerable, she wasn't so sure. If the Grysks had left a hidden comm jammer on a timer—or worse, if one or more of the incoming cloaked bombs were running jammers of their own—there would be nothing Thrawn and Ar'alani and all the rest of them could do except watch helplessly as the base was destroyed.

And if Thrawn was right about this being their best chance of finding a way to defeat the Grysks, that opportunity would be gone forever.

"Incoming!" Pyrondi snapped from her weapons console. "Large ship, bearing one thirty-one by forty-six, distance six thousand kilometers."

Thrawn and Ar'alani both spun around to face her. "Identification," Thrawn ordered.

"Configuration unkno—wait," Hammerly said, leaning close to her displays. "It's the *Steadfast*, Admiral."

Ar'alani straightened up—an impressively regal move, Faro thought with a touch of amused cynicism, that perfectly disguised her moment of raw relief—then strode back down the walkway. She stopped beside Lomar's station and unloosed a volley of rapid-fire Chiss words. A voice answered in the same language, and she sent off another string.

Out of the corner of her eye, Faro saw Thrawn beckon to her. Walking past Ar'alani, she joined him by the viewport.

"She's ordered them to stay where they are," he translated quietly, "and assured them she will give them the full story soon. Her first officer has pressed his desire to join in the operation. She has again ordered him to stay clear."

"Yes, sir," Faro said, wincing. Part of the past four hours' worth of work had been dumping the *Chimaera*'s garbage, carefully blasting the containers and contents to small particles, irradiating them to make them show up more clearly on Hammerly's sensors, and then spreading a uniform shell of that debris around the conjoined ships at a distance of twenty kilometers. Letting the *Steadfast* barge even close to the area might disturb that shell enough to destroy its usefulness. Even just coming alongside the *Chimaera*, which was itself sitting well outside the shell, would entail the use of thrusters and maneuvering jets that could send ripples into the drifting particles.

There was a breath of air on the back of Faro's neck, and Ar'alani was back. "First Officer Khresh isn't happy with the situation," she reported. "He fears a Grysk attack, and knows the *Steadfast* is too far away to offer proper support."

"But he obeys his admiral?"

"He is an officer in the Chiss Defense Fleet," Ar'alani countered stiffly. "Of course he obeys me."

"Good," Thrawn said, checking the chrono. "The time is nearly upon us. Commodore?"

"I'm ready, sir," Faro said, holding up the remote he'd entrusted to her.

A remote, and a responsibility, that she'd frankly expected Ar'alani to object to. After Ar'alani lost the argument about stationing humans on the conjoined ships, Faro had assumed she would then insist that she or Thrawn handle the final stage of the operation, citing the slightly faster Chiss reflexes.

But Thrawn had handed the job to Faro, pointing out in turn that Faro had overseen the group that had set everything in place. Faro had expected a resumption of the argument, but instead Ar'alani had accepted it without so much as a dissenting murmur.

Though now that Faro thought about it, she'd seen a subtle shift in Ar'alani's distrusting attitude toward her over the past few hours.

Maybe being thrown together into a combat situation had quieted her previously low opinion of Imperials. Or maybe watching the *Chimaera*'s crew in action had changed her opinion of humans in general.

"Impact!" Hammerly snapped. "On the board."

Faro twisted her head toward the tactical, popping the safety covers on her remote as she did so. Thirty degrees around the starboard side of the conjoined ships, the particles of the radioactive shell had suddenly been shoved aside, creating a small but clearly visible hole. Even as she watched, four more holes appeared in the shell, followed immediately by two more.

"So there were eight," Thrawn murmured. "Commander?"

"Estimated impact: one hundred seconds," Hammerly reported.

Thrawn nodded, and Faro could see him mentally counting it down. *Will make a Grysk base disappear . . .*

"Number one," he said.

Faro pushed the first button.

At the *Chimaera*'s distance, there was little any of them could directly see. But the tactical and telescopic displays, plus Faro's knowledge of the prep work, painted a picture as clear as any of the artwork holograms in Thrawn's collection.

The three armored umbilicals connecting the conjoined ships disintegrated in unison, their centers blown into dust by the explosives the Grysks had planted on the ships, which had been gathered together by Faro and the *Chimaera*'s crew and moved to their current positions. Through the viewport Faro could see the subtle yellow flash, quickly swallowed up by the clouds of debris. The tactical display told a more complete story: The two ships had been completely and violently separated.

"Number two," Thrawn said.

Faro pushed the second button.

The tanks of compressed oxygen and nitrogen stacked inside the bases of each of the umbilicals were next, shattered by smaller explosions that sent the suddenly released gases expanding violently down the remains of the tubes like the most powerful maneuvering jets in the galaxy. With the ships no longer connected in mutual rotation, and with the extra boost from the pressurized gas, the two vessels began moving apart.

But slowly. Much too slowly.

Faro waited, her finger poised over the third button. Thrawn counted off a few more seconds . . . "Number three."

Faro pressed the third button . . . and deep within the no-longer-conjoined ships, the motors that drew in the tethers to the massive triad poles were activated.

The laws of angular momentum had been known since long before the first beings ever took to the stars. Faro had seen the physics in action many times, not just in tactical situations and maneuvers, but also with spinning dancers who drew in their arms in order to spin even faster.

In this case, the effect of the physics was twofold. Not only did the shortening tethers draw both the ship and its triad pole inward toward their mutual center of mass, thus speeding up the separation of the two ships, but the decrease in the distance between ship and pole also caused both their spins to speed up. Given the geometry of the system, an increase in rotational speed also translated into additional speed away from each other, moving both ships even farther from their original conjoined positions.

And in the space of a few seconds, the target the cloaked bombs had been aiming for had neatly vanished completely from the spot where it should have been.

"Occultation!" Hammerly reported. "Multiple events."

Faro smiled tightly. So the bombs *did* have rudimentary decision-making and maneuvering capabilities along with their equally simple sensor packages. Ar'alani had expected they would, while Thrawn had been less certain. Now, with their target suddenly no longer at the mutual focus of their vectors, the bombs were blasting gas from their maneuvering jets, trying to change course to compensate.

But it was too late. The newly separated Grysk ships were already too far away from their original positions for the bombs to change their vectors, certainly not in the time and distance they had to work with. Faro held her breath . . .

The explosions that had destroyed the umbilicals and separated the ships had been barely visible from the *Chimaera*'s bridge. The multiple explosions of the seven bombs as they expended their fury on empty space more than made up for that mild disappointment. The blast was big, violent, and—in Faro's imagination, at least—full of impotent rage.

The glow faded away, and for a moment no one spoke. Dobbs's voice from Fighter Command broke the silence first. "TIEs moving into sensor range," he said. "Scanning . . . minor surface damage indicated on the Grysk ships. Repeat, minor damage only."

Ar'alani turned to Thrawn and inclined her head. "Well done, Admiral," she said in Sy Bisti.

"Thank you, Admiral," Thrawn replied, inclining his own head in response. He shifted his eyes to Faro. "Excellent work, Commodore," he added. "Your placement of the explosives was perfect."

"Thank you, sir," Faro said. Ar'alani looked at her.

And to Faro's amazement, the Chiss actually smiled.

Faro smiled back.

How to make a Grysk station disappear.

Hey, presto!

This time, at least, Eli knew all the words Khresh said. He'd just never heard them strung together in that particular order before. "I told you, sir," he reminded the first officer.

"Yes, you did, Lieutenant," Khresh conceded. "I believe the word you used was *interesting.*"

Eli nodded. Privately, though, he had to admit the show was considerably more spectacular than even he had expected. Whatever was going on out there, it harked back to some of the old missions he and Thrawn had gone on together.

Frankly, he was rather sorry he'd missed this one.

"This is Admiral Ar'alani," Ar'alani's voice came from the bridge speaker. "Senior Captain Khresh, you may now bring the *Steadfast* in. On your way to rendezvousing with the *Chimaera*, you're to intercept and contain one of the two ships now floating free. Your choice as to which is easiest and most efficient to go after."

"Yes, Admiral," Khresh said. "We want just one of them?"

"For the moment," Ar'alani said, her voice going grim. "The other must be left free and visible to serve as bait for our visitors."

Khresh looked at Eli. "I gather you anticipate the Grysks will soon arrive in force?" he asked.

"I do," Ar'alani confirmed. "And when they do, Grand Admiral Mitth'raw'nuruodo and the *Chimaera* will join us in utterly destroying them."

Eli cleared his throat. "Excuse me, Admiral?" he spoke up. "Forgive the interruption, but I must speak immediately to Grand Admiral Thrawn.

"We have a slight complication to that plan."

"It's the *Chimaera*, Admiral," the woman at the comm station called. "Grand Admiral Thrawn wishes to speak with you."

"Thank you," Savit said, striding down the command walkway toward the aft bridge. At last. He reached the comm console and keyed for the contact, making a private bet with himself that Thrawn would use the display and not the holo. "Grand Admiral Savit," he said.

Sure enough, the holopad remained blank as the display lit up with Thrawn's image. "Good day, Admiral," Thrawn said. "I was informed you had attempted to contact me two hours ago."

"Indeed," Savit said, trying to read that smooth, nonhuman face. "I have a man here who claims to be Assistant Director Ronan of the Stardust project. He furthermore claims that you personally sent him to Aloxor on a secret mission."

"*Secret* may not be the precise term," Thrawn said. "But I did send him to investigate certain irregularities in the Stardust shipping operation."

"What sort of irregularities?"

"Theft and destruction of Imperial property," Thrawn said bluntly. "Manipulation of records. Consorting with pirates." He paused. "Treason."

"Interesting," Savit said. *Treason.* That word was bandied around far too frequently these days. "He's been rather secretive about his mission and its results."

"I'm certain his reticence is not personal against you," Thrawn assured him. "When would it be convenient for you to deliver him to me?"

"For *me* to deliver him?" Savit shook his head. "Sorry, Thrawn, but that's not how it works. If you want him, you'll have to send a shuttle to get him."

"And the freighter that holds the evidence he discovered?"

Savit felt his eyes narrow. How did Thrawn know about the freighter? Had Lochry mentioned it? "I thought it would be best if I held on to that for the present," he said. "Governor Haveland is most insistent that I turn the evidence over to her. *And* she wants Assistant Director Ronan, too. She claims that since the evidence was discovered in Esaga sector, she has full jurisdiction over the matter."

"You believe otherwise?"

"I won't know what to believe until Coruscant has ruled on it," Savit said, letting some contempt into his voice. "This sort of thing always boils down to politics." *Which you know so little about,* he added to himself. "Bottom line: You can send a shuttle, or you can wait until Ronan is shipped off to Haveland and take your chances on getting him back from her."

"I would think Director Krennic would also have a say in this."

"I wouldn't count on it," Savit said. "Krennic needs the Esaga supply line. It's too late for him to set up another one elsewhere if he wants Stardust finished on schedule. That means he needs Haveland, which means he has to play nice with the woman. If playing nice means one of his bureaucrats has to sit under house arrest in her mansion for a few months, that's what he'll do."

"That doesn't sound very loyal."

"*Loyalty* is a slippery term these days," Savit said. "Right now, the question isn't what Krennic might do for Ronan, but what *you're* going to do for him. Once he's in your hands, you can return him to Stardust if you want and neither I nor Haveland can do anything to stop you. So. What do you want to do?"

"Unfortunately, I can't send a shuttle to your current position," Thrawn said. "My ship and all of its resources are heavily committed at the moment. However, if you could rendezvous at the system whose coordinates I'm sending you, I can spare a shuttle and crew that long."

Frowning, Savit pulled up the system data Thrawn had sent.

And felt his breath catch in his throat. What the *hell*? "That's not really part of my patrol circuit," he said. "Why there?"

"It's a system you might find interesting," Thrawn said. "From your current position, you can be there in two hours. My shuttle will be waiting to retrieve Assistant Director Ronan."

"I'd like to oblige you, Thrawn," Savit said. "But I *do* have other duties."

"Then allow me to add to the incentive," Thrawn said. "That system also holds evidence of a threat against the Empire. An even larger threat is imminent, one that we together could easily face and defeat."

Savit pursed his lips. An isolated system, not even important enough to have a name, without inhabitants or probably even solid HoloNet access. A good spot for an ambush.

But the alternative was to turn Ronan over to Haveland.

And then there was Tarkin's veiled request that Savit assist Thrawn if he could. There should be a way to use that request to turn this situation to Savit's own advantage.

"Very well," he told Thrawn. "I'll be there."

"Thank you," Thrawn said. "My shuttle will be waiting." He reached off cam for the switch, and his image vanished.

For a long moment, Savit stared at the coordinates Thrawn had sent him. Then, with a brief scowl, he keyed them to the helm. "Helm: Set course for the indicated system," he called as he strode back into the bridge. "Best possible speed. Captain Boulag: Prepare my ship for hyperspace."

"We're abandoning our pirate campaign, sir?" the *Firedrake*'s commander asked, frowning.

"The pirates will wait," Savit assured him. "Signal the *Harbinger*, *Stormbird*, and *Misthunter* and send them the helm's coordinates. If we're going all that way, we might as well make a party of it." He smiled tightly at Boulag. "Grand Admiral Thrawn says there's a threat out there. We might as well look like we believe him."

For a long moment, the *Chimaera* conference room was silent. Carefully, worried that the slightest move might break the moment, Eli looked around at the others: Thrawn, Ar'alani, and Faro. The three most powerful people currently in this system.

So why was he here with them?

"So you're convinced?" Ar'alani asked.

Thrawn nodded. "I am."

"Yet you still intend to go through with it?"

"He must be given the opportunity," Thrawn said. "If he could be persuaded to join us, there would be no doubt about the outcome of the coming battle."

"And if he doesn't?" Ar'alani persisted. "Do you really know him?"

"I believe I know him well enough," Thrawn said.

"If you're wrong, one against many is a perilous situation to be in."

"Understood," Thrawn said. "But it has certain advantages."

Ar'alani raised her eyebrows. "Such as?"

"Heavy odds can create overconfidence in the enemy."

"Often that's not enough."

"But sometimes it is."

Ar'alani eyed him a moment, then turned to face Eli. "Lieutenant? Your comments?"

"I can't anticipate the end result, Admiral," Eli said carefully. "But I believe the plan is sound."

"And you believe the TIE Defenders will obey your orders?"

"I knew Captain Dobbs back when I was aboard the *Chimaera*," Eli said. "I think he'll trust me. More important, he's an officer of the Imperial Navy and immensely loyal to Grand Admiral Thrawn. Once he's received his orders, he and the others will obey them."

Ar'alani shifted her eyes to Faro. "And you, Commodore? Do you agree with your admiral's plan?"

"Yes," Faro said.

"You have no qualms?"

Faro's lips twitched in an almost-smile. "One always has qualms, Admiral. The key is to prepare as best you can, and not to let the doubts stop you."

Ar'alani looked again at each of them. Then, reluctantly, she inclined her head. "Then I, too, accept it," she said.

The words were firm. Her expression wasn't. To Eli's mind, it was obvious she still wasn't happy with the situation, or with Thrawn's proposed solution. But she was willing to go along with it.

"Then let us prepare," Thrawn said. "Lieutenant Vanto, another moment of your time, if I may."

"Of course, sir," Eli said, a knot forming in his stomach. What could Thrawn possibly want to say to him that he couldn't say in front of the others?

The two of them remained seated, Thrawn with his eyes on his datapad, waiting as Ar'alani and Faro left the conference room. The door closed behind them, and Thrawn raised his eyes to Eli. "I understand from Admiral Ar'alani that you'd hoped for more command authority aboard the *Steadfast*."

So it was going to be a dressing-down. "I didn't realize it was that obvious, sir."

"It was to her," Thrawn said. "You must understand that such things take time."

"Yes, sir," Eli said, thinking back to Thrawn's own long climb through the Imperial ranks. Then, it had been Thrawn who'd been the stranger among the humans of the Empire. Now it was Eli who stood as the foreigner among the Chiss. "Time, plus experience and trust." He frowned. *Trust.* "Is that why you asked Admiral Ar'alani to let me handle the Defenders for this battle?"

"That was a welcome side effect," Thrawn said. "But no, not directly. As you stated earlier, the primary reasoning was that Captain Dobbs knows you." He smiled slightly. "*And* that he trusts you."

"I hope so," Eli said, wincing. Because if he didn't—

"He does," Thrawn said. "I've already spoken to him. He is eager to play his part in the upcoming battle, and welcomes the chance to serve with you again." He paused. "And of course, you're also the only one aboard the *Steadfast* who speaks Basic with any fluency."

"Yes, sir," Eli said. He should have expected a solidly practical side to this, as well.

Still, Thrawn didn't *have* to have assigned the Defenders to the *Steadfast* for their coming battle with the Grysks. In fact, proper Imperial protocol probably forbade him from doing so.

But it was clear that he didn't want to leave Ar'alani to face the Grysks alone. And the Defenders would be a surprise, a hoped-for edge toward a hoped-for victory. "I hope I'll justify your confidence."

"I'm certain you will." Thrawn cocked his head to the side. "The project you're working on for Admiral Ar'alani. She hasn't yet told you its purpose, has she?"

"No, sir," Eli said, thinking back to his private resentment at being saddled with such a mundane task. Numbers, organization, analysis.

"Ask her after the battle," Thrawn said. "I believe she'll then be willing to tell you." He gestured toward the hatch. "And now Captain Dobbs and his pilots are waiting in the TIE ready room for you to give them their final briefing."

"Yes, sir," Eli said, standing up.

"In the meantime, I have to speak one more time with Colonel Yularen," Thrawn said. "The battle stands before us, Lieutenant Vanto. May warrior's fortune be with us all."

CHAPTER 19

Savit had expected Thrawn's coordinates to bring his four ships into the unnamed system somewhat closer to the primary. To his surprise, the *Firedrake* came out of hyperspace much farther out, beside an asteroid cluster.

Near a darkened space station clearly of unknown design.

Savit stroked his lip thoughtfully as he studied the bridge displays. So that part of the information he'd wormed out of Tarkin's office, at least, had been true. "Signal the *Harbinger*," he ordered. "I want Captain Pellaeon to move over to that station for a close-in sensor sweep." A thought occurred to him—"Tell him he can send over boarding parties if he wishes. We shouldn't need him out here."

"Yes, Admiral."

Savit turned back to the viewport, searching the sky for signs of the promised shuttle. Pellaeon was a good officer, but he'd never had quite the degree of personal loyalty that Savit liked in his subordinates. Sending him off to the station, away from what was about to happen out here, was simply a prudent thing to do.

"Shuttle approaching, sir. Bearing two seventy-two by fourteen."

Savit turned to face the indicated direction. A Lambda shuttle, by the looks of it, favored transport of high-ranking officers and politicians all across the Empire. "Signal the shuttle, Lieutenant," he ordered the comm officer. "Inform him he's to dock in Number Seven."

"Yes, sir. The shuttle is hailing you, Admiral."

Savit frowned. A humble, low-grade shuttle pilot had the gall to ask to speak personally to a grand admiral? "You can tell him—"

"Good day, Admiral," a calm voice came from the speaker. "This is Grand Admiral Thrawn. I'm here for your passenger."

For a fraction of a second Savit's tongue seemed paralyzed. He'd expected Thrawn to send one of his people, not to come here himself.

And suddenly the whole plan had gone off vector.

"I trust you will have him ready when I arrive?" Thrawn continued.

Savit found his voice. "Of course," he said. "I'll deliver him to you personally."

"Thank you, Admiral. I shall see you shortly."

It was a short walk to the detention center where Ronan and his pilot Mole had been sequestered. Ronan had been furious about being dumped in a cell; Mole had barely come up to full awareness for the procedure before drifting away again into his own private dreams.

Ronan was in his cell when Savit arrived, his earlier seething coming back to full glower as he saw the grand admiral's face. Mole, to Savit's surprise, was gone.

"It says he was taken away for further interrogation," the chief warder said, peering at his displays. "No name attached to the order."

Savit scowled at the record. Whoever had taken the pilot had indeed forgotten to log himself into the order. Unforgivably sloppy, and Savit would make sure Captain Boulag brought down the full wrath of navy procedure when they caught up with the culprit.

But there was no time now for that. Anyway, a no-name, no-future drifter would be relatively easy to dispose of. "Find him, and get him back in his cell," he ordered the warder. "I'm taking this one to the hangar deck for transfer to the *Chimaera*."

Out of the corner of his eye, he saw Ronan's face light up with fresh hope as he picked up his neatly folded cape from the sleeping ledge and fastened it around his neck. Good—that anticipation and relief should keep the prisoner docile along the way.

"Yes, sir," the warder said. "Let me get you an escort."

"No need—I can handle him," Savit said. "Just give me a blaster." If there came a moment when he and Savit were alone and Savit could plausibly claim the prisoner had tried to escape . . .

A moment later, a blaster belted at his right hip, his left hand firmly gripping Ronan's upper arm, they headed out.

Normally, the route Savit had chosen had several places where they were unlikely to be observed. Unfortunately, not knowing what Thrawn had had planned for him, he'd had the *Firedrake* put on full alert before they arrived. With no imminent threat, Boulag had scaled back the alert, and the corridors were unusually active as people moved back and forth between stations.

Which meant that Savit and Ronan arrived at the hangar deck without a single moment when they were alone.

Which was now going to be a problem. Savit's original plan had been to put Ronan and Mole aboard the shuttle and then shoot it down as it headed for deep space, claiming new information that showed the shuttle's pilot to be an imposter whose plan was to kidnap the Stardust official. At that point, he would express deep regret that his attempts to bring the shuttle to a halt had led instead to its destruction, accept the slap on the wrist the High Command would deliver, and the matter would be closed. He would take what he already had, shut down his private operation, and move on to something else.

But that was before Thrawn decided to come here personally. There was no way that the lone Chiss in the fleet could be mistaken for anyone else, and an equally zero chance that someone could or would impersonate him. Savit was going to have to come up with some other way to make this work.

Two of the *Firedrake*'s navy troopers were standing guard at the shuttle ramp when Savit and Ronan arrived. Thrawn himself was nowhere to be seen.

Savit permitted himself a small smirk. Probably still inside, wrapped up in the latest of the artwork studies that had made him the butt of so many jokes in the navy's upper ranks. Thrawn's supporters claimed it helped him learn his enemy's tactics; his critics figured he just liked pretty pictures.

Which didn't in any way excuse this breach of protocol. The *Firedrake* was *Savit's* ship, and Thrawn should have been waiting on its commander, not making Savit wait on him. "Tell him I'm here," he ordered the troopers as they came to attention. "If he's not out in ten seconds—"

"He's already gone, sir," one of the troopers cut in nervously before Savit could finish the threat. "He said he'd meet you on the bridge."

Savit stopped dead in his tracks. Thrawn was *gone*? "Why didn't you stop him?" he demanded. "*I* give the orders on this ship, not him."

"We—" The trooper looked helplessly at his companion. "He was just standing over there beside the fueling station. We thought he was joking."

"And then he was just gone," the second trooper said. "We thought—he knew you were coming, Admiral. We thought he would be back."

Savit's comlink signaled, and he yanked it from its holder. "What?" he snapped.

"Sir, this is the bridge," Boulag's voice came, his tone a little uncertain. "Ah . . . Grand Admiral Thrawn is here."

Savit clenched his teeth. "Tell him I'll be right there," he ordered. "And make damn sure he *stays* there."

Thrawn and Boulag were talking quietly together on the command walkway when Savit and Ronan arrived. Standing at the aft end of the walkway were a pair of stormtroopers, their E-11 blaster rifles held in ready positions at their waists. Keeping his grip on Ronan's arm, Savit walked between them and strode up to the two officers. "Admiral," he greeted Thrawn as civilly as he could manage. "I thought you were going to wait in the hangar bay."

"I reconsidered," Thrawn said coolly. "It occurred to me that our conversation would be better held here."

"We have nothing to talk about," Savit said. "You're here to pick up a prisoner, and that's all."

"With all due respect, Admiral, I think a conversation would be good," Boulag put in. "The *Harbinger*'s advance survey team has boarded the station, and Captain Pellaeon says—"

"That will be all, Captain," Savit cut him off. "The aft turbolaser status report should be finished. Go make sure everything is in order." He let go of Ronan's arm. "And take this one with you."

"I would prefer that Assistant Director Ronan stay with us," Thrawn said.

"This is *my* ship, Admiral," Savit countered.

"So this *is* the real Ronan?" Boulag asked, eyeing Ronan with new eyes. "We thought he might be an imposter. My apologies, Assistant Director."

"Admiral Thrawn's statement notwithstanding, that's what we still have to determine," Savit insisted.

"Along with other truths," Thrawn said. "Admiral?"

Savit glared at him. Unfortunately, whether by luck or design, Thrawn had effectively outmaneuvered him. Ten seconds ago, before Thrawn gave Ronan his stamp of approval, there would have been little to lose by letting the pompous fool say whatever he wanted to Boulag. But with that identification, even Boulag was smart enough to take Ronan's babblings seriously. "Fine," he said, taking Ronan's arm again. "He stays here. You have your orders, Captain."

"Yes, sir." With a final speculative look at Ronan, Boulag headed back down the walkway. He passed the two stormtroopers and disappeared into the aft bridge.

"Thank you, Admiral," Thrawn said.

"Yes, I'm sure you're welcome," Savit said. He made a show of looking around. "What, no death troopers? I'd have thought the least you could do after the Emperor so graciously assigned them to you would be to keep them around."

"Sometimes it's best to leave them behind."

"I suppose," Savit said. "A point of curiosity: How did you get from the hangar deck to the bridge without being seen?"

"Of course I was seen," Thrawn said. "Did you expect any of your officers would interfere with the activities of a grand admiral?"

"No, I don't suppose they would," Savit said, his lip twisting in contempt. "I see I'll have to have a conversation with them later about that. Now, what's this about an enemy threat?"

"We will speak of that presently," Thrawn said. "First, though, I wish to know why you have been stealing cargoes from the Stardust project."

Beneath his hand, Savit felt Ronan's arm muscles suddenly tighten. "I have no idea what you're talking about," he said, keeping his voice even and doing a quick mental survey of the bridge. He, Thrawn, and Ronan should be far enough forward on the walkway that no one in the crew pits could hear them.

"I believe you do," Thrawn said. "The first indicator was the incomplete data you gave me on the grallocs. You did not want us to realize the creatures were drawn to Clouzon-36, which was the lure you used to bring them to your chosen freighters. The second indicator was the fact that the turbolaser parts being stolen were from a new model. Only a high-ranking official would know of its existence, let alone which parts were required to build one."

"A moff would also have access to that information," Ronan put in. "Governor Haveland, for instance."

"The third indicator," Thrawn said, ignoring the interruption, "was your sudden interest in pirates in this region. While a reasonable enough undertaking for the Third Fleet, its actual purpose was to clear out competition so that your operatives could more easily work the relevant spaceports."

"Indicators aren't proof," Savit said. "And as Assistant Director Ronan has already pointed out, all of those paint Governor Haveland as well as they do me."

"No," Thrawn said. "The records of your ships' locations and their pirate raids correspond precisely with the list of spaceports the stolen freighters departed from. Governor Haveland has no power to order your activities so precisely. We also have records of which pirates you raided and which you did not, the names of the technicians working the spaceports, their affiliations, backtracked records of payments, and other means of linking them to you."

Savit snorted. "Coincidence and speculation. All of it. Nothing you could ever prove to a board of inquiry."

"Perhaps," Thrawn said, his voice going even quieter. "But there is one final indicator. The encryption your pirates were using to communicate with you and one another, and which the Grysks gained access to after the capture of the way station. Do you recognize the G77 encryption, Admiral?"

Savit dug his fingers into Ronan's arm. The fools. They'd had strict orders to erase not just the encryption but also all references to it in case of capture. Clearly, they hadn't.

"The encryption is reserved solely for use by the twelve grand admirals," Thrawn said. "No governors or moffs have access to it. Moreover, a search of the HoloNet records will be able to again make connections to the times and places of the stolen freighters."

His manner seemed to darken. "I suspect you blame the pirates who failed to erase the encryption before their capture. That is unfair. The Grysks are extremely efficient, and no doubt overwhelmed them before they knew what was upon them."

"Is he right, Admiral?" Ronan asked, his eyes now on Savit.

"I am," Thrawn assured him. "The only question remaining is *why*. Why did you subvert Stardust this way?"

"That doesn't matter," Ronan bit out.

"I disagree, Assistant Director," Thrawn said. "The reason matters very much."

"To whom?"

"To everyone in the galaxy except you, Ronan," Savit said contemptuously. "Tell me, Thrawn: Do you know how much of the navy's budget is being poured into Krennic's precious Stardust project?"

Thrawn shook his head. "No."

"I do," Ronan said. "And in my opinion, it's worth every credit."

"Then you're a fool," Savit retorted. "It's a horrendous sum, an incredible percentage of overall spending. And it's all for nothing."

Ronan's eyes narrowed. "What are you talking about?"

"I'm talking about the fact that Stardust is doomed," Savit said. "It may survive five years, or ten, maybe even fifty. But somewhere during its service lifetime, someone will figure out a way to disable or even destroy it."

"No," Ronan said firmly. "It's far too powerful for that. Too well defended." His face hardened. "Or it would have been before you started siphoning off the new turbolasers."

"Don't make me laugh," Savit growled. "I have the components for twenty-two of them. That's less than half a percent of the five thousand you're planning to install."

He looked at Thrawn. "Can you imagine what the twenty-two I've saved would add to the *Chimaera*'s defenses? Or the *Firedrake*'s, or the new *Star Dreadnought* class Lord Vader's been pushing for? What could you do with the weapons and matériel—with the sheer number of credits—that are going into Stardust? The TIE Defenders, certainly; but how many other vital projects have been scrapped to feed Krennic's insatiable appetite?"

"So you steal from Stardust in order to equip other ships?" Thrawn asked.

"I steal from Stardust so that not everything Krennic has poured money into goes up in smoke and flame or scrap metal," Savit said. "I want *something* from Stardust to end up being useful to the navy."

"So ultimately you did this out of loyalty to the Empire," Thrawn said.

"Is *that* how you see this?" Ronan demanded. "No. What he did was treason, pure and simple."

"Treason, yes," Thrawn said. "But hardly simple. Tell me, Admiral: What would you do if I offered you a chance to redeem yourself?"

Savit studied him. That blue face and those red eyes were hard to read, but he seemed sincere. "Explain."

"You have seen the evidence of enemy intrusion," Thrawn said, nodding in the direction of the distant station. "Those same beings are coming in force to another system nearby. Together our five Star Destroyers would turn a perilous situation into a decisive victory."

"Really?" Savit countered. "The way I hear it, you've already colluded with an enemy intrusion. That's not going to sit well with Coruscant."

"That situation can and will be explained to the Emperor's satisfaction," Thrawn said. "The fact remains that if we do not join in defending against the Grysks, the Empire will be put at risk."

"And you're offering me absolution for my crimes if I now march to your flute?" Savit shook his head. "Sometimes your childish innocence surprises even me. If this was your plan, you don't know me at all. You should have stuck to tactics and art and stayed out of politics."

"There is no chance you will alter your decision?" Thrawn asked.

"Don't beg, Thrawn," Savit said severely. "It doesn't become your rank." He rested his hand on the grip of his holstered blaster. "This conversation is over. I don't know what you imagined you could gain by forcing this to the bridge instead of waiting for us in the hangar bay. But it doesn't matter, because that's where we're heading now."

"Admiral, we've got an incoming Star Destroyer," the comm officer called. "It's the *Chimaera*."

Savit looked at the displays in disbelief. It was the *Chimaera*, all right, facing nose-on to the *Firedrake* and coming slowly but steadily toward him. "What the hell—?"

"Admiral Savit, this is Commodore Karyn Faro, commanding the ISD *Chimaera*," Faro's voice came stiffly from the bridge speaker. "I call on you to surrender yourself and your task force to me, and to prepare your defense on charges of treason."

"You asked what I hoped to gain by meeting you on the bridge, Admiral?" Thrawn asked softly.

Savit looked back at Thrawn. The blue face was still calm, but the glowing eyes seemed to have taken on a new intensity. "So tell me," he invited.

"It's very simple," Thrawn said.

"I wished for a better view of the coming battle."

―――――

". . . on charges of treason." Faro gestured, and Lomar muted the transmitter.

And with that, the chance cube had been thrown.

The bridge, Faro noted, seemed unusually quiet. Everyone could see the odds they were facing, and knew how much of a gamble this was.

Or was it? Was it truly a gamble?

After all this time serving under Thrawn, Faro still didn't have a solid answer. Did Thrawn routinely take incredible chances, like most people assumed? Or was everything coolly and meticulously planned out in advance, leaving the illusion of uncertainty but without its substance?

It was probably a combination of both, she decided. He planned where he could, and tried to stack the odds where he couldn't.

In this case . . .

Faro looked at her datapad. She'd read his instructions a dozen times since he'd boarded the shuttle and headed out for his meeting with Savit.

Time to find out how good those instructions actually were.

"Lieutenant Pyrondi?" she called. "Stand by first slingshot."

"First slingshot ready, Commodore."

"Slingshot: *Go*."

Considering the relative masses, there was no way Faro would feel any lurching beneath her feet as the tractor beams caught hold and accelerated the object toward the bow. But in her imagination she felt the lurch anyway. There was a slight, perfectly timed pitch of the *Chimaera*'s bow to move the ship up out of the vector, and it was done.

"Lieutenant Lomar, send the package," she ordered. "Then unmute me."

"Package sent. Mute off."

"Commanders and officers of the Third Fleet," Faro said. "I've just sent you the evidence we've collected showing Grand Admiral Savit's complicity in illicit activities. I call on you to review the material, and if you find it persuasive I urge you to join the *Chimaera* in demanding that Admiral Savit surrender himself for a board of inquiry."

No response. But she hadn't really expected one, at least not this soon. She headed over toward the weapons station, gesturing to Lomar to cut the transmission as she walked. "Are we set, Pyrondi?" she asked.

"Yes, ma'am," Pyrondi said. She was trying to hide her nervousness, but wasn't quite as good at it as Faro was. "Major Quach indicates TIEs are ready." She looked sideways at Faro. "I hope you realize, Commodore, that on pure balance-sheet analysis this can't possibly work. A single Star Destroyer against four is called a mauling."

"That presumes that all four are enthusiastic about joining battle," Faro pointed out. "The admiral doesn't think that will be the case."

"Commodore, *Misthunter* and *Stormbird* are moving up to support *Firedrake*," Hammerly called.

"You were saying?" Pyrondi asked with a ghost of a smile.

"Courage, Pyrondi," Faro said, smiling back. She raised her voice. "What about the *Harbinger*?"

"Still back at the Grysk observation post."

"There's your first crack, Pyrondi," Faro said. "Captain Pellaeon's not a blind follower, and Savit knows it."

"So we just have to hold off the other three long enough for Pellaeon to sift through the data?"

"Don't worry," Faro assured her. "Savit will wait for us to fire first. That gives us time."

She stepped back to the command walkway. "Lieutenant Pyrondi: Prepare for second slingshot. Quach: Prepare TIEs for Marg Sabl."

"Slingshot ready," Pyrondi confirmed.

"Marg Sabl ready," Quach confirmed.

"Lieutenant Agral, pitch twenty degrees down," Faro said. She watched as the *Chimaera*'s bow dipped, putting the hangar bay out of view of the three Star Destroyers in the distance. "Marg Sabl: *Go.*"

She waited, peering out the starboard viewport, counting off the seconds. The Marg Sabl was one of Thrawn's best-known maneuvers: deploying a group of TIEs unseen from the hangar bay, giving them time to assemble and then swoop around the hull in all directions and converge on the enemy.

Of course, being well known also meant that Savit was certainly aware of it. In fact, given that Faro was Thrawn's senior officer and protégée, he was almost certainly expecting it.

Which was, really, the whole point.

"Second slingshot: *Go*," Faro ordered. Through the viewport she saw the starboard group of Marg Sabl TIEs appear and sweep toward Savit's Star Destroyers. "As soon as the TIEs are clear, bring the bow back up to face the *Firedrake*."

With the first slingshot, there hadn't been anything for Faro to see. This time, though, the four darkened TIEs were visible for a moment as they passed the *Chimaera*'s bow, disappearing into the enveloping blackness as they continued their steady path toward Savit's force. In the distance around them, the Marg Sabl TIEs blazed blatantly through the sky, hopefully drawing all of Savit's attention.

Faro looked at her datapad. *Savit will not want it on the record that he attacked first. He will therefore wait for the* Chimaera *to do so. Begin with a Marg Sabl. Savit will recognize the preparatory maneuvers and watch for those TIEs to appear. That will mask your second slingshot maneuver of four dark TIEs.*

She looked up again, watching as the main group of TIEs began their leisurely sweep toward the *Firedrake*.

And hoped that Thrawn had indeed left her only the illusion of uncertainty.

CHAPTER 20

The *Steadfast* had been waiting, ready for action, for longer than Eli really felt comfortable with.

Waiting was always a chore. Waiting for combat was excruciating.

Now, at last, things were starting to move.

"There," he said, pointing at the tactical display.

"I see it," Ar'alani said calmly. "Mid Commander Tanik?"

"Small ship, too small to be heavily armed," the sensor officer reported. "Probably a scout. Definitely Grysk design."

Eli studied the ship as it cut across the *Steadfast*'s line of sight in the distance. If the main Grysk force came in at that same spot . . .

But of course, there was no guarantee that it would. In fact, once the scout popped back into hyperspace and delivered its report, there was every chance that the Grysks would decide to come out closer to the *Steadfast*, and from an entirely different direction.

Which left Ar'alani with a risky choice: to wait here beside the remaining ship of the Grysks' forward base, or to move away and avoid being jumped if the attackers decided to come in right on top of them.

First Officer Khresh was obviously wondering the same thing.

"That scout has seen us here, Admiral," he said. "We might want to change position."

On the tactical, there was a flicker as the scout jumped back into hyperspace. "We might, Senior Captain Khresh," Ar'alani said. "I turn the question back: Will our enemy *expect* us to move?"

"That depends on how smart he is," Khresh said. "Or perhaps how smart he *thinks* he is."

"As well as on his knowledge of Chiss and Chiss battle maneuvers," Ar'alani said. "Let's see just how clever he thinks he is."

"We stay here?"

"We stay here," Ar'alani confirmed. She raised her voice. "All stations: Prepare for battle. The enemy will soon be upon us."

She looked at Eli. "Lieutenant Vanto, are your fighters and your slingshot tractor operators ready?"

"Yes, Admiral, they are," Eli said. Or at least they were as ready as tractor operators could be who'd never actually performed the maneuver.

But they'd had no real choice. They had only the one cloaked gravity-well generator and couldn't safely practice with it. And without knowing if or when a Grysk scout might show up, practicing with anything else might give the enemy commander a glimpse of the operation and conceivably allow him to anticipate the maneuver Eli and Ar'alani were planning.

And that would be disastrous. That part of the battle plan depended on complete surprise, right up to the point when the attack was launched.

"Good," Ar'alani said. "Navigator Vah'nya?"

"I'm ready, Admiral," Vah'nya replied from the navigation station. She hesitated. "Admiral, may I have a word with Lieutenant Eli'van'to?"

Ar'alani sent a speculative look at Eli. But she merely gestured him toward the young woman.

Eli unstrapped and crossed to Vah'nya. She didn't look up as he joined her, but continued staring at her board. "I'm here, Navigator," Eli said. "Is there a problem?"

"I don't know," Vah'nya said, her voice low. "Perhaps. Tell me, do you think Grand Admiral Mitth'raw'nuruodo will win his battle in time to come to our aid?"

Eli hesitated, sensing a verbal and philosophical trap. For a proud people like the Chiss, even the idea that they would need to be rescued by anyone could be taken as an insult. "I don't know," he said. "But we don't need Grand Admiral Mitth'raw'nuruodo. We have Admiral Ar'alani and the warriors of the Ascendancy Defense Fleet ship *Steadfast*. We can defeat anything the Grysks choose in their folly to throw against us."

A small smile briefly touched Vah'nya's face. "You've learned the Chiss credo well, Lieutenant Eli," she said. "But you are still human." Her throat tightened. "Could you kill a navigator?"

Eli felt his mouth drop open. "Excuse me?"

Vah'nya took a deep breath, let it out in a soft sigh. "I've touched the mind of Un'hee," she said, almost too quietly for Eli to hear. "I've seen what the Grysks did to her. How they probed deeply into her mind and soul. How they found her deepest desires and fears, her most comforting memories and her most cherished hopes. How they twisted and tarnished and bent all of them to their will.

"How they broke her soul."

She paused. Eli remained silent, wishing that he had something of comfort to say. Knowing that he didn't.

"They are a terrible enemy, Eli," Vah'nya said. "Your Empire—your former Empire—forces its will on its slaves through soldiers and weapons and warships. But the Grysks . . . three can command a nation. A hundred can rule an entire world. Billions of beings, their hearts and souls broken, ready to fight and die at the order of a handful of aliens. No resistance, no revolt, no dissent, no hope."

She looked up at Eli, and he flinched a little at the sudden intensity in her eyes. "I won't let that happen to me, Eli. I won't let it happen to my four sister navigators. Nor will I let it happen again to Un'hee."

"I know how you feel," Eli said, a chill running up his back. Now, finally, he saw where she was going. "What do you want me to do?"

"You're aware that it's an immediate capital crime to kill a navigator," Vah'nya said. "It's been that way since the beginning of the Ascendancy. It's so ingrained in our society that no Chiss could even conceive of such an action."

"But I'm not a Chiss."

"You're not a Chiss." Vah'nya looked him straight in the eye. "If the time comes when there is no hope, when the *Steadfast* is a broken and dead hull, when the Grysks swarm through hatchways and breaches . . . will you promise to kill me and my sisters?"

And there it was. The question Eli had known was coming.

A question that had no good answer.

But now, as he gazed into Vah'nya's eyes, he knew what his answer had to be.

"I would never do anything to harm you, Vah'nya," he said quietly. "You're probably the only friend I have aboard the *Steadfast*, and I would give my life without hesitation to save yours." He braced himself. "But there are worse things than death, and being forced into service to the Grysks is one of those. If the *Steadfast* is truly without hope, I pledge to you that you and your sister navigators will never have to endure that living hell."

Vah'nya closed her eyes briefly. "Thank you. Let us both hope and work to ensure it doesn't come to that."

"Indeed," Eli said. He touched her shoulder reassuringly, started to draw his hand back.

Stopped as she reached up and took his hand in hers. For a moment she held it, and he could feel the tension in her muscles and the coldness of her skin. Then she let go and bowed her head slightly. "Thank you," she said again.

"Lieutenant Eli'van'to?" Ar'alani called, rising from her chair. "Return to your station."

"Yes, Admiral." Touching Vah'nya's shoulder one last time, Eli crossed the bridge again.

Ar'alani was waiting for him. "She spoke to you of her fear and request?" she asked.

Eli looked at her sharply, wondering how much she knew. But her face wasn't giving anything away. "Yes, she did."

"And you're prepared to deal with both?"

Eli swallowed. She knew, all right. She knew everything. And if Eli admitted that he was even considering a capital crime . . . "Yes, Admiral," he said. "I am."

Ar'alani's eyes held his a moment, then shifted to the status boards. "Then stand ready, Lieutenant. And let us hope that Grand Admiral Mitth'raw'nuruodo is as prepared for his battle as we are for ours."

Eli nodded. "He is, Admiral. He always is."

"Good." With a final look at him, Ar'alani walked back toward her command chair.

Eli watched her go. *She might die today.* The dark thought twisted into his heart. She might die. Vah'nya might die. But if they did, he was determined to do everything in his power to make sure they didn't die in vain.

And they absolutely would not die alone.

"This is madness," Savit said, his voice and expression puzzled.

His fingers were still locked into the flesh of Ronan's arm. But at this point, Ronan hardly noticed.

Because it *was* madness. The *Chimaera* couldn't take on four Star Destroyers by itself. That was simple mathematics. He knew it, Savit knew it, and presumably Commodore Faro knew it.

And yet not only was the *Chimaera* still moving toward them, but it had launched a squadron of TIE fighters.

Was Faro running a bluff? It was the only answer.

But she was a commodore, and Savit was a grand admiral, with all the gulf of rank and experience and competence such a difference implied. Savit was going to call that bluff, and the *Chimaera*'s entire crew was going to pay for Faro's folly.

"Why do you call it madness?" Thrawn asked. His voice, in contrast to Savit's, showed complete calmness. "Do you not believe I could defeat you?"

A barked laugh rose reflexively from deep within Ronan. But to his surprise, it vanished before it could pass his lips. The sudden change in Savit's expression—

"You could probably defeat me one-to-one," Savit said, his tone suddenly cautious. "But this is four-to-one. And you're here, not on the *Chimaera*."

"Your statement assumes three things," Thrawn said. "First, that your captains will refuse to accept the evidence gathered against you. Second—"

"You have no *evidence*, Thrawn," Savit cut in. "Only hints and theories and innuendo. My captains are smart enough to see through that sort of smoke screen."

"Second," Thrawn said, "you assume that I don't know you."

Savit frowned. "What's that supposed to mean?" The frown cleared. "Oh. Right. Your famous learn-the-enemy-through-his-artwork technique. Unfortunately for you, I don't possess any artwork, and all the pieces at my family home were chosen by my parents. Or do you think I learned my battle tactics from my father's favorite art dealer?"

"Third, you have three Star Destroyers, not four," Thrawn continued, ignoring the jibe completely.

Savit snorted. "What, your people count differently than we do?"

"You have three here at hand," Thrawn said. "You chose to leave the *Harbinger* and Captain Pellaeon out of the confrontation."

Savit's fingers tightened briefly around Ronan's arm, then relaxed. "Pellaeon is completely loyal."

"I agree," Thrawn said. "But his loyalty is to the Empire, not you."

Ronan took a deep breath. Thrawn was wrong. It was time to put an end to this. "All right, enough is enough," he said. "We need to stop this, right now."

"Do you disagree that Grand Admiral Savit's crimes deserve to be examined?" Thrawn asked.

"Not at all," Ronan said. "But they're not worth getting a lot of good men and women killed. So he stole a few turbolasers—so what? Stardust can handle such a minor loss."

"And the principles of broken faith and treason mean nothing to you?" Thrawn persisted.

"*You* were about to absolve him of all crimes if he came and fought the Grysks with you," he pointed out. "What's the difference between your offer and mine?"

"The difference is that I had no intention of absolving him of his crimes," Thrawn said. "I merely offered a way for him to give balance to those actions when judgment was pronounced."

Ronan felt his lip twist. Like Savit would ever have accepted a short-end deal like that. Savit was right; Thrawn really *was* incompetent in the political arena.

"But I appreciate your concern for the men and women currently at risk," Thrawn continued. "Would you feel better if I told you I can defeat Admiral Savit's forces without a single loss of life?" He raised his eyebrows. "Admiral?"

Ronan frowned, flicking a glance at Savit. The grand admiral's eyes had gone narrow, his face hardening.

But there was something else there, as well. Amid the anger and determination, Ronan could see a hint of growing uncertainty.

Ronan had heard the stories about Thrawn. Even if only half of them were true . . .

"Maybe *you* could," Savit conceded. "But as I said, you're not there. You're here."

"True," Thrawn agreed. He cocked his head. "Do you think that makes a difference?"

"It makes all the difference in the universe," Savit retorted. He gestured to the comm officer to open a channel. "Captain Rasdel?" he called.

"Yes, Admiral?" Rasdel's voice came from the bridge speaker.

"Move the *Misthunter* up," Savit ordered. "Prepare an ion cannon attack against the *Chimaera*. Full salvo, all six cannons."

There was just the slightest pause. "Yes, sir," Rasdel said.

Savit heard the pause, too. "Are you questioning my order, Captain?" he demanded.

"No, sir, not at all," Rasdel hastened to assure him. "It's just . . . it doesn't look good, our attacking someone who's raised questions about you."

"Would you rather wait until the *Chimaera*'s in range to launch a full-scale turbolaser attack against us?" Savit growled. "Would it salve your bruised conscience in the final seconds of your life and the lives of your bridge crew to know Faro fired first?"

"No, sir," Rasdel said stiffly.

"Besides that, the *Chimaera*'s already launched TIE fighters," Savit reminded him. "That by itself constitutes a hostile move."

Ronan pursed his lips. Yes, Faro *had* launched some of her fighters. And he could see how that could be considered an invitation to combat.

On the other hand, those fighters seemed to be taking their time coming around in their individual arcs toward the *Firedrake* and Savit's other ships. Certainly they weren't charging to the attack.

"Understood, Admiral," Rasdel said. "Bringing the *Misthunter* to attack range now."

"Good. Fire when ready."

Savit will not attack personally at the beginning. He will not wish to directly involve himself, not at first. He will also wish to test his subordinates and learn their expertise before offering them more challenging tasks. He favors the left side, so the attack will most likely come from that direction.

Faro looked up at the viewport. The *Misthunter* was off the *Firedrake*'s portside, so that was presumably Savit's chosen surrogate attacker.

The first attack will be ion cannons. Savit prefers to begin cautiously, and will also bow to the qualms and uncertainties of those who wish to disable the Chimaera *without permanent damage. Your defense will be your own ion cannons.*

"Ion cannons: Target the *Misthunter*'s ion launchers," Faro called. "As soon as they launch their volley, launch one in return."

"Acknowledged, Commodore."

Faro squeezed her datapad a little tighter. Like Thrawn's earlier slingshot trick, this one also had solid science beneath it. On the other hand, she'd never heard of anyone countering an ion cannon burst with one of their own.

Of course, part of that was most defenders wouldn't know when or from where an ion attack would be launched and would therefore not have enough time to aim and respond. In this case, the *from where* had been provided by Thrawn.

If he was right.

And *that* was the real question. There were a handful of high-ranking officers, Faro knew, who fancied themselves amateur artists, and others who maintained extensive collections of other people's art. Give Thrawn an hour in their showrooms and Faro had no doubt he could take them apart piece by piece if he had to.

But Savit had no such artistic leanings. She'd heard he wrote music, but music had never been part of Thrawn's unique talent.

On the other hand, Savit's family owned a large collection of art. If there were some pieces that Savit had particularly liked, some that he'd perhaps kept in his own suite in the family mansion—and if Thrawn had somehow been able to get a list of those artworks—maybe that would be enough.

"Ion bursts!" Hammerly snapped. "Six shots from the *Misthunter.*"

"Counter bursts launched," Pyrondi snapped back. "Running true."

Faro held her breath as she watched the two sets of ion bursts closing on each other. The leading edges of the bursts intersected.

And as the containment fields crossed and annihilated each other, the suddenly released ions exploded outward in a spectacular fireworks display.

Someone in the portside crew pit huffed out a startled-sounding oath. "Agreed," Faro called back.

If the first salvo fails, there will be a second and most likely a third attempt. Both will be more intense. Your probable defense against them . . .

"Second attack is imminent," Faro said. "And if it gets through, it won't be just you—we *all* may very well be damned. So stay sharp."

"Fire!" Savit ordered. *His voice holds command. His face and body language hold disbelief and growing anger. His fingers and hands move to his left, their stiffness holding impetus.*

The Chimaera's *ion blasts fly to meet the* Misthunter's *attack. The gunners are quicker this time, and the ion blasts' mutual destruction takes place closer to the* Misthunter.

"Again!" Savit ordered. *His fingers again twitch left and forward, holding more energy and will. His body stance holds fresh determination.*

Misthunter *fires more ion bursts. All but one is destroyed by the* Chimaera's *answering burst. The remaining shot runs wide and misses its target.*

"Again," Savit ordered. "Make it *work*, Rasdel, damn it." *His fingers twitch now to his right.* "Stormbird, why are you just sitting there? Full ion cannon spread—*now*."

"Yes, sir," Lochry said. *His voice holds tension, possibly disbelief that the attacks are failing, possibly concern for his admiral's state of mind.*

Savit's *fingers point right, then point ahead.* "Enough is enough," he said. *His voice holds anger and determination.* "Lochry, prep a squadron of TIEs. Continue with ion cannon fire; I'll tell you when to launch." *The hand still holding Assistant Director Ronan's arm twists a few degrees, eliciting a momentary spasm of discomfort in the assistant director's face.* "Let's see how bloody Commodore Faro is prepared to get."

The second or third ion attack will include volleys from the ship on Savit's right flank as well as the one on his left. He himself will not yet join in the attacks.

"Ion volley from *Misthunter*," Hammerly reported.

"Countering," Pyrondi confirmed. "Ion bursts—"

"Second volley from *Stormbird*," Hammerly cut in.

And there was no way the *Chimaera's* own ion cannons could intercept both salvos. Faro knew it, and presumably so did Savit.

Fortunately, Thrawn had anticipated this one, too. "Quach?" she called.

"On it, Commodore," the TIE commander said briskly. "Left flank on intercept vectors."

Faro watched, again feeling the itching sense of uncertainty. Theoretically, TIE fighters should be able to survive the same intensity of ion blast that could disable sizable sectors of capital ships.

But Thrawn's projected scenario involved running the fighters through multiple hits. If the charge from the later bursts leaked through the outer shell instead of bleeding off into space, the pilots could suddenly find that all of the electronics in their vac suits had been fried, as well as the systems in the fighters themselves.

Faro had tried to cover for that by putting an extra oxygen bottle in each cockpit, emergency supplies that could be screwed into the suit's intake without relying on the usual mixers or scrubbers. But if enough charge got through the shell and the suit to stun or paralyze the pilot, even that backup would be useless.

The portside TIEs were nearly in position now, angling hard across the path of the *Stormbird*'s ion volley. Fortunately, the *Misthunter*, unlike the *Stormbird*, hadn't pulled ahead of Savit's *Firedrake* but had instead stayed behind the flagship's position. That meant a longer travel time for the six ion bursts it had sent toward the *Chimaera*, which gave the six TIEs on that flank enough time to move into intercept positions. Faro held her breath . . .

The timing was perfect. The TIEs swept squarely into the ion volley, intercepting five of the bursts full-on and catching the sixth a glancing blow. The bolts splashed into the fighters' spheres and wings like ocean waves before scattering and dissipating, while the sixth burst managed to hold together for another hundred meters before it, too, disintegrated. Faro threw a quick look at the status boards, confirming that the systems of all six TIEs had been completely shut down by the massive electrical jolts.

All of their systems, including the comms and bio readouts. Until one or the other of those came back up, there would be no way to know if the pilots were alive or dead.

But there was nothing Faro could do about that. The *Chimaera*'s own ion bursts had again intercepted and neutralized those from the *Misthunter*, but Savit was unlikely to give up now.

There will be a final ion attack from the two ships. Having seen one flank of TIEs disabled, Savit will attempt the same attack in the hope of disabling the other flank.

"Starboard TIEs: *Go,*" Faro ordered.

"Right flank TIEs, acknowledged," Quach confirmed.

Faro turned back to the viewport. Even as the freshly blasted TIEs from the *Chimaera*'s portside group continued their unpowered flight across the combat field toward Faro's right, the starboard TIEs crisscrossed past them, heading toward the *Chimaera*'s portside and the original sentry positions of the now neutralized TIEs. "Cannons and tractors stand ready," Faro warned. If Savit was playing according to Thrawn's expectations, he would now attempt to neutralize the rest of Faro's Marg Sabl sentries.

Sure enough. Even as the starboard TIEs raced past the *Chimaera*'s nose, heading for their new portside positions, the *Misthunter* and *Stormbird* again opened up with the now familiar ion volleys.

He will assume you will use the same defense against this attack. Instead, you will counter by . . .

"Cannons firing," Pyrondi called. "Tractors locked."

Ahead, the *Chimaera*'s TIEs continued their race to portside, toward the bolts now arrowing in from the *Stormbird*—

Just as the *Chimaera*'s own ion cannon bursts met and disintegrated that salvo, leaving the TIEs untouched.

Faro shifted her attention to the volley coming from the *Misthunter* toward the *Chimaera*'s starboard side. The drifting, lifeless TIEs moving in that direction abruptly sped up, their vectors angling now toward the *Chimaera* as Pyrondi's tractors grabbed them and reeled them in. The *Misthunter*'s ion bursts were nearly there—the TIEs were still angling in toward them—

And with another multiple splash of ionic energy, the TIEs slammed across the bolts, dissipating their energy.

"Roll starboard!" Faro snapped. The helpless TIEs were careening on their new tractor-driven vectors straight toward the *Chimaera*'s starboard wing—

And shot past without impacting the hull as Agral rolled the ship, dipping that side of the wedge out of their way.

Faro felt her lips compress. So far, Thrawn had predicted Savit's actions perfectly.

But now the initial dance was over. Savit had tried to play nice and use non-lethal force, and been humiliated for his trouble.

These attacks will be followed immediately by a launch of TIE fighters.

"Right," Faro said under her breath. "Bring it on."

CHAPTER 21

Finally, the waiting was over.

"Two Grysk warships have emerged from hyperspace," Sensor Officer Tanik reported, his voice stiff and formal.

Big ships, too, Eli noted with a twinge of apprehension. The warships that had been protecting the observation post and the conjoined forward base ships had been slightly smaller than the *Steadfast*. These two, in contrast, were each half again as big, running the on-profile odds to something closer to three against one than two against one.

The ships were big enough to carry up to thirty fighters each, as well. Eli had studied Imperial military history enough to know that in melee battles, a fighter wing or two could make the difference between victory and destruction.

"Bearing thirty left, twelve up, distance sixteen hundred," Tanik continued.

So less than a quarter of the way around from the spot where the scout had popped in and out of the system earlier, and at about half the distance from the *Steadfast*. The Grysk commander had apparently expected Ar'alani to move to a new vantage point and had hoped to catch her off guard.

In fact, if she'd moved in to guard the scout's insertion point, the attackers would have arrived into an almost perfect flanking position.

Which didn't mean the Grysks couldn't try again. This far out from any sizable mass, they could pop back into hyperspace, come around, and try to catch the *Steadfast* from behind.

But they probably wouldn't. Microjumps without nav computers were all but impossible—hyperspace navigators like those used by the Grysks didn't usually work that way. Besides, that kind of bouncing around had always struck Eli as being beneath Grysk dignity.

That, or Grysk commanders simply preferred standing toe-to-toe with their enemies as they beat them into dust.

"Swing ship to face them," Ar'alani ordered. "Prep plasma spheres, both starboard and portside. Lieutenant Eli'van'to?"

"Tractors ready, Admiral," Eli confirmed. "Awaiting your command."

"Hold," Ar'alani said, her eyes narrowed as she watched the two warships gliding toward them, one pulling ahead as the other took up a more protected position behind it. "Hold . . ."

"Lead Grysk launching fighters," Tanik reported. "Twenty targets."

And that was what Ar'alani had been waiting for, Eli knew. With the majority of its fighters loose and preparing to attack, the lead warship, at least, had committed itself to staying in this area for the immediate future lest it risk losing two-thirds of its fighter force. Now the *Steadfast* could launch its secret weapon with reasonable confidence.

"Lieutenant Eli'van'to: Execute slingshot."

"Executing slingshot," Eli confirmed, keying the order to the tractor operators. For a second there came the faint whine of overstressed engines as the tractor beams grabbed the cloaked gravity-well generator floating beneath the *Steadfast* and sent it flying toward the distant Grysk ships. A slight rise of the warship's bow to let it sweep past, as Thrawn had specified, and the generator was on its leisurely way.

Eli had already concluded the Grysks couldn't do a microjump. Now, assuming the Grysks stayed on their present course toward the *Steadfast,* they would soon find themselves unable to make any hyperspace jumps at all.

Which also assumed, of course, that they didn't have a way of detecting their own cloaked devices.

He hissed softly between his teeth. That one hadn't occurred to him until just now. If they could see through their cloak tech and spotted the gravity generator, this whole thing could come crashing down.

Still, given how much the Grysks used client surrogates in their battles, it seemed likely that their most closely guarded secrets would be kept out of their warships, lest a defeated ship's wreckage yield unexpected bonuses to the winner. A detection method for their cloaking fields would probably be considered just such a secret.

All the same, it was a possibility he needed to be aware of.

A multitone trill sounded, indicating that Ar'alani's comm was now live. "This is Admiral Ar'alani of the Chiss Ascendancy, commanding the Defense Fleet warship *Steadfast,*" she called. "The Grysk Hegemony has intruded into the Galactic Empire and has furthermore committed multiple criminal acts against it. You are hereby ordered to withdraw immediately from this system and from the Empire and return to your own territory."

There was a moment of silence. Then the speaker gave out a soft clattering noise.

Eli frowned. Anger? Defiance?

Amusement?

"Has the self-important Chiss Ascendancy then extended its jurisdiction deep into Palpatine's Empire?" a cold, dry voice came. "Or does your vaunted Admiral Mitth'raw'nuruodo now rule in Palpatine's stead?"

"Palpatine's Empire will make its presence known soon enough," Ar'alani promised. "I say again: Withdraw immediately to your own provinces or face destruction. The same destruction that all those sent before you have already suffered."

"You amuse me, Admiral Ar'alani," the Grysk said, and there was no mistaking the contempt in his voice. "A scientific study post, a simple communications relay station, and a poorly armed supply freighter? Victories over such helpless craft are the proud triumphs you claim?"

"You conveniently forget the two warships," Ar'alani reminded him.

"Not at all," the Grysk said. "Destruction of the first required the aid of one of Palpatine's warships. Destruction of the second was accomplished entirely without your aid or presence."

"Without our *military* aid, perhaps," Ar'alani said. "However, Admiral Mitth'raw'nuruodo did require Chiss interrogation methods in order to locate the communications base."

There was another silence. Eli watched the tactical, tracking the paths of the twenty enemy fighters as they made their leisurely way toward the *Steadfast*. The majority of Grysk attacks, at least the ones the Ascendancy had records of, were akin to the pounce of a predator: quick, vicious, and decisive. The fact that this commander had decided to talk first suggested he still didn't have a complete picture of what had happened out here and very much wanted one.

Eli could sympathize. The freighter Thrawn had allowed to escape the observation post would have reported the post's capture, but would have been unable to confirm that the two Grysk overseers and their slaves had all been killed. That, plus Ar'alani's casual comment about Chiss interrogation methods, had to have the commander wondering how the forward communications base had been located.

As for that second battle, only the first few seconds could have been transmitted before the triad was wrecked, with the warship's destruction quickly following. Now, of course, the second of the conjoined ships currently floating beside the *Steadfast* was silent proof of the fact that even the Grysks' final self-destruct system had failed.

Possible Grysk prisoners, possible effective Chiss interrogation, definite capture of potentially vital Grysk hardware. The commander could pretend contempt and amusement as hard as he wanted, but Eli had no doubt that he was worried. He was here for answers, and if talking to the hated Chiss got him those answers, he would do it.

Eli smiled grimly. Fat chance of that. Ar'alani had no intention of sending back any answers.

But with warrior's luck, they *would* soon be delivering the Grysks one final message.

"Fighters accelerating," Tanik said. "Angling outward for a closed-fist sweeping attack."

"Parameters?"

"Dual lasers, quad missiles, light electrostatic barriers."

So: somewhere in the mid-range of the Grysk fighter arsenal. Not unreasonable for a secret foray deep into enemy territory, where a commander would want a powerful fighter force, but not something top-line that might be captured. Not as bad as it could have been.

But not exactly good, either. Four missiles each meant a full eighty missiles that could be unleashed on the *Steadfast,* far more than its defenses could handle if they were launched in rapid succession. Dual lasers meant the fighters could stay on the attack even after all their missiles had been expended, while the electrostatic barriers meant each fighter could take at least one and possibly two laser or plasma sphere attacks without serious damage.

Still, an incoming fighter was easier to hit with a plasma sphere than with the much narrower laser beam, so that was probably where Ar'alani would start.

"Fighter spread halting," Tanik said. "Holding position . . . moving to attack."

"Spheres?" Ar'alani called.

"Primed and ready," Khresh confirmed.

"Yaw ninety degrees to portside," Ar'alani ordered. "Lock targets and prepare full starboard salvo."

The sky outside the viewport shifted as the *Steadfast* turned its right flank toward the incoming fighters. "Salvo: *Fire,*" Ar'alani said.

"Spheres fired," Khresh said. "Rolling to starboard."

Again the stars careened wildly as the *Steadfast* rolled to bring its portside plasma launchers to bear.

"Missiles away!" Tanik snapped. "Ten missiles from the ten star-board fighters, running intercept vectors. Portside fighters holding from attack."

"Spectrum lasers, lock on missiles," Ar'alani said. "Fire at will."

Eli held his breath as he watched the missiles converging toward the *Steadfast* and the tracks that marked the warship's lasers. Hitting something that small usually required multiple shots, and Ar'alani was taking full advantage of the time and distance she had available.

Which immediately brought up the question of why the fighters had fired so soon instead of waiting until they were closer. The first salvo of plasma spheres swept across the missiles—

Five of the missiles abruptly skittered off course as the plasma enveloped them, disrupting their electronics and partially burning into their control jets.

An instant later the other five missiles exploded, bursting outward in overlapping clouds of dust and debris.

The clouds were still there as the second plasma sphere salvo slammed into them. For a second the spheres held shape as they ripped through the dust; then they burst apart and dissipated.

Eli made a face. So that was why the fighters had fired early. The Grysk commander had deliberately sacrificed ten of his missiles in order to protect his fighters from the *Steadfast*'s first plasma sphere attack and let them move in closer.

It had protected most of them, anyway. "Two hits on fighters," Tanik reported. "First shows barrier down, no other damage. Second has barrier down and is drifting with drive and electronics temporarily deactivated."

"Portside launchers ready for another salvo," Khresh said. "Starboard launchers fifty percent recovered."

"Debris clouds still pose a threat to spheres," Operations Officer Velbb warned.

And plasma spheres, Eli knew, weren't an unlimited resources like spectrum laserfire. The *Steadfast* carried only a limited amount of the highly specialized concoction that went into the plasma generators, and when it was gone, it was gone.

The Grysk commander had now goaded Ar'alani into wasting two salvos. Maybe his strategy was to force her to drain the *Steadfast*'s supply completely.

Given that he had another entire warship's worth of fighters, missiles, and other resources waiting behind him to attack, it wasn't an unreasonable plan. At this point, he could afford to trade one-for-one with the *Steadfast*.

Ar'alani, unfortunately, couldn't. Not unless Thrawn managed to finish his business with Grand Admiral Savit early and come to the *Steadfast*'s aid.

Such an unexpected rescue would be timely, dramatic, and utterly devastating to the Grysks. But Eli and Ar'alani both knew it was an appearance they couldn't rely on.

"So he enjoys playing games, does he?" Ar'alani said, her voice still calm. "Very well. Let's see if we can change the rules. Officer Khresh, can the tractors get a lock on the neutralized fighter?"

"I think so, Admiral," Khresh said, a little uncertainly. "But it could regain full power at any moment, including laser and missile control."

"Then we'd best not give it time to do that," Ar'alani said. "Tractors: Grab that fighter and bring it in."

"Bring it—?" Khresh broke off. "Admiral, you did hear what I said? If it comes back to full power too close—"

"And when it gets close, run the tractor to full power and slam the fighter as hard as you can against the hull," Ar'alani continued. "Hard enough to kill or at least to stun."

Eli looked over at Khresh in time to see a sudden understanding come into his eyes. "Understood, Admiral," he said, his hesitation gone. "Tractors? Lock on, and bring it in."

It took nearly half a minute for the Grysk commander to react—probably, Eli suspected, he assumed the fighter's new movement meant it was coming out of the plasma sphere's effects and trying to get back into the battle. All around it the other fighters continued to swarm, maintaining a cautious distance from the *Steadfast* as they dodged its lasers, throwing missiles in twos and threes in their continuing effort to drain the Chiss plasma sphere resources.

Ar'alani seemed perfectly willing to keep the Grysk thinking it was still his game. She replied to the Grysk missiles mainly with laserfire, but threw enough plasma spheres to keep the enemy focus on that part of the battle.

Twenty-eight seconds after the *Steadfast*'s tractors locked on, the Grysk commander suddenly seemed to wake up to the unexpected threat. But by then it was too late. The captured fighter was too far out of range of the other fighters for any of them to catch it, and it was moving too fast for their missiles to take it down. Their only hope was to destroy it with laserfire, but with the *Steadfast*'s tractor operator continually and randomly tweaking both power and direction, they couldn't calculate its trajectory well enough to get a clear shot at it.

Even as the laserfire became increasingly frantic, four of the fighters launched missiles in one final attempt, missiles the *Steadfast*'s plasma spheres made quick work of. The fighter arrowed toward the *Steadfast*—

And with a jolt that rattled the ship all the way to the bridge, it slammed into the hull.

"Bring it aboard—quickly," Ar'alani ordered. "Senior Commander Cinsar?"

"We're ready, Admiral," the voice of the *Steadfast*'s fifth officer came over the speaker. "Tech teams and equipment are in position."

"Good," Ar'alani said. "Secure the pilot if he isn't dead, then get busy."

She looked at Khresh. "Every war machine—warship, fighter, or missile—has at least one fatal weakness that can be used against it," she continued.

"Find it."

The minutes dragged by. Eli watched as the Grysks continued their war of attrition against the *Steadfast*, the fighters pushing forward and then retreating, trying to goad the Chiss into wasting resources they would desperately need once the warships themselves made their move. Ar'alani, for her part, continued to keep them on the string, doling out just enough of the irreplaceable plasma spheres to keep them busy and buy the techs as much time as she could.

A movement across the bridge caught Eli's eye: Vah'nya, looking at him and beckoning, a worried look on her face.

Eli hesitated. But at the moment he had nothing to do in the battle. Unstrapping, he made his way across to her station.

He could feel Ar'alani's eyes on him as he walked, as well as the eyes of some of the other officers. There was no way to know what they were thinking about him leaving his assigned position, but none of them ordered him back.

"Is there a problem, Navigator Vah'nya?" he asked as he reached her side.

"A question, Lieutenant Eli," she said. "The Grysk ships are our enemies, and they seem very determined to destroy us. Yet they continue to just rest there, outside combat range. Nor do they bring their fighters in for true battle. What are they doing?"

Eli hesitated, wondering how much he should tell her. Defense Fleet General Orders stated flatly that strategy, tactics, and weaponry were not to be discussed with navigators. Eli wasn't sure whether that prohibition was to keep the young girls from worrying, which might affect their ability to utilize Third Sight, or whether it was because navigators, of all the Chiss going into battle, were the prizes an enemy was most likely to try to take alive.

But Vah'nya was smart, and had been performing her duty for a good deal longer than any of the other navigators aboard. Along the way she was bound to have learned more than anyone really wanted her to know.

"They're trying to drain the *Steadfast*'s defenses," he told her. "We can keep firing spectrum lasers forever, or at least as long as we have power, but plasma spheres and Breacher missiles are limited resources. If they can get us to waste the spheres on their fighters, we'll be more vulnerable when they finally bring their warships into play."

"But we can simply jump away, can't we?" Vah'nya asked. "I can be ready to guide the ship whenever Admiral Ar'alani gives the order."

"In theory, yes, that's a warship's last-ditch option," Eli said, again wondering how much to tell her. "At least if we're not too close to a planetary mass."

"Which we aren't."

"Right." Eli hesitated. But she deserved to know the truth. Besides, the two of them had already decided they wouldn't survive long enough to be captured. "But the Grysk have a method of creating artificial gravity wells that work the same way as that kind of mass. The supply ship that we chased away from the observation post had one."

"Yes, I remember," Vah'nya said. "They dropped it behind them to keep the *Steadfast* from following them into hyperspace."

"Right," Eli said. "I'm guessing that either they've already seeded this area with some of those, or else the warships themselves have larger directed generators to keep us here. One way or the other, they seem pretty sure we're not going anywhere."

She thought about that a minute. "The supply ship's small generator," she said. "We've already thrown that at them, haven't we?"

"Yes," Eli confirmed. One more bit of strategy that Vah'nya wasn't supposed to know about. "Admiral Ar'alani figured that if we weren't going to cut out of the fight early, neither should they."

Vah'nya gave him a small smile. "My brothers used to fight that way," she said. "Neither giving ground, neither admitting defeat." The smile faded. "Often they worked together against me in the days before the fleet took me from my family and brought me to itself. Those fights often ended with blood."

"Yours, or theirs?"

"Sometimes both," she said. "Mostly mine."

Eli sighed. "I'm sorry."

"It's all right," she assured him. "The fleet is my family now, and has treated me well." She nodded toward the viewport and the Grysk ships waiting silent and motionless. "I wonder now whether that life and family will continue beyond today."

"It will," Eli said. "Just remember that when you fought your brothers, you didn't have Admiral Ar'alani standing at your side."

Another small smile, maybe a shade bigger this time. "Nor did I have Grand Admiral Mitth'raw'nuruodo to come to my aid?"

"That, too," Eli said, mentally crossing his fingers. No, she hadn't had Thrawn.

But there was a very good chance that the *Steadfast* wouldn't, either.

"Looks like they're swapping out ships again, Admiral," Khresh commented.

Eli looked at the tactical. Three of the Grysk fighters had broken off their distant attack and were heading back to the warship. As they approached the hangar bay, three other fighters appeared and passed them on their way to the battle line. The newcomers swung close to one of the fighters already on the line, all four of them clustering briefly together like grav-ball players getting instructions from the center striker before spreading out again and moving to the positions of the fighters they'd been brought out to replace.

That had been the pattern the standoff had settled into. The *Steadfast* would disable a fighter, possibly even damage it, and the warship would bring it back in and exchange it for a fresh craft and pilot.

"The commander must sense that the final confrontation is coming," Ar'alani said. "He's bringing out everything he has left."

Eli frowned. There'd been something about that brief huddle, something he'd gotten a hint of in the earlier fighter exchanges. "Mid Commander Tanik?" he asked. "Can you give me a full sensor bracket for the three newcomers since they emerged from the hangar bay?"

Tanik half turned to Ar'alani. "Admiral?"

"Yes, give it to him," Ar'alani confirmed. "Navigator Vah'nya's station. You have something, Lieutenant?"

"Possibly, Admiral," Eli said. The sensor data came up on one of the helm displays, and he leaned over Vah'nya's shoulder, sifting quickly through the spectrum brackets. "The new fighters came right up to one of the others before deploying."

"Probably getting their final orders," Khresh said.

"But they shouldn't have had to come that close for such a briefing," Ar'alani said thoughtfully. "Interesting. Full analysis, Commander Tanik. Tell me what they were all doing."

"I was thinking they might be passing off cloaked gravity generators," Eli said. "They got close enough for a handoff like that."

"Why bother?" Khresh pointed out. "Just leave the generators with the new fighters and rearrange the line to put them wherever you want them."

"That was my thought, too," Eli said. "But there might be something else they were passing across. We know the Grysks have a strong military hierarchy. Maybe they were passing over a weapon that only the senior commander has the authority to use."

"Wait a minute," Tanik said, a mix of puzzlement and cautious excitement in his voice. "The newcomers' electrostatic barriers shifted slightly after their brush with the other one."

"Shifted how?" Ar'alani asked. "Strength? Positioning?"

"It's a little unclear," Tanik said. "The closest I can figure is that it's a frequency shift."

"Senior Commander Cinsar?" Ar'alani called. "Did you hear all that?"

"Yes, Admiral," Cinsar's voice came from the speaker. "I concur with Mid Commander Tanik—there's definitely a tuning capability for the barriers we've got down here. Best guess is that tuning all the barriers together lets them reinforce one another when the fighters are close together."

"So if we can figure out how to retune some of them, we might be able to create interference?" Khresh asked.

"I think so, yes," Cinsar said. "Provided we get them far enough apart and then figure out how to remotely affect their barrier generators."

"Or there are other possibilities," Ar'alani said. "Have you found anything else useful?"

"We've found something, though I don't know how useful it is," Cinsar said. "There are some plastic flex seals between the fuselage and the wing-mounted lasers and missile launchers. They're protected by flanges from laser attacks from in front, but the material itself is highly susceptible to the acid mix in our Breacher missiles."

"*How* susceptible?" Ar'alani asked.

"Highly," Cinsar repeated. "Get even a small splash on them, and the seals and whatever power or control lines are behind them will start disintegrating within a couple of seconds. And of course, the electrostatic barrier only follows the metal parts, so that leaves the seals completely open to attack."

"But that's wonderful, isn't it?" Vah'nya asked quietly, reaching up and touching Eli's arm. "Why did he say it wasn't useful?"

"Because we don't have nearly enough Breachers to spend one on each of the fighters out there," Eli told her.

"Lieutenant Eli'van'to is correct, Navigator Vah'nya," Ar'alani said.

Eli turned. The admiral was leaning forward in her chair, her eyes narrowed as she gazed out at the Grysk ships facing them. Two against one, just like Vah'nya's brothers.

"But there are other ways," Ar'alani continued. "Helm, prepare the thrusters for full power.

"It's time to take the battle to the enemy."

CHAPTER 22

"*Stormbird*, launch a squadron of TIE fighters," Savit ordered. "Faro wants to play games? Fine. Let's see how she does against *real* weapons of war."

Ronan's stomach was tight enough to hurt. Up to now Faro had been incredibly lucky, managing to turn the *Chimaera*'s ion cannons against Savit's attack and keep things from escalating.

But with Savit's order for a fighter attack, the mutual restraint was over. Faro couldn't stand against that kind of attack without responding in kind.

And once things crossed that line, they could never go back. Ronan looked at Thrawn, wondering if he had any idea how much grief he'd set up his ship's commander to have dumped on her.

He frowned. Thrawn wasn't showing any signs of regret or even second thoughts. Instead, he was gazing at Savit with an intense, steady expression.

As if sensing Ronan's eyes on him, Thrawn shifted his attention to him. His hand, hanging loosely at his side, made a small motion.

Ronan looked down, frowning, wondering what Thrawn was trying to say. He seemed to be pointing to Savit's right hand, the hand that wasn't holding Ronan's arm.

Ronan craned his neck. Savit's right hand was making small motions: a twitch of a finger, a slight curl of the whole hand, a small circle of fingertips.

Secret signals? But to whom? Ronan leaned forward a little farther, trying to get a better look.

He'd hoped the movement would be small enough to escape Savit's notice. He was wrong. "Where do you think *you're* going?" Savit snapped, tightening his hold on Ronan's arm and shifting his glare to him.

"I was hoping to talk some sense into you," Ronan said, wincing. Savit's frustration was coming out in his grip, and the grand admiral clearly had a hell of a lot of frustration right now. "This isn't going to end well for anyone. Please, *please,* stop before someone gets killed."

"You think I should meekly pull back and allow some alien traitor's accusations to stand?" Savit snarled. "An alien traitor *and* his tame assistant director imposter? Is *that* what you think?" He snorted. "Besides, you heard our traitor. He's already promised no one's going to get killed."

"*Stormbird* has launched TIEs, Admiral," Captain Boulag announced. "TIE commander requests orders."

"Let's keep it simple," Savit said. "Attack and disable the *Chimaera.* Destroy anything that gets in their way."

Ronan clenched his teeth. "Admiral—"

"Shut up or I'll turn you over to my stormtroopers," Savit cut him off.

"Admiral, *Chimaera*'s TIEs are moving to intercept *Stormbird*'s," someone called from the crew pits.

"And so Faro's lucky streak ends," Savit commented, half turning both himself and Ronan around to face the tactical. "Six functional TIEs against twelve from the *Stormbird.* I trust you know how to do that kind of math?" He looked at Thrawn. "I daresay even our legendary Grand Admiral Thrawn would have trouble with numbers like that."

"Perhaps," Thrawn said calmly. "You really do not understand, do you?"

Savit's eyes narrowed. "Understand what?"

"You said earlier I didn't know you," Thrawn said. "On the contrary. I know you perfectly. Commodore Faro is not simply reacting to your moves to the best of her considerable ability. The truth is that I have already given her the tools, the insights, and the instructions necessary for your defeat."

Savit snorted. "You don't seriously expect me to believe that, do you? I know all about your allegedly magical talent for reading your enemies. I also know you need art for that, and I'm not an artist."

"Of course you are," Thrawn said. "Music is most certainly a form of art."

Ronan frowned. Thrawn could read people through *music,* too? Why had he never heard about that?

"Normally, of course, music is useless to me," Thrawn continued. "There is too much interpretation in performance and direction, too many variables creating uncertainty and bias and all but eliminating focus."

Ronan felt his breath catch as he suddenly understood. "But he doesn't just compose music," he said. "He also plays *and* conducts it."

"Indeed, Assistant Director," Thrawn said, inclining his head. "Moreover, he has done so in public where both visual and auditory recordings have been made."

His eyes went somehow distant. "I have followed it all, Grand Admiral Savit," he said quietly. "I have searched back to the beginnings, when you performed simple keycurve pieces at your parents' home for the amusement of their guests. Later compositions, as you were commissioned in the navy, incorporating first the high winds, then the strings, then the deep winds, moving finally to full orchestra."

Ronan stole a look at Savit. The grand admiral's face had gone rigid, the expression of a man who is belatedly starting to understand what has been done to him.

"I saw how the number of instruments you added into each new composition mirrored your successive commands," Thrawn continued. "First a single ship, then a ship plus support vessels, then a task force, and finally the Third Fleet. I watched how you favored the different instruments, or even the different sides of the assembly. I saw you write more complex lines as the performers proved their ability to handle them. I observed which lines of melody you assigned to others, and which you reserved for yourself."

"You're insane," Savit breathed. "You're spitting out words with no meaning."

"Am I?" Thrawn asked. "But most important of all, no matter how your expertise and ambition grew, you were always there in the midst of it. You conducted, you arranged, and you continued to perform your creations in tandem with your other performers. That combination, that total immersion in your craft, is what has defined you." He nodded toward Savit's hands. "Indeed, even now your hand moves with your orders as if you are conducting this latest of your grand creations."

"Admiral, *Chimaera* TIEs have pulled away to the sides," someone called.

Ronan looked at the tactical. Faro's six TIE fighters, which had been flying wing-to-wing toward the twelve *Stormbird* fighters, had suddenly broken formation, sweeping outward to all sides.

And coming up right behind them, visible only now that the TIEs had moved out of the way—

"Proton torpedoes!" Boulag snapped. *"Stormbird—!"*

"TIEs: *Evasive!"* the *Stormbird*'s TIE commander's voice came sharply from the *Firedrake*'s speakers. "Four proton torpedoes incoming!"

But it was too late, Ronan realized with a sinking heart. The *Stormbird*'s TIEs had been running too tight a formation, and the sudden reveal had left them without sufficient time to spread out and get clear before the torpedoes reached them. If even one of them struck—or if Faro had set up proximity fuses—the twelve TIEs were doomed.

Ronan was still staring at the imminent disaster, contemplating the terrible line Faro had crossed, when four turbolaser blasts flashed out from the *Chimaera*. The blasts converged with breathtaking precision on the proton torpedoes—

And with a stuttering multiple explosion the torpedoes detonated, creating a roiling cloud of light, fire, and debris.

A second later the twelve *Stormbird* TIEs drove straight through the cloud.

For a long moment, the *Firedrake*'s bridge was silent. "I promised there would be no deaths," Thrawn said calmly into the hush. "I did not promise there would be no damage."

Savit's fingers tightened around Ronan's arm. "Damage report," he called. "Damn it all, *damage report.*"

"All *Stormbird* TIEs showing debris damage," someone spoke up hesitantly. "Combat fitness down between fifteen and forty percent."

"*Chimaera*'s TIEs?"

"No damage, Admiral. They were already far enough out from the torpedoes when they were detonated."

"Because they knew the detonation was coming," Ronan murmured.

Savit twisted around toward him, and Ronan shied back from the raw fury on the admiral's face. "Damn all of you," he hissed. "I will see you in *hell*—"

"Admiral!" Boulag cut in. "Two of the *Stormbird*'s TIEs have lost all power and maneuvering. Heading at high speed toward a projected impact on the *Chimaera*'s hull."

Savit spun back around. "Time?"

"Twenty-two seconds," Boulag said. "I don't know if the *Chimaera* can get out of the way in—just a moment. TIEs slowing . . . coming to a halt." He turned to Savit, a relieved look on his face. "*Stormbird* managed to grab them with tractors. Reeling them back now."

Savit nodded. "Well done, Captain Lochry," he called. "Excellent work with the tractors."

"Thank you, Admiral," Lochry's voice came back. To Ronan's ears it sounded a little bemused. "But it wasn't all us. The *Chimaera* fed us the fine-tune coordinates."

Savit turned to Thrawn. "No loss of life," Thrawn reminded him.

"I remember," Savit said. His voice had gone suddenly calm, with a softness that sent a shiver up Ronan's back. "But I think you'll find you're no longer in any position to make that promise." He raised his voice. "Captain Boulag, move us toward the *Chimaera* and prepare turbolasers."

Boulag looked at Thrawn, then Ronan, then back at Thrawn. "Admiral, if you're contemplating an attack on the *Chimaera,* I strongly advise against it."

"So noted, Captain," Savit said. "You have your orders. Carry them out."

"Yes, sir." Boulag took a deep breath, throwing one final surreptitious look at Thrawn. "Helm: Move us toward the *Chimaera.* Turbolasers . . . Prepare to fire."

The TIE attack may be followed by a second, in which the TIEs will be more cautiously spread out. You will counter by keeping your TIEs tight and rotating them to fire on the enemy TIEs' wings as they pass. Warn the pilots to avoid the cockpits to prevent loss of life.

More likely, the next move will be a turbolaser attack from the Fire-drake *itself, directed at the bridge deflector sphere. Your counter will involve the TIEs you slingshotted earlier, which should now be brought into play . . .*

"Major Quach, signal Lieutenant Watkin," Faro said. "He's to bring his squad to full power and prepare for action."

"Acknowledged, Commodore," Quach said. "Signal sent . . . dark TIEs coming to power."

Faro shifted her gaze back and forth between the tactical and the viewport. Thrawn's instructions had assured her that Savit wouldn't notice the four dark fighters drifting toward him on their ballistic vectors. But she hadn't been so sure.

Especially since this was one of the most marginal pivot points in Thrawn's plan. If Savit had paid better attention to his inner security sphere, he could have overturned this next phase right at the start. Such carelessness really should be inexcusable in a grand admiral.

Thrawn would have spotted the TIEs—hell, even Faro would have noticed them. Apparently Savit was a big-picture sort who relied on people and instruments to collect the minutiae for him to make his decisions on.

So far Thrawn's assessment of the man had been square on the money. However it was he'd anticipated Savit's actions, he'd done an impressive job of it.

In the distance, she could see the thruster glows now as Watkin and his TIEs ramped up to full power. Another moment, and even Savit couldn't fail to spot the threat poised right beneath his nose.

An instant later the *Firedrake* spat out a salvo of green turbolaser fire at the *Chimaera.*

Faro twitched reflexively as the bolts appeared to arrow straight toward her. They flashed past the bridge—

"Starboard bridge deflector hit," Pyrondi called. "Deflector holding at sixty percent."

Faro nodded acknowledgment. "Watkin: *Go.*"

Ahead, the TIEs angled up toward the *Firedrake*'s portside. A few shots from the point-defense lasers spattered around them as the Star Destroyer's gunners suddenly noticed the threat.

But the response was too little and too late. Watkin's TIEs evaded the attack with ease, spiraling up and leveling out along the portside wedgeline.

And even from her distance, Faro had no trouble seeing the multiple flashes of green fire as the TIEs systematically destroyed the turbolaser targeting sensors on that side.

Another burst of turbolaser fire flashed past the *Chimaera*'s bridge viewports. Faro glanced at the systems monitor, noting with grim satisfaction that the shots had missed her ship completely.

Savit does not trust human gunners, but prefers to rely on computerized sensors and targeting systems. His gunners will therefore likely prove unprepared for the sudden burden of combat operations.

"Lieutenant Agral, move us forward—one-quarter speed—and angle to starboard," Faro ordered. "Keep us on the *Firedrake*'s portside as best you can."

"Acknowledged, Commodore."

The *Chimaera* began to angle to the right. "You realize, I assume," Hammerly said quietly from the crew pit below her, "that all the *Firedrake* has to do is swivel around fifty degrees and they'll be able to bring their starboard turbolasers to bear."

"That's true," Faro agreed. "I also realize that the *Stormbird* and *Misthunter* could hit us without even bothering to turn. All I can tell you is that Admiral Thrawn doesn't think they will."

"They will if Savit orders them to."

"Also no argument," Faro said. "Let's stick with the master plan and see what happens."

"Besides which, you're curious to see if Thrawn can defeat someone without actually being aboard his ship?"

Faro shrugged slightly. "Something like that."

She pursed her lips in sudden thought. Thrawn's next orders—

The cloaked gravity-well generator you launched earlier via slingshot should be nearly to the Firedrake *now. Move to Savit's portside. He will match your maneuvers, turning to face you. That will open his starboard-bow turbolaser cluster to impact damage from the generator.*

Up to now, Faro had followed Thrawn's orders to the letter. Now, perhaps, it was time to add a little variation to his script. "Helm: Bring us a hundred meters positive," she ordered.

She watched as the *Chimaera* moved upward, rising out of the plane of battle. It was a big gamble, she knew—if Savit mirrored her movement, as Thrawn had suggested he might do, he would rise up with her, and the cloaked generator would miss the *Firedrake* entirely.

But she'd seen something else in Savit's actions, something that suggested efficiency of movement and operation. If she'd read him right . . .

She had. Instead of rising from the battle plane to match the *Chimaera*'s movement, the *Firedrake* merely pitched upward, rotating to keep its bow armament pointed at its opponent.

"Commodore, activity from the *Firedrake*," Pyrondi called. "Looks like they're launching TIEs."

Faro smiled, taking a final look at her datapad." Yes," she agreed. "It certainly does look like it."

"Really?" Savit growled. "Is *that* Faro's big plan? Moving to my blind side?"

Ronan frowned, eyeing the distant *Chimaera* as it drifted to the *Firedrake*'s portside. For once, at least, he had to agree with Savit. It *was* a pretty empty move.

Of course, Savit seemed to be ignoring the fact that Faro had slipped four fighters into attack range of his ship right under his nose, and that they'd proceeded to obliterate his portside targeting sensors. Clearly, the woman had a plan, and Savit would be a fool to underestimate her.

And now she was rising out of the plane of battle. Another useless gesture: The *Firedrake*'s response was merely to swivel its bow upward as it continued rotating to bring its starboard turbolasers to bear.

Ronan looked sideways at Savit, at the stiff expression and furious eyes. The grand admiral's earlier arrogance was still there, but Ronan could also see a growing sense of frustration and impotence. Possibly even the beginnings of panic. For the first time in Savit's career, he was being blocked at every turn.

Standing a few meters away, in stark contrast, was Thrawn.

Ronan gazed at him, marveling in spite of himself. Thrawn was his political enemy, he reminded himself firmly, the one person who stood between Director Krennic and the funding Stardust needed.

Worse, Thrawn's opposition was ultimately futile. His TIE Defenders might be useful fighters, but they would prove unnecessary in a galaxy where the Death Star shone as the ultimate power. The growing rebel nuisance would be swept away; pirates would cease to exist; even the Grysks that Thrawn seemed to fear so greatly would fall before Director Krennic and his battle station.

And yet . . .

"Admiral, this is Chief Hangar Master Llano," a frantic voice came from the *Firedrake*'s bridge speakers. "Did you order TIEs to launch?"

"What?" Savit demanded.

"Because I've got four fighters from Squadron One dropping from their cradles," Llano said. "I tried to call them for order confirmation, but they didn't respond."

"Call them back," Savit snarled.

"I tried, Admiral. But they just ignored me."

Savit flashed a look at Boulag. "Captain?" he demanded, making the word an accusation.

"I gave no orders, Admiral," Boulag protested.

"He is correct," Thrawn spoke up.

"Admiral—Captain," Llano said, cutting back in. "Admiral Thrawn's shuttle is also leaving. Did you give orders—?"

"*No!*" Savit thundered. He let go of Ronan's arm, giving him a shove that stumbled him off balance, and dropped his hand to his holstered blaster. "What did you do, Thrawn? *What did you do?*"

"Those four TIEs have been commandeered by pilots I brought from the *Chimaera*," Thrawn said calmly. "I'm afraid you'll find your pilots for those particular fighters have been neutralized."

"Impossible," Savit insisted. "There's been no report of blasterfire, and my TIE commander makes sure all his personnel are trained for hand-to-hand combat."

"I have no doubt they're quite competent against capture by pirates or rebels," Thrawn said. "Even so, I daresay your TIE commander's training is not up to a determined attack by one of my death troopers."

Savit's mouth dropped open a millimeter. "You said they were back on the *Chimaera*."

"I said I had left them behind," Thrawn corrected. "I never said how far behind they had been left."

Savit swore viciously. "Launch Squadron Two," he ordered. "They're to intercept the rogue TIEs and turn them back. No—on second thought, never mind turning them back. Intercept and destroy."

"You will find that difficult to do," Thrawn said. "My people have also disabled the remote auto-lock mechanism. You shall have to disengage each cradle manually."

"Well, then, we'll have to do that, won't we?" Savit bit out. "Hangar Master Llano, do whatever you have to, but get those TIEs in space—"

Without warning, the *Firedrake* jerked as the dull clang of an impact somewhere deep inside it rumbled across the bridge. "Hangar Master—!" Savit shouted.

"Impact in the hangar bay!" Llano's bewildered voice wailed. "Something—it's a big cylinder, Admiral. It just—we never saw anything, sir. It just slammed into the aft racks. I don't know where it came from."

"Thrawn?" Savit demanded again, his knuckles going white on the grip of his blaster.

"A tool created by the Grysks," Thrawn said. "A cloaked gravity-well generator designed to protect an area from intrusion." He waved a hand in the direction of the hangar bay. "As you see, it can also be repurposed as an offensive weapon."

Savit stared at him another moment. "Boulag, where are those stolen TIEs going?"

"They're—" Boulag paused, and Ronan saw his hands curl into fists. "They're running along the starboard wedgeline. Taking out the turbolaser targeting sensors on that side."

"Are they now?" Savit said, a dark smile tweaking the corners of his mouth. "I'm impressed, Thrawn. I really am. Faro has accorded herself very well. But she seems to have forgotten one small thing."

"What is that, Admiral?" Thrawn asked.

"The fact that I'm not alone out here." He gestured to the comm station. "Signal to the *Stormbird* and *Misthunter*."

"Channel open, Admiral."

Savit seemed to stand a little taller. "This is Grand Admiral Savit," he called. "Grand Admiral Thrawn and his officers have proven themselves traitors to the Empire. Accordingly, you are ordered to attack the *Chimaera* with full turbolasers until it surrenders or is destroyed."

"Transmitted, sir."

Ronan took a deep breath. "Admiral, I ask you again to reconsider," he said. "As Thrawn said earlier, we can find a way to make this go away. Between Thrawn and Director Krennic, we can find a quieter solution that doesn't involve the slaughter of innocent personnel."

"No one who follows a traitor is innocent," Savit shot back. "Surely an assistant director on the Stardust project can understand that."

"Admiral, please," Ronan said, shifting his eyes to the viewport and the distant *Chimaera*. He hadn't been aboard that ship very long, but he'd met some of Thrawn's officers. Commodore Faro, Commander Hammerly, Hangar Master Xoxtin, a few others. All of them loyal to the Empire. None of them deserving to die.

Especially not at Savit's hand.

Because Savit was the traitor here. Thrawn had the evidence, and Savit had all but admitted it. The inevitable inquiry—and there would be an inquiry—would surely bring that into the open.

But not before Faro and Hammerly and the *Chimaera* were dead.

Unless Ronan did something.

His gaze shifted to the blaster strapped at Savit's side. The grand admiral's hand was still resting there, the fingers still tense. If Ronan could get to that weapon . . .

But no. He had no authority to interfere in this. Not only would anything he did or tried to do reflect on Director Krennic and Stardust, but it would likely get him shot by one of the two stormtroopers still on guard at the aft end of the command walkway.

Faro and the *Chimaera* would die. The minute the other ships opened fire . . .

He frowned, belatedly noticing that they *hadn't* opened fire.

Why hadn't they?

The same question had apparently just occurred to Savit. "*Stormbird* and *Misthunter*, I gave you an order," he called. "Why haven't you obeyed?"

Silence. "*Stormbird* and *Misthunter*—"

"To all ships of the Third Fleet." Commodore Faro's voice came over the speaker. "As you can see, several of the *Firedrake*'s TIE pilots have mutinied against Grand Admiral Savit's unwarranted attack on the *Chimaera*. They have expressed their dissension by crippling his ability to bring further deadly force to bear."

"What?" Savit demanded. "No—that's a lie. Those are *Thrawn's* pilots—"

"Once again I call on you to similarly defy Admiral Savit's illegal orders and join me in demanding that he be placed under arrest and relieved of command pending a full investigation—"

"*No!*" Savit snarled. "All ships, destroy the *Chimaera*! Destroy it *now!*"

"I'm afraid they can't hear you," Thrawn said. "With your attention on the TIEs currently neutralizing your starboard turbolaser batteries, you failed to see where my shuttle went when it left the hangar bay."

"Boulag?" Savit demanded.

"Yes, sir," Boulag said, his voice strained. "Hull sensor record—quickly!"

Ronan watched as the visual record rolled backward to the point where the shuttle left the hangar bay . . . followed it as it swooped underneath the portside of the wedge and rounded the wedgeline . . . came up around and back toward the superstructure, still hugging the hull . . . came to rest against the side of the superstructure below and aft of the bridge.

"Damn," Boulag muttered.

"Indeed," Thrawn said. "As you can see, it is currently grappled to the hull directly over the *Firedrake*'s short-range transmitter, where it is now jamming all of your outgoing signals."

"Fine," Savit gritted out. "There are plenty of other transmitters on my TIEs and shuttles with enough power to reach the other Star Destroyers. I'll relay through one of those." He raised his voice. "Hangar Master Llano?"

There was no answer. "*Hangar Master Llano!*"

"I believe you'll find that Hangar Control is no longer under your authority," Thrawn said. "I believe Commodore Faro will be commenting on that fact shortly, citing it as further evidence that the *Firedrake*'s mutiny is spreading." He gestured. "But if you wish to go to the hangar bay and personally board one of the TIEs to make your transmission, you're free to do so."

"So Faro can then claim I've left the bridge because my senior officers have also mutinied?" Savit demanded. "I think I can give the lie to that one. Captain Boulag, resume your attack on the *Chimaera*."

Ronan looked at Boulag. The captain's posture was stiff, his face tortured. "I'm sorry, Admiral," the captain said. "But I don't believe the Empire is best served by continuing this course of action."

"I don't care what you believe," Savit snarled. "I'm your commander, and the commander of the Third Fleet. You will obey, or I'll have you shot where you stand for insubordination and mutiny."

"I'm sorry, Admiral—"

"This is Captain Gilad Pellaeon, commanding the ISD *Harbinger*," a new voice came over the speaker. "I've reviewed the data sent by the *Chimaera*, and have concluded that the evidence is sufficient to justify an official inquiry. Accordingly, I am placing the *Harbinger* under the authority of Commodore Faro and calling on Grand Admiral Savit to surrender his command. I also call on Captains Lochry and Rasdel to join me—"

"Cut him off," Savit snapped. "Cut him *off*!"

The speaker fell silent.

"It's over, Admiral," Thrawn said quietly. "With the *Chimaera* and *Harbinger* both against you, you cannot hope to prevail."

"Damn you," Savit said.

And suddenly his blaster was out of its holster, the muzzle leveled at Thrawn. "Enjoy your victory while you can, Grand Admiral Thrawn. I'll see you in hell."

Thrawn was Ronan's enemy. Ronan had already concluded that. Thrawn was the political and financial enemy of Stardust and Director Krennic himself. Thrawn's TIE Defenders, and Thrawn himself, were about to be made superfluous by the glory that was the Death Star.

And yet . . .

In a single smooth motion, Ronan snatched the cape from around his throat and whipped it across Savit's face.

The blaster spat out a sizzling bolt, missing Thrawn by millimeters and continuing past to shatter the edge of the starboard crew pit.

With a curse, Savit caught the cape and hurled it away, twisting to face Ronan. He raised his blaster, this time pointing it at Ronan—

And with screaming circles of blue light, a stun blast sizzled forward from somewhere over Ronan's shoulder. It caught Savit squarely in the torso and sent him sprawling to the deck.

Ronan spun around. The two stormtroopers Savit had left on guard at the end of the command walkway were sprawled unmoving on the deck. Standing between them was Dayja, a stormtrooper's E-11 in one hand and a gold-edged, shimmer-backed ident data card held high in the other.

"Everyone at ease," he called. "Major Dayja Collerand, Imperial Security Bureau. I'm ordering that Grand Admiral Savit be temporarily relieved of duty and command of the *Firedrake* turned over to Captain Boulag."

"On what authority?" Boulag asked, looking both outraged and relieved.

"Interesting fact, Captain," Dayja said conversationally as he strode toward the group on the walkway, his ID card still held high. "Not sure how many officers know it, but there's a regulation stating that all blasters on a capital ship bridge must be set on stun unless there's been a direct and previously logged order from its commander."

"To prevent exactly what just nearly happened here," Thrawn said.

"And other things," Dayja said. "Nice move, by the way, Assistant Director Ronan. Captain Boulag, you're in temporary command of this vessel. What are your orders?"

Boulag looked at Savit's unconscious form. "I assume that blaster regulation comes with a prescribed penalty, Major Collerand?"

"It does," Dayja said. "Restraint and removal from duty until a hearing can be held."

"I see," Boulag said. "Very well. I presume, Admiral Thrawn, that you'll remain aboard to testify at Admiral Savit's hearing."

"I'm afraid I have more pressing duties at the moment, Captain," Thrawn said. "There is a battle taking place even now that may urgently require the *Chimaera*'s presence."

"So you're just leaving?" Dayja asked.

"I am," Thrawn said. "Do you contest that?"

Dayja shrugged. "Colonel Yularen told me to trust you. Hardly seems worth questioning that assessment now. Captain Boulag? Any objections?"

"Grand Admiral Thrawn outranks me by quite a bit," Boulag said. "As far as I'm concerned, he can come and go as he pleases."

"Thank you," Thrawn said, inclining his head to each of them in turn. "As for my testimony, I'm sure Assistant Director Ronan will be most willing to speak to your board of inquiry."

"I will," Ronan said. "But not now." Stepping over to where Savit had thrown his cape, he retrieved it from the deck and fastened it again around his neck. "Director Krennic ordered me aboard the *Chimaera* to observe your activities, Admiral Thrawn. I don't intend to bend that order more than I already have."

"Very well," Thrawn said, pulling out his comlink. "I shall be happy of your company."

Ronan suppressed a grimace. For once, Thrawn was wrong.

Because if they were going where Ronan thought, and about to do what Ronan suspected, the grand admiral wouldn't be happy that Ronan was there.

He wouldn't be happy at all.

CHAPTER 23

And with the Grysk fighters still doing their dance of attrition as they waited for the *Steadfast* to make its move, it was time.

"Helm, your vector is straight toward the lead warship," Ar'alani reminded the helmsman. "The fighters will respond with lasers and missiles, their salvos probably partially designed to drive you off course. Ignore the attacks."

"Yes, Admiral," the helmsman said. His voice was steady, but Eli could hear the tension beneath the words. The *Steadfast* was going to get bloody on this one, and everyone aboard knew it.

"Senior Commander Cinsar, is the special package ready?" Ar'alani called.

"Ready, Admiral," Cinsar reported. "We couldn't get in and remove the propellant within your time frame, so instead we've drilled holes in the pre-mix chamber. That should drain enough of it quickly enough."

"We'll find out in a moment. Stand by."

Eli looked back, saw Ar'alani visibly brace herself. She was taking a chance on this, and everyone aboard knew that, too.

But there was no hesitation he could detect, from her or anyone else around him. The officers and crew of the *Steadfast* trusted her implicitly.

Very much like the officers and crew of the *Chimaera*, he found himself thinking. Once again, he wondered at the history and relationship between Ar'alani and Thrawn.

"Helm: Take us in."

There was a brief flicker of sensation as the ship's sudden acceleration momentarily overpowered the compensators. Then the compensators and ship's gravity reasserted themselves, and the *Steadfast* was driving toward the distant Grysk ships.

They were five seconds into their charge when the fighters opened fire.

"Laser salvo," Khresh reported. "Deflectors weakening ... deflectors gone. Secondary deflectors forming."

"Hull damage in sectors three, seven, fifteen, and twenty," a voice reported over the intercom. "Extruding ablative foam."

"Missiles launch," Khresh snapped. "Thirty missiles, running on track."

"Lasers on missiles," Ar'alani ordered. "Stand by spheres for anything that gets through. Breachers, stand by to launch."

"Breachers ready."

The *Steadfast* continued forward, its hull metal bubbling or flashing into vapor as the fighters' lasers slashed into it. The hail of missiles slowly decreased as the Chiss lasers and plasma spheres took a steady toll on their numbers, until the last one flashed harmlessly away.

But at a cost, Eli saw as he did a quick check of the numbers. The enemy still had at least forty missiles left, and the *Steadfast* was down to twenty-five plasma spheres.

And that didn't count the fighters and missiles still waiting on the second warship. On any balance sheet in the galaxy, the *Steadfast* was doomed.

"Fire Breachers," Ar'alani ordered.

There was a slight jolt as the three Breacher missiles shot out of their tubes: two normal Breachers, and the special one Cinsar's techs had created. Eli watched the tracks as the missiles accelerated toward the lead warship.

The fighters had obviously expected the move. Six of them immediately shifted their laserfire to the Breachers, trying to shoot them out of the sky before they could reach the warship. The rest angled toward the missiles' vectors, hoping to get there in time to intercept.

Ar'alani had timed the attack perfectly. With the extra speed the *Steadfast*'s charge had given them, the first two missiles shot past before the converging fighters could form their cordon. The other fighters continued to fire, and for the first time the Grysk warship's own lasers opened up in an effort to destroy the Breachers far enough out that their acid packages would be too dissipated by the time they hit its hull to do any serious damage.

The first missile flared and vanished from the tactical display as the warship's lasers got it. The second missile flickered as the fighters found the range. Three or four direct hits later, it, too, was gone.

But the third Breacher, the one Cinsar had gimmicked . . .

It had barely built up a third of the velocity a normal Breacher would achieve when its drive sputtered and went silent, leaving the missile running on a relatively slow ballistic vector toward the warship. Slow enough that the group of fighters that had been converging on the missiles' vector easily made it into position. A burst of laserfire and the Breacher was blasted into a flying glob of acid. The fighters held position, protecting the warship behind them from the attack, trusting their electrostatic barriers to disperse most of the acid before it could cause them any significant damage, and willing to take whatever minor damage it cost them to protect the warship.

The pool of acid slammed into the cluster, splashing out across the entire group. With their defensive duty now accomplished, the fighters separated again and resumed their attack on the *Steadfast*.

They got off half a dozen laser shots before their weapons and engines suddenly went silent.

"Destroy them," Ar'alani said quietly.

It was a slaughter. The fighters, unable to fire or even maneuver properly, were sitting targets for the *Steadfast*'s lasers. A shot or two each to eliminate whatever electrostatic barrier was left, then a single final shot to break, impale, or shatter the helpless fighter, and the gunners were free to turn to the next enemy in line.

The Chiss were midway through the carnage when the Grysk commander finally woke up to what was happening. The warship opened up with furious salvos of laserfire and flight after flight of missiles at the *Steadfast* in an apparent attempt to distract or otherwise dissuade it from its course of action.

Unfortunately for him, that was exactly what Ar'alani had hoped he would do. The more he drained his offensive weaponry at a less-than-optimal distance, the better.

But there was a cost. A terrible cost. And as the *Steadfast* continued to drive forward, and the range between the combatants diminished, the cost mounted ever higher. The Grysk lasers dug ever deeper into the *Steadfast*'s hull, and occasional missiles began to sneak through the defensive lasers and plasma spheres.

The *Steadfast* fought back with its own spectrum lasers, the beams from the two warships crisscrossing each other in a ferocity that rivaled the blazing fire of a solar storm. The laser blasts from the Chiss side were interspersed with the ship's remaining plasma spheres and Breachers.

Eli felt his chest tighten with each damage report that came in. Sections of the outer hull were burned off or shattered by missile warheads. The warriors on damage control did their best, but gradually they were forced inward as more and more of the outer sections were breached and the compartments behind them became uninhabitable.

The Grysk ship was hardly untouched, though. The handful of Breachers that got past the enemy defenses washed sections of hull with acid, pitting and blackening the metal and leaving it more vulnerable to laserfire. A few of the plasma spheres got through as well, and where one of them struck, a laser cluster or missile launcher would suddenly fall silent.

But the Grysk warship was larger than the *Steadfast*, with a correspondingly thicker hull and far more weaponry. It was clear to everyone that if the *Steadfast* kept up its strategy, it would be destroyed long before the Grysk succumbed to the counterattack.

And if by some miracle the *Steadfast* prevailed, the second warship waited patiently in the near distance, untouched and out of range, ready to take up where the first warship had left off.

Or so the Grysks thought.

"Lieutenant Eli'van'to, are your forces ready?" Ar'alani called.

"They are, Admiral," Eli confirmed, breathing a sigh of relief. Finally. He'd never been in a Chiss warship that had suffered this badly in combat and had no idea how much more it could handle. Hopefully, Ar'alani hadn't cut things too close. "Generator is in position, and all data has been transmitted and acknowledged." He smiled tightly. "And I've confirmed that the second warship is the same design and configuration as the first, with the same weapon and defense emplacements."

"Very good, Lieutenant. Stand ready . . . *now.*"

Mentally crossing his fingers, Eli pressed the comm key.

Two seconds passed, the time necessary for the *Steadfast*'s signal to cross the six hundred thousand kilometers to its destination. Another second passed . . . another . . . for a horrible moment Eli wondered if the Grysk attack had damaged the *Steadfast*'s transmitter—

In the distance, there was a flicker of something directly beneath the second warship: the cloaked gravity-well generator that the *Steadfast* had carefully and invisibly catapulted in that direction before the battle had even begun. The generator that the Grysks had created to detect incoming ships, snap them out of hyperspace, and then go cloaked again. The fact that it was suddenly no longer cloaked meant it had detected something approaching and was about to rudely interrupt the traveler's journey.

Only in this case, the target wasn't some hapless freighter or unaware yacht.

And as Eli watched in relief and satisfaction, twelve small ships popped into view. Ships whose vectors had been carefully calculated to converge onto that second, untouched warship. Ships that had been pulled in at the edge of the precisely defined sphere created by the generator's gravity well. Ships that were now only a few hundred meters from the warship, well inside the range of the warship's point defenses.

Thrawn's twelve TIE Defenders.

The Grysk were taken completely by surprise. The Defenders had barely returned to realspace when they launched their attack, pouring laserfire and missiles into the enemy ship.

Not simply random attacks, either. The *Steadfast*'s running battle with the lead Grysk warship, the battle that had cost the Chiss ship so much damage, had allowed Eli to pinpoint the enemy's laser clusters, missile tubes, and electrostatic barrier nodes, data that he'd continued to feed to the Defenders right up to the point of their controlled jump into battle. The result was an attack that was surgical in its precision, systematically crippling the enemy ship.

"Stand by, Lieutenant," Ar'alani said, leaning forward in her chair as she watched the Defenders' attack.

"Standing ready, Admiral," Eli said. He switched to Basic. "Captain Dobbs?"

"Standing ready," Dobbs's voice came in confirmation.

"Switch to Beta attack . . . now," Ar'alani ordered.

"Beta attack, Captain," Eli relayed.

At the stricken Grysk ship the Defenders broke off their attack, sweeping outward and fleeing the gravity-well generator's sphere of influence. With a multiple flicker of pseudomotion they jumped, disappearing once again into hyperspace.

Eli counted off the seconds. The timing on this one was more of a judgment call than anything hard and definitive. But it was Ar'alani's judgment call, and Eli was more than ready to accept it.

From the hangar nestled at the connection point between the Grysk warship's twin hulls a group of fighters appeared, driving outward to join the battle. "Tanik?" Ar'alani called.

"Thirty fighters, Admiral," Tanik reported. "Should be the warship's entire complement."

The fighters moved clear of the ship and drew together in a brief cluster as they once again fine-tuned their electrostatic barriers to one another. Eli held his breath . . .

And as the gravity-well generator once again became visible, the Defenders flashed back to the attack.

Only this time they weren't arrowing in toward the warship in a full-circuit attack sphere. This time, they were gathered beneath it, forming a hemisphere centered on the hangar bay and the newly emerged Grysk fighters.

Once again, the enemy was caught flatfooted. The Grysk fighters tried their best, half of them spinning outward in an attempt to get clear of the kill zone, the other half opening fire on the Defenders in the hope of scoring quick kills or at least trading fighters one for one.

But their tactics weren't designed for use against fighters with full shields, close-combat missiles, and heavy laser cannons. None of the fleeing Grysks got past the Imperials' encirclement before they were destroyed, and none of the fighters still in the zone got off more than a shot or two before they, too, were shattered. Once again, as it had earlier with Ar'alani's Breacher, the fighters' close-rank positioning cost the Grysks dearly, first as they impeded one another's actions, then as the Defenders' fire sent destructive clouds of fast-moving debris into the ships that were otherwise still intact.

Within a minute, the battle was over.

"Gamma attack," Ar'alani ordered.

Eli nodded. "Dobbs: Gamma attack."

"I think we can skip Gamma," Dobbs replied. "Let's move to Delta."

"Defenders want to move to Delta, Admiral," Eli said, translating back to Cheunh.

"Do they," Ar'alani said thoughtfully. "Very well, let's split the difference. Half of them to Gamma, half to Delta."

"Ah . . . yes, Admiral," Eli said hesitantly. The Alpha attack had been against the rear warship; the follow-up, Beta, against the fighters. Gamma was supposed to be a second attack on the warship, with Delta being the Defenders charging from the doomed rear warship to the lead warship, where they would join the *Steadfast* in its continuing attack.

He could appreciate Dobbs's assessment that the second Grysk was no longer a threat—after all, he and the other Defender pilots were the ones on the scene, with the clearer picture of the damage they'd caused.

But even if his conclusion was correct, splitting an already small force was a dangerous move, especially when half of them would have to fly between two enemy warships that might still have lasers or missiles that could be brought to bear.

"Send your fighters back to hyperspace," Ar'alani continued. "Six are to come back around immediately and converge on the rear warship. The others will wait thirty seconds, then follow them in." She raised her eyebrows. "This time aiming slightly closer to the *Steadfast*."

Eli frowned . . . then suddenly he got it. "Yes, Admiral," he said. Switching back to Basic, he gave Dobbs the order and a terse explanation of what was about to happen.

On the tactical, the Defenders turned and disappeared again into hyperspace. "Tractor Control: Stand ready," Ar'alani ordered. "Your window on this will be very brief."

In the distance, the gravity-well generator reappeared. "Now!" Ar'alani snapped.

"Got it, Admiral," Khresh confirmed. The six Defenders popped into view, their weapons again blazing at the rear warship as the generator again disappeared into its cloaking field.

"Bring it in," Ar'alani ordered. "Straight toward us and underneath the lead warship."

With both the generator and the tractor beam invisible, there was no way for Eli to tell whether it was working. He counted down the thirty seconds Ar'alani had specified . . .

And then the generator became visible again, hugging the underside of the lead Grysk warship as it was pulled steadily back toward the *Steadfast*. An instant later, right on Ar'alani's mark, the remaining six Defenders appeared, their laser cannons and missiles once again tearing into their target. The warship fired three or four ineffective blasts at the fighters in response, then sent half a dozen equally useless wild shots at the *Steadfast*, then fell silent.

"Stand ready, Lieutenant," Ar'alani said, again leaning forward in her chair. Another judgment call, Eli knew, this one just as crucial as the last. "Stand ready . . . call them back."

"Dobbs, pull out," Eli ordered.

"Acknowledged," Dobbs said. "Defenders—get scarce." The Defenders turned and vanished again into hyperspace.

Just as the two Grysk warships exploded.

Eli grimaced. They'd seen the Grysk warship at the observation point pull the same scorched-ground maneuver: self-destructing their ship rather than letting it be taken. He'd hoped this commander might put off that decision too long, and that there might be at least a partially intact ship left for the Chiss to study.

Now, instead, they would have to make do with wreckage.

"Secure tractor beam," Ar'alani ordered. If she was disappointed by the loss of her potential prizes, she wasn't letting it show. "Move us off the generator's vector—we don't want the Defenders running into us when they return." She turned to Eli and gestured. "A word, Lieutenant Eli'van'to?"

"Yes, Admiral," Eli said, unstrapping and walking over to her.

"I want you to arrange accommodations and refreshments for the Defender pilots," she said. "We don't know how long until the *Chimaera* arrives to retrieve them, and I want them made comfortable."

"Yes, ma'am," Eli said. He started to turn away, then stopped as she raised a finger.

"Navigator Vah'nya," she said, lowering her voice to just above a whisper. "Tell me what exactly you promised her."

Eli hesitated. But there was no way out of it. "She said that if the battle went against us she didn't want herself or the other navigators to be captured by the Grysks."

"I know. Did you promise to kill her?"

A capital crime. For an instant Eli considered denying it, or at least slanting the truth.

But this was Admiral Ar'alani. It would be useless to lie to her. "Yes, ma'am, I did."

"How would you have done it?"

Eli looked straight back into her eyes. The glowing red eyes of a

Chiss . . . the viewports into the heart and soul of a Chiss warrior. "I would have taken her and the others into an escape pod," he said. "Along with as much explosive as I could gather. I would have waited until the pod had been taken aboard the warship, then detonated the explosives."

"Thereby fulfilling your promise to Vah'nya and also taking as many of the enemy to their deaths alongside you as possible?"

The soul of a Chiss warrior . . . "Yes, Admiral."

For a moment Ar'alani gazed at him. "You wish a command position," she said. "You chafe under the analysis task I assigned you."

Useless to lie . . . "Yes, ma'am, I do."

"Do you know what it is you're studying?"

"No, ma'am. I assume it has something to do with logistics or transfer operations."

"No." Ar'alani nodded across the bridge at Vah'nya. "You're studying her."

Eli felt his eyes go wide. *"Vah'nya?"*

"Vah'nya, Un'hee, and all the other Chiss navigators," Ar'alani said. "You're examining their histories, genetics, family flow, and everything else about them we could codify sufficiently to be reduced to numbers. You're searching for a pattern—which Mitth'raw'nuruodo assured me you are quite good at—with the ultimate goal of anticipating where future navigators may arise and perhaps how to nurture more of them."

She looked across at Vah'nya. "And if we are *very* fortunate, you may even unlock the secret of how Navigator Vah'nya has held on to Third Sight so long past the time when it usually fades."

She looked back at Eli. "Does your assignment seem quite so insignificant now, Lieutenant Eli'van'to?"

"No, ma'am, it doesn't," Eli said, feeling like a fool. He should have known that Thrawn wouldn't have sent him to Ar'alani and the Chiss without an exceptionally good reason. "My apologies, Admiral. I shouldn't have questioned your orders, or my assignment."

"No, you shouldn't," Ar'alani agreed. "I presume you will take that lesson to heart?"

"I will, Admiral."

"Good." Ar'alani gestured out the viewport. "I see the TIE Defenders have returned. You may start bringing them into the hangar bay and then arrange for their comfort."

"Yes, ma'am." Eli stiffened to attention. "Thank you, Admiral."

"You are welcome." Ar'alani inclined her head to him. "Carry on . . . Lieutenant Commander Eli'van'to."

CHAPTER 24

The *Chimaera* arrived at the site of the battle into an immense field of debris.

To Faro's relief, the debris wasn't from the *Steadfast*.

Though it was quickly clear the Chiss ship hadn't exactly come through the battle unscathed. Its hull was mottled and blackened, with parts gone completely, and there were huge gouges in a couple of places where she remembered seeing laser clusters.

But the ship was alive and functional. More important, at least from an Imperial point of view, all twelve TIE Defenders had made it through unharmed.

"I'm afraid we haven't been able to sift much from the wreckage," Ar'alani said. She'd come over with the Defenders, riding in one of the Chiss shuttles, apparently with an eye toward delivering them personally to the *Chimaera*.

Faro had rather expected Eli Vanto to come over with her, if only for a last goodbye to his former commander. But aside from the shuttle crew, Ar'alani had come alone.

"We have saved a few of the more interesting pieces out for you, if you'd like them," Ar'alani continued. "You are welcome to come over and look at the rest if you have time."

"I'm afraid I don't," Thrawn said. "But I will accept the pieces you've brought for my later study."

"I will instruct my shuttle crew to unload them before I depart," Ar'alani said. "I believe you will find two of the pieces to be particularly interesting. Both appear to be sections of artwork."

Thrawn's eyes narrowed. "Indeed. Artwork of Grysk origin?"

"Unknown," Ar'alani said. "Perhaps you will be able to identify the source."

"I will look forward to examining them," Thrawn said. "If they aren't Grysk, they are at least artworks that some Grysk warrior found interesting or pleasing. Even that much will be useful."

"I pray your study bears fruit," Ar'alani said. "We will need all possible assistance if we are to prevail against them."

"I will do whatever I can," Thrawn promised.

Faro suppressed a grimace. *Whatever I can.* Did that promise include activities or assistance in direct opposition to his oath to the navy and the Empire?

Thrawn had proven that Savit was a traitor. Was his relationship with Ar'alani and the Chiss taking him along a dangerously similar path?

And if he was, even if it was for the best of reasons or intentions, would it be Faro's duty to call him on it?

"Tell me of Lieutenant Vanto," Thrawn said. "Has his study achieved success?"

"Not yet," Ar'alani said. "But he continues with determination. If success is possible, I have no doubt he will be the one to achieve it." She cocked her head. "You haven't asked about his role in the battle."

"The safe return of my TIE Defenders suggests his role was a positive one."

"It was indeed," Ar'alani said. "My official report will feature Lieutenant Commander Eli'van'to most prominently."

Thrawn's lips might have twitched in a small smile at Vanto's new rank. Faro couldn't tell for sure. "I'm glad my faith in him was not misplaced," he said. "And now, since you speak of reports, it is time for Assistant Director Ronan to make his. Commodore Faro, if you will summon him to the bridge?"

"Yes, sir," Faro said, pulling out her comlink.

"Then I take my leave, Mitth'raw'nuruodo," Ar'alani said with a nod. "A safe voyage to you."

"Another moment of your time, if you please," Thrawn said. "I should like you to be here until the assistant director has finished his report."

Ar'alani frowned. "I have my duties, Admiral."

"You may soon find those duties to be slightly expanded," Thrawn told her. "Commodore? Assistant Director Ronan, if you please."

Thrawn and Faro were waiting by the aft bridge comm station when Ronan arrived.

So, to his surprise, was Admiral Ar'alani.

"Admiral," Ronan greeted Thrawn cautiously, throwing a speculative look at Ar'alani. "You asked me to join you?"

"The TIE Defenders have returned from their service to Admiral Ar'alani," Thrawn said. "The Grysk task force has been obliterated, and with it this particular threat to the Empire."

"That's good news," Ronan said, keeping his tone neutral. The threat was gone . . . but the price of that victory had been collusion with alien forces.

"Very good news," Thrawn agreed. "I understand that Captain Boulag is returning Grand Admiral Savit to Coruscant for an inquiry, with the *Misthunter* as escort, and that Captain Lochry and the *Stormbird* are proceeding to Aloxor to supervise operations against the pirates who were complicit with him in the thefts."

He raised his eyebrows. "As time is growing short, I thought it would be useful for you to take this opportunity to deliver your report to Director Krennic and Grand Moff Tarkin." He gestured to the comm display.

Ronan felt his lip twitch. He'd assumed he would have some more breathing space to figure out how exactly to present this whole thing to Director Krennic.

Apparently, Thrawn thought otherwise.

"Captain Lochry told me the HoloNet didn't work in this system," he said, stalling for time. "Don't we need to travel back to the transfer point?"

"Captain Lochry was mistaken," Thrawn said. "I received his transmission. I merely declined to answer."

Ronan frowned. "Why? All he wanted was for you to confirm my identity."

"Which I did not wish to do," Thrawn said. "I needed him to send you to Grand Admiral Savit, so that you would be present to witness his confession."

He reached to the comm board. "They await you." He tapped a switch.

Two of the displays lit up: one with Tarkin, the other with Director Krennic. "Assistant Director Ronan," Tarkin said smoothly. "Grand Admiral Thrawn tells me you're ready to deliver your report on the lost supply ships." His eyes bored into Ronan's face. "And to tell us whether or not Admiral Thrawn fulfilled the terms of his bargain."

"I am," Ronan said, his thoughts skidding like an insect on ice. Ar'alani, standing outside the cam's view but watching him closely. Faro, also out of view, watching him with equal intensity. Thrawn, standing beside him, awaiting his word on whether his Defender project would rise or fall.

Thrawn, colluding with an alien government and using Imperial resources to assist an alien military. Treason?

The Defenders themselves, apparently pivotal in the defeat of another alien threat to the Empire. A useful, even vital project?

Grand Admiral Savit's threat to Stardust, identified and eliminated. Success?

But it was all mental gymnastics. Ronan had long since decided what truly mattered, and knew what he had to say.

"I regret to inform you," he said, "that Grand Admiral Thrawn has failed his part of the bargain."

Out of the corner of his eye he saw Faro stir as if to speak, then subside at a small hand motion from Thrawn. "The stipulation was that he would destroy the grallocs harassing the shipping vessels," Ronan continued. "He did not succeed in doing that."

"Really," Tarkin said, eyeing Ronan closely. "I was given to understand that with the arrest of Grand Admiral Savit, the problems with the Stardust shipping had been resolved."

"Irrelevant to the terms of the agreement," Ronan said firmly.

"And what of your reports that he was in contact with alien military forces?" Director Krennic asked.

It was a crucial question, Ronan knew. A potentially devastating one. But he also knew it was reflexive, a response to the reports Ronan had sent, and that Director Krennic didn't really care about the answer. Ronan's final report had eliminated the possibility that any of Stardust's funding would be lost to Thrawn's Defenders, and that was all the director cared about.

"Those contacts turned out to be minor and of no importance," Ronan said. "My final report will describe them in detail." A report that, if fully truthful, would once again bring the treason question back to the forefront.

But only if anyone read it. Ronan had dealt with enough bureaucracy to know how to file a report that would all but guarantee that no one ever would.

"I will look forward to it," Tarkin said. Another automatic response, Ronan knew, with no real determination or interest behind it. He'd lost this latest bid to wrest Stardust from Director Krennic's control, had accepted his defeat with his usual ill grace coated with surface politeness, and would now move on to his next ploy. "Admiral Thrawn, have you anything to say in rebuttal?"

Beside Ronan, Thrawn stirred. "No," he said.

"Then I'm afraid I have no choice but to rule in Director Krennic's favor," Tarkin said. "But rest assured I will continue to speak to the Emperor on your behalf. Lord Vader, too, has expressed interest in the Defenders. I have no doubt that once Stardust has been completed and additional funding becomes available, your project will be a priority."

"Thank you," Thrawn said. "Regarding Stardust, may I make a suggestion?"

Director Krennic's eyes narrowed, just slightly. "I would be interested in hearing it," he said warily.

"Considering the importance of the project, it occurs to me that as the moment of activation approaches it may come under heightened scrutiny and potential attack, both from without and within."

"What exactly are you suggesting, Admiral?" Director Krennic asked, an edge of warning in his voice. "My assistant directors and senior officers are all completely loyal to the Empire."

"I do not suggest otherwise," Thrawn said calmly. "Yet an enemy could potentially find a way aboard where he could create serious problems."

"My security arrangements—"

"What do you suggest, Admiral?" Tarkin interrupted.

"I submit that there is one person in the Empire who would not only recognize all threats to Stardust, but also have the capability to deal with them," Thrawn said. "My suggestion is that Lord Vader be assigned to watch over the project until at least the first shakedown cruise."

Director Krennic gave a small snort. "I hardly think that necessary."

"An excellent idea," Tarkin said smoothly. "I will most certainly submit it to the Emperor at my earliest convenience."

"Thank you," Thrawn said. "If we are finished, I have received word that the situation on Lothal has become critical. I must return there immediately."

"So I've also heard," Tarkin said, his expression hardening. "With command of the Third Fleet in disarray, I've ordered the *Harbinger* to accompany you." His expression cracked in a small smile. "I have no doubt Captain Pellaeon's presence will be unnecessary to your final victory against this current rebel activity, but he may prove useful to you."

"Thank you again," Thrawn said. "Director Krennic, I will return Assistant Director Ronan to you at his earliest convenience."

"Thank you, Admiral Thrawn," Director Krennic said. "I'll look forward to working with you in the future." He reached offscreen, and his image disappeared.

Which was, Ronan knew, a lie. Given Thrawn's participation in this latest of Tarkin's schemes, no matter how innocently the grand admiral might have been drawn into it, Director Krennic would never trust him again.

"I'll return you to your duties now, Admiral," Tarkin said. "And look forward to the report of further successes at Lothal." Tarkin reached offscreen.

And just before his image vanished Ronan thought he saw a small, satisfied smile.

"Commodore Faro, return to the bridge and contact the *Harbinger*," Thrawn said. "Coordinate with Captain Pellaeon for a rendezvous at Lothal."

"Yes, sir." For a long moment, Faro's eyes lingered on Ronan's face, eyes that said clearly and passionately that she wanted him dead, and not only dead but dead in the most lingering and painful way possible. Then, finally, she turned, keeping her eyes on Ronan's as long as she could, and strode under the archway separating the aft bridge from the bridge and headed for the comm station.

"You'll make arrangements at once to return me to Stardust?" Ronan asked. Faro's departure had left him alone with Thrawn and Ar'alani, and after that death-wish look from the commodore he was suddenly feeling uneasy about being alone with a pair of aliens.

"Yes," Thrawn said. "If you wish to return."

Ronan frowned. "What do you mean?"

"You heard Grand Moff Tarkin," Thrawn said. "He is going to recommend that Lord Vader be assigned to Stardust. There, he will work closely with you."

"And with Director Krennic and a hundred others," Ronan said. "What's your point?"

"My point, Assistant Director," Thrawn said quietly, "is that you may hide your contempt for the Emperor from Director Krennic and those hundred people you mention. But you will not be able to hide it from Lord Vader."

A fist seemed to close around Ronan's heart. "I don't know what you're talking about," he protested reflexively.

"Of course you do," Thrawn said. "You have three choices. You may return to Director Krennic and hope you can hide your true feelings from Lord Vader. Or you may resign from Stardust and travel as far away from the project as you can."

Ronan grimaced. Only he couldn't. The mere suggestion that someone at his level wanted to leave would raise warning signals all the way to Wild Space and back. He would be taken in and questioned . . . and the end result would be the same.

Which he had no doubt Thrawn knew perfectly well. "And my third choice?" he asked between stiff lips.

"You travel with Admiral Ar'alani to the Chiss Ascendancy."

Ronan felt his mouth drop open. "*What? Why in the galaxy would I do that?*"

"Because you've seen the threat the Grysks pose to the galaxy," Thrawn said. "Because you have worked with many non-human species, and your insights into how others think and act could be of great value in the coming conflict." His eyes seemed to bore into Ronan's. "Because if you remain within the boundaries of the Empire you will eventually be hunted down and killed."

Ronan looked at Ar'alani. As far as he knew she couldn't speak any Basic. But the expression on her face made it perfectly clear that she understood what was going on. "You're insane," he said, turning back to Thrawn. "I'm loyal to the Empire. Any questioning—any interrogation—will confirm that."

"Of course you are," Thrawn said. "That is why I know you would fight the Grysks with all your mind and heart. Because they are as dangerous a threat to the Empire as they are to the Ascendancy."

Ronan shook his head. "I can't leave. Do you understand? I *can't*."

"Then you die," Thrawn said flatly.

Ronan glared at him. Yes, he was loyal. Yes, he was invaluable to Director Krennic and Stardust.

And yes, he felt nothing but contempt for the Emperor.

"Bear in mind that your decision to leave would not be irrevocable," Thrawn continued. "As you see, the Chiss are quite able to slip into the Empire without detection. If you or Admiral Ar'alani decide that you will not be useful in the coming war, she can bring you back."

"The most useful thing I can do for your war is to make sure Stardust is operational on schedule," Ronan retorted.

"Then return to Director Krennic," Thrawn said. "And Lord Vader."

For a long moment Ronan just stared at him. Surely he didn't really expect Ronan to take him up on his insane offer. To leave the Empire and embrace an alien civilization that could easily become an enemy to everything he'd ever known—no. There was no way he could ever do something like that. Better by far to return to Director Krennic and take his chances with Vader.

But even as he opened his mouth to say so, a memory flashed back. Looking into the *Chimaera*'s bridge, watching the woman Vah'nya twitch in reaction before there was anything to react to.

Could that be Thrawn's real plan here? To send Ronan with Ar'alani in the hope of embedding an ally into his and the Emperor's secret plan to seek out and destroy the Jedi among his people?

Ridiculous. Thrawn hadn't even been facing Ronan at the time of that incident. There was no way he could know that Ronan had witnessed Vah'nya's action, or that he'd come to the correct conclusion.

But the fact that Thrawn didn't know Ronan was a potential ally didn't mean Ronan couldn't become one anyway.

In fact, sometimes a secret ally was the best kind to have.

"Fine," he said. "I'll go. But only for now, and only if Ar'alani can give me hard evidence that the Grysks are a threat to the Empire."

"Understood," Thrawn said. "I will so instruct her." He gestured to the pair of death troopers standing silent watch at the end of the command walkway. "One of my guards will escort you to Admiral Ar'alani's shuttle. Lieutenant Commander Vanto is waiting there and will begin your orientation. I will send the admiral down momentarily. If you change your mind before she arrives, you have but to step off her shuttle and you will be escorted to a different vessel for transport to Stardust."

"I'll remember that," Ronan said.

No, he wouldn't change his mind, he thought grimly as he headed into the turbolift car, the death trooper close behind him. Not yet.

But if it turned out Thrawn wasn't working with the Emperor on this Jedi thing, but was secretly working against him, the grand admiral would find he hadn't sent a pawn or even a secret ally to his people. He would instead have sent an enemy.

And while Ronan would make an excellent ally, he would also make a very, very dangerous enemy.

Ar'alani watches the turbolift doors close. Her expression holds thoughtfulness and uncertainty. "You're taking a terrible risk, Mitth'raw-'nuruodo," she said. *Her voice holds warning and disapproval.* "He is unhappy, unwilling, and unconvinced."

"I know. That's part of the framework."

Ar'alani shakes her head. Her expression and body stance now hold worry. "Dangerous," she said. "Harboring a potential traitor is bad enough. Knowing you're harboring a potential traitor is worse."

"Not at all. One can make sure a potential traitor is prepared with the information and expertise one wishes the enemy to know."

"Is that your plan for Ronan?"

"It's merely my suggestion. He's yours now. What you do with him is up to you."

Ar'alani purses her lips. Her body stance now holds some dark amusement. "Someday, Mitth'raw'nuruodo, you'll overthink and overplan, and it will come crashing down all around you. When that happens, I hope someone is there to lift you back to your feet."

"You, perhaps?"

Ar'alani shakes her head. Her expression holds regret, perhaps even pain. "I very much fear I will never see you again. The growing chaos in the Ascendancy warns of coming war. If you don't return quickly, there may be nothing left for you to return to."

"I understand. But for now, I must remain here."

"Then do what you deem right," Ar'alani said. *Her expression is stiff but firm, holding farewell.* "And may warrior's fortune be ever in your favor."

———

The brief conversation ended. Faro watched out of the corner of her eye, seething, pretending to be engrossed in her datapad as Ar'alani and the death trooper escorting her entered the turbolift.

Doubly seething now, actually.

She'd been aching to get Ronan alone, even for a single minute, just enough time to tell him exactly what she thought of his petty behavior toward Thrawn. Not just his betrayal of Thrawn and the Defender project, but also his steadfast and stupid refusal to see the larger picture. His childish petulance, his narrow-minded decision to play Krennic's games instead of rising above petty politics and serving the Empire.

She'd already planned out her speech, in fact, for once not even caring whether or not she stepped over the line into insubordination. Ronan needed to hear this, to hear every bit and piece and nuance of it, and the hell with any damage it might do to Faro's own career. For the Empire—hell, for the entire galaxy—Thrawn needed Ronan to speak up on his behalf to Krennic and Tarkin and even the Emperor if necessary. If she couldn't strangle the bastard with her bare hands, she could at least offer him one last chance to make things right.

Only now, Thrawn had unexpectedly sent Ronan away with a death trooper escort, presumably to the hangar bay and his escape back to Stardust. Faro would probably never even see him again, let alone have the chance to deliver her verbal salvo.

Damn it.

Thrawn waited until the turbolift door had closed, then turned and walked back onto the bridge. "Commodore," he said in greeting as he walked up to her. "Have you made the arrangements with Captain Pellaeon?"

Faro squared her shoulders. *One must never dwell on failure,* Thrawn had once told her. *When defeat has come, a true warrior accepts it, learns from it, and continues on.*

More than that, Faro added to herself, a true warrior should never complain about that defeat. "Yes, sir, I have," she said. "The *Harbinger* should arrive at Lothal shortly before we do."

"Good," Thrawn said. "You seem disturbed. May I ask the reason?"

Should never complain about defeat . . . "It's not important, sir."

"I presume you were unhappy to hear from Assistant Director Ronan that I had recommended against your appointment as commander of Task Force 231."

And there it was, right out in the open. With everything else that had happened in the past few days, she'd managed to compartmentalize that nagging bruise into a back corner of her mind.

But now that conversation came thundering back to the forefront. At the time she'd concluded that Ronan was lying, and had tried to put it aside.

Was Thrawn now confirming it?

"Permission to speak freely, sir?" she asked.

"Of course."

"Yes, sir, to be honest I was," she said, rather surprised her words were coming out so calmly. But then, after Ronan's betrayal of Thrawn, such minor things as her future career didn't seem all that important. "May I ask why you did that?"

"Because you are far better than that," Thrawn said. "A better administrator, a better tactician, simply a better officer. I therefore requested that you be removed from consideration for Task Force 231 and instead be considered to command the Eleventh Fleet."

Faro felt her eyes widen. "The Eleventh *Fleet*? Admiral, I'm just a commodore."

"Perhaps that will change."

"Sir, this is hardly a joking matter," Faro insisted.

"I wasn't joking, Commodore," Thrawn assured her. "The point is that you are an exceptionally competent commander, and the Imperial fleet needs to recognize and reward all such people. Your performance today against Grand Admiral Savit merely underlines that ability."

Faro took a deep breath. "Sir, I appreciate your confidence. But we both know that the action against the *Firedrake* was all yours."

"Was it?" Thrawn countered. "Tell me, why did you deviate from my instructions regarding the impact point of the cloaked generator?"

Faro felt her throat tighten. She'd hoped he would put that down to a simple mistake or miscalculation. Clearly, he knew the change in his plan had been deliberate. "Up to that point, the *Firedrake*'s TIE fighters hadn't been brought into play," she said. "I remembered your comment that Savit didn't really trust other people, but I'd also seen him use the *Stormbird* and *Misthunter* against us instead of doing the dirty work himself. I knew he would eventually have no choice but to use his own forces, so I thought it might be better to add some confusion to his hangar bay instead of just taking out one of the starboard turbolasers with a wedgeline impact. Especially since your commandeered TIEs were already on their way to handle the turbolaser targeting sensors."

"Excellent reasoning," Thrawn said. "I had already minimized the danger of a fighter threat, but you had no way of knowing that. What you did was observe your opponent, weigh his strengths and weaknesses, think several moves ahead, and plan your strategy accordingly. Those are all signs of a good commander."

He regarded her thoughtfully. "You also have a far better sense of Imperial politics than I do. I presume you were the one sending anonymous reports to Grand Moff Tarkin?"

"Yes, sir," Faro said. Oddly enough, on this one she felt less need to apologize. "Regulations require a report to be filed whenever contact with an unknown species is made. Since Tarkin is the grand moff of this region and holds direct control over it, I thought it would make sense to send the reports directly to him instead of Coruscant."

"And you also thought that such reasoning could be logically defended should the need arise?"

"Yes, sir," Faro said. "It could also be seen as pure accident that no name had been attached to the reports."

"At which point, should the question arise, you would claim you had filed them on my behalf?"

"Yes, sir," Faro said. "I also knew Ronan would be sending reports to Krennic that would be as negative as possible. I thought it would be useful for someone to balance that a little."

"Indeed," Thrawn said. "As I said before, you have a much better instinct for such political matters."

"Thank you, sir," Faro said, not entirely sure whether that was a compliment, but deciding to treat it as such. The useful tool sometimes called *plausible deniability* was hardly something the Empire had invented. "I appreciate your efforts on my behalf regarding my reassignment," she added. "I'll look forward to hearing the High Command's decision."

Thrawn's eyebrows rose slightly. "You misunderstand. Your reassignment was approved earlier this morning. You'll be leaving the *Chimaera* at Lothal for Coruscant and orientation on your new command."

Faro felt her eyes bulge. "My new—*sir*?"

"Indeed," Thrawn said, and this time there was no mistaking his smile. "Congratulations, Commodore Faro. May you serve the Eleventh Fleet as well as you've served the Seventh."

"Thank you, Admiral," Faro managed. "It—sir, it's been the greatest privilege of my life to serve under you. I can only hope my officers will feel even a tenth of that pride and satisfaction under my command."

"They will that, and far more," Thrawn assured her. "And now, Commodore, one final time: You may prepare my ship."

EPILOGUE

The face that appeared on the Emperor's private comm display was a familiar one. Grand Admiral Thrawn.

But was it the face of a senior Imperial officer? Or was it the face of a quiet traitor? The Emperor no longer knew for certain.

But he was determined to find out.

"So," he said. "Grand Admiral Savit is a traitor."

"So it would seem, Your Majesty," Thrawn said.

"Believing he was serving the Empire," the Emperor continued, "while merely serving himself."

"Yes," Thrawn said.

"And what of you, Grand Admiral Mitth'raw'nuruodo?" the Emperor demanded. "What of you and the Chiss? Tell me how that is not a similar situation."

"It is not at all similar," Thrawn said. His voice was calm, but the Emperor could see the lines of tension around his eyes and mouth. He was walking dangerous ground, and he was fully aware of it. "Admiral Ar'alani's force arrived in the Empire without my permission or knowledge. When they revealed themselves, it was to warn of an unknown threat against the Empire."

"Yes, Lord Vader has already spoken to me about these Grysks," the Emperor said. "He tells me the threat is distant. He also tells me the danger is primarily against your Chiss Ascendancy."

"Lord Vader's assessment is correct," Thrawn said. "But I respectfully submit that it is also incomplete. The Grysk presence we uncovered in Kurost sector is proof of their active interest in the Empire. Particularly dangerous is the fact that their observation and research post brought them perilously close to Stardust."

"Hardly close to Stardust," the Emperor scoffed. "Merely to one of Krennic's many supply lines."

"But even the most insignificant supply line leads eventually to the center," Thrawn pointed out. "May I also remind His Majesty that the Grysks at the post were already seeking to learn the ways and means of suborning Imperial citizens. Consider the possibility of the Death Star in enemy hands, and you will surely understand my concern."

The Emperor scowled. He and Krennic had gone to great lengths to keep the words *Death Star* out of any but the most secure communications among the most senior of Stardust personnel. The fact that Thrawn had managed to ferret out the battle station's name still rankled. "No one but the Empire will ever control Stardust," he said flatly. "Not the Grysks. Certainly not the Chiss."

"I do not seek Stardust for the Chiss," Thrawn assured him. "Indeed, I would fight with all my skill and strength to make sure that did not happen."

"Would you?" the Emperor countered. "Your loyalty is in question, Grand Admiral Mitth'raw'nuruodo."

"My loyalty remains firm, Your Majesty," Thrawn said. "There is no conflict with my service to the Empire and my recent cooperation with the Chiss."

"You made the same statement and claim to Lord Vader," the Emperor said. "I wonder perhaps if that excuse is wearing thin."

"If you wish to remove me from my rank and position, that is of course your right," Thrawn said, his voice now showing the same strain that was evident in his face. "But I continue to maintain my commitment and loyalty to you and to the Empire."

For a long moment, the Emperor gazed into those glowing red

eyes. Thrawn was a useful and formidable servant. But he would make an equally formidable enemy.

And a servant with divided loyalties was no servant at all.

There was an even more intriguing question, however. If the Chiss also recognized that fact, and if Thrawn was indeed loyal to the Empire instead of the Ascendancy, would his own people decide he was a potential threat to them? If so, would they move to eliminate that threat?

And what of the Grysks? Lord Vader had dismissed them as a distant threat, one that could be ignored for the present. But he'd been unable to hide the fact that they *were* a threat.

Perhaps Thrawn was pointing in the right direction. Perhaps an alliance between the Empire and the Ascendancy was what the future held.

With himself, the Emperor, in command of both.

It was an intriguing thought. Perhaps Thrawn could be made an even more valuable servant.

If he committed treason against the Empire, he would surely die. If he was loyal to the Empire, perhaps he could be persuaded or manipulated into treason against the Ascendancy.

Another intriguing thought. One that would require additional meditation.

But for now there were other more urgent matters to deal with. The Lothal rebels . . . and the young Jedi Ezra Bridger.

"We will speak of this another time," he told Thrawn. "I'm sending you instructions on a chamber I wish for you to construct aboard the *Chimaera*. After you reach Lothal, and put down the rebel activity, you will bring Ezra Bridger to that chamber." He smiled. "I'm sure you'll find a way to persuade him to join you."

"I will endeavor to do so, Your Majesty," Thrawn promised.

"Then I leave you to your duties," the Emperor said. "And Grand Admiral Mitth'raw'nuruodo?"

"Yes, Your Majesty?"

"When the business on Lothal is finished," the Emperor said softly, "you will return to Coruscant.

"Where you and I will have a long, long talk."

ABOUT THE AUTHOR

TIMOTHY ZAHN is the author of more than fifty novels, over a hundred short stories and novelettes, and five short-fiction collections. In 1984, he won the Hugo Award for best novella. Zahn is best known for his *Star Wars* novels (*Thrawn, Thrawn: Alliances, Heir to the Empire, Dark Force Rising, The Last Command, Specter of the Past, Vision of the Future, Survivor's Quest, Outbound Flight, Allegiance, Choices of One,* and *Scoundrels*), with more than eight million copies of his books in print. Other books include *StarCraft: Evolution,* the Cobra series, the Quadrail series, and the young adult Dragonback series. Zahn has a BS in physics from Michigan State University and an MS from the University of Illinois. He lives with his family on the Oregon coast.

Facebook.com/TimothyZahn

ABOUT THE TYPE

This book was set in Minion, a 1990 Adobe Originals typeface by Robert Slimbach (b. 1956). Minion is inspired by classical, old-style typefaces of the late Renaissance, a period of elegant, beautiful, and highly readable type designs. Created primarily for text setting, Minion combines the aesthetic and functional qualities that make text type highly readable with the versatility of digital technology.